RECKLESS

RECKLESS

R. J. McBrien

WELBECK

Published in 2021 by Welbeck Fiction Limited, part of Welbeck
Publishing Group
20 Mortimer Street London W1T 3JW

A CIP catalogue record for this book is available from
the British Library

Paperback ISBN: 978-1-78739-618-0
Ebook ISBN: 978-1-78739-619-7

Printed and bound by CPI Group (UK) Ltd., Croydon, CR0 4YY

10 9 8 7 6 5 4 3 2 1

For PH and EM

'Our sins change us more than our virtues'
Brenda Griffin

PART I

**BRITISH
TRANSPORT
POLICE**

EXTRACT FROM OFFICER'S REPORT

Report of:	Detective Constable S. L. Talbot
To:	Incident Room – Operation 1765/Y/C9
Subject:	Discovery of Body at Network Rail Railway Cutting S72/B South, Beckenham
Date:	15/06/2019

Sir/Ma'am,

At 02.18 hrs on 15 June 2019, police received a 999 call from a mobile telephone. The caller, who asked to remain anonymous, reported coming across the deceased body of an IC1 male at a railway cutting near Ravensbourne railway station. The caller appeared to be intoxicated by an unknown substance but was lucid and distressed. His mobile number has not been traced.

At 02.32 hrs PS Kemble and PC Jordan attended the scene. It was immediately apparent that the person was deceased and had suffered injuries consistent with a glancing blow from a train. There had been no reports of any train versus person collisions in the area.

PS Kemble requested paramedics attend to declare life extinct which they did at 03.07 hrs. Scenes of Crime Officers were called to record the scene with both still and video photography, and a search of the immediate area was carried out.

There appeared to be no suspicious circumstances and, due to the location and lack of obvious signs of violence or drugs misuse, the initial hypothesis was that this was either suicide or an accidental death.

The body was recovered to Princess Royal Hospital mortuary for post-mortem. On arrival the body and clothing were searched. There were no tattoos, piercings or distinguishing marks. No wallet, wedding ring, phone or jacket and no identification on the body. A lip salve, stick of chewing gum, wet section of cardboard and some tissue were recovered from the front trouser pockets. These have been sent for forensic examination.

At the time of writing, the body remains in Princess Royal Hospital mortuary, its identity unknown.

Statements from PS Kemble and PC Jordan attached.

Report submitted for information.

When Did It Start?

The roads are empty at this time of day, the pavements deserted. Nobody else is up so early on a Saturday morning in June. I stare out of the car at the Taj restaurant with its graffiti-covered shutters, at the Co-op's blank face and the estate agent's window, eerily lit by a screen endlessly scrolling through local properties. It could be any row of shops on any suburban London street, on any street in the country come to that. But I know these places, they've punctuated my marriage. Mark and I sat opposite each other in the Taj most Friday nights, for years. Lamb jalfrezi for him, tandoori prawns for me. A large bottle of Kingfisher between us, planning our perfect life. Later, in silence, hands held, tears never far away, telling ourselves children don't define happiness. Then, with the birth of Jess, knowing they do. The Taj was replaced with dashes to the Co-op for last-minute nappies, pints of milk, the occasional loaf of bread. And cheap Bulgarian red, until that stopped too.

How many times had we peered through Cartertons' window at the latest houses for sale, fantasising about life in a five-bedroom mid-terrace with 'mature garden'? Beyond our means then, for ever now. But we were happy; rooted in the complacency of busy young parents. So, when did it start? When did the first hairline crack appear, which would later widen so far I'd fall through it entirely?

The car lurches forward. I tell myself that I'm in a mini-cab on my way back from a night out, a fun dinner with friends. The back seat has the same sad, soggy feel of an overused mattress, the plastic door fittings shiny from a thousand greasy palms. But the smell is different. A nauseating cocktail of sweat and industrial disinfectant. Sweet and cloying. When I ask to open the window, I'm told it's not possible; doors and windows in the back of patrol cars don't open from the inside. As if I'm going to run down the high street in kitten heels and a pencil skirt.

We stop by a roundabout. A couple of workers in reflective jackets are hooking strings of lights to lamp-posts. The summer parade will be on later today, the one Jess used to love as a child. A man sways high in a cherry-picker, pulling cables up from the pavement below. I wonder why they do it so early in the day. Maybe so nobody sees. To keep the magic magic; the advice earnest agony aunts trot out to jaded women in jaded relationships week after week. Rekindle, become new to each other.

I did try. Many times, in all manner of ways: as a joke, an aside, in company, alone. But Mark would be busy or tired or preoccupied with vital tasks, like changing a plug or installing a new app. It could wait. I could wait. Why the hurry? We were married. No one was going anywhere.

One damp evening last November we found ourselves watching an old movie in the same room at the same time. There must have been a lull in emails, the lure of checking yet another web page momentarily satiated. I think the film was in French, certainly subtitled, not that much explanation was required. The plot focused relentlessly on an implausibly beautiful couple having sex in glamorous locations.

Time was, we'd have laughed and cuddled up and one thing would have led to another. But twenty-odd years of marriage creates its own enclaves. Mark had migrated to the beaten-up armchair he'd inherited from his parents, while I stretched out on the sofa, buffered by cushions, feet up. Long-won territories, intimacy-free.

As we undressed for bed, images from those scenes were still playing in my head; the man squatting between the woman's legs, her thighs clamped round his sweating temples, back arched, face contorted with pleasure. I leant against the bathroom door, heady from too much wine, brushing my hair as I watched Mark go through his flossing routine. White tape wound tight across his index fingers, mouth pulled wide, then the careful see-saw motion, a bloody line of dribble meandering across his chin.

'When did we stop going down on each other?' I said.

Mark moved on to his upper molars.

'I know you went off it first, but I can't remember when.'

He caught my eye in the mirror. 'Kirst.' The single, dismissive syllable. That's the problem with being married to someone who doesn't drink any more. They're no fun, not even in an argument. Luckily, I'd had enough for both of us.

'We used to do it all the time. I couldn't get you out of there,' I said. Mark spat in the basin, rinsing away the red-stained saliva with a jet of cold water. 'And then you made me ask and then it stopped altogether.' I steadied myself against the door jamb. 'Why do you think that was?'

'Sex tapers off.'

'Tapers?'

'As you get older, it . . . subsides.'

'Does it?' I said, trying to keep the accusation out of my voice. .

'When people get together they're at it all the time and then . . . '

'They stop?'

'They do it less often.' So calm, so reasoned.

I could feel myself going pink, knew my neck would be blotching up. 'When was the last time we made love, Mark?'

He placed his electric toothbrush back on the charger. 'I don't keep a record.'

'Take a guess.'

He turned to face me. 'What's this really about, Kirst?'

I stared at him. He just had to hold me, give me a cuddle like he used to, and everything would be fine. All the worries, the tensions, the petty arguments, they wouldn't matter any more. Reach out, you bastard!

He turned away with a tiny shake of the head. I knew what that meant: 'When you're sober, let's talk it through, have a rational discussion.'

Maybe that was the beginning. Or one of them.

* * *

The reception area at Bromley Police Station is empty except for an old woman moaning incoherently in a corner. She's not much more than a bundle of rags rocking back and forth. I wonder if I should check that she's OK, or at least ask the police officer behind the counter to help. She could be someone's mother, someone's wife. Someone's child once. Would it be too much to see what she wants? But before I can say anything, a man in a sharp suit appears, hand extended. We've met before, Detective Sergeant Withers and I, though this time he's wearing a tie. He ushers me down a corridor into an interview room, asking if I'd like a tea or a coffee, some water maybe. The thick door thuds shut, blocking out the old woman's ramblings.

When we first met, DS Withers had turned up on my doorstep in an informal, open collar and introduced himself as a detective from the British Transport Police. He urged me to call him Mike, but all I could think of asking was if he was a real policeman. Weren't transport police like those volunteers you see on the high street? Amateurs who fancy the uniform and a belt heavy with gizmos? 'Mike' assured me he had the same responsibilities – and powers – as any other police officer. He asked if I minded being called Kirsten or preferred Mrs Norton. I said I went by Ms Callaway, but Kirsten was fine. I'd been the one to offer a drink then, had even dug out a plate of digestives for him and his partner, DC Chowdhury. They'd smiled but declined, sitting politely in my kitchen as they asked their innocuous questions. No one's smiling this time.

'We're grateful to you for coming in,' says Withers. 'I know the weekend isn't always the easiest.'

I didn't have much choice, I think, with a couple of cops on the doorstep and a police car ostentatiously parked outside. Chowdhury asks if I'd like to call my solicitor, as if I keep one on standby, like a Mafia boss. The last time I employed a lawyer must have been over eighteen years ago when Mark and I bought the house. I shake my head, trying to look unconcerned. Inside, my stomach cramps like it used to when I still had periods.

DC Chowdhury slides a photograph across the table. A man lying on his front, arms spread, one leg straight, the other kinked at a sickening angle. I try to focus on other details to keep myself from reacting. Is he lying on a road? Or a path perhaps? There are tufts of grass by one of his knees. Another photograph appears.

Someone's turned the man over. Half the face is intact, the other mangled beyond recognition. One eye pulped, the nose almost entirely gone, no more than a mass of red, blobby meat. I look away, nauseous. Are they allowed to show me stuff like this?

'Do you recognise this man?' asks Chowdhury.

'No,' I say, my stomach now so tight it takes all my concentration not to wince.

They stare at me, their faces blank, neutral. Chowdhury edges the photograph forward an inch, forcing me to look again. Despite the horrific injuries, the man's collar and tie remain untouched, Liberty pink against a striped blue shirt. I imagine him standing in front of a mirror, tightening it, wiggling the knot until perfect, as I'd seen him do a hundred times.

'He was found early on June the fifteenth, at the bottom of a railway cutting.' It's Withers this time. 'But we have reason to believe the body had been there some time.'

I close my eyes. Please God it was quick.

'Are you all right, Ms Callaway?' he says.

'It's just the thought of it. Sorry.' I picture him in the dark, frightened and alone, knowing nothing could save him. What did he think of in those final moments? His wife? His child? Me?

'Would you like a drink?' Chowdhury pushes a flimsy plastic cup across the desk, the water vibrating inside, forming perfect circles.

'You're sure you don't recognise this man?' asks Withers.

'I'm sorry,' I say. 'I've no idea who he is.' Which is true, even though I've been having an affair with him for the last six months.

CHAPTER ONE

If disappointment is the original sin of infidelity, mine did not start with a Merlot-fuelled argument over a smutty film. We need to go way back, to times faintly remembered, even purposefully forgotten. Certainly to the buff envelope lying on the rough coir matting by my parents' front door. I recognised the postmark at once, had been looking for it every morning for weeks. I squeezed the contents and could feel the outline of a paper clip. A good sign, surely. A rejection slip wouldn't require several pages.

The house was deserted, just our old spaniel, Jeep, quietly snoring in his basket by the stairs. I held the envelope up to the light, but the paper was too thick to make anything out. I stared at the printed address, knowing my future was moments away, that once I read what was inside, my life would be mapped out. Medical school with its gruelling exams, years of hard work, then hospital rotations and more exams until finally the words I'd imagined since I was a child: Dr Kirsten Callaway.

I pushed a finger under the flap, tore it back in a toothy rip. Typewritten. The university's crest. 'I regret to inform you . . . in light of your exam results . . . you will appreciate the number of applications . . . '

I stared at the indecipherable signature of the Head of Admissions. Nothing had changed. The sun still poured through the window, spilling a pool of golden light on to the wooden floor. Jeep went on snoring. Outside, cars whooshed by. In the distance, a police siren, or maybe it was an ambulance. But nothing could ever be the same again. I was no longer who I thought I was, who I thought I would become.

My parents were sympathetic, though behind the concern and warm words of advice, my father couldn't suppress a trace of smugness. I often suspected he enjoyed his disappointment in me. Easier than being proud; at least this way, I couldn't let him down. And now he'd been proved right, yet again.

Helen was the bright one, effortlessly breezing through every exam she ever sat. No one was surprised when she wanted to study law, nor when she was awarded a first, back when – as she liked to remind us – firsts meant firsts and weren't handed out just for turning up. But me, a medical student? Absurd. A fantasy indulged and now regretted. My father should have smothered it earlier, put us all out of our misery. As it was, he had a moping daughter leaching disappointment into the family like a polluted well.

Had I succeeded and swanned off in the autumn to medical school, thirty years later a life might have been saved. I would never have met Mark, and without that, none of what followed could have happened. Even if we *had* somehow met, the rest might not have been inevitable; I could have walked away, taken a different path. Instead, on a bone-chilling beach in Cornwall, when he placed a nugget of sea-glass in my palm, I told Mark I loved him. Not just with my body or my mind but everything I possessed, everything I was and ever would be. Was that the moment a man's fate was sealed?

The only way I can make sense of it is to go back to when my discontent was so far beneath the surface, not a ripple showed. When I was bobbing along in the mainstream, temporary regrets swept away by the busy current of family, friends and work, innocent of the roaring rapids ahead. The whirlpool that would destroy everything.

* * *

A few days before Christmas, I was in my treatment room in the prosthetics wing of St Mary's Hospital, watching a twenty-eight-year-old paraplegic struggle on the parallel bars. He grimaced as he swung his torso forwards, forcing the metal leg to follow, his cheeks puffy-red with exertion.

'Remember to breathe, Jamie,' I said. 'Use your hips. You're doing great.'

Face scrunched in pain, he slid one hand along the rail, then the other, now the torso swing again. But the pylon on his left leg dragged, the false foot twisting sharply.

'Fuck, fuck, fuck!'

'OK, enough,' I said.

'No! No breaks.' He tried to drag the foot back, sweat beading on his forehead.

'Jamie, it's enough!' I held out a plastic chair. He slumped into it with a grunt.

'That was great,' I said.

'Bollocks.'

'You're right, you were shit.'

He managed a smile. I'd been helping Jamie Fletcher for the last three months, ever since he'd contracted gangrene and had both legs amputated a few inches below the knees. His original injuries had been from a landmine outside Camp Bastion in Afghanistan. The army surgeons had managed to save his legs, but a few years later infection set in and he'd needed another operation.

He grabbed a bottle of water, gulping it down.

'Will I ever be able to waterski again?'

'People do.'

'Cool, because I never learnt.'

'That's a great one, Jamie,' I said. 'Never heard that before. Usually it's playing football or the violin.'

He laughed, dropping the bottle into a holdall. Then he fixed me with his soft brown eyes.

'I want to walk again. For Michelle.'

'And you will. I promise.' That was my job, to take torn-apart humans and teach them how to walk or feed themselves or put their clothes on, then hand them back to their loved ones. Michelle in this case.

The surgeon had told her about the second op on a cold day in August. I'd been down the corridor, wrestling with our temperamental vending machine. Balancing a couple of paper cups of tea in one hand, I was making my way back to the treatment room when Michelle almost ran into me, sending scalding liquid slopping over my fingers. She tried to say sorry but could only manage an incomprehensible blub of catarrh. I didn't need a translation: the streaming mascara and red eyes said it all. She'd just been told the man she loved was about to be cut in half.

I'd seen it far too many times over the years. First, the disbelief and horror, both for themselves and their partners. Then, once they were over the initial shock, a determination to throw themselves into the relationship with renewed commitment; sympathetic, loyal, swearing it made no difference. Finally, there would be time to think. To lie in bed picturing the scenes: on the beach, by the pool, down the pub. Dealing with kids. They'd met a fit, handsome young man and now this. Some split up, some came back, most didn't. But who was I to say Michelle wouldn't be a sticker?

'How are you this afternoon?'

I turned to see a woman in a white coat marching towards Jamie. In the six months since her appointment, Dr Svetkova had addressed barely fifty words to me, half of which were to ask the way to the ladies on her first day. She had studied at Plovdiv Medical University, though God knows what qualifications you needed to get in there. Google said Plovdiv was Bulgaria's second city and had a Liebherr factory, which coincidentally was one of Mark's favourite makes of fridge, the other being an unaffordable brand from New Zealand whose name I always forgot.

Despite my repeated efforts to warm her up, Dr Svetkova remained unrelentingly chilly. The odd thing is, as a teenager I'd wanted to be like her, exactly like her. Confident and aloof; admired and feared. If I hadn't screwed up back in the day, maybe I could have been. She examined Jamie's clipboard.

'All OK?' she said in her accented English.

'They haven't grown back yet,' he said, winking at me. Dr Svetkova remained engrossed in her charts.

'What is this you say?' she said.

'Still got the stumps.'

She looked up and I thought she might laugh, but her face stayed impassive. Smooth, wrinkle-free.

'I see you have constipation,' she said. 'This will be the morphine.' She clicked on her pen. Heavy, expensive, the sort you get for passing exams. 'I will reduce it to five mil diurnally.'

'Thought it went into my arm.' Jamie winked at me again.

'Diurnally means daily.'

'As in, "Rolled round in earth's diurnal course, With rocks, and stones, and trees,",' said Jamie.

Dr Svetkova stared at him blankly.

'I'm not just a grunt,' he said. 'I did Wordsworth for A level.'

'We will monitor how the new dose works, yes?' she said, ignoring him. She whipped a signature across the notes and hung the clipboard back up. As she bent forward, I caught Jamie staring unashamedly down her front. She was wearing a red lacy bra. I turned away, conscious of my buttoned-up blouse, keeping my own sensible greying underwear safely hidden from view.

As Dr Svetkova click-clacked out on her heels, I squirted the parallel bars with disinfectant before wiping them down. I didn't even possess underwear like that, let alone wear it to work. I tossed the soiled paper towel into a bin, cross with myself for thinking such crass thoughts. She was a confident young woman who dressed as she pleased, for herself. Good for her. Wish I'd had that confidence when I was her age. Wish I did now.

'You don't like her,' said Jamie. I turned to face him, smile back in place.

'We're bosom buddies,' I said. 'But we've agreed to ignore each other at work. Makes things easier.'

'You're much more attractive than her if that's what you're worried about,' he said.

'Not appropriate, Jamie,' I said.

'Just saying.'

'Can we concentrate on getting you to walk?' I said. Helping him up, I noticed he didn't carry an ounce of fat. Solid muscle. Jamie was a good-looking man. And I was a married woman of twenty years. A happily married woman with faded underwear.

* * *

Outside, the sky was heavy and dull, the hospital buildings streaked with patches of grey. There was no sign of the promised white Christmas, just another drizzly London evening. Faffing with my umbrella, I sensed someone behind me. I knew it was Kevin, from the noise his headphones made.

'Hello, Kevin,' I said. He did this most days, crept up as I was leaving for home. With a ponytail and unruly, curly beard, Kevin had worn the same ex-army camouflage jacket ever since I'd known him. He ran the IT department for our wing from a windowless office three doors down from mine, carrying his laptop around in an old Lidl bag.

'I saw *Body Double* last night,' he said, pushing the headphones down round his neck. 'You were great in it.'

'I'm sorry?'

'Melanie Griffith!' he said triumphantly. 'You look exactly like her!'

I sighed; if only. Back in the day, there might have been a vague resemblance, but rather than Melanie's gorgeous blonde tresses, I had mad red hair which I had wasted many fruitless years, and considerable sums of money, trying to tame. The comparison would be a stretch for anyone but Kevin.

'Will you be gracing us with your company tonight?' he said.

I must have looked puzzled because he added, 'The nurses' Christmas party? Should be good.'

'Sorry,' I said, finally forcing my umbrella up and stepping into the drizzle. 'Family commitments.'

I took the same route every day: cutting through the underground car park then along a couple of side streets to the Tube. I liked glancing into the familiar front rooms, imagining what it would be like to live a different life. Most had put up twinkling Christmas trees, a few had gone to town with strings of flashing lights, one even had a neon Father Christmas climbing up its chimney. My mother would have called them vulgar, which is probably why I liked them.

A wolf whistle cut through the rain. I spun round, searching for the culprit and spotted a scaffolder perched halfway up a building. I fired him my most withering glare, the one that says, 'Really? In the twenty-first century?' Then I saw the object of his attentions, a young woman in a micro skirt and skimpy top. *She was smiling back at him, for God's sake!*

I stomped into the Tube station, trying to convince myself anonymity was a good thing. One of the perks of reaching a certain age; not having to put up with that crap any more. Hit your forties, and you become invisible. These days I could walk in public without every man sliding his eyes all over me. Which had to be a plus, didn't it?

I squeezed on to a train, opposite a poster of a woman in bra and knickers advertising an internet provider ('fast enough for you?'). Why the fuck did it have it to be so relentless? I stood pressed up against the curve of the door, silently fuming that the whole world was obsessed with sex. Fuming and invisible.

CHAPTER TWO

I arrived home to find Mark in the kitchen, layering slices of potatoes in a shallow dish. When we met, he'd struggled to produce a decent spaghetti Bolognese, but after Jess was born he took up cooking with the dedication men of my father's generation applied to DIY or classic car restoration. As the bookshelves filled with increasingly obscure recipe books, and the cupboards with expensive gadgets, I lost interest in cooking. How could I compete? The run-of-the-mill dishes my mother had insisted on teaching me were pale and limp compared to Mark's vibrant, exotic concoctions. I knew most of my friends would be delighted to have a husband like Mark and I was, too. Mostly.

'Good day?' he said.

'Not too bad. How about you?'

'I cycled over to Greenwich and had lunch in the park.'

'Lucky you,' I said, opening the fridge. 'Where's the white gone?' He gestured to a pan on the back burner. 'Mark! I was looking forward to that.'

'It's better for you this way,' he said, throwing in a pinch of salt.

'I think I know what's best for me,' I said, pulling a bottle of red from under the counter. I hadn't meant to snap but this time of year was a tripwire for us. Mark would have knocked off at noon and could now look forward to two and a bit weeks' holiday, while I had to go back to work the day after Boxing Day. As far as I could see, teachers were never more than three weeks away from a break. They had either just been on one or another was coming up. Compared to Mark, I worked slave hours, whatever he said about PPA (Planning, Preparation and Assessment, to the uninitiated). Half the time he PPAed in front of the telly anyway. What I wouldn't give to do my job half watching a box set, feet up, a glass of wine to hand.

I could tell by the way Mark stirred the sauce that he was resisting saying anything back. Here he was, making a special meal and all I could do was snipe. I took a sip of wine and considered apologising. It wasn't as if he was having a great time at work himself.

Last summer, after two decades of unstinting service, Mark had been passed over for Deputy Head and Director of Studies. Rachel Winters, ten years younger, with half his experience but double the ambition, beat him to it. She would, Mark calmly assured me, reinvigorate the school, bringing new and exciting ideas. He was looking forward to working with her. He didn't mention what everyone knew, that the head, a white man in his fifties with the unfortunate habit of leaving bits of food stranded on his jumper, had come under intense pressure from the governors to appoint at least one woman to a senior position. Which, of course, I'd normally be all in favour of, but this was my husband we were talking about.

For the last term, after more than a decade of having his own classroom, Mark had become part of Ms Winter's peripatetic initiative, or PI as she insisted on calling it. What is it with teachers and their silly abbreviations? They're worse than the NHS. Designed to bring pupils and teachers closer together, in practice PI meant Mark slogging across the school grounds – sorry, campus now – carrying a back-pack heavy enough for an SAS recruit. I told him to resign, he deserved better. We deserved better. As I pointed out after a heavy evening of two-for-one Riojas, Mark could get a job in a private school in a trice. More money, longer holidays, grateful parents and kids who gave a shit. Mark, on his third elderflower spritzer, said if a child didn't give a shit, it was because they had a shit teacher. That put me in my place.

Mark, naturally, had no problem with CPD – Continuing Professional Development – or come to that, WFAW – Working for a Woman. Or even SBTFS – Shafted by the Fucking System. Hoisted by his own political correctness, there was nowhere to put his disappointment except back inside himself, from where it set to work like lemon on a cut, tightening and drying and stinging like hell. I under-stood all this, knew what it was like to be eaten away by resentment. But it was worse for him; he was raging at an injustice he couldn't admit existed. Which is why I was about to apologise for being chippy, but then I glanced into the sitting room.

Our beautiful Jess lay slouched on the sofa, tapping at her phone while Jack, her floppy boyfriend, nestled up to her. He shuffled a bit more upright when he saw me.

'Hello, Mrs N.'

'Hello, Jack. Everything all right, Jess?'

'Yup.' She didn't look up. Time was, Jess would fly into my arms every time I came into the room. 'Mum, Mum, look what I've done!' Now she barely acknowledged me. My best chance of a response was a text.

I hadn't been thrilled when they'd found each other. Six months older than Jess, Jack left school with one A level in Business Studies and was now a 'Sales Executive' for a 'major international player in the B to B space'. Which meant he worked in a stationery shop. Although Mark would never say as much, I knew he felt the same as I did, namely Jess could do better and hoped, once she went to university, she would.

Not that I didn't see the attraction. Jack was a good-looking lad, with his big green eyes, open face and, I must admit glimpsing once, impressive six-pack. I don't remember anyone having a six-pack as a teenager. If a boy wasn't too spotty and didn't smell, that was enough. Now they needed to look like models and have perfect teeth. Who'd be a teenage male in the twenty-first century?

'Psst!' It was Mark, gesturing from the stove. Mellowed by the wine, I went over to tell him his concoction smelled great, as it bloody should have done with the remains of my Chablis in there. I refilled my glass with red as he slid a dish into the oven.

'She wants him to stay over,' he whispered.

'What? No way!'

'It's not such a big deal,' said Mark.

We'd been round and round this for weeks. I wasn't naive enough to think they weren't having sex, but sanctioning it by allowing Jack to stay over felt altogether different. A similar issue had flared up a few months before Jess's last birthday, when I was driving her to school one morning.

I'd made the mistake of suggesting she was too young to be sleeping with boys.

'What am I supposed to be waiting for? We could all be dead tomorrow,' said Jess.

'We won't be, though, will we? We'll all be alive, and you'll have thrown away something invaluable.'

'Do you ever listen to yourself, I mean really listen?' she said, jamming her feet against the glovebox.

'Can you not do that, please?'

Huffing, she slid her feet down. 'What am I saving myself for? A grateful husband?'

'All I'm saying is . . . '

'I'm nearly seventeen, for God's sake. Most of my friends were shagging at thirteen. You should be happy.'

'That your friends are more slutty than you?' I regretted it the moment I said it. She stared at me, contempt and amazement flashing across her face. She was right. Why shouldn't she have sex? It's a natural, beautiful thing and she should enjoy it freely, without guilt. Isn't that what I had always believed? But she was my daughter. My precious, gorgeous daughter.

We drove on in silence. I had become precisely who I swore I wouldn't: the heavy-handed, angry mother who refuses to listen, let alone understand. When I dropped her off, Jess got out without a word. No slamming the door, no yelling she hated me. Just a dignified, silent exit. As if to say, 'You're not worth the effort.'

The argument had stayed with me all day, like a lump of undigested cheese, heavy and globulous, an ever-present reminder of what a useless parent I had become. I crept up to her room that evening, stood on the landing, watching her through the half-open door. I took in her perfect face as she stared at her laptop. Her long limbs, her slim figure. Such easy beauty. Age has always envied youth, maybe that's why it spends so much effort trying to crush it. I pushed the door open.

'Hi,' I said.

'Before you start,' Jess said, 'it's work. I'm not playing "some dumb game".' She held up her laptop. 'Chemistry revision.'

'I want to apologise,' I said. 'For this morning in the car.'

She nodded.

'It's your body, and you're old enough to make your own decisions. But be careful, OK?'

'Mum, careful's my middle name.' She got up and hugged me. It felt like a damn bursting.

After that, we were close for a while, then Jack appeared on the scene, and I became increasingly redundant. I tried not to resent it, to understand this was a phase, and, for the most part, managed quite well. Except when she rubbed my face in it, like tonight with her request skinny Jack stay over.

I looked at the two of them again, curled up on the sofa like newly-weds. Like us, once.

'Would it be such a disaster?' said Mark. 'He's a nice boy.'

'I don't care what they get up to elsewhere,' I said. 'I just don't want them shagging in my house.'

'Our house,' Mark corrected. 'You'd rather they did it down a dingy alleyway?'

'You know what? Yes!' I said, knowing that was the last thing I wanted but feeling boxed in, as I often did when we argued.

'You're dressing up squeamishness as morality.' Classic Mark, distancing himself from the problem by making it abstract. Framing life as an exam question. 'The issue,' he added, squeezing worms of tomato puree into a bubbling sauce, 'is should hypocrisy trump morality.'

'I don't care,' I said. 'I want him out of here by twelve.'

'Kirsten!'

I strode into the living room, preparing my ultimatum to Jack when the kitchen phone rang. There was only one person who still used the landline. I picked up.

'Helen.'

'So, what are you wearing?'

'Sorry?'

'For the reunion. Don't say you've forgotten. I told you months ago!'

She had. Back in the autumn. We'd been looking for the last of the blackberries in the park, our fingers running scarlet with juice and blood when she'd mentioned our old school was organising a sixth-form get-together.

'Why would you even think of going?' I'd said, fishing out a fat berry from deep within a mess of thorns. 'You didn't like school. Or anyone there. Why on earth would you want to see them again?'

'Because it would be fun, because I never get out, because I'm on my own.'

I popped the berry in my mouth, winced at the sourness of it. 'It's all right for you,' said Helen. 'You have a built-in social life. I have nothing. I have to work at it.'

As if it was my fault that, in her mid-forties, with two kids to support, Helen was back on the market. To keep her quiet, I'd agreed. It was months away; she'd have a better offer by then.

Turned out she didn't. So here she was, telling me she'd booked a babysitter and I had twenty minutes to get ready.

'It's been a long day, Helen,' I said. 'I'm knackered.'

'Take a shower, make a cup of coffee.'

'I've got nothing to wear. And my hair needs washing. Why don't you come over, have something to eat? We'll make a night of it.' Which is when she dropped her bomb.

'Khanda's going to be there.'

I felt a rush of excitement. 'Khanda Matthews?'

'You know anyone else with that stupid name?'

So maybe that's when it started.

CHAPTER THREE

Khanda Matthews. Long-limbed, blue-eyed, smelling of rollups and patchouli oil. Irresistible to every girl, envied by every boy, he sauntered down school corridors, smouldered in classrooms and lay languidly on benches, sketchbook in hand, mysteriously exempt from the afternoon sports the rest of us were forced to do. And the most seductive thing about him? He wasn't interested. In anyone. Not gorgeous Sarah with her amazing boobs or Katy and her endless legs, certainly not pimply me. His passion was art. Giant, messy portraits, thick with slathered oil paint slapped on with a palette knife. The headmistress was rumoured to have one in her kitchen, had actually paid for it. Half a dozen more hung in various prominent locations around the school, each signed with a single, flamboyant 'K'.

Khanda had appeared in the sixth form, no one knew from where. Some said California, others that he'd been home-schooled in Ireland, but most thought he had been expelled from a posh school for an unspecified though undoubtedly sexy scandal. Like most of the girls, I was besotted but knew nothing would ever happen between us. How could it? Khanda was our Bowie, the school Morrissey, desirable but for ever unattainable. Which made what happened between us all the more disconcerting.

After leaving school, I spent the summer zig-zagging across Europe by train. Like thousands of teenagers before me, I half slept in sweaty couchettes, washed in tiny WCs with no hot water and gagged at the ones blocked with clumpy balls of soggy, stinking tissue.

It had started with three of us. Sally, bubbly, loud and determined to have a good time whatever the cost; Bridget, with her list of galleries and museums to tick off, and me, still stinging from my poor exam results, trying not to show how much I cared. Sworn friends on the greatest adventure of our eighteen-year-old lives.

By the time we reached Rome, Bridget was no longer talking to Sally, who had spent the entire nineteen-hour train journey speculating about whether George Michael was gay or not. Added to which, Bridget had period cramps the whole way and couldn't find a bin that wasn't already overflowing. As we pulled into a stifling Roma Termini, Bridget finally snapped, calling Sally an intellectual lightweight and cultural dwarf (it didn't help that Sally came in at four ten dead). Sally retaliated by telling Bridget no man would ever love her because she was the most tedious, stuck-up person on earth and she'd end up alone, dying in a flat smelling of wee, her corpse half-eaten by her own cats.

Two days later, Sally left for Capri with a slick-haired boy she'd met outside the Colosseum. Bridget and I took yet another overnight train, this time to Naples, and limped around Pompeii in the searing heat, trying to persuade ourselves we didn't care, that we were still a team. But it wasn't the same. Without Sally's chitter-chatter to kick against, we didn't have so much in common after all. Bridget went back to Rome and took a plane home. I considered joining her but could see my father standing by the front door, his knowing gaze saying, 'Couldn't last a fortnight, knew you'd be back.' So I carried on alone, taking a bus to Bari as planned, then the overnight ferry to Dubrovnik.

If I'd been my own daughter, I'd have told her it was stupid and dangerous; an eighteen-year-old girl travelling alone in a country where she didn't speak a word of the language. What the hell was I thinking? That I was invincible, of course.

Standing on the prow of the ferry watching the last of the sun dissolve into the Adriatic, I tried to convince myself this was what I needed: independence, licence to be myself, free from the inhibiting gaze of childhood friends. As night fell, I went in search of food and found a vast cabin on a lower deck lined with wide, plastic seats. Every one was full of figures snuggled under blankets, eye masks on, settled in for the ten-hour crossing. I threaded my way through a tangle of protruding legs towards the queue by the snack bar. Drawing closer, I realised it wasn't a queue but half a dozen people watching a young woman as she sat motionless, eyes focused on some invisible distant object, hands clasped in her lap. Opposite her, crouched down, sketchpad in hand, squatted Khanda.

I stared mesmerised, unable to process this most unlikely of coincidences. He worked fast, a stub of charcoal casual in his fingers, constantly shifting his gaze from the girl to the paper, occasionally smudging a line with a stained thumb. It could only have been a month or so since I'd last seen him, but he looked totally different. Not just the long hair and tan; he was fuller, more complete. In a few weeks, he'd turned from boy to man.

Khanda held up the finished drawing to a smattering of applause. The woman blushed, embarrassed by what he'd seen: a nascent mix of timidity and sensuousness, an emerging sexuality which once on paper was obvious to us all.

Her father passed over a handful of cash, and the crowd dispersed, the girl huddled with her friends, giggling at her newfound identity. It wasn't until Khanda had packed away his pad that he looked up and saw me. He smiled.

'Kirsten.'

I was so surprised he remembered my name, all I could manage was a mumbled yes.

'Don't move,' he said, pulling out his pad again. Not a word about why I was there, how weird it was to meet like this. His fingers worked the charcoal, his eyes flicking over my face. Swift, thick, confident lines. Time stalled. I could hear the scratch of charcoal on paper, the distant hum of the ship's engines, feel the gentle swell of the ocean below. And Khanda Matthews' eyes on my face, looking at nothing but me. It was the most intimate experience of my life. Perhaps still is.

'Want to see it?' His words pulled me back to the swaying room, the faint smell of cabbage and diesel.

'Sure.'

The drawing was surprisingly simple, my face caught in a few, spare lines, the hair piled up on my head perfectly rendered. It was nothing like his work at school; no bold, extravagant swathes of colour, just a few decisive sweeps of black and grey. I gazed into my own eyes, pupils wide, heavy, sleepy eyelids. I felt myself welling up.

'Are you OK?'

How could I explain? It would sound absurd, vain. He'd made me beautiful to myself. Khanda took the pad back, said he was sorry, it was a silly sketch, that's all. He ripped the sheet off, was about to scrunch it up. I reached my hand on to his.

'No.'

* * *

The snack bar had run out of hot food, so we bought the last apple, a packet of peanuts and a couple of beers. I dipped into the ladies to unpin my hair, greasy after two days without washing, but at least if it was down it might cover the remnants of my spots.

I found Khanda on the top deck, sitting on a wooden bench tucked under a suspended lifeboat. He had the apple in his hand and suddenly twisted it in half with a sharp crack. I thought it the coolest thing I had ever seen. As we bit into our respective halves, he told me he had been travelling for three weeks, working his passage with sketches and the occasional caricature ('They pay more for a cartoon. No one wants to see how they really look'). His only luggage was an achingly trendy ex-army rucksack. I cringed at the thought of the over-pocketed, brightly coloured version my mother had insisted on buying. Khanda's plan was to island-hop for a few months then see what happened. I didn't mention my deeply uncool, highly organised trip, with its long-booked hostels and carefully timetabled itinerary.

I must have eventually dozed off because the next thing I remember was being nudged awake, Khanda holding out a steaming cup of thick, black coffee. We stood together on deck as the ferry pulled into port, watching dawn spill over the walls of Dubrovnik, our hands millimetres apart on the steel rail. One raised finger and his would have brushed mine. But Khanda was watching a sailor tossing a line to someone on the dock. The man quickly pulled it across, then attached a thicker rope and finally a massive one, dripping with saltwater. He swung the sodden loop over a bollard and the ferry pulled it taut, sending droplets pinging into the pale sunlight. Khanda turned to me, beaming.

'Isn't this amazing?'

I nodded, hoping that included me.

'I love this light. It's so, I don't know . . . honest.'

If I had been with Bridget, she would have snorted in derision. How can light be dishonest or honest, she'd have said, it's just light. But on Khanda's lips, the words didn't sound absurd or even pretentious. There *was* something uncompromising about the way the sun struck the stone buildings. Nothing hidden, everything simply what it was. I'd never understood that before.

We found a dingy café up a back street where I chose the smallest table, hoping our legs might touch. But Khanda perched delicately on his stool as we ate sweet pastries washed down with more intense black coffee. I told him what had happened with Sally and Bridget, exaggerating and embellishing, stupidly thrilled when he smiled.

'You got a place at the Slade, didn't you?' I asked disingenuously, knowing his scholarship had been the talk of the school.

He nodded. 'I'm not sure I'm ready, though. Not after this.'

'This?'

'Travelling, drawing. I'm learning too much to go back.'

'You're going to turn it down?' I tried to keep the disappointment out of my voice. I already had us sharing a studio flat somewhere off Tottenham Court Road.

'Perhaps. I'll see. How about you?'

'Oh, you know, medical school.' The lie slipped out before I noticed. I've often asked myself why I said it, and why then. I eventually decided it was because he seemed so sure of himself, so unequivocal. Who was I? The class swot who'd put all her efforts into exams and come up short. If I wasn't going to study medicine, who was I? Just . . . a girl.

'You are so smart!' He leant forward, gave me a peck on the cheek. I could feel the blood rush to my face. I fumbled for my guidebook and breathlessly read out lists of must-see places: the Onforfrio fountain, the Cathedral of the Assumption, the Sponza Palace. Khanda's hand covered the page.

'We don't need someone between us and what we feel,' he said. I could hear Bridget snorting again but pushed the thought away. 'Cities are for wandering,' he said, tossing my book into a nearby bin. We both laughed. But as we left, I fished it back out.

After checking our rucksacks into a locker at the bus station, we spent the day meandering through old Dubrovnik as the whim took us, or rather as it took Khanda. If I'd known that in a few years so many of the exquisite streets and buildings would be obliterated by pointless, spiteful bombing, I might have paid more attention to them. As it was, my focus was almost entirely on him. Once or twice, when he stopped to sketch, I snuck a photograph, sure one day I'd need proof any of this had actually happened.

By dusk we were walking the city walls, watching the evening ferry pull out on its way back to Ancona. Khanda hadn't mentioned anything about where we were going to stay, not the romantic little place he happened to know, nor the boutique hotel he was happy to splash out on. In the end, I felt I had to broach the subject.

'We booked this place out in the suburbs,' I said. 'There'll be a couple of spare beds if you want to tag along?'

'Yeah?'

'I can't guarantee what it'll be like,' I added, trying to sound spontaneous, despite having practised the line to myself for the last four hours.

'Sounds cool.'

And that was it. No reaching out, no touching, no looking into each other's eyes. Just, 'Sounds cool.' I felt more uncertain than ever.

*　　*　　*

The hostel was over an hour's ride on a packed bus heavy with diesel and sweat. Quaint narrow roads quickly gave way to dusty highways lined with dark, brutal high-rises. As night fell, the bus emptied, finally leaving only the two of us, bunched up on a narrow-slatted seat. I stared out at half-finished buildings, intensely aware of Khanda's thigh inches from my own, sensitive to every jolt, every accidental press of flesh. When I pulled out my battered guidebook to check where we were, he gave me a sardonic glance but said nothing.

A few minutes later, we stepped on to a broken pavement in front of a squat, Art Deco villa, hemmed in between grey apartment blocks. A single bare bulb lit up its faded oak door, and, when we rang the bell, a gangly guy with a ponytail appeared. He spoke to us in what I assumed was Croatian and then, seeing our bafflement, German. I explained in loud, slow English that we had a reservation and pointed to Bridget's name in his ledger. He shrugged and showed us up to what he called the '*Wohnheim*'. It turned out to be a large, high-ceilinged room with three metal beds arranged along one wall. Khanda paced from one end to the other, fascinated.

'Was this the ballroom?' he said.

'*Iche versteh nicht*,' said the gangly guy.

'You know, for dancing?' Khanda said. 'This is a sprung floor.' He demonstrated by jumping up and down, doing a twirl. I laughed. 'And check out those windows!' The guy shrugged again, took out a pen and pad and made it clear we owed him forty dinars per bed. To be paid in advance.

In an echoey bathroom, I examined my face in the rust-stained mirror. My hair was greasy and flat from the night on the ferry, though at least the sun had tamed my spots. I pushed a tarnished lever on the antiquated shower, and a surprisingly powerful spray shot out, soaking my arm.

There was no soap, but the water was hot, and I still had half a bottle of shampoo left. I was rinsing off the suds, eyes tight shut, when I heard the rattle of the shower curtain being drawn back. Khanda. Naked apart from a towel round his middle, his cool blue gaze on my body. I opened my eyes. There was no Khanda, only the yellowing shower curtain flapping in the breeze.

I dried off, pulled on a T-shirt and a pair of loose cotton trousers. As I padded back along the corridor, I heard a scraping noise from the dormitory. Was Khanda pulling the beds together? Would I walk in to find him standing resplendently naked by the window?

He lay propped up in the far bed, drawing. I didn't know which bed to take for myself – if I chose the one nearest to him would that look too forward? But if I left one between us, I'd be sending an equally clear message, precisely the opposite of the one I so wanted him to understand. Modesty won out, and I made for the bed by the door.

'This is a great place you found,' he said, glancing up from his pad.

'Bridget chose it, actually.' I stood motionless, hoping he might reach out and tap the mattress next to him, but he went back to his sketch. I slipped into bed, pulling the sheet up to my chin.

'I'm knackered,' I said. 'Can you turn off the light when you're ready?'

'Sure.'

I turned to face the wall, listening to the soft scrape of charcoal on paper. Maybe, when he'd finished, he'd creep over, his hand stealing between the sheets, finding my breasts, my legs, his whispering voice on my neck. The light clicked out.

'Night.'

'Night.'

I must have lain awake for at least an hour, listening to the soft rhythm of his breathing. Finally, groggy with disappointment, I fell asleep.

* * *

I woke near dawn, my throat dry, desperate for a pee. Tiptoe-ing to the bathroom, I gulped handfuls of water, hoping to God it was safe to drink. When I came back, a shaft of light had found its way through a crack in the shutters, a triangular slice cutting across the floor and up on to Khanda's bed. He lay on his back, naked, the sheet scrunched down by his feet.

I stared at his brown torso, the band of white with its black patch at the centre, at the pale, thin curve of his penis. My eyes flicked to his face. Eyes closed, lips slightly parted, steady breathing. Was he really asleep? Or had he heard me get up and artfully arranged himself for my return? I stood still, watching his flat, tanned stomach rise and fall.

Slowly, noiselessly, I pulled off my T-shirt, bunching it up over my head before letting it drop softly to the floor. He didn't move, the same steady breaths. I undid the cord on my trousers, eased the waistband and let them slip to my feet. One step forward and I'd be bathed in the light from the shutters. A gambler sliding all her chips on a single throw. I could feel goosebumps forming on my breasts, my heart pounding, a giddy warmth spreading between my legs.

This was ridiculous. It could only end in humiliation. I stepped back, felt the coarse material of his rucksack against my calf. It tipped over, landing with a thud. Khanda's eyes slowly opened. I could almost see them focusing, taking in my nakedness. He didn't move, didn't utter a word. Then his penis slowly came to life, like someone stretching after a long sleep. It unpacked itself, eased into its full shape.

'Hello,' he said.

'Hello.'

* * *

I lay awake for hours afterwards, curled against Khanda's warm, soft body, listening to his breathing, trying to understand what had happened, make it coherent to myself. I thought how I'd tell the story to Sally and Bridget, as if turning it into an anecdote would convince myself it had really taken place.

Eventually, I drifted off. When I woke, it was midmorning, the room stifling despite the shutters. I was still naked, my skin sticky in the humid air. Khanda had gone. He'd probably be downstairs; the guidebook mentioned a restaurant. I pulled a handful of fresh clothes from my rucksack and headed to the bathroom.

In the shower, I let the water sluice over me, trying to remember every detail. His hands on my body, his delicate fingers brushing my shoulder, my neck, my breasts. I remember him asking if he should use something and me telling him I was on the pill (an attempt by my mother to deal with my acne) and after that, we were lost in silence. Unlike me, Khanda seemed experienced. He took his time, paying attention to every part of me, his tongue swift and confident. I came quickly. When he finally slid inside, I gasped. He stopped, asked if I was OK. I pulled him towards me, ignoring the pain, knowing this was what I wanted more than anything else. Afterwards, I stared up at the ceiling, woozy from pleasure, unable to believe what I had done. Then I snuggled in close and watched him until his eyes drooped and he fell asleep.

I turned off the shower and stepped out on to the tiled floor, feeling for the towel. It was only when I had rubbed my hair dry that I saw it: the sketch from the ferry, wedged into the frame of the mirror. Khanda must have crept in, put it there while I was asleep. It was all the words I needed.

I eased it free, stared at the person I had been just a few hours ago and never could be again. A droplet of water fell from my hair, landed silently on the paper, seeping out in a blurry circle. I shook the paper and saw writing on the back.

'Sorry. I need to be here and you need to be there. Best end now while all is beautiful. K.' That lovely, curling K.

I had to read it a couple of times before I understood. I laughed. A stupid mistake! A lie which had slipped out despite myself, an untruth which could so easily be put right. I had no place at medical school, I didn't need to be anywhere. I could stay here. With him.

Pulling on my clothes, I hurried back to the room to see his rucksack had gone. I ran down to the 'restaurant', a tiny room with a couple of faded wooden tables and a tired buffet of pastries and sweaty ham. There was no sign of Khanda. I tried to get sense out of the gangly guy, but he mumbled something incomprehensible in German.

I told myself to keep calm. Khanda would have seen the breakfast on offer and gone to a nearby café. He'd be there now, sipping coffee, waiting for me to rush in and explain how I'd failed my exams, that I was free to follow him wherever he wanted. Except there was no café near the hostel, only a deserted road which seemed to extend for ever in either direction.

I spent the day in the centre of Dubrovnik, searching galleries, scouring museums, hurrying through obscure squares. By sundown, my feet were blistered, my shoulders aching from the weight of my stupid, multicoloured rucksack. I thought of going back to the hostel but couldn't face another night in the same room. I headed for the bus station. Three days later, I was standing on my parents' doorstep.

Now, after all these years, I was about to see Khanda again.

BRITISH
TRANSPORT
POLICE

EXTRACT FROM OFFICER'S REPORT

Report of:	Detective Constable P. V. Chowdhury
To:	Incident Room – Operation 765/Y/C9
Subject:	Post-mortem Outcome – Action 129
Date:	17/06/2019

Sir/Ma'am,

As directed, at 09.00 hrs on 17 June 2019, I was present at Princess Royal Hospital mortuary to observe the forensic post-mortem examination of an unknown male, recovered from the railway line at Network Rail Railway Cutting S72/B South, Beckenham, on June 15th 2019, being carried out by Home Office forensic pathologist, Dr Sheila Aston.

Dr Aston observed signs of autolysis as well as traces of blood-containing foam at the mouth. There was a build-up of gas in the internal organs and the colour of the skin was red. Dr Aston determined the time of death to be within the last ten days, with the probability it occurred at the further end of this period but no earlier than 5 June 2019.

On further examination, Dr Aston determined that injuries and disruption of the body were the cause of death. Considerable trauma was observed on the left side of the head, consistent with a collision with a train. Catastrophic injuries were also found to the lower part of the body.

Examination of the internal organs revealed massive haemorrhaging consistent with being hit by a large, heavy blunt instrument but inconsistent with impact from a train.

It was Dr Aston's view that the unknown male's head injuries were sustained post-mortem, rather than ante-mortem and the victim was dead before he was impacted by the train.

Traces of soil material were found in the hair which suggests the body may have been moved after death.

Dr Aston noticed traces of paint on the cadaver's clothing and recommended further forensic examination to determine the cause of the internal injuries.

Report submitted for information.

DC P. V. Chowdhury

CHAPTER FOUR

I had never washed my hair so fast and had to ask the taxi driver to turn the heating up full in an attempt to dry it, while at the same time trying to do my make-up in Helen's compact.

'Keep still!' I said as we jerked to a halt at traffic lights.

'You think I'm not trying to?' she said, jiggling the mirror on purpose. 'That's what trying not to looks like.'

I could already feel my hips going numb from a skirt which barely fitted me any more, and my top kept riding up, too. The last time I had worn this combo must have been years ago, my life since measured out not so much in coffee spoons, as pastries and bottles of Merlot. Still, if Khanda was going to be there, what was a little discomfort?

As Helen and I stepped into the school hall, we were hit by the familiar acrid whiff of industrial disinfectant. Three decades on and they were still using the same stuff, or maybe it had so impregnated the worn floorboards that they gave off the odour permanently, like giant perfume sticks.

'My God, even the curtains are the same!' said Helen, pointing at the faded chintz affairs hanging in dusty clusters. A wilting Christmas tree stood in a corner, decked out with the same flashing, multicoloured lights I remembered from my adolescence. I scanned the room for Khanda but couldn't see him amongst the crowd of middle-aged bodies huddled near the stage.

'Hi!'

I turned to see a slim woman in a tight crop top, standing behind a trestle table covered with name tags. 'Helen and Kirsten, right? Charlie Haycock – Grantham as was!'

'Charlotte?' said Helen.

'It's Charlie now. So good you could make it,' she said, holding out a tag. 'And here's yours, Kirsten.'

I looked at the remaining rows of names. Over half had already gone.

'Has Khanda Matthews arrived?' I said.

'Khanda, there's a blast from the past! Whatever happened to him?' Charlie ran her finger down a printout. 'Not on the list but loads of people are just turning up.'

'Let's get a drink,' said Helen. 'He's probably already here.'

'Think I'd have remembered that!' said Charlie, turning to a middle-aged man behind us. 'Hi! So good you could make it!' He smiled, his eyes flicking from her chest to her face then back as she leant over to attach his name tag. A wave of sadness swept through me. When was the last time a man had looked at me like that? How long since anyone had seen me at all?

'Come on,' said Helen, pulling me away, then adding in a loud stage whisper, 'Cow!'

'Who?'

'Charlotte bloody Grantham,' she said, glaring back at her.

'I didn't recognise her.'

'Because she's had a shedload of work. Must have married money.'

'It's like Simone de Beauvoir never existed, isn't it?' Helen squinted at me. 'Maybe she made her own money? Paid for it herself?' I said.

'Do you remember nothing?' said Helen, taking a couple of plastic glasses of wine from a makeshift bar. 'Pussface, Miss Zity? Volcano Features?'

It came back to me, the endless name-calling, invariably before class so I'd be red-eyed and reeling for the next forty-five minutes. I looked back at slim, smiley 'Charlie' Haycock, pushing out her perky chest, flashing her over-white teeth at another balding ex-pupil. 'So good you could make it!'

'I'd forgotten,' I said.

'Yeah, well I haven't. Hope her face unravels.'

I smiled, my little sister still defending me after all these years. 'Cheers.'

'Cheers.'

We knocked back the lukewarm wine, then Helen refilled our glasses while I peered around the room, looking for Khanda.

'He's not here,' said Helen.

'He might be,' I said.

'I lied about him coming. Sorry.' I stared at her. 'I knew you wouldn't come otherwise!'

'Helen . . . '

'Hey, there's Katie Rignall! My God, look at her hair!' She tottered off on her stilettos, waving and shouting. 'Katie, Katie!'

What a fool I'd been. As if Khanda would turn up here, in a stifling school hall reeking of disinfectant and crisps. His idea of a Saturday night meeting up with people he could hardly remember, reliving years he'd probably entirely forgotten.

I had no idea what I would have said, anyway. Told him how, after he disappeared, I'd been convinced my life was over, that I could never love again? It was a quarter of a century ago. More. I was married, a mother, a middle-aged woman for fuck's sake. And he'd probably be a middle-aged bloke in elasticated trousers and sensible shoes. Or at a hip party in New York with a supermodel on his arm. It wasn't good either way.

I looked over at the gaggle of women stomping to 'Pump Up the Jam', hands in the air, gyrating, wiggling, wobbling. I had a flash of myself at fifteen, standing on the sidelines of a disco in this very hall, too embarrassed to step into the light, let alone dance. I felt the same now, squeezed into an uncomfortable skirt and itchy top, my mass of red hair all over the place and my face, I knew, shiny with sweat.

It didn't help that as I left, Jess had asked if I was off to an eighties fancy dress party and wouldn't going as a Rubik's cube have been a better choice. Jack thought that hilarious, then pretended not to. If I hadn't been in such a rush, I'd have asked Jess why her frequent rants about body shaming never extended to her own mother.

Now the dancers were singing along to the inevitable 'Come on Eileen'. I wished I hadn't come, that I was back home in my comfies with Mark, where I belonged, wolfing down Bolognese in front of mindless TV, not chasing a decades-old fantasy.

'Kirsten?'

I turned to see a stocky woman in a sensible skirt and white blouse. 'It's Dianne. Dianne Hendon.'

'Of course, Dianne! How are you?' An image of an intense girl in a patched, hand-me-down uniform drifted back.

'Really well. You? You look great.'

Dianne had been one of those girls who fell through the tight net of school friendships, always on the periphery, never part of the crowd. We'd bonded one term after finding ourselves in the fourth netball team, a double humiliation since all the other girls were a year younger than us. For a couple of months we were inseparable, then puberty hit and I met Sally and Bridget. I cringed at the memory of how casually I had dumped Dianne. She hadn't come back after the summer holidays and I never had a chance to apologise.

'So, you're a doctor now?' she said.

'Not exactly.'

'I thought . . . '

'I didn't get the grades.'

'You were so clever!'

'Not clever enough.' I smiled. My whole life smiling away one massive failure.

'Married?'

I held up my wedding ring. 'Mark. He's a teacher, history and sociology.'

'Trust you!'

'Sorry?' I said, not sure I'd heard properly above the blaring music. Dianne gestured for me to follow her and we went back into the entrance hall where Charlie was still behind her desk, expensive smile in place.

'What were you saying?' I asked.

'You and a teacher – it makes sense.' I must have looked puzzled because she added. 'Belisha Bacon? You had such a crush on him!'

'That's not true!' But I was already laughing at the memory; Mr Bacon had been straight out of university, tall and earnest and with an unfortunate propensity to turn bright red at the slightest provocation. We never tired of seeing who could make him go the most scarlet, particularly the girls: 'Do you like my top, Mr Bacon, do you think it suits me, sir? Or is it too tight?' 'Do you have a girlfriend, sir? Would you *like* a girlfriend, sir?'

'Whatever became of him, do you think?'

'He's here,' said Dianne. 'Want me to introduce you?'

I could feel myself blush, and then she was laughing. 'Gotcha!' I could see Charlotte in the background, hoping to be included but Dianne turned her back on her.

'If I'd known she would be here, I wouldn't have come,' she said in a loud whisper. 'She used to call me Stubby.'

'And me Zit Face.'

We laughed.

'Shall we pour our wine over her?' said Dianne.

'That seems entirely reasonable,' I said.

'Waste of even this crap stuff,' she said, knocking back the contents of her plastic cup.

'How about you? Married, kids?'

''fraid so,' she said, taking out her phone. 'Eleven-year-old twins.'

I squinted at the screen. A bushy-haired man beaming at the camera, hugging two sweet-looking girls. *You must have started late*, I thought, trying to do the maths. She told me she had a company making nail varnish bottles. I couldn't think what to say to that.

'And you, Kirsten,' said Dianne, suddenly serious. 'Are you happy?' She fixed me with her pale eyes. For a moment, I was thrown.

'Sure. Absolutely. Tired sometimes. You know. Work, kids. Life.'

She put a hand on my arm. 'I've never been happier,' she said. 'I feel I've finally arrived.'

I smiled, pretty sure she was about to tell me she'd discovered God or Scientology or colonic irrigation. Her phone buzzed.

'Excuse me,' she said, glancing at the screen, then back at me. 'Sorry, my lift's early, I have to go. Have you got a pen?'

I felt in my bag, came out with a chewed biro. Dianne took off her badge, scribbled a number under her name. 'Let's keep in touch,' she said, giving me a quick kiss on the cheek. Then she was off, texting as she went.

I hurried back into the main room before Charlotte could catch my eye. Someone had cranked up the music, turned down the lights. A heaving mass of middle-aged bodies bobbed up and down to Queen's 'We Will Rock You'. I saw a vaguely familiar woman with short hair waving her arms above her head, glass in hand. Could that be shy Suzy Peters, the fresh-faced girl who used to come for sleepovers? She'd been so scared of the dark, my mother had to escort her from room to room, proving there wasn't a burglar hiding in every cupboard, or a maniac lurking in the larder with a steak knife. I pushed through the crowd until I spotted Helen.

'I'm bailing,' I shouted.

'What?'

'Going,' I mimed. Helen pulled me tight, shouting in my ear.

'It's hardly started!'

I shrugged, turning to leave. She grabbed my arm.

'Is this about Khanda? Because that is not fair!'

'Just knackered,' I said. 'I'll call you tomorrow.'

* * *

Outside, drizzle had turned to snow, the deserted road covered with fine white dust. There were no cabs in sight, so I opened my secret Uber account (Mark disapproved, he was a fan of the Knowledge). Within seconds it told me my driver, Zankia, would arrive in ten minutes. I thought of going back inside but didn't want to bump into any more dimly remembered alumni, so tramped around the building to keep warm. What used to be the playground seemed to have become a car park.

I was checking my phone again when I heard a squeaking noise coming from one of the cars at the back. Stepping forward to get a better look, I saw a man bent over a bonnet, a woman's legs beneath. It looked unreal, staged almost, like something out of a film: the man pounding with such vigour the whole car shook. I should have stepped back into the shadows, but it was oddly compelling. Then the woman twisted her head round and looked right at me.

Dianne.

We stared at each other for what felt like minutes, but can only have been a few seconds. Then I scuttled off, breath blooming in the cold. I hadn't seen the man's face but knew one thing for sure – it wasn't her husband. His shiny bald head bobbing up and down gave that the lie.

'Kirst? Kirsten?' It was Helen, hovering by the school door.

'Thought you were staying?' I said.

'Had enough. You ordered a cab?'

I nodded.

'They're all tossers anyway. If I hear one more person tell me how bloody marvellous their kids are, I'll vomit.' She started towards the corner of the building. 'Are the swings still here? I loved them!'

A couple more steps and she'd see everything. A residual loyalty to Dianne kicked in and I grabbed Helen's hand, led her away.

'We should see if the car's here,' I said. Compliant from too much wine, Helen followed me onto the road.

'The fuckers have all got villas in Spain and kids on grade eight violin.' She swayed, steadied herself on the side of a parked car, checking her hair in the wing mirror. 'Why do I put myself through it?'

I said nothing, imagining Dianne a few yards away, legs splayed, head thrown back. And what might have happened if Khanda had appeared. A horn hooted; a white Prius had slid silently up to the kerb. I gave Helen's address and got in next to her. The driver glanced anxiously in his mirror as she slumped into the corner.

'Fifty quid if she throws up – on your card.'

'I never throw up,' said Helen, turning her bleary eyes on me. 'Why couldn't I be more like you? The perfect family, the perfect job, the perfect fucking everything.'

I said nothing, knowing what was coming next. Alcohol wrote a script for Helen; the life and soul quickly gave way to melancholy then bitterness and belligerence and finally a sullen stupor. Challenging her only delayed the inevitable, welcome, progress to silence. 'When you get back, you'll cuddle up to lovely Mark. And me, I'll raid the fridge and watch crap eighties reruns till I pass out.'

'You're going through a bad patch . . . '

'You know how long since I had a shag? *Any* sort of shag?'

I could see the driver pretending not to listen.

'Three years. Three fucking years! And that lasted less than five minutes. A mercy screw from my bastard of an ex-husband.'

'You'll meet someone,' I said.

'Where? In my kitchen? Walking through my sodding sitting room? Driving my kids around? Because I'm never anywhere else.'

Helen's marriage had ended when Tom admitted to a one-night stand at a conference in Edinburgh. Devastated, she'd agreed to counselling which dragged on for the best part of a year. Then she slept with her Czech tennis coach in the hope it might even things out (and perhaps improve her backhand, I suppose). It didn't work on either count, and when she confessed all to Tom in one of their sessions, he announced he was leaving and moved into a bedsit in Pimlico which, it turned out, he had been renting for the last three months.

After the family home was sold, Helen found herself ferrying her boys between flats at opposite ends of town. Pulled out of the local school they loved, they had to take two buses a day to a massive comp where they felt lonely and intimidated and bitter. It hadn't helped when Tom remarried within the year, to a woman in finance with long legs, a five-storey house in Clapham and a seventy-two inch TV – which the boys loved.

I peered out at a side street to get my bearings. Still a few miles from Helen's flat.

'I know it's not easy,' I said, 'but things *will* get better.'

'What the fuck do you know, hmm? What. The. Fuck. Do. You. Know? With your perfect fucking everything!'

If it hadn't been such a long day, if I hadn't seen Dianne on that car or got my hopes up about meeting Khanda again, I might have let it go. But it all came tumbling out.

'My teenage daughter's shagging her boyfriend in my house, at work I'm doing three people's jobs, and I haven't had sex for more than a year. So, not so perfect.' The driver's eyes widened in the mirror. Helen laughed, a burst of mirth exploding through her nose. 'It's not funny!'

'Sorry . . . sorry.'

I looked away, wishing I'd kept quiet, knowing this wouldn't be the last I'd hear of it. Helen grabbed my hand.

'Really, I am sorry.' The words slurred out with the sincerity of the drunk. 'I thought you guys – you know . . . '

I shrugged, not trusting myself to say anything else. 'It's not easy after years with the same person,' she said. 'Have you tried fantasy or toys? A butt plug maybe?'

'For Christ's sake, Helen!' I fired a look at the driver, but he'd turned up Magic FM to block out any more confessions. I peered through the window again. Almost there, thank God, only a couple of streets away now.

'One word of advice, sis. Check his history.'

'I already know his history,' I said.

'His computer history!' she said, suppressing a belch. 'It'll be porn. When a man's off sex, it's always porn.'

'Not Mark. He wouldn't.'

'Kirst, it's like peeing in the shower. All men do it, whatever they say.' She sat back in the seat, case closed. 'Unless there's someone else. You think he has someone else? Not Mark, surely! No, it's porn. Has to be.'

I leant forward to talk to the driver. 'Anywhere here's good.'

Helen tried to make sense of the door handle. 'Are you going to be OK?' I said.

'Apart from dying unloved and unfulfilled? Sure.' She rummaged in her bag for money.

'It's fine, it's on my account.'

'You are a good sister, you know that? A *good* sister.' She tumbled out on to the pavement, managing to right herself against a lamp post just in time. Her face leered up at the window. 'One word: history!' She turned and staggered up the steps to her flat. I watched as she wrestled with the front door, before disappearing inside with a backward wave.

*   *   *

By the time I arrived home, the house was dark. Stepping over the creaking floorboard in the hall, I padded into the kitchen to check the fridge. I hadn't had a chance to eat before I went out and the only things on offer at the reunion had been fingered crisps and greasy peanuts. I reached for a chunk of cheese and the bottle of mayo, found a couple of wrinkly tomatoes in the bottom drawer.

As I pulled open a packet of oatcakes, I pictured Dianne back with her husband, telling him how dull the reunion had been. Or maybe she was in a trendy nightclub, dancing the night away with her lover. What would it have been like, lying on that car, the cold metal pressing against my thighs, Khanda between my legs? I hadn't slept with anyone except Mark since our first night in his absurdly narrow single bed over twenty years ago. There hadn't been any offers, to be honest. I'd had the occasional creep trying to grab a feel, of course, and one spring a registrar with long hair and delightful green eyes had flirted with me for a while. I was flattered, but never seriously considered betraying Mark. Besides, back then, we'd rush home to make love and to hell with what was on TV. I took a bite of my makeshift sandwich, sending a spurt of tomato down my top.

Sponging it clean, I remembered the expression on Dianne's face as she'd looked back at me. She wasn't particularly attractive; the plain girl had grown into an equally plain woman. Heads did not turn when Dianne Hendon entered a room. Yet there she had been, her face transformed by pleasure.

To be wanted like that, just *for* that, was horribly thrilling. Turning the thought over in my mind made my stomach feel light and hollow, the same sensation I'd had peering over the edge of the Eiffel Tower on my only school trip. To let go, sail through the air, hair billowing, eyes streaming and to hell with the consequences. But I always did think of the consequences. Who wanted to be spread out in a mess of blood and bone on a Parisian pavement? Or risk a successful and, for the most part, happy marriage for a few intense moments with an ex from decades ago. It would be insane. Yet here I was, standing in my kitchen, contemplating precisely that.

I cleaned up and was heading for bed when I spotted Mark's computer on the counter. Helen's words about checking his history came back to me. I couldn't. It would be like opening his mail, reading his diary, and I had never been a snooping wife. I turned off the lights and started up the stairs.

Less than a minute later, I was back in the kitchen, trying to remember Mark's password. Something to do with the cat's name. Ruby 4 maybe? The screen jiggled. I tried without spaces. More jiggling. Then I remembered the class Mark taught at school, 3B. I typed Ruby3B and the desktop popped into focus. Neat rows of labelled folders: Finances, House, Holidays, Jess. I opened Safari, hovered the mouse on the History menu, not sure if I wanted to know.

I clicked. The page filled with web addresses going back weeks. I scrolled through the first few entries: news, weather, orders from Amazon, Google searches for unshrinkable hosepipes, villas in Italy (that made sense, we had been discussing where to go in the summer), best sports cars under £35,000 (Mark interested in cars? I never knew), then several Wikipedia pages including surviving Beach Boys and Ironman Triathlon. Not one mention of sex, girls, nudity or porn.

I went back a couple more weeks. More shopping sites, TV listings, history periodicals, maps, traffic reports, hardy perennials, how to fix an electric toothbrush. I gently closed the lid. As if I didn't know my own husband. Absurd.

Upstairs, Mark was lying in bed with his face to the window, mouth open, snoring. As I slipped in next to him, he grunted, turned over and patted my bottom. Then he was snoring again. The reassuring sound of the man I'd been married to for over twenty years. I closed my eyes and tried to remember what I needed to order for Christmas, how many beds I'd have to make up, where the spare pillows were – anything to block out the image of Dianne on the bonnet of that car.

CHAPTER FIVE

That night I dreamt of Khanda. A confused jumble of images: him painting me nude in oils, the two of us swimming in a bright blue lake, lying naked in a hammock together, none of which ever happened. The truth was, I never saw him again. It took three days on buses, trains and ferries to get back home, days numbed by vodka, then, when money ran low, cheap beer. By the time I appeared on my parents' doorstep, I'd lost ten pounds and looked as if I hadn't slept for a week.

To her credit, my mother didn't probe but threw herself at the 'shortcoming', as she named my exam fiasco, with an energy she usually reserved for raising funds for monsoon victims. She contacted my godmother, Jocelyn, a terrifying woman with short hair and raw-red knuckles, who happened to work for the Department of Education. Over a tea of white bread and butter in her austere flat, Jocelyn went through 'our' options. Within a fortnight, I was offered a place at UCL to read biochemistry, a subject in which I had no interest but, Jocelyn assured us, was one of the easier transfers into medicine. My mother's ambition for me remained as unforgiving as ever ('medicine is the only *real* job, the only one which leaves the planet a better place'). Meanwhile, my father restricted himself to disappointed looks and the occasional sigh.

In my first year, I flirted with a lot of things: drugs, men, even religion after one particularly humiliating break-up. Despite my efforts at anaesthesia, the memory of Khanda was always there, ready to sabotage any attempt at a proper relationship. I knew it was absurd, to allow a single, one-night stand to loom so large, but I felt powerless in its shadow. It didn't help that Yugoslavia was constantly on TV, brutal images of the civil war filling every news bulletin. I watched in horror as the bombs rained down on Dubrovnik, callously destroying one of Europe's most beautiful cities – and backdrop to the greatest drama of my life along with it.

At the end of January, after yet another lost weekend, I woke to the unsurprising insight that I functioned best when undiluted by casual sex, pharmacology or doctrine. Best might not mean happy, but it was a start. I drifted through interminable days, attempting to concentrate on dull lectures and deadly practicals but it wasn't until nearly nine months after our one night together that perspectives finally began to shift and whole days slipped by without the name Khanda echoing through my mind.

I began to realise that when he'd looked at me with those painfully blue eyes, he hadn't seen *me* at all, only his drawing, his rendering of me. I'd made the innocent's mistake of confusing art with the artist. Beauty is rarely created by the beautiful and eyes that see it may not see anything else. Behind Khanda's talent, the almost superhuman ability to reach beyond the prosaic and catch it on paper, there lay – nothing. It was a bitter lesson, though probably one best learnt early. Perhaps I should have been grateful for that, at least.

It was Mark who saved me. Not emotionally, though that too, later. He saved me from being arrested. We met at a noisy student party where neither of us knew the host and after which he offered to walk me the three miles back to my shared basement flat. I didn't invite him in for a nightcap, nor did he kiss me passionately under the yellow street light by my front door. All we shared was that long tramp through the cold, during which he spoke eloquently about his plan to become a human rights lawyer, determined to fight for the poor and oppressed.

I knew my friends would think Mark comically earnest, and I surprised myself by finding him attractive. We met up a couple more times for coffee or a walk into town. I liked him, with his mop of brown hair and dark, serious eyes. He couldn't have been more different from Khanda, not only because he was compassionate and interested in other people, but because I sensed he was good. It sounds risible now, but it made a profound impression on me at the time. Then he proved it.

I had been going through a phase of rebelling against the industrial-military complex by relieving local department stores of items small enough to fit into a large handbag: nothing expensive, just the odd knick-knack or handy kitchen utensil. One wet Saturday afternoon, Mark and I happened to be in one of my regular target stores. I was paying for a couple of mugs, though not for a cute little yellow milk jug I'd hidden under a pair of gloves in my bag. As I rummaged for my credit card, the gloves slipped, and the shiny spout peeped out. I distracted the cashier by using a wrong

PIN, then explained my wallet had been stolen recently, and I hadn't got used to the new code. It was a ploy which had served me well on several similar occasions. The cashier had been predictably sympathetic and a couple of minutes later, I skipped on to the pavement, laughing at my ingenuity.

Mark remained coldly silent as I explained it wasn't so much stealing as fighting the capitalist conspiracy. After several minutes of frosty disapproval, I said I'd put the damn thing back if it bothered him so much, no one would ever know. But that wasn't enough for him. I needed to admit to it. To the manager. In person. I stared at him. Was he mad? Who the hell did he think he was?

'I don't want to be with someone who isn't the best version of themselves,' he said.

I didn't know where to start; with the fact we were not 'together' and never had been, or that he was a supercilious, pretentious prig with no right to judge me. I settled on telling him to fuck off.

Mark became an amusing anecdote for like-minded friends. Who'd want to go out with such a pious, self-righteous arsehole? We'd laugh and add a splash of milk to our teas from the little yellow jug.

As the weeks turned into months and still Mark didn't get in contact, I began to miss him. There was no reason to bump into each other, his course didn't take him to the science blocks, and I never ventured into the humanities buildings. Our paths had only crossed by accident, at a party neither of us had been invited to. Occasionally, I worried that I had walked away from something good, behaving exactly like Khanda, but the thought was vague enough not to be acted upon.

Then, one overcast November afternoon, I found myself walking into the department store, asking for the manager. I don't know who was more surprised, Mr Eldridge in his middle-management suit or me presenting him with a mildly used yellow milk jug.

I was sure he'd have me arrested on the spot and had already pictured myself appearing contrite in front of a disapproving magistrate; humiliated in the local press, on the awkward phone call to my parents. Mr Eldridge, though, was so taken aback by this brazen show of honesty, not to mention remorse (I threw in a smattering of the evangelical vocabulary I'd picked up from the God Soc meetings), he let me walk out of his store a free woman. I left him with a used milk jug on his desk, probably wondering what the hell had just happened.

I slipped a postcard into Mark's pigeonhole with one word written neatly in block capitals: 'Confessed'. By seven o'clock, we were squeezed into his single bed and nothing had ever felt so good. He was right. It *was* a better version of myself. And for that, I shall always remain grateful.

* * *

The morning after the school reunion, I woke before six and was navigating in the dark to the bathroom for a pee, when I heard a creaking noise. I assumed it was Mark needing one too, but when I went back into the bedroom he was splayed out, still snoring. I crept on to the landing. The creaking grew louder. I heard a sigh, then a moan. It was coming from Jess's room. What the hell! She must have snuck Jack in. Before I left for the reunion, I had made it perfectly clear he was to go home. I wanted to slam open the door, plant myself on the threshold like a disapproving Blackpool land-lady, while scrawny Jack scrambled for his jeans.

But what would that achieve? Embarrassment all round, not to mention lingering resentment. I thought of waking Mark, insisting we took a united stand, but I knew he'd shrug, say they were adults, why shouldn't they make love? Only it wouldn't be making love. It would be sex.

The noise stopped. Maybe I'd got it wrong, perhaps it wasn't Jack, and Jess was on her own, 'sorting herself out', as Sally used to call it. I stomped my way down to the kitchen and unloaded the dishwasher as loudly as I could, bashing saucepans, clanking cutlery. When I went back upstairs, the house was as silent as a disused chapel. I closed our bedroom door with a determined click. Seconds later, I heard the groan of the floorboards, the click of the front door then footsteps on the path. I peered out in time to see Jack peddling down the street. Jess had got away with it. Again.

Mark had slept through the whole thing. I slid into bed, allowed a hand to caress his tummy. He groaned.

'What time is it?'

'Doesn't matter,' I said. 'It's the holidays.' I moved my fingers down past his navel, to the fine hairs, on to the soft length of his penis. He grunted, slid out of bed. He'd need to go to the loo first. Sure enough, I heard the familiar stream of urine, the flush of the lavatory, a squeaky fart. Marriage, I suppose. Then the disappointing roar of the shower.

I lay back on the pillows, wondering how long it had been since we'd made love on a Saturday morning, on any morning. Time was we'd plan our days around it, rush back from work, rip off each other's clothes. Even after Jess, we still managed. Now Mark preferred to fart and shower than make love to his wife.

Pulling the duvet close, I opened Google on my phone and typed in 'Khanda Matthews'. Only one entry popped up and that was in what looked like hieroglyphics. It turned out to be a BMW dealership in Cambodia. I tried his real name, Andrew Matthews, which brought up 925,000 entries exactly, the first being 'one of the world's most popular self-help authors', with titles such as *How Life Works*; *Being Happy* and *144 Strategies for Success and Happiness*. I almost got distracted by that one but ploughed on with other searches, adding in the name of our school, 'painter' and even Dubrovnik. I left messages on a couple of family heritage sites and was setting up a Google news alert when Mark called from the bathroom saying the shower was free. I clicked the phone off; it was a stupid idea anyway.

When I came downstairs, Mark was making his usual Saturday morning treat, a full, if vegetarian, English. He held out a scraping of burnt tomato for me to taste, my favourite. I'd been too harsh, we were still good, what we had worked. We were going through a dip, that's all; a year-long dip.

Jess appeared in trackies and a loose top, her hair dry. *So no shower*, I thought; she must wreak of Jack, of sex.

'Morning!' I said brightly. She didn't respond. 'Sleep well?'

She shot me a look. I knew immediately she'd seen through my dishwasher performance. 'Jack got off all right, did he?' I said, unable to resist.

'For God's sake!' Jess muttered under her breath.

'What?' I said, all innocence. I couldn't help myself. Jess seemed able to press a button on me and out came the very words most likely to rile her. Every time I gave in, I swore I wouldn't do it next time, that I'd act my age and stop needling. A few days later, I'd find myself doing it all over again.

Jess didn't take the bait this time, just glared at me as she flipped on the kettle.

'I can take you for driving practice if you like,' I said. We'd given her lessons for her last birthday, and the test was coming up soon. 'We could go down by the railway, it'll be quiet around there.'

'Jack's taking me.'

'But he only passed himself last month.'

'So?'

'He's not insured for our car, sweetheart,' said Mark.

'We can put him on though, right?'

'We are not insuring Jack to drive our car!' I said, looking to Mark for support.

'It probably would be a bit expensive, Jessy,' he said.

'You're unbelievable,' said Jess, firing me a look. I was about to point out I did not personally devise the insurance company's underwriting policy when my phone buzzed. I reached for it, but Mark was too quick and held it high above his head.

'No electronics at breakfast,' he said, dodging my attempt to grab his hand.

'Mark!'

'You know the rules,' he said, laughing.

'Yeah,' added Jess. 'She knows the rules.'

'It could be the hospital,' I said, sharply. 'I need to answer it.'

Relenting, Mark handed me the phone. 'You won't have to go in, will you?'

'Hope not,' I said, glancing at the number on the screen. It was from a landline I didn't recognise. I stabbed a button. 'Hello?'

'Kirsten? It's Dianne. From last night.'

I caught Mark's eye and mouthed that it wasn't the hospital. Dianne was saying something about being sorry to bother me at home, how she'd got my number from Charlotte, but I was concentrating on the perfect plate of eggs, tomatoes, mushrooms, spinach and peppers that Mark had just slid in front of me.

'How can I help?' I said, knowing that after her performance last night there could only be one reason she was calling.

'I was wondering if you were free for a coffee?' said Dianne.

'Sure,' I said, speering a mushroom with my fork. 'I'm back at work from the twenty-seventh, but I could probably sneak out for a bit.'

'I meant this morning.'

'Today?' I said, thinking that, despite my curiosity, it was the last way I wanted to spend my precious Saturday. 'I'm sorry, but . . . '

'Please, Kirsten. It's important.'

* * *

We met in my local café, which had been draped with tinsel and Christmas lights for so long they were beginning to look tired and droopy. At first, I didn't recognise Dianne in her black polo neck, high-waisted trousers and oversized sunglasses. She must have been there a while because there was an empty coffee cup in front of her.

'Would you like something?' she said, in a voice so low I hardly caught it.

'A latte would be great, thanks.'

Dianne caught the waiter's eye and signalled for two more coffees. It was disconcerting sitting opposite someone wearing sunglasses in the middle of winter. I could make out a distorted version of myself in her lenses and wished I'd made more of an effort with my hair.

'Are you having family for Christmas?' I said, trying to keep it light.

'Probably,' she said. I waited for more, but she fiddled with her wedding ring and said nothing. The waiter appeared with our coffees, pedantically straightening the cups in their saucers before presenting Dianne with a card reader.

'Do you remember Khanda?' I said, to fill the silence.

'Who?' she said, paying the waiter then waving him away.

'Khanda Matthews, from school. He was a painter.'

Dianne looked puzzled. 'I didn't take art.'

'He had paintings all over the place, huge canvases. Don't you remember?'

She shook her head. 'Sorry.'

I was about to explain how Miss Beech, the head, had one, but then Dianne took off her sunglasses. Her eyes were puffy, red.

'This is a bit . . . well, you can imagine,' she said, dipping a spoon into the froth of her coffee. 'I want to apologise about last night, in the car park.' She looked up at me.

'It doesn't matter,' I said. 'Really.'

'Have you told anyone?'

'No.'

'Not even your husband?'

'No.' I could see the relief flood into her face. 'And I won't.'

'Thank you!' All of a sudden, Dianne looked smaller, reduced. 'I love Henry, you see, and . . . ' She let the sentence drift.

'There's no need to explain,' I said. Which was nonsense; I wanted to know every last detail. Who was the bald guy, how had she met him and, most pressing of all, what was it like to be shagged like that? How did it *feel*?

'It's not how it looks,' she said.

Not like you were having the time of your life, I thought.

'The thing is, Henry and I . . . the fact is, he's disabled. Sex isn't possible between us. Not really. So sometimes, well, I go elsewhere.'

I was so shocked I didn't know what to say. All I could think of was asking if her thighs had been cold on that freezing bonnet. 'It's what keeps us together,' she said. 'I know that must sound weird.'

'Not at all,' I said.

She shot me a sceptical look and I almost told her the truth: that recently I had felt exactly the same. I wanted to be fucked like that. But I took the coward's way out. 'I work with severely disabled people,' I said. 'I've come across these choices before. Was your husband born with . . . problems?'

'God, no,' she said. 'When we met, Henry was incredibly fit. All triathlons and mountain climbing. Which is what made it so difficult for him. Four years ago, he was knocked off his bike at the end of our road.' She put her sunglasses back on, wiped her nose.

'I'm so sorry,' I said, reaching for her hand. Her fingers were trembling.

'There were a lot of operations. The doctors thought it might be OK, but unfortunately it wasn't, not in Henry's case.' We sat in silence, then Dianne pushed her chair back. 'I should be going,' she said.

'You haven't finished your coffee.'

'I need to get back.' She leaned towards me, and I felt her soft cheek against mine. 'Thank you, Kirsten. For understanding.'

She reached for her bag and hurried out before I could ask the one question I'd been burning to know the answer to: why had she told me at the reunion that she'd never been so happy? Why did she say she'd finally arrived?

CHAPTER SIX

The next two days were so hectic I had no time to speculate further on Dianne's gnomic announcements. What with two massive supermarket shops, last-minute Christmas present buying and helping Mark prepare as many of the meals as possible, I barely gave her a thought.

On Christmas Eve afternoon I found myself yet again in the Co-op, picking up a last few bits and pieces, including a bottle of Angostura bitters and a large box of Bendicks Bittermints, both of which my mother always insisted on, and which alone set me back over twenty quid.

Opening the front door, I was hit with Ella Fitzgerald's 'Let It Snow', accompanied by Mark's impressive baritone. He and Jess were decorating the tree, lacing fairy lights through branches and hanging sparkling baubles on ribbons. It looked like a scene from a 1950s movie, the only thing missing a bouncy spaniel and roaring log fire. And another child. This is what family life should look like, I thought, and had a flash of Dianne kneeling by her husband's wheelchair, feeding him with a spoon. How lucky we were to be together, all in one piece.

Mark draped a string of tinsel around Jess's neck, and she giggled like she used to as a child, her face scrunched up, shoulders pressed to her ears. Immediately, I felt guilty about my performance the other morning. So what if she had snuck Jack back in, I'd done worse when I was young. She was having sex, good for her. Life is for living and she should grab it with both hands. Enjoy her body while she could. Look at Dianne's poor husband, ambushed in his forties by a freak bike accident, sentenced for ever to a neutered existence. But if skinny Jack ever hurt Jess, I'd personally cut his cock off.

'That looks great,' I said.

Jess ignored me, the giggles gone, her face blank. I felt the familiar dread of losing her, then she was laughing again, putting the tinsel on her head like a Greek garland.

'Does it suit me?'

I was forgiven.

'Everything suits you,' I said, relieved. And it did; everything.

'Couldn't find the star,' shouted Mark above the music. 'I've looked everywhere.'

'I know exactly where it is,' I said, heading for the stairs. I'd spotted it months ago, in the attic, incongruously muddled up with old towels and discarded swimming costumes.

Hooking down the loft hatch, I gingerly climbed the aluminium ladder and felt about for the light switch. A fluorescent bulb flickered on, its harsh light picking out wispy cobwebs strung between beams. When we first moved in, we had made a half-hearted attempt to convert the place into an extra room, but only managed to board a third or so before accepting it was beyond our DIY abilities. Now the planks soon gave way to rafters and tufts of yellow insulation. Mark used it to store boxes of school reports which, he insisted, had to be kept for six years, though not a single pupil had ever asked to see their so-called confidential files.

The star was where I remembered, buried under a pile of towels, wrapped in tissue paper. Mark and I had bought it our first Christmas together. It had survived well, considering, apart from the hairline crack where a two-year-old Jess had sat on it.

I was about to head down when I spotted half a dozen dusty cardboard boxes balanced precariously on rafters right at the back of the attic, where the roof sloped down. I recognised the large square one that my Pioneer turntable had come in. I had spent months saving up for that, then virtually worn it out playing Bowie albums over and over in my tiny university room. I picked my way across the beams, trying not to touch any of the yellow insulation as a muffled version of 'Little Drummer Boy' boomed up from below.

Ducking under a truss, I pulled back the flaps. Inside was a pile of LPs and for a moment I thought I had the wrong box, but as I lifted out Blondie's 'Parallel Lines', I saw what I'd remembered: a red, plastic-covered photo album.

The cold fluorescent light bounced off the faded photographs: me on a bicycle, posing in the shortest of shorts, doing a handstand on a beach in a bikini. I must have been in my early twenties, post-Khanda, pre-Mark. So young, so thin! I was striking poses the way people did before every gadget had its own camera, when photographs were a delayed pleasure only seen weeks after the event, the day a yellow Kodak envelope dropped on to the doormat.

I turned a couple of warped pages to see a festive table with my father in a paper hat tolerating jollity as if it was part of his job description as head of the family. In another, my mother tilted a trifle, looking earnestly into the lens, while Helen sulked in the background, wearing the tie-dye T-shirt she and I had made together. I flipped to the back, to the page I had been remembering ever since the reunion: six black-and-white photographs of Khanda, taken on that long summer's day in Dubrovnik.

Even after all this time, the sight of his perfect face, his languid, graceful body, stirred something in me. I could feel my cheeks burning, my stomach skipping as it used to at the very thought of him. In one shot, Khanda was staring straight at the camera, a pencil held delicately in one hand, the other curled round his chin, his lips in the half-smile that used to turn my insides to jelly – and, disconcertingly, still did.

I wondered where he was now, and if he still had those gorgeous cheekbones. Slade's 'Merry Christmas Everybody' drifted up from below, dragging me back to reality. I threw the album into the box, sending up a cloud of dust. I should never have opened it. After Christmas, I'd clear the whole lot out, take it to the dump, though even as I made the promise to myself, I suspected I wouldn't keep it.

As I picked my way back to the safety of the boards, I thought the past isn't just a foreign country, it's a whole fucking different universe; an illusion, like the light from an ancient star we know burnt out aeons ago.

Suddenly, the room plunged into darkness. I swore at myself for not remembering the light was on a timer – one of Mark's relentless energy-saving measures. I fumbled for my phone but slipped, my foot scraping past a rafter, sinking ankle-deep into the insulation. I managed to turn the phone's flashlight on and was trying to brush the spiky fibres off my leg when I saw something glinting, something metal. I reached in, gave it a tug and found myself staring at my old Dell laptop, the one Mark said he'd recycled when I'd splashed out on the MacBook.

I opened the lid and pressed the space bar, thinking it couldn't possibly still work. The screen came to life, throwing an eerie glow on to the beams above me. It was a search page, but not Google, another one I had never seen before. A hollowness grew in my stomach as I clicked on the history tab. A naked woman stared out at me, sandwiched between two men, their penises in her hands. The next page started to play a video . . .

'Any luck?' It was Mark, shouting up from the landing. I could hear his foot hit the bottom rung of the ladder. 'Need a hand?'

I stared at the screen – a man was having anal sex with a faceless woman.

'It's fine,' I said. 'I found it.'

'Cool,' said Mark. 'I'll fetch the extension from the garage.' His steps receded as he made his way across the landing.

I closed the laptop and carefully slid it back under a layer of insulation.

* * *

I managed to get through the rest of the afternoon without mentioning what I'd seen or giving in to the temptation to creep back up to the attic. I needed time to work out what I felt beyond that initial fury. There'd be an explanation.

Mark had probably only visited those sites once, out of curiosity, no more. It was no big deal. Though how come the laptop was charged up?

By six, the house was ready for the onslaught of the next day. Jess opened a bottle of Prosecco and insisted we eat in front of the TV, watching *The Sound of Music*, the way we had done every year since she was a toddler. Although I must have seen the film dozens of times, I never before realised how shoddily von Trapp treated his fiancée. Ousted by a younger woman parading her sexuality right in front of her, it amazed me the Baroness managed to be so gracious. I'd have shoved that naval whistle right down the Captain's throat.

Mark and Jess loved every minute, singing along to the songs, checking their phones to see what had happened to the actors (one became an interior designer, another a florist). As the credits rolled, Jess went to have a bath, and I found myself alone with Mark at the kitchen table facing a pile of toys, toiletries and an oversized stocking. He picked up a tangerine.

'I can't believe Jess is still into this,' he said. 'One minute she wants her boyfriend to stay over, the next she's leaving notes for Father Christmas. How does that work?'

Like a man filling his daughter's stocking with mini bubble baths after browsing X-rated websites, I thought, reaching for a pack of chocolate coins.

'The other day, I read that over half of the men in the UK watch online porn at least once a week,' I said, without looking up.

'How do they get statistics like that?' Mark said, without a hint he was one of them.

'Do you?'

'Of course not.'

He said it with such conviction I wondered if I'd made a mistake, if it had been someone else's browsing history.

'You must have looked once or twice.'

'Not really.' He picked up a clockwork penguin, wound it up and set it click-clacking across the table. 'I love these things!'

'Not really?' I said.

'Maybe years ago.' He put the penguin into the stocking. 'Do you wank?'

He stopped, a tin of Crazy Soap in hand. 'Do you?' I said.

'Occasionally.'

'Do you think of me?'

He gave me the weary look he reserved for when I've said something particularly inappropriate in front of his friends. But there were no friends here, only us. He sighed, picked up the bulging, lumpy stocking.

'I should take this up.'

I stared at the table, littered with torn-off labels, discarded paper bags, a dusting of green glitter from the wrapping paper. I tipped the remains of the wine into my mouth, felt its dull taste on my tongue. 'Occasionally.' What did that mean? I should have taken more notice of the dates in his history. I did remember the last one, though, because it didn't have a date. It just said 'yesterday'.

*   *   *

One of the many reasons I loved Helen was I could ring her any time of night, and she'd still be up. At first, she thought it hilarious I'd found 'fuddy-duddy Mark's porn stash', then she caught the wobble in my voice and stopped laughing.

'It's just pictures, Kirst. He hasn't been shagging the school secretary.'

'He disapproves of porn.' I could hear her sceptical silence. I tried to explain Mark wasn't puritanical. He had, or used to have, a healthy interest in sex and had been quite open about it, but this was different, this was porn and porn is exploitative. I felt myself wince as I said the words. They sounded self-righteous, po-faced. Joyless.

'It's not all bad, Kirsten. Lots of women use porn, too.'

'I know.'

'So, what's the problem?'

'I don't know,' I said, suddenly confused by my outrage.

'He's a bloke. That's how they are.'

I bit my lip, stopped myself saying I had never felt that was much of an excuse for anything.

'You want advice from a woman who made a total success of her marriage?' said Helen. 'Confront him. Tell him what you saw. It won't be pleasant, but it's the only way, otherwise it'll fester. And you don't want fester, believe me.'

'I can't.'

'Sure you can.'

'Not now, it's Christmas.'

'Then right after.'

I said nothing. 'Kirsten, promise me you'll tell him. Promise!'

'OK,' I said. 'I promise.'

'Happy Christmas.'

'You too. See you tomorrow.' I hung up, glanced over at the tree with its off-centre star, the note for Father Christmas on the mantelpiece next to the milk, the biscuits and the carrot. Our traditional family Christmas.

* * *

Helen arrived at eleven the next morning, her kids and our mother in tow. Amidst the chaos of present opening, we didn't have a chance to talk, but she did squeeze my hand and ask if I was OK.

Mark and I gave Jess a pair of noise-cancelling earbuds which, he assured me, she had lusted after since trying his. I slipped in a bottle of Ted Baker perfume and a box of bath bombs as a little extra. I got Mark a shirt, my mother bought us both a subscription to the *New Statesman* – a little jibe to remind us we didn't take life seriously enough, I imagine – and Helen gave everyone Amazon vouchers ('I'm a single mother, I don't have the luxury of swanning around shopping malls'). Mark, very generously, bought me a Fitbit.

'It's top of the range,' he said, taking it out of my hand before I had a chance to try it on. 'I checked all the reviews, and this came out top across the board. It tracks your pulse, your calories, your steps, even your blood oxygen levels.'

Marvellous, I thought. And so much more useful than those diamond earrings I had pointed out a couple of months ago. 'Thank you,' I said, kissing him on the cheek. 'I'm sure it'll be very useful.'

The mayhem of Christmas dulled my fury at finding the secret laptop. Too many presents, too much food and way too many bottles of wine, they all helped. I began to see Mark's porn dabblings for what they were: harmless fun.

Why not at our age, after so many years? I'd overreacted, turned into the prescriptive, judgmental partner I swore I'd never become. So Mark had a guilty secret. As peccadillos go, it wasn't so bad. Our sex life had deteriorated, and Mark had simply done something about it, taken it into his own hands, you might say.

Occasionally, serving up the turkey or scrubbing out a pan, I'd get flashes from the videos: a girl bent over, a tattooed man with his face buried between a redhead's legs. They couldn't have been much older than Jess. I wondered where those girls were now, what they'd had to do to end up on the screen of a sad-sack middle-aged man in South London. Then we'd pull crackers or open another bottle or collapse laughing at my mother's hopeless attempt at charades, and the images would be gone.

We finally packed everyone off to bed, settling Helen's boys in the living room on a makeshift mattress of sofa cushions. A swaying Helen gave me a hug.

'It's not so bad.' I could feel her hot whiskey breath on my ear. 'At least he's still here.' She staggered off to Jess's reluctantly vacated room, giving a wayward wave of the hand as she closed the door.

I brushed my teeth, staring at my bleary reflection, aware I'd pay a price in the morning. As I spat into the basin, I remembered something from way back. The next minute I was standing on a wobbly stool, rummaging in the top cupboard on the landing. I pulled out a glossy carrier bag. Inside was the crimson box exactly as I'd left it. I eased off the lid, peeled back the layers of tissue paper, and there it lay, curled and gorgeous. A red lace basque. Mark and I had bought it together in Agent Provocateur years ago, trying not to giggle like a couple of newly-weds as we wrote out the cheque. I touched the delicate fabric. I couldn't possibly still fit into it . . .

I did, more or less. I checked myself in the bathroom mirror. Not bad, pretty damn good in fact, after a child and a decade of overindulgence. I turned off the light and stepped into the bedroom. Mark was reading. Creeping to the end of the bed, I struck a pose and coughed. He looked up.

'Hi!' I twisted to one side, giving him what I hoped was a sexy smile.

'What the hell is that?' he said. I turned the other way, peeped over my shoulder, the way I'd seen girls do in a thousand fashion shots.

He laughed. An explosive, nasal laugh. The sort of laugh you reserve for a pratfall, for someone tripping, falling on their face, making an utter fool of themselves. I froze, too numb to move, then I grabbed my dressing gown and rushed into the bathroom, determined not to cry. I yanked the horrid thing off, tearing at the fabric, ripping the silk with my nails.

'Sorry!' he called out. 'It was a shock, that's all.'

I pulled on my winter pyjamas, dabbing at my tears with a sleeve. 'You don't need that sort of stuff.'

'Is that right?' I stood in the bathroom doorway; my hands clenched to stop them shaking.

'Kirst . . . '

'I found your laptop. The one with the porn on it.'

He stared at me, clearly baffled by this change of direction. 'Aren't you going to say anything?'

'I'm . . . I'm sorry you had to see that.'

'That *I* had to see it?'

He sighed, pinched his nose where his glasses had been. A weary teacher facing a particularly obtuse child.

'Why, Mark?'

He shrugged as if it was self-evident.

'Because you want sex with women who aren't your wife, is that it?' I said.

'You can't have sex with a photograph.'

'Always the semantics.'

'What do you want me to say?'

'Don't you dare put this back on me!'

He sighed again. 'Yes, I look at porn occasionally . . . '

'How often?' I said.

'I don't know. It varies.'

'Today? Yesterday?'

He said nothing. 'What time? The morning, the evening. Both?'

'It's not a crime to view porn.'

'Mark, we haven't had sex for over a year, then this. How do you think that makes me feel?'

'It's not about you.'

'Who else could it be about?'

'Me. It's about me.'

I stared at our linen curtains, determined not to lose it. We'd chosen them together one wet Sunday afternoon, leafing through giant fabric books. I looked back at him.

'But we're a we,' I said.

'I can't talk about this now,' he said.

'Why the hell not?'

'We have visitors. And you're drunk.'

'So easy, isn't it? "She makes no sense. She's barking." You're smarter than that, Mark. You teach gender politics, for Christ's sake!' I wanted to stomp out, hole up in the spare room and cry myself to sleep. But the house was full. I had nowhere to go.

'What I'm trying to say is . . . '

'Forget it,' I said, getting into bed. 'Forget the whole fucking thing.' I pulled the duvet over me, turned over, shut my eyes and hoped to God the alcohol would do its work.

CHAPTER SEVEN

I woke hungover and achy. Picking up my phone I saw it was five fifty. Too early to get up, too late to get any meaningful sleep. I could hear Mark's rhythmic breathing next to me. I turned away, determined not to think about last night, instead concentrating on how many people there would be for breakfast, what we were having for lunch. But as I stumbled into the bathroom for a glass of water, the argument came back to me with sickening, overwhelming clarity.

I cringed at the memory of swaying drunkenly at the end of the bed, crammed into that stupid basque, but I was also furious with Mark for humiliating me. If he had giggled or grinned or even just smiled, I would have been fine. It was the snort of derision that felled me. I grabbed my dressing gown and went downstairs in search of painkillers.

Rummaging in a kitchen drawer, I thought that whatever Mark might claim about desire tapering off, he was still interested in sex, just not in having it with me; he preferred watching strangers do it. I tried not to have a problem with porn per se; I'd read *The Sceptical Feminist*, accepted the problem lay in the means of production, not the product itself. Knowing Mark, he probably restricted himself to sites with a Kitemark guaranteeing they were owned and controlled by women, the same way he sought out organic vegetables and sustainably caught fish. But the bottom line is porn exploits young women for the pleasure of men. End of.

As I laid the table for breakfast, it occurred to me that maybe Mark and I were not so different. Recently, I'd begun to feel more sexual than ever. I hadn't felt so horny since my teens. In my thirties and early forties, I'd thought about sex, but not like this. Then it had been a background hum, rising to the occasional crescendo. Now it was incessant, an infuriating melody I couldn't get out of my head. Perhaps Mark felt the same and found a simple cure, the way men do.

My ever-present thoughts about sex were not welcome, an uninvited guest demanding a five-course meal when the only thing on offer was a TV dinner. Another cruel joke played by nature; the moment I reached the age when men, my husband included, found me invisible, I was obsessed by the sex I was never going to have. Maybe there was a remedy somewhere on the internet, a bitter Chinese herbal infusion guaranteed to dampen my urges down. But I wasn't sure I *wanted* to be damped down. Not completely.

At fifteen, I had an aunt who remarried when she was seventy. She delighted in embarrassing Helen and me by announcing she was having the best sex of her life. I wasn't yet fifty. If things didn't change soon, I could be looking at decades of this. I should see last night's humiliation as an opportunity, not a disaster. I'd sit down with Mark and have an adult conversation, address the real issue, get ourselves back on track. If we both wanted the same thing, how difficult could it be?

* * *

On Boxing Day, we always went up to town to see a play as a family. When I was a child, it had meant dressing up and being on our best behaviour. Now Helen's kids wore what they liked and had to be bribed to leave their phones behind. As a peace offering to Jess, I had managed to buy an extra ticket for Jack (at double the face value, naturally). It was the first time I'd seen him since his squeaky performance and hasty exit the week before. They sat next to each other in the theatre, bolt upright, concentrating brightly on the farce which Mark had opted for this year, because it would 'appeal to all ages'. I noticed neither of their hands were visible, buried under artfully placed coats. I looked away, tried not to think about what they were up to.

My mother fell asleep as soon as the lights went down; Helen laughed so loud I knew it was out of loyalty and her kids spent the entire time kicking the seats in front of them. Helen half-heartedly asked them to stop, but soon gave up. Since the divorce, she had been reluctant to discipline either of them. Tom showered them with gifts and treats while she countered by letting them do whatever they liked. A disaster all round.

In the interval, Mark handed me a glass of red which he'd had the foresight to pre-order.

'Sorry about the play,' he said. 'The reviews said it was hysterical fun for all the family.'

'Just not our family.'

He smiled, and I found myself smiling back as a red-faced man barrelled towards us.

'I got rid of that computer,' said Mark, letting him pass.

'Got rid of it?'

'I hit it with a hammer; apparently it's what you're supposed to do.'

I laughed, the image of Mark attacking an inanimate object somehow incongruous. 'I'm sorry,' he said. 'The whole thing must have been awful for you.'

I nodded. 'I don't understand why, that's all.'

'I suppose sometimes it's easier.'

'Easier?' I said. Like having sex with me was complicated?

'Quicker.'

Before I had time to make sense of that, work out how sneaking up to the attic to toss himself off could be either quicker *or* easier than making love to me, he reached for my hand.

'I'm sorry. It won't happen again.' He held my gaze.

'I probably overreacted,' I said at last.

'No. You were right.' He squeezed my fingers; I felt myself squeezing back. And that was it: our adult conversation over and done. A bell rang. The performance would resume in two minutes.

We should have had a proper talk but it was too late when finally we made it back home. I had to make my mother a warm glass of milk ('Too hot! You think my mouth's made of asbestos?'), then put her to bed ('This mattress is like a brick! And why is it so big? Who needs a bed this big? What a waste of money.') By the time I crept into our own bed, Mark was asleep, and I was so tired I couldn't face an earnest discussion about why he felt it necessary to watch other people having sex.

* * *

After the chaos of Christmas, it was a relief to be back at work. Approaching the OT block, I spotted Kevin by the fire exit, talking to Aaden, the Somalian porter. Kevin was gesticulating with his Lidl bag, no doubt trying to explain one of his corny jokes. I couldn't face a blow-by-blow account of his hilarious Christmas, so hung back in the hope they'd go inside, but then Dr Svetkova appeared, marching over to them with her usual determination. Giving up, I doubled back and went the long way round. When I eventually made it to the treatment room, Jamie was waiting for me, holding a potted plant, a poinsettia by the look of it.

'I thought you could keep it here,' he said. 'Place could do with cheering up.'

'So it's a present to yourself?'

'To us both,' he said, grinning.

We set to work and for the first half hour made more progress than we had for weeks. For the first time, I could see him walking unaided by Easter. We were taking a break when Dr Svetkova appeared, announcing she had the results of his last batch of tests.

'Don't tell me,' said Jamie. 'My legs aren't going to grow back.'

'This is not the result,' she said humourlessly. 'Sexual functionality is unlikely to return.' She sounded like a garage mechanic telling someone their car had failed its MOT.

'Functionality?'

'You will not be able to have sex.' She glanced at her clipboard before adding, 'Penetrative sex.'

'But you said that would be fine, you said it would come back!'

'I said it was possible. Unfortunately, the nerve damage is too great. I am sorry.'

Jamie stared at her blankly. 'You mean I won't be able to get it up?'

'You will still be able to have children,' she said, giving him one of her thin smiles. 'The testes continue to produce sperm.'

Jamie shook his head in disbelief. Then turned to me, glaring. 'Did you know about this?'

'No, of course not,' I said.

'You've seen enough blokes with their legs blown off! You must have had an idea.' He almost spat it out.

'It is unusual,' said Dr Svetkova. 'You have been unlucky.'

'Unlucky?' He swept his hand across the table, sending the poinsettia crashing to the floor.

'You might consider counselling,' said Dr Svetkova, without missing a beat.

After she'd gone, I made tea and cleaned up the mess. Jamie remained slumped in his wheelchair, picking at the skin around his thumbs. I desperately wanted to fix things for him, make everything OK.

'How the fuck am I going to tell Michelle?' he said at last.

'I'm sure she'll understand,' I said, emptying the dustpan into a bin.

'Course she'll understand,' he snapped. 'It's not difficult to grasp, is it? We can't have sex, end of.'

'Not that kind of sex . . . '

'Don't start!' he said. 'I don't want to know all the inventive ways we can satisfy each other, because the fact is, I won't be able to. Not the way it counts. And she won't be able to do anything for me, either.'

What could I say? Sex wasn't everything? Relationships do survive without it?

'Should have fucked everything that moved when I had the chance,' he said.

I couldn't argue with that.

* * *

As I was locking up the office, my phone buzzed from inside my handbag. Thinking it would be Mark asking me to pick up some shopping on the way home, I took it out and kept walking down the corridor as I opened the mail app. When I saw the subject headline, I stopped dead. Khanda Matthews. I fumbled to open the email. It was from one of the family heritage sites I had left a message on, a copy of an obituary. I laughed. It must be a different Khanda – for a start it was from an obscure local paper in upstate New York. I scrolled through the rest of the article.

The details began to add up: his date of birth, his graduation from the Slade, the name of our school. I felt faint. Closing my eyes, I tried to steady my breathing, then looked back at the phone. It had been a freak accident. He'd fallen in the snow when trying to get into his car late one night. The coroner's report concluded Mr Matthews had been knocked unconscious by the fall and died of hypothermia. It didn't say how he'd ended up living – and dying – in the middle of nowhere. Just the bald fact that on February the eighteenth six years ago, Andrew Collins Matthews had died on a country road, alone and cold.

'Bad news?'

I spun round to see Kevin, his mouth turned down in a caricature of sadness.

'I'm sorry?' I said, stupidly thinking he resembled one of Jess's emojis.

'You look like you've had a shock. Are you OK?'

'I'm fine,' I said. The last thing I needed was Kevin commiserating. 'I'll see you tomorrow.' I headed into the dark, not knowing how I was managing to put one foot in front of the other.

It was only on the train home, as I creaked my way over warped Victorian tracks, that a truth I had never before acknowledged became instantly obvious, like a slide projector snapping an image into focus: I had never given up on Khanda. I had assumed somehow, somewhere, he and I would meet up and all would be resolved. I'd tell him how I lied about medical school and he'd tell me how he regretted running away and had thought about me for years. Now none of it would be possible. A piece of me died with him that night and I knew I could never be quite the same woman again.

CHAPTER EIGHT

The next day, I had hardly any appointments in the afternoon, which was normal between Christmas and New Year; people were unwilling to give up a day's holiday when they could wait a week and bunk off work. I sometimes took advantage of lulls like this to sneak home for an early bath, curling up with a glass of wine and a good book, but after the basque fiasco, I had other plans. I'd seen an ad for a gym offering a New Year deal: no joining fee, thirteen months for twelve and an entirely new you within eight weeks. What wasn't there to like? I'd get fit, invest in new clothes and give up alcohol. The new me would be so sexy Mark wouldn't care if I wasn't as 'quick and simple' as his internet buddies, in fact he'd welcome it. Though, of course, I quickly reminded myself, I wouldn't be doing it for him. As the well-thumbed women's magazines in my waiting room were keen on stressing, you need to be attractive to yourself to be attractive to others.

I'd walked past the gym every day for years without being tempted to investigate further, put off by processions of skinny young women sashaying in with their ostentatious water bottles. But an offer's an offer, and *something* had to be done.

The receptionist was a reassuringly normal size, probably chosen so as not to frighten away people like me, but then she introduced me to Marina, their 'Fitness Consultant': six foot, without a trace of fat, let alone cellulite. This gorgeous Amazonian with perfect teeth took me through my health assessment. Did I exercise? How was my diet? Did I drink? Only to forget. I fired her a smile. She remained impassive; how many units a week would I estimate?

She had me strip down to my underwear and stand on scales that measured my weight, BMI, water content and fat percentage (higher, I noticed, than a tub of Flora). It wasn't until she produced a menacing pair of callipers that I began to have doubts. She jammed them on to a couple of inches of underarm fat I didn't even know I possessed.

'Always a problem area,' she said, pinching hard. 'You'll be amazed what a few weeks targeted weight training can do.'

Now she held a wodge of my tummy in her perfectly manicured fingers. I caught sight of myself in the mirror: a woman of a certain age, a certain curviness, being assaulted by a long-limbed stick insect. I would never look like Marina, however many free months they gave me. Twenty minutes later I was in the pub with a double gin and tonic. And a packet of crisps.

*　*　*

Pressing a licked finger on the last fragments of salt and vinegar, I promised myself I *would* exercise, but in my own way. Get off the Tube at Bayswater, maybe Notting Hill in good weather, and walk the rest. Besides, it wasn't New Year yet, I had plenty of time to draw up a proper set of resolutions. I glanced out of the window, at the rivulets of rain running down the glass. No point getting wet, it would clear up soon. I ordered another double and a packet of dry roasted peanuts. It's important to line the stomach.

I tried to imagine what it'd be like if I did get fit, lost the weight I had accumulated over the years. Would Mark rush home after work, throw me on the bed like he used to? Were a few extra pounds here and there all that was stopping him? The truth was, we had grown apart in other ways, too. It began after a particularly boozy summer holiday after which we both resolved to give up drinking for the rest of the year. I lasted six weeks until the temptations of Helen's birthday bash proved too much. Mark was still going four years later. As Oscar Wilde might have said on a slow day, 'There is only one thing worse than a partner who drinks too much, and that's one who's given up altogether.' Every time I poured myself a glass of wine, I could sense Mark looking at me, even when he wasn't in the same room.

After abstinence came running, which for me was something you did as a kid, then for an occasional bus and finally not at all. But for Mark, it rapidly became an obsession. It wasn't enough to pull on a pair of plimsolls and an old tracksuit; now the shoes alone cost two hundred quid and had to be specially fitted by a fancy shop off the Fulham Road. Last Christmas, he'd asked me for a course on how to run. What was his first lesson? Today we will focus on putting one foot in front of the other. Slowly. We don't want to run before we can walk.

I emptied my glass. It was still raining. A single wouldn't hurt, in pubs they're mostly fizz anyway.

My problem, as Mark liked to remind me, was I had no outside interests. I thought I had plenty: listening to music, reading, drinking wine, going to the cinema, the theatre, attending the occasional concert. Drinking more wine. Apparently, they didn't count; those are just things people do. Mark, on the other hand, had 'interests': cuisine (different from plain cooking, you understand); running; cycling (don't get me started on how much *that* gear costs. The bike alone was worth more than our car); photography (I took snaps on my phone, he had a camera suitable for a professional wildlife photographer) and, most recently, learning Arabic via the world's most expensive online course, streamed live from Cairo. Three months ago, Mark had announced that, 'If we want to understand them, we need to understand their language.' I missed the old days when we didn't give a shit about understanding anyone and were happy to sit together rubbishing cliched TV drama. And then had sex.

As far as I could fathom, the main difference between my pastimes and Mark's hobbies was mine only needed the clothes I stood up in, while his required hours on the internet to make sure he bought the best lens or saucepan or shoelace. Maybe *that* was the problem. I didn't require enough kit to be interesting. If sex with me needed a couple of grand's worth of gear, my guess is we'd be at it the whole time.

I looked out of the window again and saw the rain had finally stopped. Perfect. I drained my glass, crunching the last ice cube as I headed out on to the street.

* * *

It was a beautiful evening; the sky a beguiling mix of dark clouds and feathered sunset. Inured against the cold by gin and crisps, I resolved to walk to Victoria. It would be fun. I'd cut through the park, dodge the smuggies on bikes with their silly helmets, zip across Hyde Park Corner, skirt Buck House and pop out by Victoria Station. Easy.

Ten minutes in, it started to rain again. Freezing, sleet-like needles that stung my face and sought out every weakness in my shoes. The park rapidly emptied, leaving only the occasional cyclist struggling against the piercing rain, a spray of filthy water flaring up their back from the rear wheel. Whatever happened to mudguards?

By the time I reached the road, my clothes were soaked, my hair matted and my face numb. Across several lanes of belching traffic, I could make out the haven of a coffee shop. Ignoring horn blasts and silent swearing from inside cosy cars, I zigzagged through the traffic and pulled open the door.

The air was heavy with the smell of damp wool, like a winter classroom at the end of a long day. There were no free tables, so I stood by the door, looking round in the forlorn hope somebody might be about to leave. I spotted a seat by a man on the other side of the room, and was tempted to ask if I could join him, but he looked vaguely familiar and I couldn't deal with bumping into a patient. As I watched him fill in a crossword, it came to me who he was. A little older than in the photo Dianne had shown me at the reunion, but there could be no mistaking the wide face and bushy hair. It was Henry, her husband. He had the broad shoulders and powerful upper body typical of men who spend their lives in a wheelchair. He looked up and smiled at me. How could that be? He couldn't possibly know who I was.

Then Dianne appeared, bending down to kiss him, and it all made sense: he had been smiling at her, not me. She pulled out the free chair and, as she sat, raised her head a fraction. Seeing me, she broke into an awkward smile. I had no choice but to push my way over.

'Kirsten!' she said, proffering her face for a kiss. 'How nice.'

I puckered my lips and held my breath as we embraced, hoping she wouldn't smell the gin. 'What are you doing up here?'

'On my way back from work,' I said.

'I thought you were at St Mary's?'

'Finished early, thought I'd do some shopping.' As soon as I said it, I realised I only had my handbag. 'Window shopping!' I gave a snort of laughter which turned into a coughing fit.

Dianne squinted at me. Maybe she'd caught a whiff of alcohol and was worrying what I might let slip. I reassured her with a smile. Henry looked at her expectantly, waiting to be introduced, though I could sense that was the last thing she wanted to do. I saw he had a scar running across the top of one eye, presumably from his accident. Lucky not to have lost his sight, too, I thought.

'Sorry, this is my husband, Henry,' Dianne said finally.

'I thought I recognised him,' I said. A look of concern flashed across her face, a tiny tightening of the muscles around the mouth. Henry held out his hand without getting up. 'Kirsten,' I said, noticing how soft his fingers were. 'Dianne and I were at school together.'

'Was she *very* naughty?'

'Very,' I said.

He laughed. A warm, inclusive laugh, old-fashioned somehow.

'Sounds like it was quite a party the other night,' he said, folding his paper. Out of the corner of my eye, I could see Dianne firing him the look any couple would recognise, the visual equivalent of a kick under the table. I took the hint.

'I should be going,' I said. 'Good to meet you, Henry.'

'You, too.'

Dianne stood up, wearing the relieved smile of a host seeing off one last, recalcitrant guest.

'We should meet up properly,' she said. 'I'll give you a call.'

'Great,' I said. As I made for the door, I imagined her whispering a hasty explanation: 'can't hold her drink, bit of a pain, dodged a bullet there'.

I couldn't face the thought of walking another twenty minutes to the station, so put out my hand for a taxi. Miraculously, a black cab pulled up, its rained-smeared window silently winding down.

As I settled into the warmth, the driver said something about Grosvenor Place being chocker and pulled us round in a U-turn. Glancing out of the window as we passed the coffee shop again, I saw something that stopped my breath: Henry, standing next to Dianne, fighting with an umbrella. Henry, the man who'd had a tragic bicycle accident, the man who was paralysed from the waist down. Standing on his own two feet.

And that's when it really started.

PART II

BRITISH TRANSPORT POLICE

Criminal Justice Act 1967 s9
Magistrates' Courts Act 1980 ss 5A (3) (a) and 5B
Criminal Procedure Rules r27.1 (1)

EXTRACT FROM STATEMENT OF WITNESS

Statement of:	Jayden Matthews
Age of Witness:	Over 18
Occupation of Witness:	CCTV Operator
Date:	18/06/2019

This Statement, consisting of two pages, signed by me, is true to the best of my knowledge and belief, and I make it knowing that, if tendered in evidence, I shall be liable to prosecution if I have wilfully stated in it anything which I know or believe to be false or do not believe to be true.

At 13.20 hrs on 18 June 2019 I was on duty in the police CCTV Monitoring Centre at Croydon when DS Withers asked me to review footage recorded from Network Rail camera ID 74B, which covers an area adjacent to Ravensbourne Station, Beckenham.

I was asked to review images recorded between 00.00 hrs on June 5th through to 02.18 hrs on 15 June 2019. DS Withers provided me with photographs of a deceased male and asked for any images of the subject over the ten-day period specified above.

At 10.26 hrs on 8 June 2019, camera ID 74B records a male resembling the subject in the photograph. I would describe him as in his thirties, above average height, dressed in jeans and leather jacket with a scarf at the neck. Due to the angle of the camera it is not possible to see the face of the man.

He approaches a woman holding a paper cup, which I assumed contained a hot beverage. I would describe her as being in her forties, dressed in sports leggings and running top, wearing trainers.

The two individuals engage in conversation. Whilst there is no sound, the conversation between them appears heated. After seventeen seconds the woman walks away. The man remains in view for a further eleven seconds before stepping back and therefore out of view of the camera.

I downloaded this footage on to a DVD, which is now marked as item JM/1 and I handed it to DS Withers at 17.00 hrs on 18 June 2019.

Signed,

Jayden Matthews

Bromley Police Station

DC Chowdhury has brought me a cup of tea (almost black, Mum would approve) and a biscuit wrapped in plastic (Jess would not). She did offer 'breakfast', some sort of cheese roll in clingfilm, but the thought of it made my stomach turn. Then she left without saying when she would be back. Maybe there's a legal requirement to give suspects a break every few hours, but I suspect it's more to spook me. They're probably watching right now through a two-way mirror, telling each other they need to let me sweat, like cops do in the movies. I look round for a camera or mirror but can only see a couple of torn public notice posters and a cracked thermostat.

I unwrap the biscuit and take a bite. Ginger. Not bad. Perhaps there's nothing sinister about this at all, maybe they've gone for a 'comfort break'. They kept assuring me I was here on a voluntary basis and I wonder what would happen if I walked out, if a heavy hand would land on my shoulder halfway across the car park. Perhaps it's a test. What would an innocent person do? Sit meekly eating a biscuit, get up and go, or bang on the door and demand to see a lawyer?

I close my eyes, trying to remember what Withers and Chowdhury have on me. Not much, judging by what they've let slip so far, but then they might be a whole lot smarter than I give them credit for. When they first came to the house, I was caught on the hop. They claimed there had been some 'activity of interest' on my debit card and, like a fool, I'd handed it over. But since when did card fraud need two officers to investigate, in person?

'Has someone been using it?' I said, showing them into the kitchen. 'We had the same problem before, on holiday. They copied it and bought twenty tickets for the Holyhead ferry. Apparently, they're easy to cash in because they give full refunds.' I stopped, conscious I was talking too much. 'How about some tea?'

Withers sat at the table, propping an iPad against a couple of Jess's textbooks.

'Are you familiar with Ravensbourne Station, Ms Callaway?'

'Of course,' I said. 'It's the nearest one to us.'

'So you use it to go to work?'

'I go from Beckenham Junction, it's a bit quicker. Has someone been using my card to buy train tickets or something?'

'Do you know the coffee stall at the station, Cappa's Cuppa?' he said.

'I know where you mean,' I said, remembering to smile. 'But I didn't know that's what it was called.'

'Do you think you might have bought a coffee there recently?'

'We're talking about the eighth,' added Chowdhury, handing me back the card. 'Saturday the eighth.'

My stomach lurched as if I'd dropped hundreds of feet. After so many precautions, such elaborate subterfuge, to be tripped up by one trivial mistake seemed almost unfair. Think, I told myself, think!

'Our records indicate a Visa card registered in your name was debited £2.65 by Endline Ltd, trading as Cappa's Cuppa at 10.22 a.m. on Saturday June the eighth,' said Chowdhury, reading from her notebook. 'Can you confirm that was you?'

'Probably,' I said. 'I mean, yes that sounds right.' My left leg began to jiggle. Rapid, tiny vibrations, like having a live wire jammed into my thigh. I crossed my legs, forcing a heel into my toe. The pain brought momentary clarity. 'I sometimes go running in the park, there's an entrance by the station.'

'So I understand,' said Withers, swiping a finger across the screen. I couldn't help noticing his neat, square-cut fingernails as he tapped on a folder, then a file.

'This is from the Network Rail camera at that location,' he said, as the screen filled with grainy footage of the entrance to the station, a time code racing across the bottom. A woman in running gear was pushing a lid on to a takeaway coffee, earphones dangling round her neck. The same earphones that were on my hall table. Withers and Chowdhury must have walked right past them on their way in. 'Could you confirm the individual on the screen is you, Ms Callaway?' he said.

I squinted at the frozen image, not daring to look up in case I involuntarily glanced into the hall. They must have seen the earphones as they stepped through the door, unless I'd thrown my coat over them. Had I done that? My mind was blank. I could hear a rushing noise in my ears, like static on a radio.

'Madam?'

When I tried to speak, it felt as if I had a furball in my throat. There was no point denying the obvious.

'Yes, that's me,' I said. Now another figure appeared, a man wearing a leather jacket – and a scarf. He tapped me on the shoulder, I turned and we had a brief conversation, me shaking my head, him being insistent. I saw myself turn away, disappear from view, leaving the man staring after me. Twenty minutes later, I'd see him again – for the last time.

'What did you talk about?' asked Withers.

'I'm sorry?'

'Looks like you had quite a conversation. I assume you knew each other?' He brought up a still of the two of us leaning in to each other. The shot was blurry, our features difficult to make out, but the intimacy was undeniable.

'No,' I said, trying to sound casual. 'We didn't.'

'Really?' he said, genuinely surprised. 'But he did talk to you?'

'He wanted money,' I said quickly. 'I refused and that was it.'

'He was begging?' Chowdhury didn't disguise the incredulity in her voice. I had no idea where any of this had come from; it was like a different person had stepped in with a barely credible story. But it was too late to go back now.

'He told me he'd lost his wallet and needed money to get home. He said he'd give me his address, but I've been ripped off like that before.' I tried to look knowing, then added, 'Did he try it on with other people, is that why you're here?'

Withers leant back, staring at me in silence, scepticism written all over his face. I refused to be thrown. They couldn't prove anything, I just needed to hold my nerve.

'Do you remember what clothes he was wearing?' said Chowdhury.

'Clothes?' I said, confused. 'You can see, some sort of leather jacket.' The same one I had clamped my arms round so many times.

'Besides that,' said Withers. 'Can you describe anything else he had on?'

'I don't really remember, sorry.' Not the designer jeans, the trainers, the silk boxer shorts. 'I didn't get much of a look at him.'

'Despite him asking you for money?' said Chowdhury, unblinking.

'Constable,' I said, trying to sound both weary and empathetic, 'we both know that's probably not what was going on.' I glanced at Withers. 'The guy was hitting on me, OK?' I felt relieved to have come up with something a tiny bit more believable and noticed a satisfying flicker of doubt cross Chowdhury's face. 'Can I ask what this is about?'

'We're trying to reconstruct this man's last movements,' said Withers.

'Last?' I said.

They exchanged another look.

'You may have heard of a death on the railway recently? We believe this was the individual concerned.'

I felt pummelled, bruised from within. Withers was saying something about wanting to let the next of kin know.

'What do you mean, you have reason to believe?' I said. 'Don't you know for sure?'

'The victim had no ID on him. Which is why we checked local CCTV footage,' said Chowdhury, as if this was obvious to any fool.

'But if, as you say, his wallet had been stolen,' added Withers, more kindly, 'that would make sense. Perhaps he was telling you the truth after all.'

I felt myself getting hot, my palms sweating. None of this added up.

'The problem is,' cut in Chowdhury, 'when he was found, he wasn't wearing a jacket, yet when you spoke to him, he clearly was.' She tapped on the still from the CCTV camera. 'As you can see.'

'What's this got to do with me?' I said.

'Probably nothing,' said Withers, giving me a reassuring smile. 'It does seem odd, though, him asking you for money when he did. It would make more sense if he'd already mislaid his jacket, don't you think? Along with his wallet and phone.'

I had no answer, could only manage a shrug. 'There is something else,' I said.

They leant in, their hope of a breakthrough almost comically obvious. 'He smelt of alcohol. Might that have anything to do with it?'

* * *

I take another bite of biscuit. Looking back, I should have thought of something more substantial than him being pissed. Now I'm stuck with a story I made up on the hoof. I consider coming clean, laying it all out, but dismiss the idea – it would only make things worse.

I finish the biscuit, scrunch up the wrapper and look around for somewhere to put it. There's no bin in here. Health and Safety, I bet. We have the same rule at the hospital: nothing in the room which could be used to assault a member of staff. I'm pushing the wrapper inside the plastic cup when the door opens, and Withers steps in.

'All right?' he says.

Right on cue. They must have been watching me after all.

CHAPTER NINE

By Thursday, the Christmas break felt weeks ago. The weather had remained dull and cold with no sign of sun for days on end. At work, there were rumours of yet more cuts, with at least two vacant posts in the department now unlikely to be filled for another twelve months. I'd had a full-on morning trying to squeeze in extra appointments and hadn't had time for lunch by the time Jamie turned up. I asked if he'd spoken to Michelle, but only received a grunt in reply.

'You could bring her in for a chat,' I said.

'I don't need your fucking help, OK?'

Patients often lashed out at me, they needed someone to blame for their situation, and I was conveniently close to hand. I understood that, but, foolishly, thought I was more to Jamie than an emotional punchbag who happened to help him walk.

We spent the rest of the session more or less in silence, Jamie pushing himself hard, refusing breaks, forcing himself to practise the leg swing over and over. By the end of the hour, he was exhausted, his T-shirt streaked with sweat. He wheeled himself out without looking at me. I thought of referring him for therapy or even to Chaplaincy, though they'd both probably start by telling him to talk to

Michelle and I already knew how he'd react to that. Best to let him work it out on his own.

Between appointments that afternoon, I googled Dianne Hendon. Companies House listed her as a director of an obscure company which had never traded or posted any accounts. There was no mention of nail polish bottles; all it had was her name and a registered address for the business. She didn't appear to have any other public profile or be on social media sites. On the other hand, nor was I, so that didn't set off the alarm bells, which in retrospect perhaps it should have.

* * *

After work, I drove over to the Sainsbury's near my mother to do her shopping. As I pushed a trolley down the cereal aisle, I thought of Henry standing on his own two feet next to Dianne and wondered why she'd made up the story about his accident – and in such detail. Perhaps she thought I'd be less judgemental if she had a disabled husband. But it was still cheating; it would be cheating if he was in a coma.

Putting a box of All-Bran in my trolley, I went in search of denture adhesive. Why would Dianne even care what I thought? It wasn't as if we were great mates, we hadn't seen each other for years, not since school. Maybe the story was for her benefit, not mine. I'd had patients with phantom limb syndrome stare at the place where their leg should be and swear they felt it itch. Perhaps you can have phantom beliefs, too.

* * *

When do old people's homes start to smell? For years my mother's house had the faint scent of flowers and wood polish but now, opening the door into her hall, I was hit by the depressing odour of stale clothes and bleach, with undertones of urine. I found her in the sitting room, a cold cup of tea by her side, trying to do the crossword while an inane property programme played loudly in the background. A tattered dictionary lay on the side table, its cover long gone, the pages worn and yellow. I'd bought a new one for her last birthday, but she refused to use it, said she couldn't get to grips with the thumb holes. Although I knew it was the intransigence of age, I'd felt annoyed she wouldn't let me help her.

'Hi, Mum,' I said.

'There you are,' she said. A three-word tirade of resentment and accusation: why are you late; why don't you come more often; why don't you love me as a daughter should? Determined not to react, I cleared up the tea things, filled the kettle and put the shopping away.

'Peas?' she snapped.

I turned to see her in the doorway, stick in hand. She'd been using it since her hip operation last spring and now just the sound of its innocent click click click drove me mad. She pointed it at the packet of Birds Eye. 'I don't like peas.'

'You do.'

'You think I don't know what I like?'

'You've had them all your life.'

'Nonsense! I've never liked peas. Never.'

'Fine,' I said, shoving the damp packet into my bag. 'I'll take them home.'

Driving back, my hands gripped the steering wheel until they ached. Why did she have to be so irritating, so bloody critical? Underlying it, of course, lurked her unspoken judgment that I had thrown my life away, become an OT, a second-rate, quasi-medic rather than the high-flying consultant she longed me to be. Why did I let her get away with undermining me the whole time, just because she was my mother?

Yet the thought of her sitting alone in that sad chair, staring at the television, waiting until it was time to heat her quiche, made me want to weep. While I'd be in the bosom of my family, laughing and chatting and enjoying a glass of wine, she'd be hauling herself upstairs, struggling to get out of her clothes before slipping into the cold bed she'd shared with my father for forty-three years, to face another lonely night.

I'd be nicer next time, of course I would.

I had told my mother I needed to get back for Jess, which was not strictly true; she went to revision club on Wednesday evenings and wouldn't be home until eight at the earliest. On a whim, I took a left at the big roundabout and headed for the address I'd found for Dianne on the Companies House website. I had expected an office block or maybe a unit on an industrial estate, so had to check twice when Waze had me pull up outside an impressive, detached house. Was this really where Dianne ran her nail polish empire? The windows were dark, no one seemed at home. I should probably have driven off right then, but instead I parked opposite and settled in to wait.

It was a gorgeous house, flat-fronted white stucco with tall sash windows and those impossibly thin wooden struts.

Mark once told me Americans call them muntins. It was the kind of useless information we both used to love.

I had always wanted to live in a house like that and, early in our marriage, it felt a real, if distant, possibility. A doctor and lawyer, both on decent salaries, if we worked hard and invested wisely, we too could hold dinner parties in a Georgian home with a two hundred foot garden. But I never reapplied to medical school, and Mark never practised law. After seven months of articles, he announced he had become disillusioned with the legal profession and wanted to retrain as a teacher. In love and not a little in awe of such certainty, I put my plans of medicine on hold. We couldn't both follow our dreams at the same time, one of us needed to earn the money. I took a job with a local travel agent, organising holidays for the sort of people who lived in houses with multiple muntins. My mother took it as a personal insult while my father added it to the long list of disappointments I had brought him, starting by being born without a penis.

Despite my parents' disapproval, those years were some of the happiest of my life. Living in a tiny flat near Hounslow, with three mismatched chairs and a kitchen table balanced on paint tins, it felt as if I was finally doing something good, something worthwhile. Twenty-four years later, parked opposite a house I could never afford, I wondered how it might have been had Mark stuck to the law, and I'd become a doctor. But hey, who needs stucco and lovely windows when there are underprivileged children to educate? Muntins had long ago been filed under 'useful answers to crossword clues'.

I looked over at the tastefully matt green door of number twenty-five, wondering if I should ring the bell, and what to say if the owner turned out to be an entirely different Dianne or, come to that, the right one. This whole enterprise was mad – stalking a school friend I could hardly remember, with no idea what to say if I did bump into her. I needed to step back. It was a phase, that's all. Like my adolescent obsession with Khanda, the reckless abandon of my college years or the giddy happiness of early marriage. This too, would pass. I'd look back in six months and see it for what it was: a delayed menopausal crisis before the calm waters of later middle age. I could take up badminton or Pilates. Maybe even bridge.

I had started the car and was about to pull out when I saw them: a couple of little girls laughing as they jumped over cracks in the pavement. And behind them, smiling at their antics, Dianne. I jammed on the brakes, ducking down in my seat. A horn hooted. I bobbed up to see a gesticulating woman in a bullying 4x4. The next moment Dianne was knocking on my passenger window.

* * *

To her credit, she didn't question what we both knew was a lie: that I had been in the area and by chance had pulled over to make a phone call in her street. Right opposite her house, the address of which she had never told me. Instead, she introduced me to her children as an old school friend and invited me in.

They must have gutted the place, rebuilt it in the uncompromising style so beloved by modern architects – all hidden cupboards and austere surfaces with no concession to everyday human untidiness. Dianne led me into the massive

117

kitchen, one whole wall of which was a window, looking on to a landscaped garden where her daughters bounced on a sunken trampoline, giggling as they held hands, flying high into the air. The bottle business was clearly treating her well.

'You need to know we're mortgaged to the hilt,' she said.

'I'm sorry?'

'So if you're after money, you've picked the wrong target.'

I stared at her, baffled.

'Money? What do you—?' She cut me short.

'I saw you in the taxi,' she said. 'So you must have seen me. Seen both of us. I assume that's why you're here?'

We stood facing each other either side of her snooker-table-sized granite island. Dianne defiant and defensive; me desperately trying to think what to say when all I wanted to do was run out of there and never see her or her perfect house again.

'Could I have a glass of water?' I said at last.

She hesitated then opened a cupboard and chose a tumbler from a row of others neatly stacked upside down.

'Still or sparkling?'

'I don't mind.'

She stood there, glass in hand. 'Sparkling,' I said. 'Please.'

She pressed a button on a gleaming tap, and the next minute I was holding a tumbler of bubbling, ice-cold water. 'What a wonderful kitchen,' I heard myself saying.

'What do you want, Kirsten?'

I took a sip of the water, felt it fizz in my mouth.

'The other night, at the reunion, you said you'd never been happier,' I said. She gave the slightest of shrugs. 'That you had finally arrived. Do you remember?'

'No.'

I held her look.

'I may have done,' she said. 'I'd probably had too much of that awful wine . . . ' She trailed off as if it was enough of an explanation.

'Nothing to do with what happened in the car park, then? Or Henry?'

She turned away, wiped a few droplets of water off the shiny granite surface. Then she reopened the cupboard and took out a couple of wine glasses.

*   *   *

We sat in a living room separated from the kitchen by a huge aquarium. Brightly coloured fish swam aimlessly from side to side as Dianne described what led up to her performance at the reunion. Her marriage had started well but gradually, imperceptibly, the passion and fun drained away. While she enjoyed Henry's company, appreciated him as a companion and father to her children, the zip and zest had vanished.

'And we hardly ever had sex.' She stared at the floor and for a moment I thought she might cry, but then she looked up, dry-eyed. 'Not so unusual, I suppose.'

'What didn't you leave him?' I said.

'We had two young kids and I was trying to build a business. Besides, we were married, you know? I had been brought up to think marriage was for the long haul, that sexual fulfilment was for the young or people in magazines with made-up names. I resigned myself to toughing it out. I assumed we'd come out the other end eventually. But then I met Livia.'

Livia, she explained, was an American living in London who, after several Christmas cocktails, confessed to using an 'introduction service', for people who 'shared a desire for intimacy without compromising their domestic situation'.

'They called themselves Amorem. It was an agency for people in relationships who wanted sex without strings,' Dianne said matter-of-factly, refilling our glasses.

'Like Tinder?' I said.

'A lot more discreet than that – and safer.'

'Did you sign up there and then?'

'To be honest, I thought it was a mad idea and put it right out of my mind. But then we met again, on holiday in the Isle of Wight of all places. Things hadn't improved with Henry, and when Livia's husband insisted on taking him sailing in a gale, she and I hunkered down in front of a log fire with a bottle of wine. Pretty soon what had seemed bizarre and weird was sounding increasingly attractive. By the time Henry returned, I had told Livia I was in.'

'My God, Dianne!'

'I know, crazy, huh?' She looked out of the window at the twins, now sitting on the trampoline, swapping the intimate secrets of eleven-year-olds. 'I never saw myself as the sort of woman who cheats, I still don't really. But it works, you know?' She looked back at me. 'I suppose that's what I meant about being happy, about arriving.'

We sat in silence, the sound of her children's laughter wafting in from the garden.

'What was it like, the first time?' I said.

Dianne stared at the condensation on her glass as it coalesced into a drop and ran down the stem.

'You remember the feeling you get when you lie flat on your tummy on a swing?' she said at last. 'The hollow, empty feeling deep inside? That's what it was like. Both thrilling and awful.'

'Did you feel guilty?'

'Not immediately. But a couple of days after my first encounter, when Henry and I were watching the girls in the park, I nearly confessed, told him everything.'

'Why didn't you?'

'Because I wanted to do it again.' She smiled. And then we were both laughing, out of control. It was like being back at school, sharing a risqué joke at the back of the classroom. As our laughter finally subsided, Dianne poured the remains of the wine. 'They say orgasms are like opiates,' she said. 'Apparently they deliver the same rush of dopamine. The more you get, the more you want. It can be difficult to stop.'

'And Henry?'

She twisted the stem of her glass between her fingers for a moment. 'I've always loved Henry, and I've never wanted to leave him. Now I don't have to.' She looked totally sincere.

'Do the two of you still . . .?'

She nodded. 'And it works. In many ways, better than ever. I can dedicate myself entirely to Henry's needs. It doesn't matter if I don't get much out of it, I know I can get the real thing any time.'

'Always with the same guy? The one I saw?'

'God, no.'

I must have looked shocked. Dianne shrugged. 'The last thing I want is to get involved with any of them, or them me. Not being exclusive keeps things simple, understood.'

I looked at the smear of lipstick on my wine glass.

'Mark and I haven't had sex in over a year,' I said suddenly. It was a relief to say it out loud.

'I thought it might be something like that,' said Dianne. 'Have you tried—'

'Talking, counselling?' I interrupted. 'It makes no difference, or if it does, only for a few weeks, a month at most.'

'You could move on, find someone else.'

'I don't want to find someone else.'

Dianne picked at the label on the wine bottle like a distracted teenager. At last, in a voice so quiet I had to strain to hear it, she said, 'Once you cross the line, Kirsten, that's it.' She looked up, held my gaze. 'There's no way back.'

'I don't want to go back.'

CHAPTER TEN

First thing the next morning, before even getting out of bed, I checked my phone for messages. I'd left Dianne's with an email address for Amorem scribbled on an old receipt and sent off my enquiry the moment I got back to the car, before I lost my nerve. Despite Dianne warning it might take a while to receive a reply, I had been checking my mailbox obsessively ever since. Nothing had appeared.

I came into the kitchen to find Jess surrounded by ring-binders, earbuds in, intently studying a textbook. Recently, she had taken to getting up before six to revise. I could trace her enthusiasm back to September, when Mark and I had attended a parents' meeting at the school. Mr Weatherby, who taught maths and had disconcerting bug eyes which he blinked every few seconds, had launched into an energetic description of how well Jess had been doing.

'She's a talented girl.' Blink. 'She's worked very hard this term.' Blink. 'She has a good chance of excellent grades.' Blink blink blink. As we headed for the physics table, I whispered to Mark could this be the same Jess who howled at long division and refused to learn her times tables? Maybe Mr Weatherby had muddled her up with another girl.

'Why do you have to belittle her?' said Mark.

'It's a joke,' I said, surprised at his sharp tone. 'I'm very proud of her, you know that.'

Mr Sanchez, Head of Biology, turned out to be equally enthusiastic, and Ms Brady and Mr Pinkerton. As we were leaving, the head came bustling over. In the last four years, we'd probably spoken to her less than five times. I was amazed she knew our names.

'I wanted to say how pleased we are with Jess's progress.' She wore one of those condescending smiles professionals reserve for the rest of us. I had my own version at work. 'We're very excited she's considering medicine.' Which was news to me.

Walking across the frozen car park a few minutes later, I was still trying to take it in.

'Did you know about this?' I said to Mark, getting into the car. 'The applying to medical school thing?'

'She's hinted at it a couple of times,' he said, turning on the windscreen wipers. They juddered across the frosted glass.

Not to me, I thought, pulling on my seat belt and clicking it into place.

'It's mad,' I said.

'I don't know . . . '

'All those extra exams, the personal statement, not to mention having to get three A stars.'

'Her teachers seem confident she can handle it,' said Mark, fiddling with the heating controls. I pushed his hand away and flipped the defroster on.

'Do you have any idea how many people apply to medical school every year?' I said. 'And how many get in?'

Mark eased the car into the road. 'I know how difficult this must be for you, Kirsten.'

'What's that supposed to mean?'

He shrugged. 'Not being offered a place yourself.'

'I think I'm over it now, Mark. It was decades ago.'

'You don't regret not trying again?'

Every day, I thought. *Every fucking day.* 'This isn't about me,' I said. 'I don't want Jess to be disappointed, that's all.'

'She's doing brilliantly,' he said, slowing at a roundabout. 'And we should support her in whatever she chooses to do.'

'Of course we should,' I said, staring out at the sleet. 'Absolutely.'

As we drove through the freezing night in silence, I tried to work out what I felt. I *was* proud of Jess; it was a great achievement even to be thinking of medicine. She would be stupid not to grab the chance with both hands. No one would be more delighted than me to see her become a doctor. No one.

And I felt the same now as I watched her bent over her textbooks at the kitchen table. She looked up, smiled, then went back to her studies. My beautiful, clever daughter.

* * *

At work, I was midway through helping a ten-year-old with a dislocated shoulder when I received a call from an A&E nurse. My mother had tripped while hoovering the stairs, hit her head and, they suspected, broken her left wrist. She'd managed to crawl to the phone and had been taken to triage at her local hospital, Queen Mary's in Sidcup.

I phoned Helen at work. After a tirade about how stubborn Mum was and if she had agreed to move into a bungalow, none of this would have happened, Helen announced she had to get back into court and I'd have to deal with the hospital. The fact this meant cancelling my own patients didn't seem to bother her.

To get to Queen Mary's, I had to take the train back to Beckenham Junction, pick up the car from the driveway I hired by the week, then drive for half an hour to Sidcup before spending another half an hour looking for a parking space and finally wrangling with a ticket machine for twenty minutes as it demanded to know everything from my car registration to the date Jess took her first steps. Any vestige of good mood had long gone by the time I stomped into the main block, hot and sweaty and ready to bite the head off anyone in my way. I was unforgivably sharp with a receptionist, despite knowing she was one of the unsung heroes of the NHS, on the sort of annual income some people blow on a week's skiing.

I finally located my mother as she was being wheeled into the X-ray department by a young porter.

'What are you doing here?' she said.

'I thought you might like someone with you.'

'My father was a doctor, for God's sake. Hospitals hold no fear for me.' She turned to the porter pushing her wheelchair. 'And what's your name?'

'Cabdulmajiid.'

'What's that?'

'Cab-dul-ma-jiid,' said the porter, enunciating each syllable. My mother stared at him, mouth slightly open, waiting for her brain to catch up.

'I'll call you Ken,' she said. I fired him an apologetic smile. He shrugged; it wouldn't have been the first time. I knew from the way people treated Janice in my own department how deep casual racism ran in the British public. My mother had been a young woman in the sixties, yet acted as if she'd spent an Edwardian childhood in India, not post-war Pinner. Maybe it's what happens in old age; you revert to prejudices that were out of date before you were even born.

While my mother was X-rayed, I sat in an unloved waiting room on a hard, plastic chair with nothing but a couple of STD posters for company. I checked my phone yet again. An email from Mark saying he would be late, another last-minute emergency departmental meeting, and a one-line text from Jess claiming she was 'studying with friend' that evening, for which she meant, 'up to no good with skinny Jack'. I was about to text her back when my phone vibrated with an incoming email.

I recognised the address immediately. It was from Amorem. I could feel my breath coming in short bursts as I scanned the few lines: 'Thank you for your enquiry. To take further, 12.30 Thursday, Selfridges kitchen department. Blue coat. Please confirm. Amorem'. I stared at the neat, luminescent writing as it hit me that within days I could be on my first date. I felt sick and excited, like I used to on sports day when forced to run the eight hundred metres, knowing I'd come last.

'Your mother's a remarkable woman.'

I looked up to see a twelve-year-old radiographer helping Mum out of the X-ray suite.

'Sorry?' I said, my thoughts all over the place.

'Playing on her phone as usual,' said my mother.

I shoved it back in my bag.

'She's amazing for her age,' said the twelve-year-old.

'Nonsense,' said my mother, beaming.

It always infuriated me the way she could switch on the charm, winning over strangers, convincing them she was a lovely old lady. I glanced at the radiographer's badge and thought of enlightening Gemma on just how remarkable my mother could be.

'She has what we call a Barton's fracture. It's a dislocation of the . . . '

'Radiocarpal joint, I know,' I said, unable to resist adding,' 'I work at St Mary's.'

'Right, cool,' said Gemma. 'Then you know all about it.'

'Hardly,' said my mother. 'She's an OT, not a proper doctor.'

Gemma looked from one to the other of us, not sure how to respond.

'Will she need a cast?' I said, to help her out.

'Absolutely. For about six weeks. Then you should be right as rain!'

My mother reached out, squeezed Gemma's hand. 'Thank you so much, you've been wonderful.'

'No problem,' smiled Gemma. 'I can get a porter if you'd like help?'

'It's OK,' I said, adding, '*I can tip her down the stairs on my way to the car.*' Only, of course, I didn't. I just returned her smile and said we'd be fine.

I spent the next two hours organising a plaster for my mother's arm while taking the occasional peek at my phone to make sure I'd read Amorem's message correctly.

I speculated endlessly why they'd want to meet in a department store of all places, why not in their offices or a coffee shop? And if I did agree to go, what should I wear? Was I interviewing them, or they me? The whole thing seemed so bizarre as to be bordering on the unreal. Maybe I should call Dianne, ask if this was normal.

On the journey back, I found myself wondering what sort of sex life my parents had had, conversation with my mother having lapsed after I lost the argument to have her stay with me for a few days ('I am perfectly capable of looking after myself, thank you very much. I am not a child').

When Helen was sixteen, she'd claimed to have heard Mum and Dad at it one Sunday morning, though to me her description sounded suspiciously like a scene we'd seen the week before on *Play for Today*. As far as I could tell, they were entirely asexual. I never saw them kiss, hold hands or so much as touch each other unless by accident. How they managed to conceive two children was a complete mystery. Hardly a mystery, I corrected myself. For all I knew, they could have been the same as Mark and me, at it the whole time until pregnancy, whereupon sex was put aside, like a child giving up stamp collecting or keeping seashells. Maybe one of them even had an affair. A mad part of me wanted to ask, but by then my mother had fallen asleep. Maybe another day.

I arrived home to an empty house. Grabbing an apple, I poured myself a glass of wine and called Helen to update her on Mum. She was predictably outraged that I had taken her back to her own home: how did I expect an old woman to look after herself with a broken arm?

'Wrist,' I said.

'How is she supposed to clean her teeth, brush her hair? Cook?!'

I explained it was her left hand, that we had been through it all together and both felt she'd be fine. Besides, she had refused to come back with me.

'You should have insisted,' said Helen. I could hear her boys rampaging in the background.

'If you're worried, Helen, you could drive over yourself and see how she is.'

This elicited another tirade along the usual lines of did I have any idea how difficult it was to be a single mother and a professional woman, but I wasn't listening – I'd put her on speaker and was staring, yet again, at the message from Amorem.

* * *

I spent most of the weekend rehearsing arguments for and against going to the meeting. Should I follow Dianne's example, or dismiss the idea as an embarrassing fantasy? It was like looking at one of those optical illusions which flip between an old woman in a shawl and a girl with flowing hair; I could see two versions of my future though never both at the same time.

I tied myself in knots trying to tease out what constitutes cheating. Looking, fantasising, remembering? I had done my fair share of those over the years. Maybe it has to do with what you would like your partner to know. Cheating isn't cheating unless it's secret. Which made Mark serially unfaithful, albeit with an old laptop and a box of Kleenex.

That was pure sophistry. Everyone masturbates, and while porn might not hit the spot for me, I did have memories of Khanda, amongst others, to rely on when needed. Making love, though, was different. The whole point is to lose yourself, to meld and merge and flow into the other. Masturbating is the opposite, the ultimate reminder we are alone. And I was fed up with feeling alone in a houseful of people. A house that would soon have one less person in it. I didn't have to put up with it any more. But if I did take this step, I might lose everything. I went to bed as confused as ever.

CHAPTER ELEVEN

The next day was New Year's Eve. I was wrangling with Mark's espresso machine, trying to get it to produce a simple cup of coffee when Jess appeared, carrying the Fjällräven backpack Mark had bought for her sixteenth birthday.

'You don't know how to stop this thing frothing, do you?' I asked. She leant in and pressed a couple of buttons, then picked her coat off the back of a chair.

'You off somewhere?' I said.

'Yup,' she said, wrapping a scarf round her neck.

'You have remembered Helen's coming over tonight, to see the New Year in? Dad's cooking a special meal.'

'Sorry, going to a party.'

'You said you'd eat with us.'

'I changed my mind.'

'Jess . . . '

'What? It's not a big deal. It's only Aunty Helen.'

'And us.'

'Exactly.'

I took a breath, determined not to rise.

'So where is it, this party?'

'Why do you have to know everything?'

'It's perfectly reasonable to ask my seventeen-year-old daughter where she's going,' I said, knowing I sounded like my own mother. I remembered how infuriating I'd found her endless quizzing, yet now couldn't help myself doing exactly the same. What makes mothers and daughters go through this ritual rhetoric as if they have been handed lines by a bossy director who will tolerate no deviation from the script, however overblown it is?

'I'm staying at Mel's. Satisfied?'

All I knew about Mel was she had a 'super cool' place in Chelsea, courtesy of working as a so-called 'live-in guardian' for an old lady, who seemed remarkably tolerant of guests partying in her basement. 'See you tomorrow,' said Jess, and then she was gone. I caught a glimpse of her striding down the road, face to the wind.

She used to love New Year's; being allowed to stay up, watch Big Ben on the telly, sing 'Auld Lang Syne' with the adults. Now she preferred to celebrate with people I hardly knew. I could feel the tears rising. Images of her as a toddler crowded in: her first day at school, a trip to A&E with a cut big toe, summer holidays on the beach, buying her first pair of high heels. What the hell's happening to me? She was going to a party, not emigrating. The tears kept coming, though.

It was Mark who'd suggested having Helen over, knowing she didn't have the boys this year. Tom and the Horse, as Helen called the new Mrs Fordwell, had taken them skiing, a pastime Tom had previously claimed was poncy and too expensive. I agreed it would be kind to include her, though had my reservations. Helen in her cups could bring out the sanctimonious in Mark. The more she lost herself in self-pity, the more he felt compelled to explain what she should do with her life. There is nothing quite as wearing as a sober man lecturing a pissed woman. Give me two drunks any day.

Helen arrived earlier than planned, I was only just out of the shower. She claimed she wanted to 'discuss Mum', then proceeded to hoover up the remains of the sloe gin before segueing effortlessly on to red ('No need to change glasses, saves on the washing-up'). The holidays were a dangerous time for Helen; Tom had broken the news about leaving her on a Boxing Day, so the whole of December – and January – had become toxic.

She used to be a high-powered defence lawyer, defending the indefensible Mark called it. She made a small fortune, or so it appeared to us. I once worked out Helen's hourly rate was the same as a trainee nurse earned in a week.

Six years into their marriage, Tom made partner in a firm of accountants and they moved to the suburbs for a better quality of life, good schools and a garden you could sit in. Helen downsized her job and took on a lot of pro-bono work for the local community. She said she wanted to give something back and the pressure was less. Besides, life is not all about money, is it? She could spend time with the boys, take up other interests, become 'more human', whatever that meant. Mostly Pilates classes followed by bitching in coffee shops with other yummy mummies it seemed to me.

When Tom left, the dream move became the worst decision of her life, forced on her by a husband who couldn't handle being married to a successful, empowered wife earning (at one time) more than him. Not only had he apparently dragged her kicking and screaming from a London life she adored, but by sequestering her away in the back of beyond, sabotaged her career, too. She couldn't afford to move back to central London, and the commute, with two young kids, was impractical. Besides, once you drop off the cliff face of a 'proper' career (a dig at me, there), you can never get back. Tom, as she liked to say after a couple of glasses, had fucked her, then fucked her.

For most of the evening, I managed to keep Helen distracted with chit-chat about my work, mutual friends and Jess's plans for the summer, but by the time we started on the cheese, with still over an hour to go before midnight, the subject inevitably turned to Tom. I tried to head it off by suggesting we play a game, but she'd have none of it. Helen, naturally, laid the blame at Tom's door. The guy was a two-timing bastard, end of. Mark, sipping his elderflower pressé as it if were Grand Cru, pointed out that Helen had chosen him, not the other way round.

'You can't help who you fall in love with,' said Helen, refilling her glass.

'Of course you can,' said Mark.

'You *chose* me, did you?' I said, trying to arrange the cutlery in the infuriating top tray of the dishwasher.

'I chose to go ahead, yes.'

'Like a mobile phone contract?'

'You meet someone, you're attracted to them, you hang out,' said Mark, emphasising each point with a tap of the cheese knife on the table. 'If you're lucky, you fall in love and *that*,' a louder knife tap, 'is when you exercise choice. If you find an axe in their cupboard, you opt out.' He laid the knife back on the cheese board as if the gesture made his argument incontrovertible.

'Tom didn't have an axe in his cupboard,' said Helen, pouring herself more wine. 'Not that I ever saw, anyway.'

'He was going out with another woman when you met him though, right? He cheated on her to be with you, I seem to remember.'

'Mark!' I said sharply, gesturing at him with a dirty spoon.

'I thought we were adults here?' he said innocently.

'So it's *my* fault?' slurred Helen. 'He's the arsehole, but I'm the one to blame.'

'No . . . '

'Like it's the woman's fault if she gets raped because she wore a short skirt.'

'You know that's not what I'm saying, Helen,' said Mark. I winced at his patronising tone. 'My point is, we all have choices.'

Helen reached for the now-empty bottle. 'You have any more of these?'

Mark headed for the utility room, ignoring my look. What happened to our agreement to limit Helen's intake? He came back with a fresh bottle.

'The difference between happy people and unhappy people,' he said, removing the foil with his special cutter, 'is the happy ones don't allow lust to trump judgment.'

I froze, dirty plate in hand. It had to have been directed at me; somehow he'd found out about Amorem.

'What does that even mean?' I said, trying to sound casual.

'You sound like a bad self-help book,' said Helen. 'And I should know, I've read enough of them.'

Mark laughed, and relief swept through me. I was imagining things, it hadn't been directed at me at all, just another of his provocative statements designed for effect.

'The problem,' said Helen slowly, 'is you *don't* have a choice. Not when you're properly in love. It's not that you don't care about the axe, it's you can't see it. You open the cupboard, and all you see is old clothes on hangers. You don't realise there's an axe there until it's too late. Way, way too late.' She started crying, huge tears rolling down her face, dropping on to the tablecloth, spreading out in dark uneven patches like miniature Rorschach tests.

* * *

Too much had been said to see the new year in. Mark and I cleared up in silence while Helen blew her nose and helped herself to the remainder of the brie, washed down with another glass of red. Once the dishwasher was on, Mark mumbled something about getting up early, wished us both a Happy New Year and disappeared upstairs.

Helen and I sat on the sofa watching the crowds in Trafalgar Square on TV as they cheered and splashed about in the fountains.

'I did that once,' said Helen forlornly. 'With Tom.' She reached for the nearly-empty bottle.

'Is that a good idea?' I said.

'Nope.' She tipped the lot into her glass. 'I shouldn't have come,' she added before swallowing a hefty mouthful.

'Don't be silly,' I said.

'You guys could have had a great night, then I turn up. God, I hate my life.' She heaved herself off the sofa. 'I have to pee.'

The TV was showing a close-up of Big Ben. As the minute hand crept towards the twelve, I remembered being told it was fourteen feet long, or had I seen that on *Blue Peter*? The bells began to ring, and the commentator trotted out the usual platitudes. How had it come to this? My daughter partying with God knows who, my husband self-righteously asleep underneath an eye mask and my sister throwing up in the loo, hating her life, knowing her ex would be toasting the New Year in a swanky chalet while a nanny looked after her kids.

Maybe I was seeing my own axe for the first time. If I left Mark, how would next New Year be? Potentially worse, but I wasn't sure I could face another twelve months of the same, either: doing nothing, changing nothing, feeling frustrated and useless and dead inside.

Dong! Big Ben struck the first chime as fireworks burst over the Thames. Dong! Couples hugged and kissed. Dong! Friends danced with their arms around each other. Dong! I could hear Helen retching in the downstairs loo. Dong!

Enough! I pictured my diary for the week. If I juggled a couple of appointments – and put up with the inevitable harrumphing from Janice – there was no reason why I couldn't make Selfridges on Thursday. I picked up my phone, found the email from Amorem and typed 'Confirmed'. Then I pressed 'send', deleted the chain and downed the remains of Helen's wine. Job done. Happy New Year.

BRITISH TRANSPORT POLICE

Criminal Justice Act 1967 s9
Magistrates' Courts Act 1980 ss 5A (3) (a) and 5B
Criminal Procedure Rules r27.1 (1)

EXTRACT FROM STATEMENT OF WITNESS

Statement of:	Michael Henning
Age of Witness:	Over 18
Occupation of Witness:	Forensic Scientist
Date:	18/06/2019

This Statement, consisting of two pages, signed by me, is true to the best of my knowledge and belief and I make it knowing that, if tendered in evidence, I shall be liable to prosecution if I have wilfully stated in it anything which I know or believe to be false or do not believe to be true.

On 18 June 2019 I was asked to examine the contents found in the pockets of clothing item marked MH/10-13, recovered in the course of a post-mortem examination carried out on 17 June 2019 by Dr Sheila Aston on an unknown male.

Item 1, marked MH/10, was a used lip salve manufactured by Carma Laboratories. Item 2, marked MH/11, was a stick of chewing gum manufactured by Wrigleys. Item 3, marked MH/12, was fragments of a tissue, degraded by contact with water. Item 4, marked MH/13, was a folded section of cardboard, also degraded by contact with water.

I was able to unfold the cardboard and further examine it under an infra-red light source. This revealed the presence of printed matter. I enclose a photograph, marked MH/14, which shows a magnified section of print with the words 'Imperial College Healthcare'.

Cross-referencing with items provided by Imperial College Healthcare NHS Foundation Trust, led me to conclude this was part of a printed guide to St Mary's Hospital, London.

Signed,

M Henning PhD

CHAPTER TWELVE

The morning of my appointment at Selfridges turned out to be one of those bright January days when the sun pings off buildings and, for a few hours, they resemble the artist's impressions which inspired them. I walked the last hundred yards to work gulping down the cold, invigorating air to calm myself. I hadn't felt this way since taking my exams at school, that intense sense of consequence, knowing that by the end of the day nothing could be the same again. It would either be a new start or the welcome end to a dangerous fantasy.

Checking my pigeonhole, I heard the familiar tisk tisk of Kevin's headphones.

'Hello, Kevin,' I said, dumping a pile of flyers in the bin.

'How did you know it was me?' he said, pulling off his headphones so they dangled round his neck.

'Intuition,' I said, turning round and firing him a brief smile.

'You and me, we're on the same wavelength!' There was something different about him today; not the camouflage jacket or Lidl bag – it was his hair. The ponytail had gone, along with his unruly mop, tidied up into a slicked back undercut. His beard had been trimmed, too, and was now a neat goatee. I must have been staring because he shuffled from foot to foot, saying, 'Thought I needed a change.'

'It's certainly that,' I said.

'Think it suits me?' he said, leaning so close I could smell the spearmint gum he endlessly chewed.

'Absolutely,' I said, before hurrying off in search of Dr Svetkova. I eventually tracked her down to the Albert Ward, where she was tapping at a terminal in the nurses' station.

'Hi, could I have a word?' She didn't look up. 'Dr Svetkova?' I said, louder.

A couple of nurses looked over. She kept typing.

'Yes?' she said at last.

'Could we have a chat?' She stared at me as if I'd accused her of malpractice. 'If it isn't a good time . . . ' I trailed off.

'It is fine,' she said, marching off down the corridor. 'You wish to discuss James Fletcher?'

'No,' I said. 'It's my daughter, Jess. She's applying for medical school, and I was wondering . . . '

'If I will give her work experience?' She stopped and fixed me with those clear eyes of hers.

'Yes,' I smiled. 'How did you know?'

'I do not believe in nepotism,' she said, placing the accent on the last syllable. 'It is divisive, unfair and immoral.'

I had no idea what to say. 'Why should your daughter be helped when a child whose parents do not know people, is not? You understand this is wrong?'

'It would only be a couple of days,' I said. 'More to see if it appeals than anything else.'

'This will give her an advantage on her application.'

She was right, it would be unfair. But this was Jess we were talking about. I started to say a day would be fine, a few hours even, but Dr Svetkova had already pushed through the swing doors, adding as she went, 'Your daughter must download the forms from the hospital website. Like everyone else.'

Humiliated and embarrassed, I felt like shouting after her, 'She didn't go to private school! People like us need all the help we can get!' But she was long gone.

* * *

Letting myself into the treatment room, I saw a man standing by the window – tall, mixed-race, in white T-shirt and jeans.

'Yes?' I said, irritated Janice hadn't warned me someone was already there.

'Greg Wheately,' he said, hand extended. 'I'm a friend of Jimmy's, from the army.' Now it made sense: the toned biceps, the firm handshake.

'Is he OK?' I said, worried Jamie might have done something stupid. It was a thought never far from my mind with patients who had suffered life-changing trauma.

'Just taking a leak. But he's told me all about you.' He flashed me a smile as the door banged open and Michelle appeared, pushing Jamie in his wheelchair.

'Jamie!' I said, relieved to see him alive and well.

'See you've met the dickhead then,' he said.

'He thinks he's funny. No really, he does,' said Greg, as Michelle helped Jamie stand. There was no sign of the despair I'd seen the last time we'd met when Dr Svetkova had so tactlessly announced her prognosis. Jamie must have talked things through with Michelle, and she'd been fine about it, as predicted.

'Hope you don't mind me butting in like this, Doctor,' Greg said to me. 'Only I had a few days leave and thought I could give these guys a lift.' I didn't have the heart to tell him I was a lowly OT.

'Typical,' said Jamie. 'Always offering help when it's not wanted. Can I give you a lift? Mind if I tie a tourniquet around your legs . . . ?'

'What can I say?' said Greg. 'I'm a nice guy.'

'Interfering arsehole more like.'

'If it hadn't been for Greg, Jamie wouldn't be here,' said Michelle.

'Bollocks,' said both men together, though from their faces I could tell it was true. Greg and Michelle stayed half an hour, watching as Jamie took five steps unaided, the most he'd managed so far. I knew how much it must be hurting and, as soon as they left, he collapsed into a chair, his top soaked with sweat.

'That was amazing, Jamie,' I said. 'I'm so proud of you.'

'Would you give him one?'

'Sorry?'

'Greg. He's a good-looking bloke.'

'Very,' I said, before moving on quickly. 'I'd like to change your home exercises, concentrate more on flexibility now you have the basics down.'

'Bastard!'

I looked over at him, surprised by his bitterness. He stared at the pylons where his feet should be. Did he suspect Greg and Michelle? They'd certainly smiled a lot, shared the odd glance, but I'd assumed it was nothing more than the usual chemistry between attractive people, the conspiracy that keeps the rest of us at bay. 'Fucker,' said Jamie, under his breath.

'You're tired . . . '

'Yes, I'm fucking tired! You know why? Because I haven't got any fucking legs!'

I said nothing. Early in my career, I made the mistake of telling a young woman who had been in a motorboat accident she wouldn't always feel like this, that plenty of people in her position led fulfilling, happy lives. She threw a crutch at me, catching me above the eye. I still had the scar, and reached for it now, a useful talisman to stop me trotting out sanctimonious crap.

'I'm sorry,' I said. 'It's shitty not having legs. And even shittier about the sex thing.'

'Yeah,' he said quietly.

'Have you told Michelle yet?'

'So, where are you off to?' he said.

'Sorry?' I said, thrown by the change in tack.

'You keep looking at the clock every two minutes. You got a secret lover?'

'Hardly secret if you know,' I said, turning away, kicking myself for being so obvious. 'I'm meeting my daughter at Selfridges.'

'Isn't she at school?'

'It's an inset day.' The lie popped out so easily I almost believed it myself.

* * *

I took the Edwards Mews entrance into Selfridges, figuring there would be fewer people, but had forgotten about the January sales; the place was teeming with affluent bargain hunters. As I stepped off the escalator into the kitchen department, I scanned the crowds for a blue coat. The message hadn't said if it would be long or short, leather or wool. I didn't even know if I was meeting a man or a woman.

I made my way down an aisle full of gadgets, the sort you use once before they end up in a tangle at the back of an overcrowded cupboard. I wandered past mothers and daughters arguing about wedding lists ('Mummy, nobody uses napkin rings any more'), negotiated my way around a retired couple comparing toasters and a single man puzzling over what knife to buy, until I ended up in the pottery section. I clocked a store detective eyeing me up, my old instincts kicking in, I suppose. Picking up a side plate, I pretended to examine it in detail until she looked away. As I put it back on the shelf, I saw something familiar: a yellow milk jug, just like the one I stole all those years ago. Looking closer, I realised it wasn't quite identical; for one thing, the handle was different, moulded in one piece, not joined separately as we had been taught by Miss Jameson in ceramics. The lovely, squat lines were the same though, and the colour. I thought of slipping it into my handbag. Perhaps Mark could persuade me to bring it back.

'One can't have too many milk jugs, can one?'

I turned to see a short woman in a blue plaid coat. Sixty if a day, her grey hair in a neat pixie cut. 'Kirsten isn't it?' she said. I could feel myself reddening. 'I thought I recognised you.'

Her accent was difficult to place. Borders? The sort of warm, reassuring voice call centres use to tell you they've doubled your insurance premium. 'Why don't we have a bite to eat?'

She marched us confidently over to a corner lift as I wondered how she'd recognised me. Dianne must have given her a description, maybe even sent a photo. Waiting for the lift, I snuck a look at her. She had the pink, healthy glow every Englishwoman of a certain class used to have before cheap holidays and tanning machines. Her lipstick was a subtle shade of rose, and I could make out a hint of powder on her cheeks. My mother would have approved. Could this really be the woman about to lead me down the path to my worst intentions?

The doors pinged open, and we stepped inside, next to a weary-looking man with a baby strapped to his chest.

'Gorgeous,' said the woman. 'Let me guess. Three months?'

* * *

The restaurant was on the roof, with spectacular views across the London skyline. A smiley young waitress appeared and showed us to our table, weaving past immaculately groomed women hemmed in by oversized carrier bags.

'I've never been up here before,' I said, sitting down. 'I did once have a sandwich on the ground floor. Salt beef, with American mustard.' I was gabbling like a nervous teenager on her first date. The waitress handed us each a tall menu, said something about the dish of the day which I didn't catch, then disappeared again. The woman unfolded her napkin and I caught sight of a rose tattoo on her inner wrist.

'So tell me, Kirsten, why do you want to cheat on your husband?' I glanced around, terrified someone must have heard. The woman gave me a reassuring smile.

'That isn't what I want,' I said quietly. 'I mean, I realise it's what I will be doing, but it isn't why I'm doing it.' I could feel my thoughts slipping away, getting tangled as they used to when I was stoned and tried to explain why Sartre was still relevant to a sceptical, sober Bridget. I wished the waitress would come back and give me a chance to straighten myself out. The woman smiled.

'You understand once you take the first step, there's no way back?'

'Are you trying to put me off?' My laugh came out too high, almost a squeak. She didn't flinch.

'This sort of thing isn't for everyone. Not for most people.'

The waitress had returned now, thank God. I chose the first things on the menu and took a welcome gulp of the water she poured. The woman waited until she left. 'Many people like the idea, and, more often than not, the event itself,' she said. 'It's the rest of their life they find challenging. Not the fear of being found out, we would never let that happen, but because they lose sight of themselves.'

'How do you mean?' I said.

'Infidelity changes people. They're no longer the person they thought they were, and that can be unsettling.'

The waitress brought our starters. I seemed to have ordered sauteed calamari, its little suckers looking up at me accusingly. I flipped it over with my fork.

'I think I'd be all right,' I said, risking a mouthful.

'You need to be sure. Are you sure, Kirsten?'

I nodded, still chewing my squid.

'If you're looking for emotional attachment, then . . . '

'I'm not,' I said quickly. 'I already have that. What I want is . . . ' I hesitated, unexpectedly embarrassed.

'Satisfaction?'

'Yes. I suppose that's it.'

'And if you don't get it, you fear losing your marriage, which is the last thing you want.'

I stared at her, fork frozen halfway to my mouth. 'Yes,' I said quietly.

She reached over and touched my hand; I noticed she wore a slim wedding ring. 'You've come to the right place.' She slid a blank card across the crisp linen. I picked it up, cupping it in my palm, though no one was near enough to see anything. Written on the back, in neat black italics were three words: *Fifteen hundred guineas*. Who the hell charges in guineas, I thought, trying to work out what it came to in real money. Horse traders and private doctors were the only ones that came to mind. And now pimps.

'The fee provides unlimited introductions for six months. Subsequent months are charged pro rata.'

I slipped the card back on the table, determined not to betray my surprise. Dianne hadn't mentioned anything about fees; I had assumed there would be a cost, but nothing like this.

'Discretion is expensive, I'm afraid. And we are very good at what we do.'

'It's fine,' I said quickly, trying to calculate what accounts I'd have to raid.

'How will you access the money?' she asked as if reading my mind.

'Sorry?'

'It might be difficult to explain such a large expenditure to your husband,' she said, cutting neatly into a tiny quiche.

'I have my own account,' I said. 'Why should he ever know?'

'Because he could. And if he did, everything else would follow.' She dabbed her lips with a white napkin. 'I recommend you take a little from your own account then top it up with cashback from a supermarket. It will appear on your statement as groceries.'

'You're making me sound like a spy,' I said.

'You'll be cheating on someone you love,' she said, not returning my smile. 'Someone who knows you intimately. You need to be careful.'

I felt like a scolded child. 'As I said, this isn't for everyone.' She tore a roll in half. 'There's no shame in walking away. Quite the opposite.'

I stared at the remains of my calamari, knowing if I hesitated, my sensible self, the one who hedged bets, refused to take risks and never changed a damn thing, would step in and crush this dream, like she had so many others.

'Money won't be a problem,' I said, looking up. 'Why don't you tell me how the rest of it works?'

* * *

As we ate our main courses – beautifully presented tagliolini in my case, none of which I was able to taste – she explained how the service operated. If I wanted to go ahead, and assuming the funds were cleared, I would be sent a phone.

'I already have a phone,' I said.

'This one can't be traced, either to you or us. It comes loaded with WhatsApp, which I expect you're familiar with?'

I nodded. 'It uses something called end-to-end encryption – which makes it one of the most secure platforms available. Not even the police can hack it.' She went on to explain I would be sent photos of possible partners. If I was interested, I simply replied with a tick. If the person in question felt the same, contact details would be sent to both parties, who could then exchange messages directly.

'That's it?' I asked. 'A photograph?' I had imagined a lengthy interview or at least a comprehensive questionnaire. 'How can you tell we'll be compatible from a photo?'

'Look around this room. Is there anyone you find attractive?'

I glanced at the surrounding tables, full of ladies who lunch. The only man amongst them, the exhausted-looking guy with the baby. Definitely not my type.

'No.'

'Are you sure about that?' She nodded at the young man behind the bar – tall, cropped hair, with a crooked smile. He looked about twenty.

'You stared at him the moment you came in.'

'I did not stare!' But I had noticed his white shirt, the muscular shoulders, his large, sensitive eyes.

'Would you say no because he turned out to be obsessed with Formula One or black-and-white movies or spent the weekend re-enacting civil war battles?'

I couldn't help laughing.

'This isn't about shared interests, Kirsten. It doesn't matter about their politics, their hopes, where they went to school or what they do. It's about one thing only: instant, undeniable, physical attraction. And for that, a photograph is the very best guide there can be.'

I felt a quiver of excitement at the thought. Could she really find a man who'd make me feel the visceral connection I used to have in the old days?

'And if we did like each other, what then?'

'Then you'd follow the rules.'

* * *

The rules were extensive. Number one, initial contact should be in public, a place with plenty of people, where we'd both feel safe if we wanted to bail.

'If you wish to take things further,' said the woman, 'we have an arrangement with a serviced flat company in a central location. Access is via a PIN, there's no front desk and no one to see when you arrive or leave. You're welcome to visit on your own to make sure you're comfortable with it.'

'Presumably, there's a fee for all this, too?' I said.

'Seventy-five pounds for three hours. Considering the safeguards, it's not unreasonable.'

'Safeguards?'

'All bathrooms are provided with deadlocks and a phone connected to a twenty-four-hour concierge service.'

'Blimey.'

'We take safety very seriously, Kirsten,' she said sternly. 'And so should you.'

'Do you vet people?' I said, trying to claw back some credibility.

'Our service is by invitation only, and I personally interview all prospective members.' She signalled to the waitress and ordered a double espresso. I went for a peppermint tea, I couldn't deal with caffeine, my heart was racing already.

'How about criminal background checks? Do you use the CRB or whatever they're called now?'

'The Disclosure and Barring Service. And yes, we use it for our male applicants.'

'Because women aren't serial killers?'

She gave me one of her blank stares. 'With female clients, we make our own enquiries.'

'Have you enquired about me?'

'The vetting procedure only occurs on acceptance.'

'And then what? You talk to my friends? People at work?'

'Nothing like that,' she said, giving me a thin smile. 'Our business relies on discretion, Kirsten. But it's important we are particular about who we accept, for us as well as you. One wouldn't want a journalist after the next sensational story, for example.' She held my eyes.

'I'm not a journalist,' I said.

She shrugged as if that was yet to be confirmed.

'In turn, we expect clients to exercise similar caution. Transactions should be cash-only; receipts must be destroyed immediately, and your personal phone turned off or left at home. Assignations should never be at regular times, and evening meetings avoided. You cannot tell anyone what you are doing and never, under any circumstances, ask a friend to lie for you. They'll either resent it, forget the details or feel compelled to come clean.'

'It's a lot to take in,' I said.

'There's a lot at stake.' She took a sip of her espresso. 'Our priority, and yours, is to protect your marriage. The key is keeping everything else the same, even when that will be the last thing you'll feel like doing. You'll want to try a new haircut or experiment with different clothes or a change of perfume. Don't.'

'You're very confident you know how I'll react,' I said.

'Human beings are remarkably similar. You'll find yourself buying your husband a present for no good reason or having more sex with him than normal.'

'Seems unlikely,' I said, smiling. Her face remained serious.

'Your greatest challenge,' she said, holding my gaze, 'will be to explain your happiness. Remember that.' She finished her coffee, replaced the tiny cup on its saucer. 'Do you have any questions?'

Only what on earth I'm doing here, I thought, refolding my napkin, aware of feeling empty inside despite the food. There was a flash of light. I looked up to see her holding her phone. Another two flashes.

'What the hell!' I said.

'We'll need a photograph for the app.'

'Here? Like this?' I said, suddenly aware of wayward strands of hair in my face.

'You look wonderful.' She held out the phone. It wasn't too bad, though hardly flattering. 'We find this works better than posed photographs. They can lead to disappointment.' She put the phone back in her bag. 'Once you are accepted, you are, of course, free to edit your profile.'

'What if I change my mind halfway through?'

'You can suspend or cancel the service at any time. Though as you can imagine, the joining fee is non-refundable. Anything else?'

'How did you get into this line of business?' For the first time, I saw her composure fall a fraction.

'Is that relevant?'

'If I'm handing over fifteen hundred pounds, yes, I think it is. I don't even know your name.'

She smoothed her napkin, as if weighing up how much she needed to reveal to secure a sale.

'My name's Alice,' she said at last. 'My aunt started Amorem in the late nineties. When my children were small, I worked for her part-time, mostly doing the books. It was an old-fashioned introduction service back then, everybody's details kept on index cards. When the internet came along it pretty much wiped us out. My aunt retired and I was about to give up, too. Then I had a stroke of luck. The Ashley Madison scandal broke.'

The name sounded familiar, but I couldn't place it. 'It was an international dating site with the rather distasteful motto, "Life is short. Have an affair." They were very successful, until their database was compromised; thirty million highly confidential details found their way into the public domain. It ruined a lot of lives, even ended a few, I'm sorry to say.' She caught the waitress's eye, signalled for the bill. 'But for me, it was an opportunity. All of a sudden, people wanted to do things the old-fashioned way.'

'Couldn't the same thing happen to you?'

'We still don't use computers. And as I explained, WhatsApp is entirely secure.'

The waitress appeared with the bill.

'So what happens now?' I said.

'If you would like to take things further, you'll need to send us the fee. In cash, by post.'

I laughed. 'That's a lot of money to put in a letterbox.'

'The Royal Mail is remarkably trustworthy and, unlike a bank, it leaves no paper trail.'

I nodded, wondering if this could be a scam of some sort.

'Once we have processed your fee, a secure phone will be sent to an address of your choice. Shortly after, you will receive notifications of potential partners.'

'And all I have to do is choose?'

'Precisely.' She picked up the bill without looking at it and reached for her bag. 'There is one other thing. We find being clear about one's preferences saves misunderstandings.' She slid a white envelope across the table. 'Be as honest as you can, then pop it in the post, too.'

The address was a PO Box with a central London postcode. Alice held out her hand.

'It's been good to meet you, Kirsten. I hope we can work together.' She briefly touched my shoulder, and then she was gone. I watched her pay at the till before making her way to the lift, just another middle-aged woman on a shopping trip.

CHAPTER THIRTEEN

On the train home, I managed to get an aisle seat, pressed up against a man buried in a book of Sudoku and opposite a squirming toddler who repeatedly kicked me under the table while its mother stared gormlessly at her phone. I opened the envelope Alice had given me and took out a closely printed sheet of paper. There were four columns with tick boxes to the side. Taking out a pen, I scanned the first few: Heterosexual, LGBTQ, Androphilic, Gynephilic, Bicurious, Skoliosexual. They sounded like diseases, not something you'd want to do with a partner. I caught Sudoku man glancing over and snatched the paper up before he could read any more.

Pulling an *Evening Standard* magazine from my bag, I secreted the paper in the centre pages, holding it close to my face. What age groups would I consider? 21–35; 36–45, 46–55, 56–66 and 67 up. I couldn't imagine stripping off in front of anyone younger, them with their perfect body, me with my saggy bits and stretch marks. They would have to be close to my age, with their own imperfections to hide. I ticked 46–55, added 36–45 and put a cross by the last two. I wasn't in this for charity.

There were questions about ethnicity, build, hair and eye colour, even religion. I hadn't thought about the Almighty since my God Soc days and imagined it had been mutual. I ticked 'Any'. Would I accept tattoos? Yes. Piercings? I played safe, put a cross – as a student I'd once had tangling issues. Shaved genital area? I didn't know men bothered and had a problem with women turning themselves into girls. Besides, a man waxing his testicles suggests an unacceptable level of self-regard I could live without, so that was a no, too.

I stared out of the window as repetitive London suburbs flashed by, and wondered if there was an equivalent questionnaire for men. Did it stipulate weight, breast size, ratio of hips to waist? Would any man tick the boxes which even vaguely approximated to what I had to offer? A middle-aged woman who hadn't been to the gym for an age, with saggy boobs, a spreading bottom and bingo wings. I rubbed my eyes – I couldn't think like that or I might as well toss the whole thing into the nearest bin.

I turned the paper over and saw yet more options. Penis size: S, M, L. Good grief, how small was small, how large was large? At university, Bridget once dated a guy so well endowed she took a step back in surprise, fell down two stairs and broke her ankle. That would take some explaining to Mark. Besides, I wasn't sure about the sort of man who'd put down L. Or S. I stuck with medium.

Viewing Porn. I hesitated, remembering the webpages Mark visited, how I had felt looking at those dead eyes staring out from his laptop. I wanted nothing to do with men who enjoyed that sort of material. Putting my cross in the 'No' box, it occurred to me I might have driven Mark to those images, just as he had me to this packed train, coolly choosing what I'd get up to with my new lover. Perhaps complacency had made us complicit in each other's betrayal.

We pulled into Sydenham Hill, the blurry lights of the platform distorted through the rain-streaked window. The man next to me heaved himself up. As he squeezed his bulk into the aisle, he fired me a smile. Had he seen the questionnaire, despite my precautions? So what if he had? I'd never see him again. I picked up my pen.

How did I feel about Bondage, S&M, BDSM? Or Erotic Spanking, Infantilism and Golden Showers? The list went on and on: Fire Play, Cupping, Impact, Wax Play, Figging. What the hell was that? I took out my phone, opened the Google App. 'Figging, the practice of inserting a piece of ginger root into the anus or vagina.' Would I have to go to Waitrose every time I went on a date? I put crosses by the lot, folded the paper back in its envelope and shoved it into my handbag. After eighteen months of virtually no sex, vanilla would be fine.

* * *

My usual parking space at home was blocked by a plumber's van, so I had to park all the way up the road, almost to the T-junction. I grabbed an old carrier bag from the boot and, holding it over my head, made a dash through the rain. Crossing the road, I saw a figure by the front door. Probably yet another Amazon delivery for Mark, but as I moved closer, I saw it was a bedraggled Jack, hands stuffed into his skinny jeans.

'Hi, Jack,' I said, reaching for my keys. 'I'm afraid Jess isn't here, she's seeing her friend Gemma this evening.'

'I know,' he said.

Which is when I noticed his puffy, bloodshot eyes. 'You'd better come in,' I said.

Interpreting Jack's grunts and sighs was hard work, but eventually, with the aid of a hot chocolate and several biscuits, I winkled out of him that Jess had ended things. By text. No proper explanation, just a couple of lines saying it would be best for both of them. When Jack tried phoning, his calls went straight to voicemail, and she hadn't replied to his texts either. I could sympathise, remembered what it was like to be rejected with no proper explanation.

'She's met someone else, I know she has,' said Jack, dunking his biscuit then tapping the soggy edge against his mug. 'She has, hasn't she?'

His faith in mother–daughter confidences was touching but misplaced. Jess told me nothing. I watched him suck on the biscuit. I know we fought long and hard to get men to show their emotions but close up, a blubbing teenager boy is not a pretty sight.

He finished the biscuit, reached for another, his fifth by my count. 'What am I supposed to do?' It had become a mantra repeated every few minutes. He snapped the biscuit in half. 'It's not fair!'

What is fair? I thought. That I was desperate for him to leave, so I could plan how to betray my husband? That the man I loved had lost all interest in me other than as a helpmeet around the house? Or that a teenage love affair had come to its inevitable end? That seemed the least problematic.

'I'll talk to her,' I said, standing up.

'Yeah?' He sniffed loudly.

'But you should go now, Jack. Jess could turn up any minute and we don't want her seeing you like this, do we?'

He nodded, got to his feet, eyeing the remaining biscuits. 'Take the packet,' I said.

A smile crept across his face. If he could be cheered up by the thought of a half-eaten pack of Hobnobs, he'd probably be fine. 'I can't promise anything, though,' I said, escorting him to the front door.

He hugged me, his muscly arms gripping me tight. I caught a hint of sweat, not altogether unpleasant. 'I love her so much!'

Watching him wobble down the road on his bike, biscuits in hand, I knew how it felt, that intense vulnerability when everything that matters is bound up in someone else. I almost felt nostalgic for it, like a child remembering the delicious pain of their last wobbly tooth.

* * *

As I did the ironing that evening, I tried to work out how to get hold of the £1,575 Google assured me fifteen hundred guineas came to. It might be possible to move money from various accounts without Mark noticing, but it was a risk. We knew each other's PINs and occasionally made transfers to and from our sole accounts. He'd only have to come across the wrong statement to become suspicious.

I had a modest savings account with Nationwide, but it would need ninety days' notice and I didn't want to wait that long. Tacking incremental amounts on at the supermarket was a possibility, but it felt doubly wrong to finance my infidelity off the back of our weekly grocery bill.

Wherever the money came from, it needed to be clean and untraceable. My godmother, Jocelyn, had given me Premium Bonds at birth, though even if I could find them, they wouldn't come to more than a couple of hundred quid. Perhaps I could borrow it, I was always getting emails offering me loans. Then I remembered something else Jocelyn had given me.

Running upstairs, I hurried into the bedroom and pulled open the bottom drawer of my dressing table. It was right at the back, behind the unused Fitbit – a ring box covered in faded blue leather, with two gold initials on its lid: J.A.

Jocelyn Anders had been my mother's best friend at school and my only godparent. A hard-faced woman, she had never shown any interest in me, studiously forgetting virtually every birthday and, on the few occasions we met, finding fault with everything from my accent to my untameable hair. No wonder she got on with my mother.

When she died at fifty-five from breast cancer, Jocelyn left me this box and the ring inside. I'd never liked it, a chubby Cupid in Limoges enamel set in a cut-diamond frame on an impossibly thin band of gold. It had to be valuable though; throughout our childhood, my mother insisted it was the most precious thing Jocelyn possessed, which wasn't quite true: she left a flat in Balham to the Woodland Trust. I suspect she only said it to make me feel guilty for not liking Jocelyn more.

Turning the ring in my fingers, I felt a twinge of guilt, but what good could it do anyone, tucked away at the back of a drawer? It should be worn by someone who admired the workmanship, enjoyed staring at the little Cupid with his bow of gold. Most persuasive of all, Mark hadn't seen it for years and would never miss it.

Downstairs, the front door opened and closed, and I heard Jess saying hello to the cat. Pushing the box back into the drawer, I took a quick look in the mirror, almost expecting to see guilt written over my face, then headed for the landing.

* * *

Over supper, a delicious Persian dish of aubergine and chickpeas Mark had discovered on the internet, I mentioned to Jess that I'd seen Jack, but only got back a mumbled 'Yeah?'. I pressed on.

'He said you'd split up.'

'Thought you'd be pleased,' she said. 'You made it quite clear you didn't want him around.'

'I never said . . . '

'Sorry to hear that, Jessy,' interrupted Mark. 'It's never easy, is it?'

Jess shrugged. 'It's OK, Dad.'

'He couldn't understand why you ended things,' I said, determined not to let it go.

'I told him why.'

'By text. He was very upset.'

'It's not like we were in love or anything. It was just sex.'

I felt myself blush. All those frank discussions about the importance of intimacy had come to this?

'You took a brave decision,' said Mark. 'Brave and mature.'

Mr Bloody Reasonable. 'It might have been kinder to do it in person,' I said. 'At least you could have explained.'

'Stop, OK?' Jess said, getting to her feet. 'It has precisely nothing to do with you!'

Mark stepped in before I could respond. 'You did the right thing, J,' he said definitively. 'Right, but difficult.'

Which was pretty much how I felt about my own last twenty-four hours.

* * *

Later, as I tipped the cat's litter into an old carrier bag, and Mark placed the bins on the street ready for the next day's collection, he asked about my mother. Would she be able to cope at home? I knew what was behind his concern: the unspoken horror of Mum living with us. Despite all his kindness and practical help, Mark drew the line at his mother-in-law moving in, and frankly I couldn't blame him. I said she had been fine and I'd pop over at the weekend to make sure she was all right.

I poured myself another glass of Rioja, wondering if I should apologise to Jess, though suspecting we would inevitably spiral back to the same old arguments. I hated us being like this. In a few months, she would be gone, and all I'd have to look forward to would be a husband practising double root irregular verbs and watching lonely box sets. Unless I sold that ring.

CHAPTER FOURTEEN

The following morning, with Mark safely singing in the shower, I retrieved the ring box and slid it into my handbag. An online valuation service had given me a rough idea how much it was worth, and Google identified a jeweller on the Edgware Road who bought such things. I eventually found it squeezed between a kebab shop and a place offering to jail-break phones. A small, leathery woman with an enormous pile of silver hair, offered me £1,000. I told her I knew it was worth at least double that, but I'd take £1,600, in cash. She said they didn't keep that sort of money on the prem-ises. I reached across the counter for the box, whereupon she remembered they did.

I bought a padded envelope in a nearby post office, cop-ied the address from the envelope Alice had given me and slipped the money inside, along with the questionnaire. Queuing up to pay, I had a moment of doubt. Was it insane to send so much to a woman I had only met once? By post. What if I never heard from her again, or she claimed she never received the money?

'Cashier number three, please!'

'That's you, love,' said the man behind me, nudging me forwards. I couldn't back out now.

'I'd like to send this signed for, please,' I said to the bored woman behind the counter.

'Contents?'

'Books,' I said on a whim.

'Under fifty pounds value?'

'Yes.'

'Put it on the scales,' she said, without looking up from writing on a label. 'Eight fifty.'

And that was it. My fate handed over to Her Majesty's Postal Service. Along with over fifteen hundred quid.

* * *

I spent the next few days in a constant state of anxiety. The first twenty-four hours weren't too bad, I couldn't expect a response from Amorem immediately, but as it stretched to forty-eight, then seventy-two hours, I became convinced the whole thing had been a scam. I'd thrown away £1,575 for a two-course meal and a handful of tips on infidelity. It was a clever racket, designed to reel in women like me. No one was going to call the police and tell them they'd willingly handed over an envelope of cash so they could cheat on their husband. I considered marching round to Dianne's, but couldn't face the humiliation. I tried to calm down, told myself that, while I might have been a fool, at least no one else had been hurt. I was still a faithful wife, albeit a poorer one.

I threw myself into work, even agreeing to attend one of the department's deadly three-sixty 'sharing' meetings. The main topic of discussion had nothing to do with health targets or improving patient experience, but focused entirely on whether we should get rid of our expensive, unreliable vending machine and go to Costa on the third floor instead, or have the contractors replace the damn thing yet again. I thought we should buy a kettle, but that didn't seem to be on the agenda.

I was surprised to see Dr Svetkova in attendance; we hadn't spoken since she had treated me to her lecture on nepotism. She was wearing a short red dress under her white coat and spent most of the time on her phone, only looking up once, to say she didn't mind what we did as long as she could have decaf and non-dairy milk. How had her Christmas been? Full of carefree sex I imagined. The rumour among the nurses was she'd hooked up with the handsome American radiologist on secondment from UCLA. She was probably checking out condos in LA, dreaming of weekend hikes in Big Sur and Hollywood pool parties. For once, I didn't mind. Good for her, I had my own adventure to look forward to – if I ever heard back.

*　*　*

That evening, I was standing by the department's entrance looking out at the lashing rain, debating whether to wait until it eased up or make a run for it, when someone whispered in my ear.

'Birthday, is it?'

I span round to see Kevin, chewing gum glistening between his teeth. He wasn't wearing his usual camouflage jacket, but had on a tailored peacoat of all things.

'Sorry?' I said, taking a step back.

'Package,' he said, nodding at the pigeonholes. 'Hand-delivered. Thought it might be a present.'

I looked over to see a fat, padded envelope protruding from my pigeonhole. It could only be one thing. I felt my pulse race at the thought. I pulled it out – no postage, no return address. It had to be from Alice.

'So, when's the big day? Let me guess, Scorpio. Same as me.'

'Sorry, Kevin,' I said. ' I have to go.'

* * *

It took every ounce of resolution not to open the envelope on the Tube or in the train, but as soon as I reached the car, I tore at the now soggy paper, pulling out a small, plain box. My heart sank. It wasn't big enough to be a phone. It had nothing to do with Alice, was probably a gift from a patient or something dull from hospital admin.

I peeled open the lid of the box, gave it a shake and a tiny mobile slid into my palm. It looked more like a toy than anything that could actually work, my fingers easily folding round its tiny form. I found a switch on the side, pushed it up with a fingernail and to my amazement the screen came to life: a miniature copy of my iPhone, a bright green WhatsApp icon in the top corner. It was happening. Actually happening.

I tapped my forefinger on the icon. A series of thumb-print photos popped up. A dozen different men, some smiling, some serious, a few full-length but mostly close-ups. There wasn't a single one who did anything for me. They looked like the sort of middle-aged blokes you saw at the garden centre, not a lover who'd transport me to new heights of desire. The thought of having sex with any of them made me queasy. How come I hadn't been offered someone like Dianne's stud in the car park? True, I hadn't seen his face properly, but even from the back I knew he had to be better-looking than any of these saddos. Then the depressing truth hit: Alice had only forwarded the men she thought would be interested in someone like me.

I tossed the phone on to the passenger seat. How could this possibly have worked, a woman like me, an invisible, middle-aged mother with crazy hair, attracting anyone even remotely fanciable? It was delusional. I turned on the engine, cleared a swathe through the steamed-up windscreen with my sleeve, and set off into the traffic.

By the time I got home, I had decided to write the whole thing off as an interesting but doomed experience. Parking opposite the house, my only regret was not being able to show Jess that dinky phone – she'd love it. As I scooped it up to put in my handbag, the screen came to life again, with more thumbnails. A man who looked like the captain of a golf club; a young bloke with a whisky-coloured beard and then . . . then my mouth went dry.

A man around my age, blond hair, grey eyes, a trace of a smile on his lips. Nothing exceptional, nothing you wouldn't find in loads of other men, and yet I felt an instant, unmediated attraction, almost frightening in its intensity.

I put the phone down. This was madness. Not who I was. I'd stood on the precipice, peered into the depths and now I was going to have the sense to step back. I'd chuck the phone in a bin and never think of it again.

I picked it up and looked at the photo again, at the straight nose, the curving lips with their suggestion of a smile, the neat hair cut just above the ears. Before I knew what was happening, my fingers had found the screen and were tapping on the accept icon. Shocked, I threw the phone into my bag and ran across the road to the house.

Fumbling for my keys, I almost giggled at the absurdity of it all. Once inside, I headed straight for the fridge, gulping down a Peroni to steady my nerves. It would probably come to nothing. Hadn't Alice said it needed both parties to agree before she'd send any further details? What were the chances I'd get a reply? Close to zero probably. I took another swig of beer and wondered if I had time for a bath before the others got home.

Making my way through the hall, I was halfway up the stairs when I heard the ping of a phone. I couldn't tell from the sound if it was my new one or not. I ran back, scrambled to find it, managed to locate the tiny switch. The screen lit up. The other person had accepted. Did I want to meet?

I stared at the screen, at the pulsating Yes and No. Of course I didn't want to meet. That would be insane. I'd be putting my whole marriage on the line, my family, making the same mistake my sister had, and look how she'd ended up: living in a poky flat next to a railway line, weeping into her Rioja every night. My thumb tapped on the answer without any further thought.

Yes.

CHAPTER FIFTEEN

What do you wear to betray a partner of twenty years? Nothing with history, that's for sure, which ruled out my favourite – the floral, sleeveless number I'd worn to Helen's thirteenth and, as it turned out, last wedding anniversary. I went online, scrolled through dozens of outfits. It proved more difficult than I thought to find something at once both sexy and demure, attractive without being over the top. Under normal circumstances, I'd avoid anything too revealing, opt for sensible over sensuous, but this wasn't a do at work or sedate dinner party with Mark's colleagues.

I knew nothing with a pinched waist would work, that would only made my hips look too big, and no way was I going to have my bum on display – those days had long gone. In the end, I opted for a loose white top with a hint of cleavage and skinny black jeans. My legs still looked pretty good, especially if covered up, and the top accentuated my boobs, which Helen claimed were my best feature.

I typed in the hospital's address and hit the order button, briefly wondering how I had become the sort of person who makes clandestine purchases on the internet, before moving on to lingerie sites. They appeared only to cater for adolescent bodies honed by lack of food and hours in the gym. Where was the stuff for a woman who had a child and enjoyed the odd profiterole? After the disaster with the basque, I couldn't risk being humiliated again, so settled on a conservative push-up bra which would, I hoped, entice without being open to ridicule, and a pair of black knickers which covered more than they revealed. They had to be sexier than my greying M&S favourites.

I'd read enough magazine articles to know most young women waxed with pre-op thoroughness. Would a new lover expect that? I baulked at something so radical, not least because, in the unlikely event of Mark ever paying enough attention, he might notice. Admittedly it was a long shot – he rarely noticed if I cut the hair on my head let alone between my legs – but still possible.

In the spring, I usually gave myself a tidy-up, ready for the beach. Like a hedge being prepared for a summer fête, Mark used to say. When he first grew a beard, he joked he'd get stuck down there, Velcroed to me for eternity. Those were the days when sex wasn't just fun but funny. That's what porn does for you, I thought – drains all the humour out of it until you're left with nothing but the slapping sound of flesh on hairless flesh.

I confined myself to a discreet trim, more the equivalent of a short back and sides than radical remodel. Snipping carefully over the edge of the bath, it occurred to me that the man in the photo would be the next person to see me naked. I felt numb at the thought, the same feeling I'd had the day before my A level physics exam, and look how that turned out.

My new clothes arrived at work the next day, in anonymous boxes which could have contained anything from stationery to shoes. Locking myself in the bathroom at home, I tried everything on. The light cotton of the top felt good against my body, if a touch baggy around the waist, but nothing a couple of stitches couldn't sort. As I scrutinised myself in the mirror, I imagined a stranger's fingers unclipping my new bra, standing back and . . . God, condoms! I had totally forgotten. While the chances of getting pregnant were zero, no way was I going to risk unprotected sex with a stranger.

I searched the bathroom cabinet in the forlorn hope I might find some, though we hadn't used any for years. I checked old sponge bags, the bedside table and, in an inspired move, an ancient suitcase. Sure enough, I eased a crumpled Durex from a side pocket, its foil creased and crinkly. Stamped along the bottom was the expiry date: eight years ago.

* * *

I had never noticed the bewildering range of condoms in our local chemist, despite having walked past them a hundred times over the years. Early on I'd had a coil fitted, then, after we gave up trying for another child, Mark went for the op. I scanned the shelves of brightly coloured boxes: Extra-Sensitive, Lubricated, Non-Lubricated, Natural. It was trickier than choosing a coffee at Starbucks – but at least you didn't have to give your name.

'Hi!' It was the spotty assistant, a smirk on his face. Normally, he sat behind the till reading graphic novels but had clearly seen an opportunity to embarrass me. 'Need any help?' What did he expect me to say, 'Would you recommend the Tickler over the Studded?'

Kicking myself for not going further afield, I told him I was fine and moved down the aisle to the shampoo section. Once he was safely dealing with another customer, I circled back and restarted my examination of the prophylactic products on offer. What the hell did Hexagonal mean? If the guy had a penis any shape other than an aubergine, I was out anyway. Next to it were Flavoured, Textured, Warming (since when had sex been chilly?), Pleasure Shaped and Edible. I couldn't see myself sitting up in bed with my new lover, munching on a condom. If I fancied a snack after, I'd prefer a slice of pizza. Or a scone.

Right at the bottom was a bright orange box with 'Glow-in-the-dark' picked out in fluorescent orange. I pictured one of those guys at the airport guiding in planes with glow sticks. Left a bit, right a bit and . . . stop. I giggled at the thought and looked up to see the spotty assistant staring at me. I put the basket back and left without buying anything.

Back home, I did what I should have done from the start: snuck into Jess's room and pinched a couple of Durex from her secret stash under the mattress.

*　*　*

We arranged to meet at the V&A at three. Public enough to melt into the crowd if necessary and not too suspicious if we bumped into anyone we knew. I changed in the office, rolling my work clothes into a tight sausage and pressing them down into my handbag. I snuck out through the fire exit, hoping to God I didn't meet Dr Svetkova or, worse, Kevin. Then I splashed out on a black cab and sat in the back, acutely aware of the new bra pushing my breasts up, a sensation I hadn't had for years. It felt good, unlike the elastic on my new knickers which cut into my hips. It was a small price to pay.

I spotted him immediately, standing to the left of the ticket office, reading a pamphlet. Everything about him was compact and neat, like a well-made Scandinavian table. Mid-length tailored coat, cashmere by the look if it, discreet dark-blue shirt, black brogues.

The attraction was disconcerting. These days, the days of men with greying hair and creeping jowls, I rarely fancied anyone of my own generation on first sight, certainly not like I used to, when a glimpse through a crowded party had been enough to shake me, inevitably with disastrous consequences. Now I needed chit-chat, banter, at the very least an idea where they stood on the pressing questions of the day. Between me and my desire, a censorious voice demanded to know their views on Brexit, Me Too and the latest Netflix series. Which made this moment all the more unnerving – and thrilling.

I must have been staring because now he was striding towards me, hand out.

'Thomas.' A firm handshake, a salesman's smile, confident of a deal. A fat band of white gold glinted on his wedding finger. Points for honesty, I thought. When I'd slipped off my own ring, I'd expected to see an accusatory indentation left by two decades of marriage, but my flesh had turned out to be reassuringly forgetful.

'Mary,' I said. I'd gone through a series of exotic alternatives: Araminta, Henrietta, Cassandra, the porn-sounding Krystal, before settling on plain Mary. He held my gaze – grey eyes, long lashes, a hint of wrinkles.

'Did you come far?' I said. Jesus, I sounded like the Queen.

'Not very.'

'You live in town?'

'Sort of.'

'Sorry,' I said. 'We're not supposed to talk about that kind of thing, are we?'

'Verboten!' He smiled, showing neat, white teeth.

'Shall we look around?' I said.

He looked puzzled, then shrugged. 'Why not?'

I'd spent the last forty-eight hours planning our visit. I couldn't see myself shaking the guy's hand and marching straight off to the bedroom, but nor did I want an awkward coffee where we tried to find something neutral to talk about, both knowing there was only one thing on our minds. Hence my bizarre choice of an educational museum visit. I led the way through a room full of costumes, down a small flight of steps and through another room. 'You know this place?' he said.

'It's one of my favourite museums,' I said, as if I had a top ten of the things. In truth, I had been there just once, as a teenager, dragged round by an enthusiastic probationary teacher only recently out of school herself. But there's not much a few hours on an iPad can't make sound convincing.

'Is that right?' he said, taking my hand, his fingers surprisingly soft. I imagined them on my body, sweeping over me, touching me where no one had been for so long.

'There's an interesting room through here,' I said, as we dodged past a gaggle of bored foreign schoolchildren fidgeting in front of a guide. Thomas gave me a look, a mischievous smile on his lips. Would I be kissing them soon? Feeling them on me? I smiled back. Our first intimacy.

My stomach wobbled with an attack of butterflies, something I hadn't felt for years, not since school probably. It had sounded so easy in principle; I'd be swept along by desire, no time to think of anything other than the passionate present. All reservations, all guilt washed away by a tsunami of desire. Instead, I was holding hands with a man whose real name I didn't know, leading him through obscure galleries in the V&A, feeling vaguely sick. Within a few hours, this stranger was going to know me in a way no one other than Mark had for over twenty-five years. It was like being strapped into a rollercoaster, slowly climbing a vertical incline. Click, click, click. Any second, we would stop at the top. Then there would be no choice but to wait for it to tip over into the terrifying plunge.

Crossing a corridor, I panicked. What if we bumped into someone I knew? I imagined their look as they took in our entwined fingers.

'It's down here,' I said, gently pulling my hand away, leading him into a vast, vaulted hall full of Greek and Roman remains.

'What is this place?' he said, genuinely surprised.

'The Cast Courts,' I said. 'Everything in here is an exact replica of the original, cast in wax, then plaster.' Two towering Roman columns dominated the room. 'They're copies of Trajan's column,' I said. 'Cut in half so they'd fit.'

'Extraordinary,' said Thomas. I could smell his aftershave. Subtle, lemony.

'Every European museum used to have rooms like this. These are the only ones left.'

He turned to take in the rest of the exhibits: statues, busts, whole facades of buildings. 'They're all fake?'

'Every one,' I said, trying to remember what else the Wikipedia entry said. 'You could say they're more real than the originals, most of those have been worn away by pollution, some even destroyed. These things are snapshots of the past.' We walked through to another room, stopping in front of a full-size recreation of Michelangelo's *David*.

'They cast this in hundreds of sections, then put them together in situ.' I was beginning to impress myself. 'An Italian Grand Duke gave it to Queen Victoria,' I went on. 'When she saw *David* in all his glory, Victoria insisted a fig leaf be hung over his bits on two little hooks. You can see the leaf over there.'

He stared at me in silence and I wondered if I'd been bullshitting a professor of archaeology.

'And what do you insist on?' he said, leaning in close.

'Sorry?' I said, thrown by this interruption of my lecture. I hadn't reached the bit about the museum being the brain-child of Albert himself.

'What do you like in the boudoir?'

Despite Alice's comprehensive checklist, the question threw me. What the hell *did* I like? I'd never given it much thought, and certainly no man had bothered to ask. There had been the odd 'are you OK?' or 'is this working for you?' Once or twice a 'shall we try x or y', but no one had sat me down away from the bedroom and asked what sort of sex I liked. All I could think of was the things I *didn't* like. Having my head shoved into a pillow for one, or my legs bent backwards like a circus contortionist. The fact was, comfort came pretty high on my list of sexual proclivities. But how do you say to your new lover your sexual fantasy is being comfy?

'Well, there's a question,' I said, thinking I'd have to come up with *something* by the time we reached the flat.

'Why don't we find out?' he said, offering me his hand again. We navigated past clumps of Chinese tourists, emerging into bright sunshine from a side exit I didn't recognise. I looked up and down the road trying to get my bearings, eventually spotting a souvenir shop on a corner which looked familiar.

'So,' said Thomas. 'Where now?'

I was at the top of the rollercoaster, the cart at a standstill, balanced on the apex of a near-vertical drop.

'This way,' I said, leading him across a busy road. As we approached the apartment building, I told myself there was still time to bail out. The Tube was near; in less than five minutes I could be safely underground, hurtling towards freedom and sense. We were only yards from the entrance now, I could see the discreet keypad on the wall, with its neat row of buttons.

I'd checked out the place a few days before, satisfied myself the bathroom had the lock and phone as promised. The bedroom had been small and clean, dominated by a high double bed, with a window opening straight on to a brick wall. But I'd figured we wouldn't be there for the view.

'Have you done this before?' said Thomas, stopping by the door.

I looked into his eyes. He really was very good-looking.

'Once or twice,' I said, and punched in the code.

* * *

The curtains were half drawn, subtle lights bathing everything in a forgiving yellow glow. Ambient music played softly from hidden speakers. The bed, puffed with cushions, stood like a sporting arena awaiting a great contest. I glanced at the bathroom.

'I should . . . '

'Absolutely.'

Easing the bolt across, I caught sight of myself in the long mirror, then quickly looked away before I lost what little confidence I had. Sitting to pee, my left foot began jigging up and down like a nervous five-year-old's. I squished my other foot on top of it. My stomach was still wobbly with nerves. Maybe I should be taking off my clothes, ready to stride in, grab him by the lapels and pull him close. I felt nauseous. There must be a mini-bar, maybe we should start there. I slid back the bolt.

As my eyes adjusted to the gloom of the bedroom, I saw Thomas standing by the window, naked. Feet astride, hands on hips. What did he expect me to do? Applaud? Hold up a card with a nine on it, though eleven might have been more appropriate? No wonder the guy was confident.

'Say hello to Toby.'

I found myself suppressing a giggle, tried to turn it into a cough and ended up making a peculiar 'spluh' sound. Perhaps if he'd laughed it off, grinned and thrown me on to the bed, everything would have been fine. Instead, he stared at me as if I'd farted in a communion service.

'Sorry,' I said. 'Sorry. Should I take off my . . . ?'

He put his fingers to his lips. 'Shh.'

He took a couple of steps, his balls swaying like an abbreviated Newton's Cradle. I noticed his pubes were darker than his hair. Could he have dyed them? What sort of man does that? As he reached for the buttons on my blouse, I could feel Toby poking me in the tummy. The laughter began to rise again, undeniable, irrepressible. I clamped my mouth shut. What the hell was wrong with me? I turned away, our heads bumped. I could see his willy waggling about like one of those balloon sculptures at a kid's party. I laughed out loud. A proper, loud, full-on laugh.

'What the fuck?' he said.

Any residual magic vanished like a soap bubble popping in a bath. Two minutes later I was back on the street, blinking in the afternoon sunshine. Hurrying to the Tube, I didn't dare look back, convinced he'd be loping down the street after me like an irate silverback.

CHAPTER SIXTEEN

Safely back in my own lovely bedroom, I tore off my jeans and top, then the knickers and bra and stuffed the lot into an old carrier bag before shoving it into the back of my wardrobe. Sitting in a painfully hot bath, I tried to convince myself I had sabotaged things for the noblest of reasons, been overcome by moral certainty at the last moment and removed myself from danger before making an irreversible mistake. That was nonsense, of course. I'd bottled it, frozen when it looked like something might actually happen. Then another truth hit me: I was the problem, not Mark. I was the passionless one, uptight and incapable of letting go. Which is when the tears started. Hot and salty and full of self-pity.

There was a bang on the door.

'Mum? Are you in there?'

'I'm having a bath,' I said, trying to sound normal.

'It's the middle of the afternoon! Are you OK?'

'Got a bit of a cold,' I said. 'Thought a bath might help.'

'I'll make you a honey and ginger.' She sounded so adult. Just a few months ago she had been the one locked in a bathroom, sobbing, while I stood on the landing trying to console her for not being invited to the birthday party of a new girl at school, assuring her it might feel bad now but time heals all wounds. Only it doesn't. Guilt's a running sore which never mends.

'Oh, and Mum, did you talk to your doctor friend?'

'I didn't have a chance,' I said, for some stupid reason unable to admit the truth.

'You know she's one of the youngest women consultants to get a fellowship?'

Hardly a surprise, I thought. Dr Svetkova was the all-round fucking package. Accomplished, gorgeous, unafraid of her sexuality. I bet she wouldn't run out on a guy with a massive hard-on.

'That's wonderful, darling,' I said. 'I'll try to grab her tomorrow.'

* * *

A couple of hours later, perspective returned, partly down to giving myself a severe talking to but mostly thanks to a stiff G&T. Pouring myself a top-up, I reasoned that while it was sickening to have thrown away so much money, at least no harm had been done. I felt as if I had emerged from a full-on weekend, hangover gone, sour taste in my stomach replaced by a healthy hunger and a resolution never to overdo things again. I could move on now. The fever had broken, the boil had been lanced.

Determined to make amends, I ordered Mark's favourite takeaway and opened the most expensive bottle of wine we had.

'What are we celebrating?' said Jess.

'Just life,' I said, reaching to fill Mark's glass, but he slipped his hand over it.

'I don't drink, Kirsten. You know that.' He poured himself a tumbler of water. I bit back the urge to say one fucking drink wasn't going to kill him and offered the bottle to Jess instead.

'Sorry, Mum, school night.'

'Of course,' I said, pouring myself a large glass. 'Quite right.'

'How was your day?' said Mark.

'Oh, you know, the usual,' I said. Nearly shagged a guy hung like a horse. Nothing out of the ordinary. I spooned the takeaway on to the plates, and we talked about Jess's personal statement, how awful things were in Syria and if we should plan one last family summer holiday before she went to medical school. Then we cleared up, watched a bit of telly and I poured myself the last of the wine – there was no point sticking a cork in stuff that good.

* * *

Brushing my teeth, I stared at myself in the bathroom mirror. I looked the same as I had that morning. Of course I did. I'd done nothing wrong, it had been an aberration, a tiny mid-life crisis safely over. Normal service would now resume.

Mark was sitting up in bed, reading his book, glasses perched on the end of his nose. I reached over and took them off.

'Hey, what are you doing?' he said.

'Being a wife,' I said and kissed him.

'You're tipsy,' he said.

'Yes, I am,' I said and reached my hand down to his groin.

*   *   *

Making love with Mark was like watching him cook one of his favourite meals. Spicy papaya salad perhaps, or his special tofu dish with chilli. He took his time, preparing everything meticulously, in the right order, in the right proportions. No need to weigh or measure, he knew the recipe by heart: a pinch of salt here, a squirt of lemon there, a quick stir to end. The results were invariably the same. Tasty, tasteful. Reassuringly familiar.

After we finished, Mark lay back and stared at the ceiling as I snuggled into him. Things weren't so bad between us, and if I hadn't come, it was probably me being rusty. We'd get back on track soon enough. It would be fine, we needed to pay attention to each other, that's all. This was my chance to make good, explain how I'd nearly betrayed him, then at the last minute hadn't because, despite everything, I still loved him and wanted us to spend the rest of our lives together. He'd understand.

'Penny for your thoughts,' I said.

'I was wondering,' he said, 'if I should cycle in tomorrow.' Then he reached over and turned out the light.

*   *   *

Instead of leaping out of bed at the first sound of the alarm as I usually did, the next morning I lay in bed for a while, thinking. Next door, I could hear Mark practising his Arabic vocabulary while he shaved. He had set himself the target of a thousand words by summer when he planned to take us all to Morocco. Maybe by then, yesterday would seem an age ago, a silly misadventure, half forgotten.

Hearing Mark turn off the tap, I slid from under the duvet and headed for the shower. As I went past, he slapped me on the arse. He hadn't done that for years. I felt like a horse who's romped in a creditable second to be rewarded with a whack on the flanks from its trainer.

I was being too harsh. I liked seeing Mark happy, hearing him hum as he made breakfast rather than shout at the radio or grump into his laptop, but I also had to admit feeling more than a little disappointed about the sex last night. Not angry exactly, but close. He must have known I didn't come; he'd even apologised afterwards. Or rather he'd said he was sorry it hadn't worked for me, like I was the one at fault. Which might have been true; it certainly didn't help to have the picture of Thomas's impressive Toby popping up in my head uninvited, but Mark couldn't have known that. It was as if we had played a game of tennis which Mark had won six-love, six-love, and afterwards he commiserated with me, saying what a pity my serve was off.

I stacked the dirty breakfast plates, cleaned the stove and wiped down the table. I was being unreasonable. It was me who had nearly cheated, and now I had the gall to blame Mark for my inability to put it behind me. It *was* like a game of tennis, and my serve *was* off. Maybe I should try therapy, it would be a relief to confide in someone. Only I didn't have another ring to sell and suspected the NHS wouldn't be up for funding a sexually frustrated, middle-aged woman who had nearly screwed everything up for a quick thrill. I needed to sort this one out on my own.

PART III

BRITISH TRANSPORT POLICE

Criminal Justice Act 1967 s9
Magistrates' Courts Act 1980 ss 5A (3) (a) and 5B
Criminal Procedure Rules r27.1 (1)

EXTRACT FROM STATEMENT OF WITNESS

Statement of:	Bishaaro Ossas
Age of Witness:	Over 18
Occupation of Witness:	CCTV Operator
Date:	19/06/2019

This Statement, consisting of four pages, signed by me, is true to the best of my knowledge and belief and I make it knowing that, if tendered in evidence, I shall be liable to prosecution if I have wilfully stated in it anything which I know or believe to be false or do not believe to be true.

I am a CCTV operator employed by Imperial College Healthcare NHS Foundation Trust. My job is to collect, monitor and review CCTV images in and around St Mary's Hospital for security purposes.

At 09.10 hrs on 19 June 2019 I was on duty in the hospital CCTV Monitoring Centre when DS Withers asked me to review footage I had requested from several different departments across the hospital compound. Specifically, footage recorded from camera GH43, which covers the main entrance to the hospital.

I reviewed the images shown as being recorded between 09.00 hrs and 18.00 hrs between 1 May and 8 June 2019. At 09.10 hrs on 20 May the camera records a man who I would describe as in his thirties, dressed in jeans and a leather jacket, entering the hospital on foot.

He appears to be alone. He is next captured by camera GH28 at the main lifts and then walking along the corridor leading to Cardiology and Ward 7 by camera GH29. He is picked by up by camera GH51 walking towards Paediatrics.

The cameras beyond this point were not functioning on the day due to the loss of an assigned IP address and I did not see him on any camera again, specifically, I did not see him leave the hospital site.

I downloaded this footage on to a DVD which is now marked as item GO/1 and I handed it to DS Withers at 12.10 hrs on 19 June 2019.

Bromley Police Station

As Withers and Chowdhury take their seats opposite me, I catch a trace of tobacco. My guess is it's her; the only people I know who still smoke are women. For one mad second, I think of asking for a cigarette, despite having given up over twenty years ago. Withers takes off his jacket to reveal the beginnings of sweat patches under his arms. It's already hot in here. If they can't run to air con they could at least leave the door open.

'We'd like your help making an E-fit likeness,' says Withers, propping an iPad on a neat little stand. 'We're interested in the man you spoke to near Cappa's Cuppa, the coffee stall by Ravensbourne Station.' He turns the stand to face me. 'DC Chowdhury's done all the courses, I'll let her take you through it.'

She moves her chair to sit next to me.

'If I could begin with some basic questions?' she says. 'What was the skin colour of the man you saw?'

I almost say black but then remember the CCTV had showed images of his hands. 'White.'

'Age range?'

'Late-twenties? It was difficult to tell.'

'OK,' says Chowdhury, touching the screen. 'We're going to show you six different face shapes. I'd like you to indicate the one which you feel most resembles the man you saw.' The screen fills with blank outlines of faces, from round to long. I hesitate, then point at the one which looks least like Zac. 'Thank you,' says Chowdhury. 'Now let's move on to hair.'

And so it builds. Each time I make a choice, she taps the screen, moving elements, subtly changing a detail, once or twice making a feature bigger or smaller. It goes on for what seems hours, but eventually the screen fills with a remarkably lifelike image of a man I quite often see on my morning commute, though I have added a few quirks to make sure it's not too similar.

'Would you say this is an accurate rendering of the man you saw?' says Chowdhury, her finger hovering over the 'Save' button.

'I only saw him briefly, but yes, I suppose so.'

The two of them exchange a look then Withers nods and Chowdhury presses the button.

'Is that it?' I say. 'Are we done?'

'There is something else we'd like your help with, Ms Callaway,' says Withers. He leans over and taps the screen a couple of times. As it fills with a blurry still, I recognise the location immediately – the main reception at St Mary's.

'Sorry,' says Withers, 'it takes time to load.' The three of us stare at the screen as the image slowly sharpens then starts to move. I can make out Bella behind her desk, talking to a woman in a wheelchair as other people come in and out of shot. Just another day in reception, I think. Then Withers taps the screen, freezing the footage. He points at a figure in the background taking a map of the hospital from a rack. Despite having his back to the camera, I know exactly who it is. How could I not? 'What do you think?' says Withers. 'Might this be the same man who approached you near Ravensbourne Station?'

'Maybe,' I say, feeling nauseous. 'The jacket looks similar.'

'That's what we thought,' says Withers, starting the video again. Now the screen has shots of the same man in the hallway, going past the lifts, striding down a corridor. I recognise all the locations, it's the journey I've made every day for the last fifteen years. I know what comes next: Zac will pass the turning to Paediatrics then it's just twenty paces before he'll reach the door to my office. Which I will open. I feel my throat contract. I desperately want to reach for the cup of water but dare not move in case my hand shakes.

The footage suddenly stops, after Paediatrics but before Occupational Therapy.

'That's all we have,' says Withers, looking up.

'What do you mean?' I say, convinced this must be a trap of some sort.

'Coverage in the next section was unavailable,' says Chowdhury.

'It appears there was a problem with some of the cameras,' adds Withers. 'We have no idea where he went after this. He vanishes.'

I see a glimmer of hope. After taking the fire escape I'd pushed him through, Zac would have crossed the litter-strewn courtyard and exited under an archway at the other end, popping out on an alleyway near the canal, far from the prying eyes of the hospital's security cameras.

'I'm sorry,' I say, leaning back. 'But I still don't see what this has got to do with me.'

'It's odd, don't you think?' says Withers. 'The man you spoke to at a coffee stall in Beckenham – which is where you live – turning up where you work?'

All I can manage is a silent nod.

'You're quite sure you don't know him?' says Chowdhury.

'Quite sure,' I say.

They sit in silence for what feels like minutes, until I almost blurt out, 'Yes I know him, know him in ways I have never known anyone else.'

'There is another possibility,' says Withers at last, sitting back in his chair. 'He could have been stalking you.'

I nearly laugh. Can they seriously believe that?

'Not all stalkers are known to their victims,' adds Chowdhury.

It begins to dawn on me this might be a way out. 'Is that's why he did it? Committed suicide, I mean?'

'Suicide?' says Withers.

'I thought . . . '

'We're no longer exclusively pursuing that line of enquiry,' says Chowdhury.

'What do you mean?' I say, my mind spinning.

'The post-mortem suggests the victim was dead before he was hit by the train.'

They both look at me, clearly expecting a response.

'So how did he die?' I say at last.

'At this point, we're keeping an open mind.'

'Which does not exclude foul play,' adds Chowdhury looking straight at me.

My left leg takes up its furious jiggling. I push a palm on to my thigh to stop it. Only one thought keeps going through my mind – they think Zac was murdered.

CHAPTER SEVENTEEN

The first time with Zac took less than ten minutes. On the way back home, in a crowded Tube to Victoria, I had to stop myself grinning and announcing to the carriage 'I did it! I actually did it!'

I found Mark in the kitchen, Radio 3 playing in the background. I watched unseen as he extracted juice from a lemon with a fork, aware this was our last innocent moment together. Then I dropped my bag on to a chair with a thump. He turned, lemon in hand.

'You're back,' he said with a smile.

In twenty-five years, I had never lied to him – at least not about anything important – and certainly never cheated. I had imagined myself at this point seizing up, frozen as if plunged into an icy lake, unable to breathe or speak. This was the man I'd fallen in love with, promised to be faithful to, shared a child with. I should have been poleaxed by my betrayal.

Instead, I wanted to tell him what an amazing day it had been, as if I'd seen an inspiring film or eaten at a great restaurant I knew he'd like. I had to hold back from hugging him and laughing and saying how beautiful life was. He could treat himself to a new 'private' laptop, I'd see Zac, and everything would be perfect. It was only sex, after all. Gorgeous, lovely, life-enhancing sex.

'Jess is over at Gemma's so I thought I'd try something new,' said Mark, sweeping detritus into the bin. 'It's basically street food. In Arabic they call it koshri.' He pronounced it with the guttural enthusiasm of a new language student. 'Fingers crossed it works.' He picked up a pepper, fine-slicing it with the Henckels knife I'd bought for his last birthday.

'Smells wonderful,' I said. How could this be? How was I able to continue as if nothing had happened? I hadn't just crossed the Rubicon, I'd splashed about in it, kicking sand in the faces of those I loved. I reached for a bottle of wine.

'It's Thursday,' said Mark, watching me pull the cork. 'Mid-week?'

'More like nearly the weekend,' I said, feeling stupid for breaking my routine and remembering Alice's cardinal rule: change nothing, act normal. Too late now, I thought, pouring myself a large glass. 'One of my patients got mobility back in her arm today,' I said. 'Thought I'd celebrate.' Not entirely a lie, though it had happened a good two weeks earlier.

The kosh-whatsit dish turned out to be delicious. As Mark described his latest tussle with Ms Winters, I tried to persuade myself we were having a normal meal together, while knowing nothing could ever be the same again.

After we cleared up, Mark went online for his Arabic course and I ran a bath. Lying back in the steaming water, I wondered what had become of me, where the self I thought I knew so well had gone. I'd begun the day loyal, honest and true, my only crime a theoretical betrayal more comedy anecdote than anything serious. Where was that woman now? Five hours ago, while my husband was no doubt struggling with intractable timetable conflicts, I'd been with a man I knew nothing about, not even his real name. Where was the shame? The leaden sense of betrayal that should have made every word with Mark stick in my throat like a fish bone? Nowhere. Instead, lying in the embrace of my bath, I felt light and breezy and young, the only guilt, guilt at not feeling guilty.

* * *

After my brush with 'Toby', I'd resolved not to try my luck with Amorem again, to put it down to experience and to hell with the expense. For the first few days, I stuck to my resolution, but after a week or so couldn't resist the occasional peek at my little phone, purely out of curiosity, you understand. Not that there was anyone remotely attractive. I began to feel sorry for the men Alice had persuaded to part with cash – more for them, I suspected, than I had paid. Not many women would be tagging these guys.

One Thursday lunchtime, I was sitting alone in the canteen in my favourite seat by the window, enjoying a bowl of cold pasta, eating with one hand, checking emails with the other when I heard a buzz from my handbag. More out of habit than any genuine hope, I fished out the Amorem phone.

It took a few seconds to locate the tiny 'on' switch, but then the app bobbed up with a new message. I tapped the screen a couple of times, and a man's face smiled out at me: short hair, blue eyes, a wide, full mouth. There was something both amused and conspiratorial about that smile, as if to say, you and I know how bizarre this is. The clatter of cutlery jerked me back to the canteen. I looked up to see Kevin sliding his tray on to my table as he squeezed in opposite me.

'Hi!' he beamed.

'Kevin,' I said, slipping the phone back into my bag.

'Wraps have less calories than bread,' he said, fingering a bulging burrito. I resisted the temptation to say it should be 'fewer' not less, and the pack of Walkers cheese and onion would probably more than wipe out any benefit he was hoping for. 'I tried the 5:2 thing,' he went on, 'but I binged on the days off. I prefer the seafood diet – I see food and I eat it!' He guffawed – I have never known anyone more amused by their own jokes.

I glanced at my half-eaten pasta, debating whether to finish it or cut my losses and head back to the office to check the phone. But it had cost £6.95 and besides, I was starving.

'You ever been on a diet?' said Kevin, reaching for his Coke. 'Not that you need to,' he added quickly. 'Not at all.' He grinned, and I wondered if he'd had his teeth whitened. They certainly looked different. I tackled my food with renewed determination.

'Busy?' he said.

'As always,' I said, between rapid mouthfuls.

'Me too. Bonkers busy. You know why? Because people think tech is beneath them. No, really.' He leaned in as if I'd contradicted him. 'Particularly the ones who should know better. Take the MRI guys, their kit costs millions, but can they sort out their own laptop?' He looked at me for confirmation.

I shrugged, spearing the last couple of farfalle, a word Mark and I had taught ourselves on honeymoon, when we'd spent a squiffy afternoon talking nonsense Italian made up entirely of pasta names. I pushed away the memory.

'I have a theory,' said Kevin, opening his mouth so wide I thought he might shove the entire wrap in, in one go.

'I should be going,' I said, standing up.

'You haven't had your yoghurt.'

'It'll keep for later,' I said and was on my feet, tray in hand when my bag buzzed again.

'You should get that,' said Kevin. 'Could be important. Someone's leg might have fallen off.' He laughed and took an enormous bite of his wrap, squirting juice through his fingers.

I stashed my tray in the rack by the exit then took out my new phone again. The same face stared up at me, friendly, with an amused look around the eyes. The app pinged, and a message appeared.

> where are u?

I hesitated, glancing back into the canteen. Kevin was engrossed in wiping his plate clean with a finger. I tapped on the screen's tiny keyboard.

> london

> me 2!! in W2. U?

What sort of coincidence was that? I hesitated, W2 is a big area, he could be miles away. Part of me hoped he was.

> paddington

Silence. Then a string of emojis: a wine glass, a cappuccino, a bottle of champagne. I scrolled up to the photo again, took in the knowing smile, as if we were the only ones in on the joke. He didn't look like the sort of man who'd have a pet name for his penis, but then nor had Thomas. Another message flashed up.

drink?

In the afternoon? On a weekday? The very idea threw me into a panic. I had my work clothes on, my hair hadn't been washed for a couple of days and underneath everything I was wearing giant pants and a faded bra. I glanced at the photo again. I was getting ahead of myself. He was suggesting a drink, not a full-on Toby-style liaison. We'd have a quick coffee, that's all. He'd probably look nothing like his photo anyway. I texted back.

maybe

The reply was almost instant.

Lamb off Edgware Road?

I hadn't been there for years but knew where it was; at one time it had been a popular haunt with the nursing staff, before they'd moved on to trendier establishments.

when?

2.30?

Jesus! This was going way too fast.

too soon?

I bit my lip. My next appointment wasn't for an hour, I could easily get to the Lamb and back. Maybe it would be good not to have time to overthink things. Besides, what could go wrong in a pub, in broad daylight? I started texting.

ok

I pressed send, then turned the phone off before I could change my mind. I felt faint, as if I had stood up too quickly. Then I headed for the loos; the least I could do was put on some lippy.

* * *

The pub was less than five minutes' walk away. Alice would have been horrified, but I knew my NHS crowd were unlikely to be there. It was too old-fashioned for them, all dark wood and engraved mirrors with nothing to eat but bar snacks. Stepping in from the bright winter sunshine, it took my eyes a moment to adjust. The place was deserted except for a couple of old men sitting alone at wooden tables, nursing pints of bitter in dimple glasses. A young woman with piercings and a streak of blue through her blonde hair stood sullenly behind the bar.

'Latte, please,' I said.

She sighed as if interrupted doing something of immense importance rather than playing on her phone. 'Don't do coffee.'

'Oh, OK,' I said. 'Then a mineral water, please. And some dry roasted peanuts.'

Another sigh. 'Ice, lemon?' You'd have thought she was being asked to create both from scratch. I nodded, looked around at the empty tables. Had I been stood up? Maybe he'd been hovering close by, seen me going in and lost his nerve. Or interest. Taken one look at the real me and decided to knock it on the head.

'Four fifty,' said the young woman.

As per Alice's rules, I paid in cash then asked if there was another bar.

'No,' said the girl tonelessly, dropping coins into the till.

'There's not another room? Upstairs maybe?' I nodded at a faded flight of stairs leading into the gloom.

'Not open in the day,' she said, already back on her phone. 'Just this and the snug.'

'Snug?'

'At the back.' She bobbed her head without looking up.

I picked up my glass, feeling its icy wetness against my fingers as I walked round the bar, past one of the old men, and into a small, wood-lined room. The man from the photo sat facing the door, half a pint of beer in front of him, staring straight at me. I felt myself grinning, almost laughing. He smiled back and immediately we were like naughty kids bunking off school. He stood up, held out his hand.

'Zac. Not my real name obviously.'

'And I'm not Susan.'

A firm handshake, slender fingers. He pulled out a chair for me, pointed at my glass of water.

'I should have gone for that, but I panicked. Thought I might need the courage.'

'Is it working?' I said.

'No.' He smiled again, sat down. Nice teeth: even, white without being American-bonkers white. 'I've never done anything like this,' he said. 'Sorry, that must sound stupid. You're probably an old hand. God, that sounds worse. Can I start again?' Faded cotton jacket, dark shirt underneath, no tie. A wisp of chest hair. He picked up his beer, then put it down again. 'I don't even like beer, but I didn't dare ask for wine.'

'Try ordering coffee,' I said. We both laughed. 'This is new for me, too.'

'We should get out some paperwork. Did the guys at Amorem tell you that? Make it look like a work meeting.'

'I didn't bring any paperwork.'

'Damn, me neither!' he said.

'Peanut?'

'I love peanuts.'

He held out his hand as I tipped a few into his palm. Neat fingernails, including the cuticles. It was difficult to gauge his age, younger than me, but by how much I couldn't tell.

'Do you work around here?' I said.

'Not allowed to discuss work,' he said. 'Part of the "rules", remember?

'Sorry,' I said. 'So, what can we talk about? How we rate the Prime Minister, maybe?'

'What you thought of *Bake Off* last night?'

'Or if you caught the match?'

He laughed. 'The PM's a twat, I don't watch much TV and I hate football.'

'And things were going so well,' I said. My God, I was flirting. I couldn't remember the last time I had done that.

Zac stared at me, his lips slightly parted. I'd always had a thing about blue eyes. As a child, I desperately wanted them myself. A kind boyfriend once called mine hazel, they are in truth a nondescript greeny-grey, like used putty. Blue, I thought as a teenager, had to be the ultimate colour. Clear, piercing and luminous, like Paul Newman or Jude Law. Or Khanda. Their clarity spoke to me of freshness, of light and lack of guile. No man with eyes the colour of a Mediterranean swimming pool could be all bad.

'You are way, way more beautiful than your photo,' he said.

I looked away, embarrassed. I hadn't been called beautiful for years, decades probably.

'It's kind of unnerving to tell you the truth,' he said. 'I feel out my depth.'

'You're not,' I said.

Right then I knew I would have sex with this man. Maybe not today, maybe not for a while, but it would happen. It felt as if the decision had been made by someone else and all I had to do was go along with it. The relief was immense, like the quiet before an exam when there's no time left to revise. You just have to cross your fingers and hope for the best. We held each other's eyes for what felt like minutes.

'I need to work this afternoon,' I said at last.

'Me too,' he said. 'But perhaps we could meet again?'

'Yes,' I said quickly. 'Yes.'

We agreed to make a date on the app, awkwardly shook hands, then went for a peck on the cheek, me for two, him for one, bumping each other's noses in the confusion. Stupidly embarrassed, I said I needed the loo, and he said he really should get back. He pulled on a Marlon Brando-style motorbike jacket. On anyone else it would have looked ridiculous; on him it was achingly cool. He gave me one last smile, wrapped a red scarf round his neck and made for the door. A slice of light fell across the pub's faded carpet as it swung shut with a thud. I almost ran after him, imagined myself hurrying down the street, grabbing his shoulders, turning his face to mine. Instead, I glanced at his untouched beer and, for some crazy reason, downed the lot. Then I went through into the main room and asked the sulky barmaid for the loo.

'Upstairs on the left,' she said, with an uncharacteristic smile. She must have been eavesdropping. Why else grin at someone who'd bought a measly mineral water and packet of peanuts? The old man with the paper seemed to be in on it, too, squinting disapprovingly over the top of his *Standard* as I headed for the stairs.

In the loo, I turned on the cold tap and ran my hands under its gushing stream. I wanted to stick my whole head under there to cool down. I hadn't felt like this since that night with Khanda, waiting naked under my sheet for him to peel it back, lean over and kiss my naked stomach, my breasts, my mouth.

I turned off the water. Zac must be a couple of streets away by now, safe from my mad impulse to bolt after him. I mentally ran over my diary for the next week or so, trying to picture when and where we could meet. Please God let him be free soon, I couldn't bear feeling like this much longer. I looked at myself in the mirror. Beautiful, he said. And for the first time in aeons, I allowed myself to think it might be true. We are only as beautiful as those who see us, and I hadn't been seen for years. I tucked in my blouse, smoothed down my skirt and snatched a final look in the mirror before opening the door.

He was right there in the corridor: in that jacket, with that scarf – and on his face, the wickedest of grins.

He began to say something, but before his mouth could form a word I leant in and kissed him. Soft lips, the lingering taste of peanuts. I could feel his hands on my shoulders, slipping down to my waist. We pulled back, our faces inches from each other. I could hear his breath, feel it on my cheek. He smiled, turned his head a fraction and then his lips were on mine again.

The sound of laughter, footsteps. We leapt apart, bug-eyed. Two women were making their way up the stairs, chatting noisily about flights to Madrid. Zac grabbed my hand, pulling me into some sort of meeting room. We clicked the door shut as the women reached the landing. I giggled. Zac put a soft hand on my mouth.

'Shh!'

We pressed our faces against the door, could hear the muffled sound of running water. I took in the room: Art Deco lights, framed book covers of the Bloomsbury group on dark blue wood panelling, tables with leather chairs artfully arranged in front of tall Georgian windows.

'This is so much nicer than downstairs,' I said.

'Much,' he said, taking my face in his hands. I found his mouth again and the next thing I knew, was wriggling out of my skirt. He unbuckled his belt as I reached in. I could feel his finger hooking the elastic of my knickers. He reached in, too. I couldn't remember being so desperate. As he slid into me, I looked up to see Edith Sitwell staring down her nose at us.

'Wow,' said Zac.

'Wow,' I agreed.

*   *   *

Within an hour, I was back in my office, still buzzing as I tried to concentrate on manipulating a pensioner's arthritic hand. She must have been in her seventies, so twenty-odd in the 1960s. She'd probably had her own wild sexual adventures. I wanted to ask what it had been like, to compare notes. Then she winced.

'Sorry,' I said. 'Did that hurt?'

'It's OK, dear. I know it's for the best.'

I worked my way up her wrist, the skin covered in liver spots, so paper-thin I could see the blue-black veins under the surface. My hand would look like this one day, not so far off now. One had to take one's pleasures while one could. I didn't want to look back when I was frail and bent, my flesh withered and dry, and think, 'if only'. We're here for so little time, hardly any at all really. We have a duty to enjoy ourselves.

I thought back to how outrageously soft Zac's lips had been and shivered at the memory.

'Would you mind stopping now, dear?' said the old woman. 'It's beginning to hurt.'

*   *   *

I woke at three the next morning, covered in a film of sweat. Mark lay with his back to me, eye mask on, gently snoring. We must have been mad, I thought. What if someone had come in or seen us through the windows? I could have lost everything I valued for a quickie in a room above a pub.

But what a quickie. I'd never come so fast. It almost made the years of waiting worth it.

Unable to get back to sleep, I tried to reconstruct every moment, from opening the door on to the corridor and seeing Zac standing there, through to the overwhelming end. But it was a mishmash of touch and smell and glory. His skin felt soft, so different to Mark's. He probably wasn't forty, maybe a lot younger. His hot breath on my neck, his fingers inside me . . .

Bridget once told me she'd had an orgasm just by thinking of her boyfriend. Lying stock-still she'd wished herself to come and now, for the first time, I believed her. I turned over, pulling the duvet to cover me. Mark groaned and tugged it back. I held on tight.

CHAPTER EIGHTEEN

Almost exactly two years earlier, Mark and I had tried the talking cure. It was my idea, though once on board Mark embraced it with the same thoroughness he applied to choosing a new bike or the best high-pressure patio washer (an obscure Danish make, it turns out). He canvassed opinion from the few people we knew who were in therapy, carried out extensive research online and entered into lengthy correspondence with strangers in chat groups.

I did my best to like Bonnie, but Mark loved her. So he should – he chose her. They spent our first session discussing the theoretical framework she would employ. Mark was in his element: charming, enthusiastic and entirely academic.

I thought Bonnie would see straight through him and perhaps she did but had decided to play the long game. At eighty quid a shot, who could blame her. We did make some progress. We identified the problem: not enough sex. And came up with a possible solution: more sex. After five sessions, Mark announced he'd gained all the insight he needed, and I agreed, pretty sure we could find a better home for the weekly eighty pounds.

To be fair, Bonnie's strategies did work for a couple of months. We had regular, if scheduled, sex, which felt a bit of a checkbox exercise, but I hoped it might be a catalyst for the real thing to re-emerge. Then Mark spent a week in Scarborough at a conference, Jess went through a bad patch at school and I had to cover for a colleague's maternity leave. We slipped effortlessly into old ways and, without the regular focus of a therapy session, were soon back where we started. Minus four hundred pounds.

After my fifteen minutes with Zac, I could now say with authority, the talking cure is nowhere near as effective as the shagging cure. I hadn't felt so good in years.

* * *

The journey to work the day after my tryst should have been a nightmare. To start with, it was one of those overcast, matt February days when the damp seeps through to your skin, however many layers you wear. And the train guards were on strike – again. I had to take a bus into town and stand for forty minutes in the drizzle as packed double-deckers splashed by without stopping. When I did manage to squeeze on, I arrived at Victoria to find there had been an 'incident' on the Tube at Sloane Square. Some poor person had had enough and started the day by throwing themselves in front of a train, thus messing it up for the rest of us and, no doubt, leaving the driver traumatised. When I eventually made it to the hospital, I'd missed two appointments and a departmental meeting. Amazingly, I didn't care. Despite it all, the world seemed bright and new and full of promise.

It helped that first thing I'd received a message from Zac.

We spent the next hour bouncing increasingly silly emojis back and forth.

I felt like a teenager again, passing love notes between desks as Mr Robinson wrote the formula for photosynthesis on his squeaky blackboard. I tingled, vibrated and – I suspected – glowed. I tried hard to act normally, asking Janice how her birthday had been, filling out an assessment for a recent intern, forcing myself to concentrate on the few patients who had struggled in. During a coffee break, I found myself chatting animatedly to Kevin and complimenting Dr Svetkova on her shoes. They both stared at me as if I was on something. Which is when I remembered Alice's warning that happiness can be difficult to explain away.

Despite feeling more alive than I had for years, when Zac sent a message asking if we could meet again, I hesitated. I needed time to mull over what had happened, to let it become part of me, or decide it never could be. I'd once made a charity parachute jump and, when the instructor offered me another go, agreed immediately. The second time, I landed awkwardly, snapping my ankle, and was on crutches for six weeks. I should have accepted the first go as a one-off experience and moved on, not lusted after more. Maybe it was the same now. I sent Zac a question mark, then turned the phone off to stop myself doing anything stupid.

After lunch, Jess called. There had been virtual radio silence between us since New Year's Eve, when she didn't come home until the next morning, slept until four, then disappeared again without a word. Now she was asking if she could drive me over to see Gran after work. That way she'd have some practice for her test and we'd both get to see my mother. Determined to play it cool and not sound overjoyed, I said I couldn't be sure how long it would take me to get home, but in principle, yes.

As it turned out, half my appointments were cancelled, so I sneaked away early and managed to catch the first bus that came along. The rain had cleared by the time I walked from the station, sombre clouds blown south by a sharp breeze, revealing a vast, low-slung moon, intermittently visible between the trees. Jess was waiting for me, sitting on the bonnet of the car, fiddling with the broken aerial that I kept meaning to fix. I wanted to rush over and say: 'You'll never guess what I did yesterday. Had sex with this bloke in a pub!' We'd laugh, and she'd say, 'No way! What was it like?' And I'd say 'Amazing', and she'd say 'That is SO cool' and we'd be the best of friends and all would be well again. Instead, I said, 'OK?' She nodded and asked for the keys.

We drove in silence until we took my mother's turn-off. 'I'm sorry about the other night,' I said at last. 'Giving you a tough time about going out.'

She gave me a quizzical look.

'I've got to stop treating you like a child, haven't I?'

'It'd be a start,' she said, cautiously overtaking a bin lorry. She stopped at a T-junction, meticulously checking the traffic both ways. I wanted to tell how proud of her I was, how I loved her, how I'd miss her when she'd gone, but didn't trust myself to say any of it. So I pointed out some kids crossing the road up ahead and told her to slow down a little.

* * *

My mother was in the kitchen, glaring at the stove, her wrist still in its blue cast. She looked round as we came in, neither surprised nor particularly pleased.

'Hi, Mum,' I said. 'What are you up to?'

'I'm allowed in my own kitchen, aren't I? I wanted a cup of tea.'

There was no cup, no teapot, no sign of the silver strainer she always insisted on.

'Why don't I make it for you, Gran?' said Jess, reaching for the kettle. My mother looked blank, then her brain kicked in, like a computer rebooting.

'Hello, dear,' she said. 'How were the exams?'

'I haven't done them yet, Gran. Another few months of revision, thank goodness.'

'That's excellent dear, really excellent.' She took a few steps, then swayed and had to reach for the counter to steady herself. She seemed suddenly older.

'Maybe we could look out Dad's old walking frame,' I said. 'It might make things easier for you.'

'Why would I want that?' she snapped. 'I'm not a cripple!'

'We don't say cripple now, Gran,' said Jess.

'Nothing wrong with the word cripple,' said my mother. 'We used to call them spastics.'

'I'll take you through,' I said, offering my arm before Jess could launch into one of her lectures. My mother's grip felt surprisingly strong, her bony fingers digging into my flesh as we navigated the hall carpet, then the small step into the living room and finally the narrow space between the coffee table and sofa. She dropped into her chair with a sigh.

'I was wondering, Mum,' I said, 'if you had a boyfriend before Dad?'

'What's that?'

'A boyfriend,' I said louder, sounding like an English tourist asking for directions. 'Did you have one before you were married? Or even after!' I added, with a silly laugh.

'What's it to you?' she said, fixing me with her pale blue eyes. 'What are you up to, Kirsten?' Instantly, I was the naughty child again.

'I'm curious, that's all,' I said, regretting I had started this.

She gave me a sceptical look. My mother had an uncanny ability to see through me, to home in on a truth however meticulously hidden. Could she have intuited I was only interested in her indiscretions because of my own?

'If you don't want to talk about it, fine,' I said.

She tilted her head to one side. As a child, that gesture alone had been enough to make me blurt out the truth; forty years on, it retained some of its power, though not enough. I had built up immunity over the decades.

'I know what this is,' she announced triumphantly as I moved her worn dictionary to the sideboard to clear a space for the tea tray. My heart pounded. It wasn't possible, she couldn't simply have *guessed*. Somehow known that I had cheated on my husband, trashing the vows I'd made in front of him and her and my father. 'You want to squeeze everything out of me before I die.'

'What?' I said. 'What are you talking about?'

She hadn't looked so pleased with herself for weeks. 'Well, let me tell you,' she went on, 'I'm not dying any time soon!'

I didn't know whether to be relieved she had no idea what I had been up to, or appalled she hadn't followed anything I'd said. Before I could quiz her further, Jess appeared with the tea.

'Hello, dear,' said my mother. 'How are those exams of yours going?'

* * *

Jess drove back in the dark, with me trying not to jab my foot on an imaginary brake every time we approached a junction. In fact, she was a perfectly good driver, confident without being reckless. I was sure she'd pass her test first time.

'What will happen when Gran can't look after herself?' she said, turning into our road.

It was an inevitability I tried not to dwell on. She couldn't move in with us, it would drive Mark and me mad. Helen couldn't have her either, not now she lived in a shoebox on the other side of town, and we couldn't afford a care home. Even the cheapest ran to over fifty thousand a year.

'We'll come up with something,' I said, as Jess parked neatly between two cars.

'It's crap getting old, isn't it?' she said.

'It can be.'

'Me, I want to live it all and drop down dead at fifty.'

'I'm nearly fifty,' I said.

'Better start living then,' she said, opening her door and flashing me a smile. 'You've only got a few months.'

Sitting alone in the car for a moment, I wondered what she'd think if she knew I *had* started living. Would she be sympathetic, understand the forces which had driven me to seek pleasure where I could? Or would the repulsion all children feel for their parents' sex lives, combined with the ruthless moral certainty of youth, condemn me for ever? And if it did, how much would that matter to me?

CHAPTER NINETEEN

On my way to work the following Monday, I saw Jess on to the train at Paddington. She was off for an interview at Bristol, no thanks to Dr Svetkova, though when I eventually told Jess about her refusal to help, she thought that made her even cooler ('she has such a moral centre, Mum'). Watching Jess stride down the platform, overnight case in hand, a confident young woman ready to take on the world, I had a premonition of what my life would be like come October. Then she wouldn't be away for twenty-four hours but months at a time. As the tears formed, I told myself I was being absurd, self-pitying. I watched until she opened the train door and stepped in, hoping she might turn and give a final wave, but she didn't.

Later, making my way through the department's reception area, I heard Kevin's laugh echoing across the lobby. He was leaning on the desk in his new coat, showing Janice, who was laughing almost as loudly as he was, something on his phone. Dr Svetkova watched disapprovingly from the lifts, bolt upright in her pencil skirt and heels. As I made my way down the corridor, Kevin ran to catch up with me.

'You have to see this thing on Twitter,' he said. 'It's hysterical.'

'Maybe another time,' I said, determined to keep things neutral. I rummaged in my bag for the office keys.

'Are you OK?' he said. 'You look kind of different.'

'Know what, Kevin? I'm having an existential crisis which includes, though is not limited to, losing my daughter, having a mother with dementia and betraying my husband.'

Kevin stared at me, unblinking, and for a second I thought I had said it out loud. 'Late night, you know how it is,' I said.

'I was wondering,' he said, shifting his weight from one foot to the other, 'and you can say no – obviously – if you'd like to have a drink sometime?'

I'd been dreading this for a while, but it still came as a surprise.

'Sorry,' I said, 'but I'm a bit tied up at the moment.'

'It wouldn't just be me,' he added quickly. 'A bunch of us are going on Friday after work.'

'That's very kind of you, Kevin, but . . . '

'We'll be at The Lamb. Next to Lidl?'

I froze. The Lamb was where Zac and I had met.

'It's a proper old-fashioned London boozer. One of my faves.'

He couldn't have seen us! It wasn't possible. A coincidence. It had to be.

'It doesn't matter,' he said quickly. 'Stupid idea.' He practically ran down the corridor and let himself into his office. Stunned, I tried to work out if it had been an innocent attempt at a date or prelude to telling me he knew all about Zac and me. If he did know, what he did he want?

'Ms Callaway? Ms Callaway!'

I looked round to see a young woman hurrying towards me.

'Michelle?' I said, taking in the sunglasses, the overly made-up face. 'I don't think Jamie is in today.'

'I'm not with Jamie,' she said. 'I need to see you on my own.'

'I'm sorry, but I have appointments all morning. If you talk to Janice, perhaps she could . . . '

'It won't take long. Please.'

I could make out her eyes through the tint of her sunglasses, the smeared mascara. 'I have a few minutes before my first patient,' I said, opening my office.

Before I'd even closed the door, Michelle was demanding to know why Jamie had done it, how he could do this to her, what the fuck was he thinking of!

'Michelle, slow down. I have no idea what you're talking about,' I said.

She pushed a mobile under my nose. 'I can't read without my glasses,' I said, reaching across the desk.

'Jamie dumped me.'

She slumped into the nearest chair, tears seeping under her sunglasses. I took the phone from her hand. It wasn't a long message, little more than goodbye: it's my fault, not yours; this is for best; you need to be free. Another Dear John letter delivered at the speed of light.

'I'm so sorry, Michelle.'

'Has he said anything to you? I know he tells you everything.'

I glanced out of the window, noticed a pigeon trying to balance on the anti-foul spikes, and wondered why the disappointed in love felt it was fair game to unload their misery on me – first Jack, now Michelle.

'Michelle, even if I did know anything, I can't break patient confidentiality.'

'We're engaged for fuck's sake!'

'I'm sorry. NHS guidelines are very strict.'

'There's someone else, isn't there? There must be.' She searched in her pocket for a tissue, realised it was sodden and tossed it into the bin. I handed her the pack from the top of the filing cabinet, reeling off the official confidentiality guidelines, despising myself even as I went through the familiar tropes.

'You need to talk to Jamie,' I concluded. 'As soon as possible.'

'Think I haven't tried?'

'Then maybe Greg.'

She stared at me, mouth open, the tissue held between her thumb and index finger. I shrugged, not wanting to spell it out. Then she laughed.

'The guy's gay, for fuck's sake!'

'Are you sure about that?'

'Er, yes! He came out to his commanding officer three years ago.'

My head spun. 'Does Jamie know?' I said.

'He was the one who told him to get on with it.'

I rubbed my eyes. How could I have got it so wrong? Imagining Jamie sacrificing himself so Michelle could be free to be with Greg!

'I have a right to know what's going on,' said Michelle.

My desk phone rang. It was Janice, saying my nine o'clock had arrived. 'Michelle,' I said, hanging up. 'You need to discuss this with Jamie, not me.'

'Is he sick? Is his leg infected?'

'It's nothing like that, I promise.'

'You're not going to tell me, are you?'

'I can't. I'm sorry.'

She stood up. 'I thought you were a friend.' She picked up her bag and walked out. I sat in my chair, telling myself I'd had no choice, my responsibility was to my patient, not her. Outside, the pigeon had flown off to a more comfortable perch. I'd broken the most sacred vows a person can take and then refused to help an innocent, suffering woman because of some bureaucratic jobsworthy crap. That couldn't be who I was.

* * *

I caught up with Michelle as she was marching out of the main reception area, almost had to stand in front of her to make her stop.

'This is strictly off the record,' I said, out of breath. 'You can't tell anyone about it, including Jamie. You understand?'

She nodded. I went through Dr Svetkova's diagnosis, explained Jamie wouldn't be able to have penetrative sex.

'That's it?' she said. 'That's why he dumped me?'

'Yes,' I said, not knowing what else to say.

'Why didn't he tell me?'

'I don't know, Michelle. He was probably embarrassed.'

'Embarrassed! He'd rather lose me than be "embarrassed"?'

'You need to make an appointment with Dr Svetkova,' I said. 'Both of you. Get it all out in the open.'

'How? Jamie's not even talking to me.'

I watched helplessly as she straightened her skirt, sniffed back a tear. 'The hospital does offer counselling. If you like I could . . . '

Her stare silenced me.

'Thank you for telling me,' she said curtly. 'I know you're not supposed to.' She held out her arm and we shook hands. It felt strangely formal. Then she fired me the briefest of smiles and walked out on to the busy street. I wished I could help her, comfort her. But at least she had a chance of moving on now. I felt sorry for Jamie too, but he had no right to inflict his tragedy on a young woman with her whole future ahead of her. Everybody deserves a life of physical pleasure. It's a human right.

* * *

On my way to the Tube, I took a detour past The Lamb, hoping Kevin might be there so I could prove that I occasionally dropped in after work, and if he *had* seen me, it was nothing out of the ordinary. The same old man sat at the corner table, a half-pint and newspaper by his side. A young couple huddled over a phone, giggling, but there was no sign of Kevin or anyone else from the hospital. The sulky barmaid had been replaced by an equally vacant boy, whose main preoccupation seemed to be trying to grow a beard.

On a whim, I climbed the stairs to the first floor. The landing was empty, but the door to 'our' room was slightly ajar. Like a criminal making sure she'd left no clues, I gingerly pushed it open. A dozen people looked up from a round table littered with notebooks and pencils. One, a silver-haired woman in her fifties, was on her feet, reading from a sheet of paper. It sounded like a poem.

'May I help?' A serious-looking man stared at me over a pair of wire rims as the woman flustered to a halt. I muttered something about looking for the loo and scuttled out. I had seen all I needed: the wood panels, the leather chairs, the framed image of Edith Sitwell looking down her nose. It had happened. All of it.

In the safety of a cubicle next door, I switched the little phone back on to find a stream of emojis and texts from Zac. Was I OK, had he offended me, could we meet again? I felt the thrill of being wanted rush through me, as intense as any chemical high – and equally dangerous. I looked at the scratch on the back of the door, forcing myself to concentrate on the yellowing handle, the crooked hook with a missing screw. But my fingers found the screen anyway and before I knew what was happening they'd sent a smiley emoji. A text flashed up.

tomorrow 6.30?

I stared at the glowing number. I had vowed not to sin again and, besides, it was impossible – I was supposed to visit my mother tomorrow. But the thought crept in that maybe I could move Mum to Thursday, she probably wouldn't even notice. And Mark, I knew, would be at yet another departmental meeting which never finished before eight. Why not? One more time, just to prove to myself it was all for real. I sent a thumbs up.

CHAPTER TWENTY

The second time with Zac couldn't have been more different. The thought of going back to where I'd been introduced to 'Toby' didn't thrill me, so when Zac sent over an address, I didn't dismiss the idea out of hand. Google Street View showed it was in one of those new developments on an obscure part of the Thames they're always pushing in the *Standard*. Close to the City with easy transport and its own gym, it had a phoney name vaguely reminiscent of Dickens. I knew theoretically it was a risk but, after what we had shared, I trusted Zac.

At work, I felt like a child counting down the hours until a birthday party. Every other minute, I thought of his lips, his fingers, his weight pressing into me. I couldn't concentrate, kept messing up on the computer, entering wrong dates or NHS numbers. One patient asked if I was coming down with something, which in a way I was.

I hurried out of the hospital at five-thirty sharp, almost knocking into Kevin as he put on his bicycle clips. I shouted an apology, thinking, I bet Zac doesn't wear bicycle clips. I took the bus despite it being much longer, remembering Alice's rule about not using the Tube. Apparently, anyone can tap a contactless card at a station and see your whole journey history. Buses only know where you got on – they can't track where you get off.

The development consisted of a confusing maze of walk-ways, switchbacks and cul-de-sacs, designed, no doubt, so every flat could boast a sliver of river view. By the time I found the right building, I was fifteen minutes late and sweating, despite the cold. The chrome intercom had twin rows of nameplates, all blank. Zac's message had said his was the eighth button down on the left, but as I was about to press it, I hesitated. What sort of man lives in a block with no other residents? Had he removed his name to pro-tect his identity or did he rent the place by the hour? It was a stupid risk coming here, to the faceless flat of a man I'd met once, for less than half an hour. Nobody knew where I was, I'd seen to that myself. I could vanish off the face of the earth and they'd have no clue where to look.

The intercom crackled into life all on its own, Zac's face appearing on a small screen.

'You found it OK, then?'

'Yes,' I said, too amazed to say anything else.

'Saw you coming across the square,' he said, his voice distorted but recognisable. 'Give the door a shove.'

There was a loud buzz and, without thinking, I pushed the door open, stepping into a vast atrium.

'Hi!'

I looked up to see Zac peering down at me. If he was a serial killer, he was a damned attractive one. As I started up the chrome and marble stairs, my skirt rubbing my thighs, I imagined myself as he might see me, a defenceless woman climbing towards her fate.

He stood on the landing, one foot propping open the door. He wore jeans and a dark blue shirt – and that knowing, complicit smile.

'Sorry I'm late,' I said, slightly out of breath.

'No problem. It's difficult to find the first time.'

This wasn't how I'd planned it. I had us ripping each other's clothes off, staggering semi-naked into the bedroom, wordlessly possessing each other, not having a polite conversation as if I'd come for a dinner party.

Stepping forward, I thought we were going to kiss, but he stood aside, ushering me in. The flat was huge, with spectacular views across the Thames.

'Wow,' I said, quickly scanning the room for photographs of his wife and family.

'Wow, indeed.' We smiled at each other. I wanted to reach out, grab his shirt and have sex right there and then, but a bizarre abstract sculpture stood between us.

'What an amazing place,' I said, edging round it.

'The ones higher up are even better, but they're not finished yet. Would you like something to drink? Tea, coffee?'

I gave him a look, and he laughed. 'Sorry! I don't know why I said that. There's wine, beer, G&T?'

'A glass of wine would be great,' I said. 'White if you have it.' I was back in dinner party mode with no idea how to snap out of it.

Watching Zac extract a bottle from a drinks fridge, I tried to work out how old he was. Thirty, thirty-five maybe. A trace of wrinkles by the eyes, the rest of his face smooth. He could even be in his late twenties. Could he really find someone like me attractive? In daylight?

'Have you been here long?' I said. Jesus, I sounded like the Queen again.

'Hardly any time,' he said, half filling a couple of large glasses. There was nothing remotely personal in the room, no knick-knacks, no paintings, only the weird abstract sculpture that looked like a Toblerone with a hole in the middle. It must have taken him hours to depersonalise the place so thoroughly.

As he handed me the glass, our fingers touched.

'Hello,' I said, looking into his eyes.

'It's a Fourchaume Chablis,' he said. 'At least that's what it says on the label.'

Which is when I realised this man was as nervous as me, maybe more so. It made things doubly exciting.

'Are you *very* knowledgeable about wine?' I said softly, stepping in close. I could feel my legs vibrating like they do on a platform when a train rushes past without stopping. His face was so close I could see the down on his ears.

'I know what I like,' he said.

'Me too.'

'How about a guided tour?' he said, stepping away.

What the fuck? Was this a tantalising game or cold feet? 'Here we have the main room,' he was saying. 'Complete with contemporary fitted kitchen.' Who cares, I thought, as he led the way down a corridor, past half a dozen framed photographs on the wall. I couldn't make them out properly in the dim lighting; was that a couple by a pool? Maybe they were the reason for his nerves. Wild sex in an anonymous pub is one thing but in the heart of your own life, watched over by photos of family and friends? Then again, he'd chosen this place.

'Guest bed and en suite,' he said, stepping into another huge room and holding open the door to a bathroom only slightly smaller than my living room. A double shower with two huge spouts took up a whole side, large enough for both of us. Maybe that was his plan: sex under a gushing cascade of water. But now Zac was on the move again.

'And this is the main bedroom.' He stood silently in the doorway, admiring the massive bed as if it had been where Queen Victoria slept, or Churchill conceived. Music played quietly in the background, the lights were dim, the window curtained. I reached out and touched his cheek.

'I've missed you,' I said and kissed him on the mouth. In an instant, all the awkwardness and fear were gone, swept away like the sun burning mist from a pond.

* * *

We took it slowly this time, undressing each other item by item. Down to my knickers and bra, I felt suddenly embarrassed, self-conscious about my middle-aged body, with all its idiosyncrasies and irregularities next to Zac's young, flawless physique. I looked around for the light switch.

'You,' he said, 'are beautiful.'

And, in an instant, I was.

We gently swept fingers over each other, as if to reassure ourselves this was really happening. His body wasn't as toned as Mark's, no stringy muscles or washboard stomach, more a comfortable, natural softness. A flash of guilt passed through me. I turned on my side to look at him properly and caught sight of a photograph by the bed, a young woman in a bikini, her arms around two flaxen-haired children, smiling at the camera, at the man holding it. Seeing my change of expression, Zac reached out and picked it up.

'Sorry.'

'It's not a problem,' I said. 'Really.'

He laughed, holding the frame above his head.

'I've never met any of those guys in my life.'

'I don't understand.'

'We buy them from a photo agency,' he said. Then, seeing my face, 'I'm in property development.'

'You don't own this place?'

'If only! It's a show flat.'

I laughed, like someone who's been told they haven't been fired after all, it was an office joke, a silly jape on April Fool's Day.

'What if somebody comes in for a viewing?' I said.

'They'll get a shock.' He eased my knickers down. I raised my legs and closed my eyes, barely able to breathe at the thought of what would come next.

* * *

Afterwards, I stared at the neat air-con grille high in one wall and tried to work out where I had just been. Mostly it was a jumble of images and sensations, too confusing to put in any coherent order. I did remember the first time I came, with Zac's head between my legs. For a while, it felt so wrong, I thought I would never be able to finish. How could I participate in this most intimate of acts with a stranger, a man I knew nothing about, not his views, his history or his standing in the world? He was dislocated from me in every way, even as he squatted between my legs, applying himself assiduously to my pleasure.

I became conscious of the time he was spending down there, embarrassed by how long I was taking. I could feel my thighs tensing up, my fingers curled tight like they did at the dentist when I heard the whine of the drill. Zac stopped, resting his head on my thigh. He reached out and found my hand, gave it a squeeze and then he was off again. Something about that gesture, the simple, affectionate complicity of it, gave me permission. I relaxed, imperceptibly letting myself go until I was carried away on wave after wave of sheer pleasure. Eventually, I had to push him aside, unable to take any more.

'All good?' he said, looking up at me.

I couldn't open my eyes, let alone speak. I lay back and thought of nothing.

Later, I watched Zac as he dozed, half his body covered by the sheet, his chest rising and falling rhythmically, the slightest purr of air as he breathed in and out between barely parted lips. I slid out of bed and made my way to the bathroom, noiselessly closing the heavy door behind me.

I caught sight of myself in the floor-to-ceiling mirror. There were no excuses now. That time in the pub had been so fast, so unexpected, I could almost persuade myself it didn't count, like an illicit snog at a party. An aberration. What happened fifteen minutes ago was full-fat, undiluted, indefensible betrayal, deserving a dedicated level all of its own in purgatory. I had planned, anticipated and longed for every second and, now it was over, knew I wouldn't be able to stop myself coming back for more. I was lost.

I stood under the huge shower, scalding water cascading over me, washing away what remnants of rationality were left. My cautious 'what ifs' and 'what thens' slid down the stainless steel slot in the shower tray, along with the soap suds. Whoever I had been that morning was gone for ever. I knew there was no way back now. And I was grateful.

* * *

Coming back into the kitchen, I found Zac wiping down surfaces, polishing taps. There was no sign of the wine bottle, or the glasses. After what we had done to each other, such everyday domesticity felt awkward, out of keeping.

'I should be getting back,' I said.

'Me, too.' He wrung out his cloth, folded it neatly before stowing it under the sink. 'Would you like a lift?'

'It's OK,' I said. 'I'll hop in a cab.'

'You'll be lucky to find one around here. Why don't I drop you at the Tube? Any station. Your choice.'

'What about the "rules?"'

'I won't tell if you won't.'

Imagining the long tramp in the cold to the bus stop, I shrugged. What possible harm could there be?

'That would be great, thank you.'

As the lift doors silently closed, I could see blurred versions of ourselves in the polished steel, two strangers about to walk away from each other, never to meet again. Except I already knew we would.

'Are you seeing anyone else?' he said, reaching for the basement button.

'Sorry?'

'Apart from your husband, of course.'

'No,' I said, shocked he should ask. 'Are you?'

'No,' he said. 'Absolutely not!' He gave me a smile. 'You're everything I need.'

I didn't have time to work out if I should be flattered or concerned before the doors opened and he gestured for me to step out. The basement car park was vast and nearly empty, just a couple of cars hidden under protective covers and a van with Capital Drainage Services written on the side. Was that what he meant by working in property: unblocking drains?

Zac walked past the van, turned a corner and stopped by a black motorbike. Now the cool leather jacket made sense.

'You're not serious?' I said.

He unlocked a pannier, took out a helmet. 'It's the only way to get around town.'

'And the most dangerous.'

'I'm very safe.' He pressed a button, and the engine started with a deep purr. I hadn't been on a motorbike since university when I briefly dated a guy with an old Norton. He had spent most of his time covered in oil taking it to bits, but when we did go out, roaring through the countryside, it had been one of the greatest thrills of my life.

Zac held out the helmet. It would be mad to even contemplate it, I knew the statistics for motorcycle injuries, everyone who works in a hospital does. The transplant guys call them donor bikes, for God's sake.

'What station's best?' he said.

I heard myself saying Victoria, and the next moment Zac was tilting my head so he could slide the helmet over my hair, past my ears. I felt it press firmly against my cheeks, his fingers by my throat, fastening the chin strap. He took off his scarf, wrapped its cashmere softness around my neck, tucking it gently into my coat, then he handed me a pair of gloves. As I pulled them on, I wondered if his wife had been the last to wear them.

Perched on the back of his motorbike, the footpegs so high my skirt rode up, I couldn't find anything to hold on to except Zac himself. He revved the engine a couple of times, the growl bouncing off the concrete walls of the car park, then we eased past a row of parking spaces, made a turn and slowly mounted the ramp into daylight. My stomach lurched as the bike leapt forward, shoving me back in the seat. I tightened my grip on Zac's body, my head filled with the whine of the engine as we whipped past a line of cars.

The bike leant over, and us with it. We were solid, as one, leaning first one way, then another. Slowing for a junction, I pressed myself into his back, then we were off again, flying down the Embankment, the world a muffled blur. A final spurt of speed, a few turns through narrow streets I had never seen before, and we were at a side entrance to Victoria Station. As Zac helped me off with the helmet, I caught sight of myself in the wing mirror: my cheeks had pressure marks, my hair was flat and my mascara had bled into a mass of rivulets. But on my face was the stupidest grin I had ever seen.

* * *

Sitting on the train home, thinking of the pleasure Zac and I had so freely given each other, an unwanted image popped into my mind: Mark, huddled over his secret computer, face lit by the flickering images of a favourite website. I felt a wave of sadness. Despite my efforts over so many months – the therapy, the dressing up, the reaching out – he chose to take his pleasure alone, furtive and disconnected. How lonely he must have felt.

I dropped into the Taj on the way back and bought takeaway for all three of us. We hadn't had a family curry night for almost a year. It used to be a regular part of our week; we'd argue about what to order, poach each other's food, laugh and set the world to rights as the air filled with the heavy musk of coriander and garlic. Could anything ever be so simple again after what I had done that afternoon? Those innocent days were beginning to feel like someone else's history, not mine.

Over my tandoori prawns, I tried to concentrate as Mark enumerated Ms Winters' latest Stalinist attacks on the timetable. Her young deputy, Joe, unable to take any more, had resigned.

'He's off to Shanghai to tutor kids for Oxbridge. It's a great loss to the school,' said Mark.

'Bet he's coining it, though,' said Jess, helping herself to a forkful of Mark's veggie jalfrezi.

I floated above the conversation, listening but not engaged, like a parent filtering out the chatter of toddlers.

'First-class airfare, own flat, and more a month than most teachers earn in half a year.'

'What's not to like?' said Jess. 'Sounds amazing.'

'It stinks,' said Mark. 'Helping the privileged get more privileged.' He had a distaste for success and entitlement that verged on the physical.

On any other night, I'd have chipped in that it would be fun swanning around Shanghai, living off the fat of the new masters of the universe. It had to be better than earning a pittance working in an underfunded shithole run by Mein Führer. But I said none of that, nor did I tip the last of the wine into my glass. Instead, I rinsed the foil trays under the tap, the way Mark liked, and asked if he couldn't rally cross-school support against Ms Winters. If all the heads of department signed an open letter, surely she'd have to take notice. Jess agreed, and even Mark said it might be worth a try. He'd send some emails. Probably best in person, I said, emails leave a trail. Then we all went into the living room and watched crap TV.

CHAPTER TWENTY-ONE

It's a fact rarely acknowledged that the more sex people have, the more amiable they become. It was certainly the case with me. As Zac and I spent time together, I grew less snippy, more easy-going and, dare I say, more loving. I only had to look at Helen to see the alternative. Ever since Tom had left and her sex life dried up, she had developed a carping, judgmental bitterness which saw the world as hostile and pernicious. But I could hardly say, 'What you need, Helen, is a damn good seeing to.' It wasn't as if she didn't know.

At work, Janice asked if I had taken up yoga or been on a relaxing mini-break. Maybe it was the serotonin that's supposed to flood your brain when you come, or perhaps it simply felt good being wanted. Whatever the mechanism, there could be no doubting its efficacy.

Sex with Zac freed me up to be a nicer person, maybe even a better one.

* * *

It was Jess's suggestion to share the car on Wednesdays so she could practice ahead of her driving test; we could swap places at school, then I'd take the car on to my parking space near Beckenham Junction. I kept my enthusiasm subdued, saying she'd need to guarantee to be on time every day because I couldn't afford to miss the train. In fact, I was delighted. The trip to my mother's had broken the ice, now this proposal might help us return to normal. Better than normal, it turned out.

Unable to make eye contact and distracted by the banality of rush hour traffic, we slid into a level of intimacy we hadn't enjoyed for years. Maybe if Mark and I had seen a therapist in the back of an SUV rather than a book-lined study, we would have cracked it.

One morning, as Jess took a detour to avoid a burst water main, she told me why she'd ended things with Jack. He had seen something on the internet he wanted to 'try out'. When Jess refused, he gave her a hard time, saying if she loved him, she'd agree. She decided if his love and respect depended on acquiescing to his sexual curiosity, it probably wasn't worth a great deal. So much for Jack's performance with me, pretending he had no idea why he'd been dumped, while snaffling my biscuits. Bastard. I was proud of Jess. I didn't ask for specifics but couldn't help remembering Alice's list of 'preferences'. Maybe Jack had wanted to experiment with a spicy root vegetable.

I settled into a bizarre but happy routine. Jess and I exchanging confidences as she drove to school; me hurrying through work in heightened anticipation, then every few days hooking up with Zac for fifty or so minutes of sheer bliss. On these special days, I made sure to get home before Mark, jump into the shower and change out of my work clothes. I had long abandoned dressing up for our liaisons, there wasn't much point when it all came off within minutes of walking through the door. I did take to carrying a spare pair of knickers, though, and on our third meeting, Zac suggested next time we go commando. I spent the day convinced everyone knew, from the man opposite me on the train, through Kevin in the canteen to Dr Svetkova on her rounds. I had never felt so aroused. By the time we met, Zac only had to reach out and touch my thigh and I was gone.

We soon ditched Alice's convoluted rules for our own, simpler ones. I'd get myself to an agreed street corner and look for the familiar, lean figure astride the motorbike, my helmet balanced ready on a wing mirror. We'd weave through the London traffic, anonymous King and Queen of the road, before pulling up outside another upmarket property.

Zac had an endless supply of these, from Holland Park to Islington. We never used the same flat twice. All were immaculately appointed, the beds made up, the bathrooms supplied with a range of pricey toiletries. I didn't ask how he organised it, who came in to clean up after us or made the rooms perfect before we arrived. It was part of the magic, and I had no desire to know his backstage secrets.

Zac would bring a small speaker and, as he paired it to his phone, I'd unpin my hair and shake it loose, like an uptight secretary in a fifties movie. He kept saying how amazing it was and couldn't seem to get enough of running his hands through it. Then he'd press a button on his phone and the room would fill with music. I'd never heard of most of it but soon knew our 'special' songs by heart. I even asked him to put the playlist on my phone so I could listen to it on the train or at home in the bath, remembering what we had done to each other that day – anticipating what we would do next time.

Afterwards, we'd lie satiated on another super-king-sized bed and Zac would tell me how gorgeous I was. 'Gorgeous and curvy and beautiful,' was his mantra, which as mantras go, was altogether superior to the Gayatri chant I'd struggled to learn one summer at a yoga class in Beckenham Leisure Centre.

On our fourth or fifth meeting, Zac was tracing a line from my breast to my navel with his fingertips, when he asked if I felt guilty.

I sat up, uneasy at the direction this was going. Whenever we had ventured on to the personal – do you have kids, how many, what age – I had shut down the conversation, remembering Alice's warnings.

'I don't,' he went on before I could head him off. 'Though I do feel sad sometimes. That it has come to this, the fact it became necessary, you know? Sorry, that sounds stupid.'

It didn't. I felt the same. No regrets, no guilt, only a lingering sadness this joy had to be shared with a stranger, rather than the man I married.

'I wouldn't change anything, though,' said Zac. 'Not for the world.'

Looking into his face, I wondered if that was as phoney as the photographs on the wall or as true as the pleasure he gave me time after time. He kissed my nipple. I closed my eyes. It didn't matter either way.

* * *

I wasn't entirely incurious. At work, I googled the addresses of some recent places where Zac and I had met. While a few were listed with upmarket estate agent sites, none had details of the developers. I tried the Land Registry, but all the companies involved were registered offshore and no further information was available. I had the inspired idea of looking on Westminster's Planning Portal, which did contain links to developers, but just had lists of directors with no photographs. I contemplated checking each one but lost interest, unsure what to do if I did winkle out Zac's real identity. So what if I discovered where he lived, how long he had been married, the name of the woman he betrayed twice a week? I already knew everything I need to: he was the best lover I had ever known.

Sitting on the Tube one day, hemmed in by a giant rucksack to one side and an exhausted, dusty construction worker on the other, I listened to our playlist and tried to analyse why our sex was so all-consuming. While Zac could be passionate – often literally throwing me on to the bed, even occasionally pinning me to it – we didn't try anything particularly imaginative and were, on the whole, conservative. There was the excitement of a new body, of course, its softness, its smell, how it fitted together with my own, but that didn't account for everything.

As I made my way up the escalator, manoeuvring past tourists who insisted on standing on the wrong side, I thought perhaps it was precisely because our encounters didn't need to go anywhere that they were so satisfying. The sex was neither preamble to a greater intimacy nor answer to an unresolved part of our relationship. We didn't have to worry about what this might mean, how that might be taken, if we'd thought or said the wrong thing. There was no wrong thing. Our only task was each other's pleasure. Freed from the pressure of meaning, we simply revelled. A dance with no purpose other than itself.

Standing on a packed train crawling and screeching through the suburbs, I realised it was this not knowing which made our meetings so enticing. While we understood each other's bodies with almost forensic thoroughness, we had no sense of what tethered the other to everyday life. It was wonderfully liberating. Zac had no idea I was frightened of bees or had once been an accomplished shoplifter or that most days felt a fraud and a failure. He wasn't interested in any of this, just as I didn't care about his foibles and fears and frustrations. We were like two athletes meeting for a game of tennis, who enjoyed pushing each other to the limit, then shook hands and said, 'Well played, see you next week,' before going their separate ways, refreshed and loose and happy.

Driving back from these encounters felt like a dream. Often, I had no recollection of getting into the car, let alone the route home or how long it took to get there. If someone asked me my name within an hour of seeing Zac, I'm not sure I would have been able to answer. It reminded me of my drinking days at university when whole weeks vanished into a black hole. I was anaesthetised by desire.

Home life rapidly, unnervingly, also settled into a routine. Jess chatted about friends and exams; Mark cooked exotic meals and practised his Arabic vocab, while I praised them both. With good reason in Jess's case – her offer from Bristol came through and was much more achievable than we feared. She was ecstatic and I was delighted for her. My daughter reaching for the stars, aiming, as my mother would say, for the only job really worth doing. Dr Jessica Norton. Or she could take my name, Jess Callaway, MD, FRCP, even FRCS. Why not? She could be whatever she wanted to be.

At Mark's school, Ms Winter's Blitzkrieg continued its relentless progress. While the rest of the staff had welcomed his (my) suggestions, none had been courageous enough to stick their head above the parapet, no doubt terrified of having it blown off by Ms Winter. Old Rowlinson from the maths department almost agreed to make a stand but was due to retire at the end of the summer term and didn't want to miss out on the traditional parting gift of a fifty quid John Lewis voucher.

By the Easter holidays, Mark's campaign was pretty much spent. Ms Winter completed her victory by picking off the stragglers with promises of more free periods and the occasional inset day. A final appeal to the head proved futile. Ever pragmatic, Mark capitulated gracefully and spent the break buried in his laptop, wrestling the new timetable into submission. With Jess equally busy revising, I had more time than ever. Zac and I increased the frequency of our encounters.

They were not all equally exciting; we weren't always on peak form, but it didn't matter if the earth failed to move on Tuesday, we had Thursday to look forward to. I was averaging five orgasms a week. Soon, I would have come more with Zac than in my entire marriage to Mark. It was both an exhilarating and sad thought.

We were lying woozily on a waterbed early one evening (another first for me) when Zac whispered, 'I think I might be falling . . . '

'Don't,' I said, removing my hand from his stomach. I knew once the words were out, they could never be unsaid. Zac looked disappointed but remained silent. I slipped from the bed and made my way to the bathroom – a glass box with a showerhead the size of a wok. Twisting the mixer until hot water gushed out, I wondered what would have happened if I hadn't stopped his proclamation. I couldn't see myself saying it back, that wasn't how I felt about Zac at all, not even close. I liked him, enjoyed him, but there was no deeper connection than that.

The truth was, I couldn't imagine saying 'I love you' to anyone other than Mark. As I stepped into the shower, shutting my eyes against the almost-too-powerful blast of water, the awful thought occurred to me that I might not even be able to say it to him any more. When was the last time we had said that to each other? Not muttered, but meant? I couldn't remember. I knew my heart didn't miss a beat when Mark entered a room like it used to, but that didn't mean I no longer loved him. Surely that was the point of all this, it was precisely because I *did* love him and wanted us to stay together. But can you love someone you're cheating on? I knew what Helen would say.

There was a knock on the glass. I opened my eyes to see Zac's naked form fuzzily visible through the steamed-up glass.

'Room for another?' he said.

I opened the door. My angst would have to wait for another day.

* * *

I had almost become blasé about my happiness, until one Saturday morning I woke to horribly familiar music blasting from the kitchen. It was the playlist Zac and I had sex to. My mind went into overdrive. Had Mark found out and this was his way of rubbing my face in it? Would he be standing by a speaker, demanding to know how long the affair had been going on?

I crept into the hall, trying to see through the half-shut door into the kitchen but could only make out the edge of the island. Taking a breath, I marched in.

No one was there. Music blared into an empty room. I scrambled to find my phone and turn the damn thing off, searching under piles of papers, a heap of dirty dishcloths, down the side of the sofa. Where the fuck was it?

'Hi, Mum!' Jess stood in the doorway in cut-off pyjamas, swaying back and forth to the music, her own phone in her hand. I grabbed it.

'What the hell's my playlist doing on your phone?' I snapped, struggling to turn off the noise.

'It's not a crime!' she said, taking it back and shutting the music down. 'If you must know, I follow you on Spotify.'

'What does that even mean?'

'That I can see what you listen to. I've been doing it for ages.'

Jesus Christ! Zac had put the playlist on my little phone, did that mean Jess knew about that, too? What else could she get access to – all my texts?

'I didn't know you were into Mooryc,' said Jess.

'What?'

'That last song – it's "Saint-Saëns" by Mooryc, very cool. And you've got Kovacs and Angela Puxi and some

Maribou State, too. I had no idea you listened to stuff like that.'

Did she *know*? Somehow put it together: the regular late nights, the so-called visits to my mother. It would only take a few calls to blow holes in my alibis.

'I don't,' I said. 'Not really.'

'So how come they're on your playlist?' Jess stood silhouetted against the window, a 1930s investigator from a black-and-white movie.

My mind went blank then, out of nowhere, I heard myself say, 'A patient sent me a link.'

'And you really like it?'

'Why shouldn't I?'

She shrugged. 'Seems kind of young.'

'Perhaps I'm young on the inside.'

'Hey, Mum, it's cool, OK?'

My heart rate finally slowed. I was safe, but would have to be a lot more careful in the future. The thought of my daughter discovering who her mother had become was too awful to contemplate.

After lunch, I snuck out of the house on the pretence of going to the shops, and spent half an hour in the car watching YouTube videos on how music sharing worked. I managed to uninstall Spotify and was pretty sure Jess wouldn't have seen anything else, but couldn't be certain. Ironically, though, it wasn't the secret phone that got me into trouble. It was my old one.

I had offered to work Good Friday. It was predictably quiet, and by four, I was on my way to meet Zac, free to spend a full two hours with him. We'd been in bed less than twenty minutes, when I heard a phone buzzing from inside my handbag. I had already ignored it three times, letting it jiggle impotently by the bed as Zac ran his tongue up one thigh, then, after the briefest, most tantalising of incursions, down the other. Now it was vibrating again. Worried it might be Jess, I fumbled impotently in the muddle of my handbag, finally tipping everything out and feeling for around on the floor with my spare hand. Peering into the gloom, I saw it wasn't Jess. It was a text from Mark. My mother had vanished.

CHAPTER TWENTY-TWO

Mark was already at Mum's house when I arrived. There hadn't been time to shower, so I carefully positioned myself a few feet away as he explained the situation. When Helen had dropped round earlier with a couple of frozen meals, she'd found no sign of my mother. Her mobile had gone straight to answerphone and, knowing Mum never left home after dark, Helen phoned me and, when I didn't answer, Mark.

He drove over with Jess, who was now out with Helen scouring the streets. They'd started with my mother's usual haunts: the local shop, the library, the park where she used to walk our spaniel, Jeep, before he had to be put down. Mark stayed in the house in case Mum turned up, systematically working his way through her address book, contacting old friends on the off-chance she had gone to one of them. A good third had either moved away or died or both, and the remainder hadn't heard from my mother for months, some years. None had any idea where she might be. All this while I was having sex with Zac in an anonymous show flat off the Essex Road.

When I phoned the police, the operator explained they no longer had the resources to send out a dedicated team; the best she could offer was to inform nearby patrol cars and pass my contact details to local hospitals. She added that the chances were, my mother would turn up.

'And if she doesn't?'

'I'm sorry, that's all we can do.'

Leaving Mark to continue with the address book, I set off to check the streets that Helen hadn't yet covered. As I walked through the rain, past rows of identical houses, I thought how easy it would be to get lost here, even if you weren't an old lady teetering on the edge of dementia.

An hour later, we met back at the house, damp and despondent. I could see my mother's only raincoat hanging by the front door. She'd be soaked by now.

'We have to go out again,' I said.

'She could be anywhere,' said Helen.

'You want to sit here, doing nothing?'

'That's not what I said.'

Mark offered to come with Jess and me, Helen could stay in the house in case Mum turned up. We were pulling our coats back on when the phone rang. I picked up.

'Hello dear, is that you?' said my mother.

She was at a bus terminal in Norwood. She'd caught the bus from the end of her road, fallen asleep and ended up at the depot, where a cleaner took pity and helped charge her phone.

Helen and I drove over to pick her up. She spent the journey back complaining that the bus driver hadn't woken her and that my car was too hot. No apology for what she had put us through or admission she had in any way been responsible. Safely ensconced in my kitchen, Jess made her a cup of tea (too weak! Did your mother never teach you how to make a proper cup of tea? It has to sit for a *minimum* of three minutes), while I made toast (I asked for toast, not warm bread!).

Mark, needless to say, proved the most patient, gradually piecing together the story. My mother had gone to the local shop and, finding they were out of her favourite marmalade, decided to take the bus to Sainsbury's. The driver had shot past her stop without a 'by your leave' and the next thing she knew 'a strange little man' was telling her to get off. She had never been lost and could perfectly well have found her own way home.

When Helen gently suggested it might be best to stay with me that night, Mum accused her of treating her like a child. I whispered to Mark that maybe we should look into getting her formally tested, but she overheard, despite her supposedly poor hearing.

'What tests?' she snapped. 'What tests are you talking about?'

Helen and I exchanged a look. Mark leant forward. 'If you're having a problem with your memory, Dorothy, the doctor might be able to help.'

'You think I can't remember the Prime Minister's name?' She reeled off most of the Cabinet, along with some highly specific views on their shortcomings. My mother had always been obsessed with politics, in a way that put Helen and me to shame. 'I know what this is about,' she went on. 'You want to put me in a home.'

'Don't be ridiculous,' I said.

'You think I'm incapable. That I can't look after myself.'

'Mum, you've got an arm in plaster and you went missing!' said Helen.

'I won't go in a home. I'd rather drink poison.'

We finally persuaded her to stay, on the condition we took her back to her own house first thing in the morning.

As Jess helped me make up a bed, she said, 'You know Gran never went anywhere near Sainsbury's? She took the wrong bus outside the town hall.'

'Did she tell you that?' I said.

'Of course not! I checked her phone.'

I stopped, pillowcase in hand. 'What do you mean?'

'I could see where she went on Google Maps.'

'Do all phones do that?' I said, trying not to panic.

'Pretty much.'

'So you could see where I've been, and I could see where you've been?'

'Except I've changed my preferences, so don't get any ideas,' she said, buttoning the duvet cover. 'But if we put the right app on Gran's phone, we could track her from the iPad. Want me to check it out?'

I didn't answer. I was remembering Alice's warning about not taking a phone to my liaisons, or at the very least making sure to turn it off. But I hadn't. It had been with me many times when Zac and I were having sex. Did that mean Jess could see exactly where I had been and when? My erotic progress across the capital called up at the press of a button. I felt sick at the thought.

'There we go,' said Jess, spreading the duvet on to the bed. 'So, what do you think?'

'About what?'

'Tracking Gran! Haven't you been listening?'

'Sorry. Whatever you think best, darling.' I hurried past her, determined to find my phone and hide it from prying eyes until I figured out what to do.

'You haven't finished the pillows!' said Jess, but I was already halfway down the stairs.

With my mobile safely hidden in a drawer, I was able to concentrate on getting Mum to bed. Helen and I did our best to ignore her complaints that she didn't have any of her things with her, couldn't work the bedside light and that the room was too cold. It was late by the time we made it back to the kitchen and Helen insisted on a nightcap, 'to steady her nerves.' I dug out an old bottle of Jameson and made myself a cup of camomile.

'You got any cheesy things?' she said. 'I'm starving.'

Helen had been born starving and, despite living on a diet of alcohol and salty snacks, never put on weight. More proof that the universe wasn't simply uncaring but positively unjust. I found a packet of crisps and threw them over.

'Do you want me to order you a taxi?' I said.

'I'll be fine,' she said, draining her glass. 'It was a tipple, no more.'

More like half a tumblerful, I thought, but, too tired to argue, I saw her out, retrieved my phone and made my way upstairs. Mark had turned the bedroom light off, so I undressed in the dark and slipped into bed.

'Helen get off OK?' he said.

'Pretty much,' I said, sliding the phone under my side of the bed. I could sort it out tomorrow. 'And thanks for helping with Mum. You were amazing.'

'I'm just glad she's safe,' he said, giving my hand a squeeze. I was about to turn over when he leant in and kissed me. I froze. Then his hand slipped under my nightie and caressed my left breast, slowly circling the nipple.

'Why now?' I asked, thinking this was the first time he had initiated anything for years.

'Mmm?'

'After all this time?'

'Can't I find my wife sexy?' he said, sliding his hand down and across my hips. 'Is that a crime?'

I had never had sex with two different men on the same day, never thought of myself as the sort of woman who would. But Mark's advances caught me off guard and, after what he had done for my mother, it felt impossible to refuse. It wasn't unpleasant, Mark was a considerate lover. But try as I might, I couldn't come. Too many comparisons, too much guilt. In the end, I faked it, which I hadn't done since my student days. I stayed awake long after Mark fell asleep, swearing never to let this happen again. At least not on the same day.

CHAPTER TWENTY-THREE

Life became manic over the next few weeks. I had to cover for a maternity leave as well as deal with my own patients and check on my mother most evenings. The only time Zac and I could meet was on the occasional early morning. It felt overwhelmingly exciting to get dressed knowing in less than forty-five minutes I'd be whipping the lot off again.

After Jess's warning about phone tracking, I spent hours on the internet trying to understand how to edit 'Locations Services' on my old phone, before hitting on the easiest of solutions: losing it and starting again with a new one. The young woman in the phone shop was very helpful setting up my new handset, assuring me she had disabled all the settings that would enable apps to track me. I dropped the old one down a drain off Praed Street and felt a weight slip away.

As for my mother, I thought she was coping well, but Helen claimed to have found a saucer of mouldy cake under the sofa and the loo sticky with urine. We met for breakfast one morning to discuss next steps. Helen chose a café run by ex-offenders, which I couldn't help finding funny, given what she did for a living.

'Recognise him?' I asked as a heavily tattooed waiter brought our order. 'Maybe you put him in prison.'

'I'm a defence lawyer, Kirsten, not CPS,' she said, fiddling with her phone.

'It was a joke.'

'Hilarious,' she said, not looking up from the screen.

Part of me wanted to snatch it away, confess all, to share with my sister the excitement and pain of what I had achieved. Tell her that there wasn't a second of the day when I wasn't alight inside with the thought of Zac wanting me. In our twenties, Helen had revelled in my misadventures. Recently married to Tom and working the insanely long hours law firms demand of the young, she lived vicariously through me. She and Tom would invite me over to marvel at the next instalment of her wayward sister's progress through the seedier parts of London, like a latter-day Becky Sharp.

With the collapse of her marriage, however, Helen's enjoyment of other people's escapades soured into bitter judgements; men became shits, younger women sluts and as for wives who shagged other people's husbands, she'd probably want them eviscerated. Helen's moral compass had become skewed by divorce, her misery a giant magnet pulling everything else out of true. She'd hate to know her plain sister was having the best sex of her life, while she was reduced, in her own words, to lying in a bath reliving a holiday romance she'd had in Paxos with a Norwegian guitarist.

I tucked into a huge pain aux raisins as Helen went through her 'options for Mum'.

'I've made a rota,' she said, sliding over a printed sheet of A4. I glanced at the neat columns; I seemed to be going over nearly every day while Helen just did the occasional weekend. 'What?' she said, offended by my silence. 'You live closer and I have two kids to look after. On my own!'

It was like when we were young, I was left clearing away the toys and tidying up, while Helen discovered she had a maths project to finish or needed to paint her toenails.

'I'm not sure I can make all these days,' I said.

'They're after work!' she said, reaching for her coffee. 'What else have you got to do?'

Shag my toy boy, I thought. 'Work's hectic,' I said.

She shrugged, as if to say too bad, deal with it. 'Of course, the only long-term answer is a home.'

'Mum would hate it,' I said, taking a bite of pastry. 'She said she'd rather drink poison, remember?'

'But she wouldn't, would she? Not in reality. And we can't keep going on like this, the next time it could be serious. Can't you pull strings? Get her into some NHS place?'

'It doesn't work like that.'

'After twenty years of slogging your guts out, they owe you. It's payback time, baby!' Helen's American accent was appalling.

'She'd need to have virtually zero assets and no savings,' I said. 'Even then, there'd be a massive waiting list.'

'How about having a carer a couple of times a day? Get Mum up, put her to bed, make sure she's OK. Don't district nurses do that?'

'They're for people who are properly ill. Which Mum isn't.'

'Jesus, Kirst, why do you always have to be so negative? Every time, it's shoot the idea down.'

A few weeks ago, I would have hit back with a smart-arse reply, and we'd be off into our familiar exchange of jabs and counterpunches. Today, I took another bite of pastry and let the criticism wash over me. Helen almost looked put out by my lack of response.

'Doing nothing,' she said, reaching for her vape, 'is not an option.'

'I'll call a couple of agencies,' I said. 'See if we can get a private carer a few hours a day.'

'How much is that going to cost?'

'It'll cost whatever it costs,' I said, finishing off my pain aux raisins and wondering if I should have another.

'What are you, made of money all of a sudden?'

'She's our mother, Helen,' I said, catching the waiter's eye and signing I'd have the same again. Helen narrowed her eyes.

'What's up with you?'

'Nothing,' I said, immediately self-conscious. Helen had inherited my mother's uncanny insight into me; I should have been more careful, I never normally hoovered down two pastries in a row.

'You've had your nails done!' she said, grabbing my hand.

'Jess did them for me,' I said quickly, pulling my fingers away and hoping to God they didn't compare notes. In fact, it had been a place near work. Helen spent her life dealing with liars and cheats, she'd know the signs. 'Things are a bit weird at home right now,' I said, racking my brains for a catch-all explanation.

'How so?' She leant in like a sniffer dog sensing a suspicious package.

I shrugged. 'You know, with Jess's exams coming up.'

Helen nodded sceptically.

'In six weeks, she'll have finished and then she'll be off and I'll never see her,' I said. It wasn't difficult to summon the hint of a tear.

'She'll be back,' said Helen, softening. 'Kids never leave home these days.'

'I'm going to lose her.'

'You're not going to lose her, Kirsten!'

I didn't need to fake the tears now. Helen took my hand again, gently this time. 'She loves you, of course she'll come home.'

I doubted it. Jess might pop back for the occasional weekend in her first term, when she needed laundry doing or her batteries recharging. But inevitably, the visits would get further and further apart, the lure of new friends – and lovers – keeping her away. She'd tell them she had to see 'her parents', rather than 'go home', an obligation casually put off, more duty than a treat eagerly anticipated.

'And you'll still have Mark,' said Helen.

The tears came fast now, splashing on to my plate, seeping into the crumbs of my pain aux raisins. Helen came round, hugged me silently as I searched my pocket for a tissue.

'Here,' she said, handing me a serviette.

'I don't know who I am any more, Hellie,' I said, dabbing my eyes, blowing my nose. 'I have no idea who I am.'

An embarrassed waiter hovered with my second order, not sure what to do. Helen took it and shooed him away.

'Join the club, sis,' she said, taking a bite of my pain aux raisins. 'When women get to our age, none of them know who they are.'

* * *

I decided to walk to work from the café. I needed time to figure out where those tears had come from, how much of the stuff about Jess might be true. Could my recent behaviour really be traced back to the fear of losing my teenage daughter, and have nothing to do with Mark? Or was it as simple as having the best orgasms of my life?

I also wanted to work through the consequences of my performance with Helen. It would only require her to get squiffy at our house and let something slip, for Mark to follow up with awkward questions. Like why, for example, I had never shared any of my worries with him. After all the meticulous planning, the exquisite care I took in deceit, to be caught out by a weepy outburst in front of my sister felt grossly unfair. I resolved to be more circumspect. More normal.

I started with Kevin. No more out of character chit-chat at the pigeonholes. I reverted to bidding him a terse 'morning' and heading straight for my office. I kept it strictly professional with Dr Svetkova, too, offering no opinion on her shoes, restricting myself to post-operative consultations about our mutual patients.

I spent my lunch break trying to track down a carer for my mother. Demand, I kept being told, was high. The earliest anyone could offer an assessment visit was in ten days' time, with a start date of a fortnight. Unless I was prepared to pay for emergency care, in which case someone could be there tomorrow, at three hundred pounds a day plus travel, and a sign-on fee of two fifty.

* * *

Arriving home, I found Mark and Jess huddled over her laptop, scribbling in a notebook. It was like they used to play together when she was a toddler, just the two of them, me reduced to providing lemonade and biscuits on demand.

'What's up?' I said.

'Travel plans,' said Mark. I knew Jess had vague notions of going abroad once her exams were over but didn't know she had done anything about it.

'Turns out Europe is naff, South-East Asia old hat and Australia full of public schoolboy wankers,' said Mark.

'It's true!' said Jess.

'Which apparently leaves Latin America.'

'Specifically, Patagonia, Chile and Peru,' said Jess brightly, looking up. 'They have these incredible trails.'

I could feel panic rising at the thought of Jess hitch-hiking across deserts, being picked up by armed men in dusty Jeeps.

'Why don't you get a job here in the summer?' I said. 'It'd be nice to have a buffer of money when you go to university.'

'She needs to travel,' said Mark. 'See the world!'

'She could travel later,' I said.

'Mum, the course is seven years! The next time I get a proper holiday, I'll be nearly thirty.'

'Don't exaggerate,' I said.

'There is another advantage,' said Mark. I clocked him exchanging a look with Jess. 'If Jess goes, Gran could move in here.'

I almost choked. 'What? What are you talking about?'

'We've been speaking to Aunty H and . . . '

'Wait a second,' I said, feeling assaulted from all sides. 'What's going on?'

'She'd have my study,' said Mark, calmly, 'and I'd work in Jess's room.'

'Who? Who would have your study?'

'Gran! Keep up, Mum!'

'But you need your own room!' I said.

'Only in the holidays,' said Jess. 'This way Gran would be on the ground floor, near the loo. It makes total sense.'

'And where's she supposed to wash? She'd still have to go upstairs to shower.'

'Not if we put one in downstairs,' said Jess. 'It would easily fit in Dad's study.'

'Where?' I said, incredulous.

'In the corner by the window. We've measured, it would be fine.'

They'd measured it. Together. I looked at Mark. 'A whole new bathroom? How much is that going to cost?'

'Less than two months of a carer. And when we're too feeble to get upstairs, we can use it.'

'Didn't I say?' said Jess. 'I'm popping you two in a home.'

They were serious. They'd checked the space, worked out the cost, probably spoken to a plumber. All behind my back.

'You said you'd rather move out than have my mother live here,' I said.

'That was you,' corrected Mark. 'Not me.'

'No!' I said.

'Actually, it was, Mum.'

I felt I was in one of those films where the heroine wakes up and no one recognises her.

Mark pressed a key on the laptop.

'Why don't we check flights to Lima?'

*   *   *

Undressing for bed, I tried to remember our conversations about my mother over the years. Had I really been the one with the red lines, insisting she could never move in? If not, why was Mark lying? Being so bloody reasonable. Maybe he knew about Zac. No, that was impossible, we'd been too careful. Even if he did, why take it out on me like this?

I was being paranoid. Mark wasn't that sort of person. He was a thoughtful husband helping his mother-in-law in her time of need, on the eve of his daughter's exams. With whom he'd discussed the whole thing.

I tried to picture living under the same roof as my mother, the endless evenings with the two of us watching television, her complaining about actors mumbling their lines or news reporters trivialising the issues of the day. I knew Mark would create a series of convincing excuses to absent himself, a committee meeting here, a gym session there. In the mornings, I'd have to make her breakfast, bring the newspaper, lay out her lunch. I'd be another middle-aged woman looking after an elderly relative with no time for myself. Zac would grow sick of the cancelled appointments and take his talents elsewhere. I'd be on my own again. No Zac, no Mark, no Jess. Just my mother.

CHAPTER TWENTY-FOUR

At the weekend, I promised to take Jess up to town for lunch and then shopping, the sort of outing we hadn't been on since the days of her squirming in changing rooms with me insisting the skirt she lusted after was too short or the top too tight. This would be different. She could buy whatever she liked up to eighty pounds, my treat. The occasion was a post-exam party to be thrown in a week or two by Tabs, one of the most popular girls at school. She had never invited Jess to anything before, so this was a big deal, particularly now Jess was a single woman again.

We took the Tube in and, as we rode the escalator up into the spring sunshine, Jess touched my hand.

'How did you get that?'

I looked down to see a small, fierce bruise on the fold between my thumb and finger, a dark patch where Zac's teeth had pushed in deep.

'I must have caught it in a drawer,' I said, thrusting my hand into a pocket. How did I let him bite me that hard? And why didn't it hurt? We emerged on to Oxford Street and made our way into the Saturday crowds.

I'd booked a table at a restaurant in St Christopher's Place, not because the food was particularly memorable, though it was fine in a touristy sort of way, but because I wanted to share a bonding anecdote with Jess.

'I broke up with a boyfriend here,' I said, as we took our seats.

'No! What was his name?'

'Geoff. With a G.'

'What did he do wrong?'

I explained he was the kind of man who not only picked where we ate (attractive at first, I knew nothing about restaurants), the wine we ordered (ditto, it was a means to an end for me in those days), but also what I could wear, down to my necklace and earrings ('Not too dangly, they make you look African,') and, the ultimate insult, *what* I could eat ('Have you any idea how many calories there are in roast potatoes?').

'God knows what I saw in him, he wasn't even that great in bed.'

'Mum!'

'His idea of a good time was me serving his every need then telling me what a "great lay" I was.'

'Too much information!' said Jess, fanning herself with the menu.

'The final straw was right here, by the window. He wouldn't let me order pudding, so I tipped a plate of pasta on to his white trousers. He made a terrible fuss.'

'I'm not surprised. What kind of pasta?'

'Pasta puttanesca, I think. We could have it if it's still on the menu.'

Jess laughed, the first time I could remember her laughing at anything I'd said for months. My plan of showing her how much fun I could be was working. I pressed home my advantage.

'Have you heard from Jack?' I said, trying to sound casual.

'It's over, you know that.'

'Thought you might have had second thoughts. I mean some of it was good, right?'

'Mum, you called him an under-educated waste of space.'

I shrugged, not remembering the exact phrase, but the sentiment sounded about right. 'This wouldn't be because you think if we were together, I wouldn't go travelling?' said Jess.

I should have known she'd see through it. She was like Helen, with her forensic ability to home in on dissembling.

'No,' I said, 'not at all.' On to Plan B. 'So, how are you planning to pay for this trip of yours?'

'I still have the money Gran gave me for my seventeenth, remember?'

Even my mother was conspiring against me.

'Why don't we order?' I said, trying to keep the disappointment out of my voice. 'Then we can look for that dress.'

* * *

I had forgotten how exhausting shopping with a teenager could be. We visited virtually every shop on Oxford Street at least once, most twice, and still she couldn't find anything. At one point, spotting a skirt I fancied for myself, I held it up for Jess to look at.

267

'Not age-appropriate,' she said, putting it back on the rack. What would she make of my even less age-appropriate liaisons with Zac, I wondered.

'Can we try Selfridges?' said Jess, as I limped out of Urban Outfitters for the second time. After three hours of traipsing up and down, my feet were killing me.

'Not sure it's quite within our budget, darling,' I said.

'Just a quick look? Please! We don't have to buy anything.'

I didn't have the energy to refuse and found myself being hustled through the impressive revolving doors. The smell of the perfume counters brought back the last time I had been here, to meet Alice. Had that only been a few months ago? It felt like years, the woman who'd sat nervously listening to the 'rules', now a completely different person.

I stationed myself on an armchair outside a set of changing rooms and took off a shoe. There was an angry red blister on my heel. I was poking at it gingerly when a skinny woman with an armful of clothes nearly hit me in the face with a coat hanger. She was apologetic, I was conciliatory. Then I looked up – and my heart stopped.

Zac was standing twenty feet away, flipping through a rack of dresses. Or was it him? A woman with a toddler was in the way now, blocking my view. I stood up, peering through the tangle of shoppers, taking a couple of steps so I could see better.

It was him, no question. Wearing the same shirt I had peeled off two weeks ago in a mews flat near Holland Park. I sat down sharply, told myself not to panic. It wasn't a big deal. He hadn't seen me. I'd pay for whatever Jess had chosen and get out of there. In a few minutes, we'd be safe in the anonymity of Oxford Street, surrounded by thousands of people, impossible to pick out.

'Hi!'

I looked up to see Zac looming over me, a large carrier bag in his hand. 'Thought it was you!'

My face was on fire. I struggled upright, lopsided from the missing shoe.

'What the hell!' I whispered. 'What are you doing here?'

'Same as you, I imagine,' he said, holding up the carrier bag. Immediately I felt the familiar rush of desire.

'My daughter's in the changing room!' I hissed.

'No!'

'You can't be here.'

'Right. Sorry.'

He looked around, gave me a quick kiss on the lips. The world pulsed.

'Go! Go!' I said, gesturing with one hand as I glanced back at the changing rooms. He nodded and headed over to the lingerie section. Was he shopping for us, buying sexy underwear? That couldn't be it. I'd have to strip off my everyday knickers, put the new ones on, just to have Zac take them off again. He must be here with someone else, his wife probably. I scanned the room but couldn't see where he'd gone.

'This is so cool!'

It was Jess, stunning in a simple black dress. I was too frazzled to say anything. 'You don't like it.'

'It's perfect,' I said. 'You look amazing.' I glanced at the lifts, Zac wasn't there either.

'Thing is,' said Jess. 'It's kind of over budget . . . '

'That's fine,' I said.

'But you don't know how much it costs,' said Jess.

'It doesn't matter,' I said. 'I want you to have it.'

'OK,' said Jess slowly. 'Thanks, Mum.'

'Is there anything else you'd like? New underwear, tights?' I needed to give Zac as long as possible to get away. 'Are you OK?'

'I'm just pleased you found a dress you like, darling,' I said, taking it and heading for the till.

'A hundred and ninety-five sixty,' said the cashier. I hesitated, card in hand. It was over double what I had expected to pay.

'I don't have to have it, Mum,' said Jess.

'Shh,' I said, handing over my card.

'If you could put your PIN in, please?'

I tapped in my number, trying not to think of the expense.

'Thanks, Mum. It's super generous of you.' She kissed me on the forehead as the cashier folded the dress into layers of tissue paper. 'Who was that guy?'

'Sorry?'

'The bloke you were talking to. Do you know him?'

'Hang on,' I said, trying to wedge the card back into my purse. She must have seen us through the gap in the changing room curtain, maybe even saw the kiss.

'Have a good day,' said the cashier, handing me a large yellow bag. I held it out to Jess.

'I don't know about you,' I said, determined to distract her, 'but I'm ready for home. Let's treat ourselves to a cab.' No way was I going to risk walking to the Tube. As we made our way to the escalator, I looked back but couldn't see any sign of Zac. He must be well clear by now.

'He looked kind of intense,' said Jess, turning to face me from the step below.

Jesus, why couldn't she leave it?

'He was a patient,' I said, in a moment of inspiration.

'Yeah?'

'The dad of a patient,' I added, remembering Alice's rule that every lie should contain a kernel of truth. 'His daughter had an accident on a scooter he bought for her birthday and she lost her leg. He blames himself.'

'My God,' said Jess. 'That's messed up. Will she be OK?'

'Well, her leg won't grow back,' I said.

Jess laughed, gave me a gentle punch in the arm. 'Mum!'

Danger over.

'She'll get back to normal,' I said. 'Eventually.'

* * *

In the taxi, Jess chattered excitedly about the upcoming party; who was invited, who wasn't. I couldn't concentrate on the details, my head too full of Zac. It had to be a coincidence, the alternative was too weird. He would have had to know where I was going, or followed me, which made no sense. If he wanted to meet, he just had to use the app. And yet there he had been. Out of all the shops in London, out of all the floors in Selfridges, he'd turned up virtually next to me. Could that really be luck?

'All right, Mum?' asked Jess.

I looked up to see the cab had pulled into the taxi rank by Victoria Station. I paid off the driver and Jess and I wove our way through the crowds towards a far platform. As we waited for the train to arrive, Jess took photos of herself holding up the carrier bag, making faces for her friends on Instagram or whatever. I thought back to Zac standing by the rack of clothes, him leaning in and kissing me. What if Jess had stepped out of the changing room thirty seconds sooner? I wanted to be angry with him, furious for risking so much, but the truth was I'd found it thrilling, my whole body tingled just at the thought of it.

I felt a phone vibrate in my bag and knew immediately it would be him. I glanced at my watch.

'Need to pop to the loo,' I said to Jess.

'Sure,' she said, pouting into her phone.

I hurried back to the main concourse and dodged into a Costa. Scrambling in my bag for the little phone, I opened the app and saw Zac had sent a single exclamation mark. I started typing.

WTF?

NOT acceptable!!

sorry! Stupid 😣

I was about to answer when a new message came through.

got to see you. NOW!!

can't

when then?

I hesitated. I ached to see him, longed to escape into the world I knew we could create together, but meeting him in public had spooked me. I'd got away with everything so far: my husband didn't suspect, my daughter was happy, and my family was intact. Why risk all that?

A ringing sound came from my bag. I fished out my other phone and tapped the screen. It was Jess.

'Mum, where are you? It's about to go!'

'Coming,' I said, hurrying for the platform, a phone in each hand. I reached the barrier just in time, ran to the first open door and, climbing on board, shoved both phones deep into my handbag. In retrospect, I should have been more careful.

CHAPTER TWENTY-FIVE

The moment we arrived home, Jess ran upstairs to try on her new dress. A note from Mark said he'd gone to a spin class, though why he chose to cycle nowhere surrounded by twenty other sweaty people on the one day he didn't have to cycle to work, remained beyond me.

I ran a bath, threw in a capful of Olverum (last year's birthday present from my office – they'd all chipped in) and lay back in the soothing water. Images of Zac floated through my mind: me astride his motorbike as we sped through London, legs clamped on the leather seat, arms tight round his waist. Then standing outside the door to another anonymous flat while he searched for the keys, the faint smell of his aftershave in the air as his muscles moved within his shirt; our fraught progress to the bedroom.

I must have drifted off because the next thing I knew Mark was gently shaking my shoulder.

'Hello, sleepyhead.'

I opened my eyes to see him standing over me with a bunch of flowers. Still groggy, I couldn't get my head around what was going on. Had they been given to him by a grateful student? Ms Winter even?

'For you,' he said.

'Me?' Mark had never been a flower-giver; the last time he bought me a bouquet had been after my first miscarriage when we both wept as we arranged the stems in an old chutney jar.

'Why?' I said, sitting up in the now-lukewarm water water, folding my arms over my chest, stupidly embarrassed by my nakedness.

'Can't I buy my wife flowers?'

'They're lovely,' I said, getting out and quickly wrapping myself in a towel. 'What's the occasion?'

'No reason.' He gave me a quick kiss on the cheek.

No reason never means no reason, I thought, looking for my hairbrush. Had Jess told him what happened in Selfridges, described my stolen kiss?

'You've been through a tough time recently,' he said, pushing the crinkly cellophane into a wastepaper basket. 'What with your mother and Jess's exams. Not to mention Take Cover.' Mark's name for Dr Svetkova. He was being nice: attentive and kind and supportive. I felt like crying, weeping at what an awful person I had become, suspecting him of an ulterior motive when I was the one at fault. I turned on the tap to hide a loud sniff.

'Thank you,' I said, recovering. 'That was very thoughtful.' I gave his shoulder a brief pat. 'I'll be down in a minute.'

* * *

As I made my way across the landing, Jess called from her room. She was wearing the new dress, complete with her favourite suede boots.

'What do you think?' she said, twirling round. 'Too much black?'

'You look gorgeous. Amazing.' I couldn't take my eyes off her, the way you can't when confronted by true beauty. You look and look and try to figure out how that all *works*. Could this beautiful young woman be my little girl?

'I was wondering,' she said, kicking off the boots, 'if I could borrow the dubrey? As a lucky mascot, like I did for my GCSEs.'

Dubrey had been Jess's childhood name for the piece of sea-glass Mark had given me years ago, on a beach in Cornwall. As a child, she had been enthralled by it. If she cried or was grumpy or sad, I only had to press it into her tiny fingers and she'd be transfixed by its smooth curves, its bluey-green depths.

'I'll bring it down,' I said.

'Cool,' she said, reaching over her shoulder for the zip on her dress.

When Mark had given it to me, he'd said it was us. I'd had no idea what he meant, not until he held it up against the pale winter sun and then I understood. If the light caught it just so, two figures appeared, curled into each other, their heads pressed together, their limbs entwined. Countless years of tumbling waves had created a natural netsuke from an old jam jar or broken wine bottle. It became our lucky talisman. On the first anniversary of that day, I gave it back to Mark and ever since we had swapped it back and forth each year; a sea-glass reminder of our love. This year was my turn to keep it.

It should have been in the side pocket of my handbag, but when I felt inside, I could only feel my new phone where there should have been a soft, velvet pouch. I ran my fingers from side to side. Nothing. I searched the rest of the bag, hunting through tubes of make-up, my purse, a wad of tissues. I tried to calm myself, stifle the panic rising in my stomach. It must be there. I tipped up the bag, spilling the contents over the duvet, spreading everything out with the palm of my hand. There was no velvet pouch, no dubrey. An awful possibility occurred to me: in my hurry to answer my new phone at the station, I must have flipped the little bag out.

'Hey, Mum.' It was Jess, now back in jeans and a T-shirt, the Selfridges carrier bag in her hand. 'Wow,' she said, seeing the bed covered in mess.

'Sorry,' I said. 'I thought the dubrey was in my bag then I remembered it's at work. Can I give it to you next week?'

'My first exam's on Monday.'

'Sorry, darling. If I'd known earlier . . . '

'It's OK,' she said, heading for the door. 'I'll find something else.'

She could hardly be cross with me, not after what I had spent that afternoon.

'See you later,' she said.

'You're going out?'

'I want to show Gemma the dress! Won't be late.' She skipped down the stairs, leaving me to stare at the detritus scattered across the mattress, as if by a miracle the little pouch would pop up and reveal itself. Our anniversary was coming up soon. How could I tell Mark I had lost his precious gift after twenty-five years?

I slumped on to the bed. Maybe I should phone Costa, ask if someone had handed it in. But who would do that, in today's world, at a mainline station? Chances were it had either been nicked or put in a bin. I was usually so careful, keeping it zipped in my bag all year, how could I have been so careless? But then I remembered there was a time I had taken it out – and recently.

A few weeks ago, I'd been in the canteen rummaging in my bag for paracetamol. Frustrated, I upended it, spewing its contents over the table, just as I had on the bed. I was picking through the contents when a hand appeared.

'This yours?' I looked up to see Kevin, the pouch in one hand, the familiar glass shape in the other. 'It was on the floor.'

'Sorry, yes.'

'What is it?' he said.

'Only a piece of sea-glass.' I reached out my hand, but Kevin was turning it over in his fingers, holding it up against the light.

'It's a couple!' he said triumphant. 'See?'

'Yes, I know,' I said sharply, irritated he had discovered its secret so quickly. 'Could I have it back?'

He shrugged, dropping it into my palm. 'It's kind of cool. Where did you get it?'

'A beach,' I said, sweeping everything back into my bag and hurrying past him.

Kevin had mentioned it a couple of times after that, wanting to have another look, but I said I'd taken it home for safekeeping. One lunchtime, a week or so later, he appeared in the canteen again and sat down opposite me, ostentatiously placing a backpack on the chair next to him.

'And what do we have here?' he said.

I sighed, not in the mood for one of his convoluted riddles.

'Is it a new bag?' he said. 'Why yes it is. Is it a genuine Tumi? Correct first time, madam.' He gave the backpack a twirl. 'Military-grade ballistic nylon. Tom Cruise's bag of choice.' When I failed to enthuse, he added, 'It was a present.'

'Very generous,' I said, getting up to fetch a fork. When I came back, my own bag was on the table. Not so odd, except I hadn't put it there, I'd left it on the floor.

'You don't want to leave stuff lying around here,' Kevin said, handing it to me. 'Too many light fingers.'

I hadn't thought much of it at the time, now it made complete sense. Sneaky bastard, I'd confront him in the morning, demand my property back.

* * *

In the kitchen, Mark was by the stove, the flowers in a vase and a bottle of wine chilling in an ice bucket. He was up to something, no question. Maybe it had been his idea to send Jess out, as well. I'd long ago settled on a strategy if Mark became suspicious. First step, denial, as I tried to work out how much he did and didn't know. If he only had suspicions, I'd bluff my way through. If he knew but was hazy on the details, I'd admit to a fling. A one-off which I would assure him was now over. If he knew everything for sure, it was the nuclear option: a full-on, comprehensive confession with the expectation my marriage would be over.

He poured me a glass of wine.

'One of our old favourites,' he said, holding up the bottle so I could read the label. We used to treat ourselves to it when we were first married – if we were feeling particularly flush. 'I have something to tell you,' he said.

Here it comes, I thought, taking a mouthful. 'There might be an opportunity for me to teach in Egypt.'

'Sorry?'

'In Cairo, at an international school.'

He *does* know! And, rather than confront me, discuss it like adults, he's going to remove himself to a different continent. I had to admire the boldness of it.

'Is it something the school's organised?' I said, trying not to sound panicked.

'I found it myself.'

'You found a job in Cairo?' I said. 'Just like that?'

'My online teacher told me about a recruitment site, and the first vacancy that popped up was Head of Studies at the Maadi British International School in Cairo. It seemed like fate!'

'You're seriously considering it?'

'It could be great for us.'

'Us? You want me to go, too?'

'I wouldn't go on my own, would I?'

I dared not say that had been exactly what I thought. 'Think about it, Kirst! A new city, new friends. Jess will be at university, so the timing's perfect. We'd have a ball. You always said you wanted to live abroad.'

'In my twenties! I've got a job here, Mark. A career, a life.'

Not to mention a lover.

'It wouldn't be for ever. The initial contract's only a couple of years.'

'Well that's OK, then!' I could see the disappointment on his face and instantly regretted sounding so negative. 'Sorry. It's a surprise, that's all.'

'I wanted to make sure it was for real before mentioning anything,' he said. 'I've been sleuthing. The International Hospital in Cairo is looking for qualified Western staff. You could get a job there.'

'I have a job here,' I said.

'I'm sure St Mary's would keep it open for you. They'd be crazy not to.' He took my hand. 'I've had enough, Kirst. All the bullshit at school, I'm done with it. I want to do something new, with you. While we're still young enough.'

I looked into his eyes and saw no guile, no agenda, only a genuine desire to have an adventure. With me.

'What about Mum?' I said, ignoring the lump in my throat. 'Wasn't the plan to move her in here?'

'That was before I had the offer.'

'Offer?' I said, pulling my hand away. 'I didn't even know you'd applied.'

Mark hesitated. 'To be honest, I never dreamt I'd get it, so it didn't seem worth mentioning.'

Bollocks, I thought. He sounded like an actor who can't believe they've won the Oscar, despite being on a shortlist of five and having spent every waking hour since they were ten rehearsing an acceptance speech.

'The salary would be over double what I get here. Tax-free.'

Enough to afford a home for my mother, he meant. He reached out, took my hand again. 'All I'm saying, Kirst, is think about it. It could be life-changing.'

I looked at the flowers he'd given me, glowing in the late evening sun. It was as I thought. No reason never means no reason.

*   *   *

I lay awake for hours, going over all the reasons why Egypt would be a terrible idea: my mother, my job, my friends, Helen, Jess. Not to mention Zac. I also knew if we didn't go, one dark January morning on a stuffy Tube, I'd wish we had.

I imagined sipping Turkish coffee in a café on a sunny street, listening to the sound of morning prayers; strolling through markets full of seductively unfamiliar sounds and smells. I *had* always wanted to live abroad and, although my fantasy was Paris or New York, why not Cairo with its fascinating history and clash of cultures?

Then there was Zac and the pleasures his name alone conjured up. But that couldn't go on for ever. We'd got away with it in Selfridges – what if we weren't so lucky next time? I turned over to face the wall, stared at the curling patch of wallpaper I had been meaning to stick down for months. The consequences of discovery were too awful to contemplate. I could lose everything. Maybe Egypt was exactly what I needed. I could hardly fall from grace thousands of miles away. I should call it a day with Zac, move on before anything terrible happened.

At half-past one, still unable to sleep, I went to the bathroom, more for a change of scene than wanting a pee. Sitting down, staring into a gloom lit by the occasional red pulse of the burglar alarm, I made a decision. We'd go.

Together. Then, as I reached behind me for the loo roll, I pictured Mum sitting in her faded armchair with her tatty dictionary, trying to do the crossword. Could I leave her alone and lonely while I galivanted across the world? What if she died while we were away? I'd never forgive myself. However seductive Mark's mid-life adventure sounded, it would have to wait. This wasn't only about us.

CHAPTER TWENTY-SIX

I planned to tell Mark my decision in the morning, but Monday was Jess's first day of exams and what with him cooking a special breakfast and me making sure she had everything with her, there was never a good moment.

As Jess drove to school, I was again impressed by how calm she seemed. This was one of the most important days of her life, her performance in the next three hours determining much of her future, yet she behaved as if it was just another day at school. It was enviable.

We were hovering by the gates looking for parking when out of nowhere Jess announced I should go to Cairo.

'Dad told you about that?' I said, surprised he'd mentioned anything before we had agreed what to do.

'Sure. It's such a cool idea.'

'You wouldn't mind?' I said.

'It's exactly what Dad needs,' she said, nipping into a space before a lumbering people carrier got its act together.

'Needs?' I said, unclipping my seat belt. 'How can he "need" to drop all we have here and disappear to a Third World country?'

'They're called Majority World countries now, Mum.' She reached for her school bag. 'You must have noticed how unhappy he's been.'

I stopped, my hand on the door handle. Mark hadn't appeared any different from normal to me. He'd had a tough time at work, yes, was often frustrated and irritated, but not positively unhappy.

'It would do you good, too.'

'You think I'm unhappy?' I said, ignoring the fuming driver in the people carrier.

'You have been acting kind of odd recently.' She gave me a quick kiss. 'Cairo might be what you both need.' She ran off to join a gaggle of friends. It was only as I pulled out into the traffic that I realised I had forgotten to wish her good luck.

* * *

With no seats on the Tube, I spent twenty minutes pressed up against sallow commuters, deafened by screeching wheels as we navigated the labyrinthian tunnels under the city. Maybe Jess had been right about Mark; I'd been so obsessed with myself I'd taken my eye off his happiness. One of the reasons for my 'adventure' was that it was supposed to make the rest of our marriage work. Now I'd been told it had done just the opposite.

I was sifting through my mail by the pigeonholes when an unfamiliar man in a suit and tie approached. As he drew closer, I was astonished to realise it was Kevin. I had never seen him wear a jacket, let alone what looked like a fitted suit, complete with crisp, white shirt and cufflinks.

'I know,' he said. 'It feels as weird as it looks, believe me. But you have to make an effort for the Big Day, right?' He must have realised I had no idea what he was talking about, because he added, 'The CQC visit?'

It came back to me with sickening clarity – the Care Quality Commission inspection. Janice had warned me about it weeks ago.

'You forgot, didn't you?' said Kevin, a grin spreading across his face.

I was about to say no, but realised how absurd that would sound, with me in the same skirt and top I wore week in week out. 'Actually, yes. Thanks for telling me.'

He shrugged. 'Lot on your plate, I expect.' He leant in conspiratorially, 'No sweat, I've got your back.' He actually winked as he turned to go.

'Kevin,' I said. 'You remember the piece of sea-glass I showed you?'

He opened his mouth, ready to deny it.

'The one which looks like a couple,' I said.

'Yeah, right. That was cool.'

'The thing is, I can't find it. You haven't seen it by any chance?'

'How could I? You took it home for safekeeping, remember?'

Damn! That's what I had told him in the canteen, though, of course, I hadn't left it home at all, it had been in my bag the whole time. 'It's of great sentimental value,' I said.

'I can imagine.'

'How? How can you possibly imagine?' I could hear my voice tightening.

'Why else would you want to keep it safe?' He smiled, revealing the gap in his teeth. 'It'll turn up, you'll see.' He sauntered off down the corridor, his leather brogues click-ing on the concrete floor; he must have put taps in them like

Helen and I did when we were teenagers. Maybe he'd put it back, slipped it into my bag when I wasn't looking. If he didn't, I had no idea how I would explain its loss to Mark.

* * *

In reception, Janice was sitting bolt upright behind an uncharacteristically tidy desk. Wearing a smart two-piece, she'd scraped her hair back in a neat, if severe, bun. She whispered that a porter had told her the inspector had already been in the building an hour and could be here any minute. Then she looked at my hair and said she had a few clips if I needed to borrow them.

I hurried into my office, searching my handbag for lipstick and blusher as I went. There hadn't been an inspection for years, never under the new CQC regime, and I had no idea what to expect. There was a knock on the door. The inspector couldn't be here already!

'Hang on,' I said, tidying away the make-up and smoothing down my skirt. I went over to the door, took a deep breath and opened it.

'Hi.'

It was Zac.

For a second I was too stunned to say anything, then I yanked him inside before quickly shutting the door. 'What the hell are you doing here?' I whispered.

'You haven't been answering my messages,' he said, taking my hand. I shook myself free.

'How did you know where I work?'

He shrugged. 'I took you to the end of the road once, remember? I guessed it might be here.'

It was true, I had asked him to drop me nearby one afternoon when I was running late, but never outside the hospital, let alone anywhere near my office. 'I never told you which department.'

'They have photos of everyone at the main reception,' he said, adding in mock-serious tone, 'Ms Kirsten Callaway.'

It felt like being slapped. I steadied myself on a nearby chair.

'You have to leave,' I said.

'You sure that's what you want?' He leant in to kiss me, but I dodged away.

'Now! You have to leave right now!'

He moved towards the door, slid the bolt across and grinned. 'You don't mean that,' he said, reaching out to brush my left breast with his fingers. Despite myself, I felt the old rush.

'For Christ's sake, Zac!'

'George.'

'What?'

'My real name's George. Since I know yours, it's only fair you know . . . '

'You can't be here! I have an appointment any second.'

'I am your appointment. I think it might be a groin strain, doc. Do you have anything for that?' I found myself laughing even as I pushed him away.

'I mean it!'

'Are you trying to get rid of me?'

'Of course I'm trying to get rid of you. Now bugger off!'

He kissed me full on the mouth. I could feel myself swaying. Then he broke away and started for the door. 'Not that way!' I said, picturing him bumping into Janice or, worse, the inspector. 'Use the fire escape.' I fumbled with the external door, finally wrenching it open. He turned, one foot on the metal steps.

'Why don't we go out properly?'

'What?'

'See a play, a film, maybe go for a meal?'

'Are you crazy?' I said, then, seeing the hurt on his face, gave him a quick kiss before shoving him out, shutting the door and pulling the blinds.

I could feel my heart pounding. Glancing in the mirror, I saw my neck was blotchy with panic. I ran the tap, swallowed a handful of water and told myself it was OK, no harm had been done. A silly prank, nothing more. I tried to remember other places Zac had dropped me. Nowhere near home, of that I was sure, but I had once asked him to take me to my car when I had left it near Mum's. He'd made a joke about fixing the aerial and I'd pointed out that it would be difficult to explain to Mark. If he knew my name and where I worked, what else did he know? About Mark – and Jess?

A knock on the door snapped me back to the present. He must have scooted around and was standing outside my office again. I froze. Another knock.

'Kirsten?'

It was Janice. I unbolted the door to find her staring at me accusingly. We both knew it was against hospital protocol to lock an office door. 'Sorry,' I said. 'I must have . . .' What? I couldn't think of anything, so just shrugged.

'Ms Bloom is here to see you,' she said frostily. 'From the CQC.'

A severe-looking woman in a trouser suit stepped forward. She had short silver hair, no make-up and an Apple watch on her wrist.

'Hi,' I said, offering my hand. 'Kirsten Callaway, Occupational Therapy.'

'I know who you are,' she said curtly. 'Pretend I'm not here.'

'Would you like tea, coffee?' I said, trying to steady my breathing.

'No need.' She held up a small Thermos flask.

'Your first appointment's in the treatment room,' said Janice, our word for the windowless basement I had managed to carve out of a couple of storage areas over the years.

'Thank you, Janice,' I said, my breathing beginning to return to normal. I gestured for Ms Bloom to follow me into the corridor, hoping to God Zac wouldn't be lingering somewhere, ready to pounce.

'So how long are you with us?' I said.

'Long enough to do my job,' she said, in a tone designed to shut down any further conversation.

* * *

Ms Bloom perched silently on a stool as I worked with Patricia, a young woman who had lost her left leg following a scooter accident. She then sat in on a couple of appointments in my office, making numerous notes on her clipboard. By the end of the two hours, I was sweating with nerves. As I saw off the last patient of the morning, she finally put her pen down.

'Thank you,' she said. 'Very informative.' She offered me her hand. 'I'm impressed by the rapport you have with your patients, Ms Callaway.'

It felt like being praised by a teacher you're convinced despises you. 'I try to make the sessions as informal as possible,' I said.

'And you do it very well.' She smiled, her features relaxing to reveal a pleasant face. 'I used to be an OT myself,' she said. 'I know how challenging it can be.'

Soon we were swapping anecdotes like old friends, comparing notes on the frustrations of NHS life, the attractions of leaving the service.

'I should be going,' she said at last, sliding her clipboard into her bag and offering her hand again. 'I have two more inspections today.'

I opened the door for her and was casually asking which department she was off to next when she stopped to face me. 'I probably shouldn't be saying this,' she said, 'but I spoke to a patient of yours earlier this morning. Jamie Fletcher?'

'Oh yes,' I said, expecting her to say how well he was doing. 'He's quite an inspiration, isn't he?'

She fiddled with the handle on her bag. 'I'm afraid he's making a complaint to the HCPC. About you.'

I almost laughed. Was this one of Jamie's wind-ups? 'He feels you breached his patient confidentiality.'

I closed my eyes. Michelle must have told him about our conversation. But why would Jamie betray me after everything I had done to help him?

'Specifically, he feels there has been inappropriate sharing of confidential information with a third party.'

'His fiancée.'

'You don't have to tell me the details,' she said. 'You probably shouldn't.'

'Thank you for warning me,' I said.

She nodded. 'Us OTs have to stick together. Good luck.'

As she left, I looked over at the walls covered in post-cards patients had sent me from their travels, photographs of them proudly displaying their artificial limbs outside the Taj Mahal, at the bottom of the Grand Canyon, on the summit of Mount Kilimanjaro. I knew that I could look forward to months of investigations as every patient I'd seen over the last few years was contacted, every treatment scrutinised. There would be panels and reports and chances to put forward my side, but the result would be the same; I'd be demoted at best, lose my job at worst. My only hope was to persuade Jamie to retract his complaint. I called his number. It went straight to answerphone.

'How did it go?' Janice had popped her head round the door. 'She looked kind of fierce.'

'When's Jamie Fletcher's next appointment?' I said.

'What?' said Janice, clearly expecting a chatty debrief, not an abrupt question. But I didn't have time for niceties.

'Jamie – when's he next in?'

'Today.'

'He's not in my diary.'

'That's because his appointment's not with you,' said Janice sulkily. 'It's with Prosthetics. Are you going to tell me how the inspection went?'

But I was already out of the door, running down the corridor.

*   *   *

Mike Denton had been head of Prosthetics for longer than anyone could remember. He'd seemed old when I started at the hospital and was still going fifteen years later. I once came across a photo of him from way back when they were building the new wing, and he looked pretty much the same then as he did now: wispy beard, frizzy receding hair, brown eyes behind wire-rimmed glasses.

I found him in his cramped workshop, working on an artificial leg clamped in a vice, shaving slivers off the socket-head with a scalpel. Despite the hospital investing tens of thousands in the latest laser scanners and 3D printers, Denton insisted on the old-fashioned methods, virtually carving every prosthetic by hand. The results spoke for themselves.

'Ms Callaway,' he said, without looking up. 'How may I help?'

'Hi. I think you're seeing a patient of mine today, Jamie Fletcher?'

'This is his,' he said, tapping the leg.

'Is he still here?'

'Through there,' he said, gesturing at the door. 'You can tell him I'll be another ten minutes, no more.'

Pushing past piles of boxes and discarded limbs, I hurried into the next room. Jamie sat in a wheelchair, stumps visible, bent over his phone.

'Hello, Jamie,' I said, determined to keep my fury at bay.

He looked up, startled.

'I hear you're contacting the HCPC.'

'Don't know what you're talking about,' he said, going back to his phone.

'It might have been more friendly to talk to me directly.'

His phone beeped. I could see he was playing a game. 'Can you put that down, please?'

'What's your problem?' he said.

'My problem, Jamie, is I could lose my job.'

'Should have thought of that before you went blabbing to Michelle.'

I turned and closed the door – I didn't want Denton getting wind of this, he was a well-known stickler for protocol.

'She came to me!' I said. 'In tears. What was I supposed to do?'

He shrugged, went back to his phone.

'The woman was in bits, Jamie. Because *you* dumped her for no reason.'

'I had my reasons.'

'Because you were too "embarrassed"? You think that's fair on her?'

'I tell you what's fair,' he said. 'Letting her move on, find someone who isn't broken.'

'Please! You're not broken.'

He spun his wheelchair round to face me, his face red and bulging. 'What the fuck do you call this then?' he said, slapping his stumps.

'You can't take it out on Michelle,' I said, shaken by his anger. 'She's only ever loved you.'

'I'm doing it *for* her. Don't you get it?' He almost spat it out. 'And now you've fucked it all up.'

'What I've done,' I said, 'is tell the truth.'

'Like that's a good thing?'

'Yes!'

He sighed as if explaining the painfully obvious.

'If Michelle knew it was because I can't get it up, she wouldn't be able to walk away, would she? She's not that sort of person. She'd feel she had to stick by me. Which is why I didn't want her to know, so she could move on, have a life with a partner who can give her what she needs, what she deserves. But no, you had to mess it all up with your "truth". And now we're both fucked.'

I felt like someone who's been told all their most cherished beliefs are empty, superstitious nonsense.

'OK, that should do it.'

I turned to see Denton wielding Jamie's new limb. 'Let's pop it on and see how it sits, shall we?' He knelt by the wheelchair, gently manoeuvring the mechanism on to one of Jamie's stumps.

'Jamie . . . ' I started, but he shook his head. There was nothing else to say.

* * *

On the way home, I came across a young woman with a toddler and buggy stranded at the top of the steps leading down to the Tube. Impatient commuters pushed past, scowling at a mother with the gall to travel in rush hour. I offered to give her a hand, and between us we struggled down the steps, ignoring sweaty malcontents jostling us on either side. Once on the platform, the woman wheeled her child away without a word. I was furious.

'You might bloody well thank me!' I shouted after her. She walked on, oblivious, as people stepped away from the potty-mouthed madwoman.

Later, walking to the car, I pinged open the door to be confronted by a dirty coffee cup jammed next to the handbrake. Pushing it aside, I drove off, peering through the smeary windscreen. My car looked like a recycling bin, full of plastic bottles, sweet wrappers and old parking tickets, with a bent stub of wire for an aerial. How had I let it get into this state? I used to keep on top of it, now I drove around in filth. I pulled up outside the house, tears flowing. I was crap at my job, cheating on my husband, betraying my daughter and I couldn't even keep my car clean. I picked a scrap of tissue from the floor, wiped my eyes and blew my nose. This couldn't continue. I needed to talk to Mark. And then deal with Zac, once and for all.

* * *

I found Mark in the garage, pounding away on his Peloton, sweat dripping off his face to form dark commas on the concrete floor. He was still an attractive man. Lean, fit and with the physique of someone ten years younger. He didn't see me at first, lost in a podcast no doubt. I waved a couple of times until he slowed, pulling an earbud out.

'Hi,' I said.

'Hi,' he said breathlessly. 'Everything OK?'

I nodded, not trusting myself to speak. 'I'll be done in ten,' he said.

'About Cairo,' I said. 'I think we should go.'

He stared at me, one earbud in, the other in his hand, sweat still dripping from his face.

'You are doing this for the right reason?'

'What do you mean?' I said, beginning to panic.

'For us both, not just me?'

I didn't answer but stepped forward and hugged him despite his sweaty T-shirt. For the first time in months, it felt right. Now all I had to do was sort Zac.

PART IV

BRITISH TRANSPORT POLICE

Criminal Justice Act 1967 s9

Magistrates' Courts Act 1980 ss 5A (3) (a) and 5B

Criminal Procedure Rules r27.1 (1)

EXTRACT FROM STATEMENT OF WITNESS

Statement of:	Michael Henning
Age of Witness:	Over 18
Occupation of Witness:	Forensic Scientist
Date:	19/06/2019

This Statement, consisting of five pages, signed by me, is true to the best of my knowledge and belief and I make it knowing that, if tendered in evidence, I shall be liable to prosecution if I have wilfully stated in it anything which I know or believe to be false or do not believe to be true.

On 19 June I was asked to examine a red cashmere scarf, recorded as item MH/22, for traces of cellular material and, if found, extract DNA from the material and compare it with a sample of DNA from bone marrow extracted from the body of an unknown male by Dr Sheila Aston in the course of a post-mortem examination. This sample was marked ST/27.

I was also asked to determine whether any DNA from the cellular material recovered from the scarf MH/22 could have come from any other known person. I was not provided with any control samples, so I restricted this second requirement to a comparison against samples held on the National DNA Database (NDNADB).

Using a technique known as DNA 17, the details of which are at Appendix 1, I concluded that the DNA detected from the scarf MH/22 matched the corresponding components in the DNA 17 profile of the unknown male and his profile was almost fully represented.

I performed a statistical evaluation of the result from which it was estimated that the DNA findings would be in excess of one billion times more likely if DNA found on the scarf MH/22 was present from the unknown male rather than another unknown person.

This provided extremely strong support for the assertion that DNA from the unknown male was present on the scarf MH/22. Other identifiable DNA was recovered but is from an unidentifiable source.

Bromley Police Station

It must be nearly twenty minutes since they gave me another break. They did say I could have something to eat, but I said no, despite my rumbling tummy; I'm not sure I could keep it down. The room smells of sweat and fear, as if there isn't enough oxygen to go round. And it's so damned hot! What I wouldn't give for a lungful of polluted London air.

The door opens and Withers comes in with his iPad and notebook. Chowdhury isn't far behind. That trouser suit really doesn't suit her.

'Sorry for the delay,' he says. 'We've been chasing a couple of reports.'

I almost laugh – how many times have we seen that trope on TV cop shows? I bet there was nothing new at all. Withers hangs his jacket on the back of the chair. 'You do have the right for a lawyer to be present,' he says.

'You said.'

'If you don't have one,' chimes in Chowdhury, 'we can arrange for the duty solicitor to attend.'

Straight into the double act. I shake my head.

'So, just for the record,' says Withers, placing a cheap biro by his notebook, 'you are declining legal representation?'

'Yes,' I say, instantly worrying if I'm going to regret it.

'We're still puzzled by the jacket,' he says, tapping the iPad and bringing up that damn CCTV footage. 'Here is the deceased with it on and yet, as you know, when he was found by the railway track, it's gone.' Chowdhury slides a photo across the desk. The horrific shot of Zac's mangled body. 'We thought maybe we'd missed it during the search of the area. Items of clothing can get blown a long way down the tracks. A train goes by at speed, things get caught up in the vortex and the next minute they're hundreds of metres away. Up a tree even.'

'Except he had been wearing it, sir,' says Chowdhury.

'You're right, Padmaja,' concedes Withers. 'And whoever heard of wind taking a leather jacket clean off? It'd be quite a thing.'

Have they been practising this banter in the corridor?

'But we still thought it worth a try,' continues Withers. 'So we went back and looked again. Three hundred metres of track in each direction, including the trees.' He smiles, pausing for me to ask the obvious question. I'm not going to give him the satisfaction.

'We didn't find anything, not even remnants.'

'Maybe someone stole it,' I say quietly. 'It looks expensive.' I wasn't guessing. When we'd first met, I'd googled the make of Zac's leather jacket – Perfecto by Schott, not much change out of a thousand pounds.

'We did consider that,' says Withers. 'But would a thief really remove an item of clothing from a body? Most people would find that difficult. There'd be a lot of blood.'

Images of a blood-spattered jacket flash before me. I feel numb, my feet frozen despite the warmth of the room.

Withers runs a thumbnail over his bottom lip. 'You know my guess? We'll never know for sure. It happens a lot in this business, more than you'd think. We don't find stuff out. It's frustrating.' That smile again. 'Unless a witness comes forward, of course.' He pauses, perhaps to give me one last chance to confess. When I say nothing, he turns to Chowdhury. 'Our visit didn't turn out to be a total waste of time though, did it, Padmaja?'

'No, sir.'

'We did find one item of interest.' He lets it hang there. I try to stay motionless, inside desperate to shout 'What? What the fuck did you find?'

Chowdhury produces a large, clear plastic zip bag. Inside is Zac's red scarf. I feel my jaw tightening.

'We couldn't be sure this was the same item of clothing from the CCTV images, so DC Chowdhury suggested we run a DNA test. And I have to say, she was right.' Withers fires a smile at his junior colleague. 'It came back positive. For the victim's DNA, that is.'

I scrunch my toes, concentrate on my breathing. Slow down. Do not panic. There's nothing to connect me to any of this. Withers twists the evidence bag in his fingers. Could the scarf have my DNA on it, too? It must have, I'd worn it often enough. But they'd need a sample from me to check it against. Unless they'd already taken one from something I'd touched. Maybe the plastic cup from my first interview. Could they run tests without my permission? Is that legal? Maybe I should get a lawyer after all. Withers is talking again.

'Now that we're satisfied this item belonged to the victim, we can post photographs on social media. Hopefully, someone will recognise it.'

I can feel my left hand shaking, have to cross my arms to control it.

'Are you OK, Ms Callaway?' says Withers. 'Would you like more water?'

'Could I use the ladies?' I say.

*   *   *

I close the lid and sit on the loo, trying to get my thoughts straight. Whatever I tell them, it needs to be simple. Yes, this man became obsessed with me, yes he stalked me. But would Withers leave it there? What if he requests my DNA and they match it to traces on the scarf?

I rub my eyes, try to get a grip. The bottom line is, if the police had anything concrete, they wouldn't be putting me through all this. They're fishing, trying to trip me up. I need to stay strong, keep calm. I run through what they have – a guy who bothered me when I was buying a coffee, turning up at the hospital. It's nothing. If they had more, they'd have arrested me. They haven't read me my rights because they haven't got enough and don't want to start the clock ticking.

I take a breath. It'll be fine. I can handle this.

CHAPTER TWENTY-SEVEN

'You know Egypt's human rights record stinks?' said Helen, taking a swig of Peroni. I had driven over to her flat after work to break the news about Mark's job offer. We were sitting on a couple of incongruous designer stools in her cramped galley kitchen, the boys having taken over the tiny sitting room to play computer games. Now and again, an overground train roared past yards from the window, rattling the shelves and drowning out conversation. I couldn't help remembering the impressive detached house Helen and Tom used to share, with its double bay windows and pretty, hundred-foot garden.

'Imprisonment without trial; torture; rape as means of repression,' said Helen, handing me a cup of tea in one of her prized Emma Bridgewater mugs. 'You know the army overthrew the democratically elected prime minister and killed him in the dock?'

'He collapsed, Helen, there was no evidence of foul play.' I had done my share of googling over the last twenty-four hours.

'And they imprison all their journalists.'

'That would be every single one, would it?' I said. 'And how come you're an expert on Egypt?'

'I was involved in a rape case where the guy legged it to Cairo and we couldn't get him back. There'll be no legal protection for you if things go tits up. None.'

'Mark's a teacher, not a bank robber on the run,' I said.

'And when he says jump, you jump. As per.'

'What's that supposed to mean?' I said, stung. Her answer was obliterated by a train thundering past. 'What? What did you say?' I said.

'It doesn't matter.'

'No, come on. Spit it out,' I said.

'Fine. Mark wants to retrain, you drop everything; he wants to move south of the river, you give up your lovely flat, and now he gets middle-aged wanderlust, what do you do? Abandon your job, your friends, everything, just like that,' she said, snapping her fingers. 'You can stand up to him, Kirst. It is allowed.'

We stood facing each other in silence, listening to the sound of gunshots from the boys' game next door. I took a sip of hot tea, she another mouthful of Peroni.

'It might suit me to go,' I said at last. 'You ever thought of that?'

'So you don't have to look after Mum? Who I'm going to be left with.'

'I told you, we're happy to pay for carers, as many as she needs.'

'Carers are not the fucking point, Kirsten!'

I bit my lip, almost telling her if I didn't go with my husband, I risked losing him for ever. That I was terrified of ending up like her, living next to a railway line in a flat smelling of damp and despair.

'It's too late,' I said. 'I've already agreed to go.'

* * *

On the way home, I began to wonder if I had been entirely fair. Life wasn't easy for Helen, what with juggling the boys and work, then not having anyone to go home to at the end of the day. With me in Egypt, and Mum requiring an increasing amount of care, she'd be under even more pressure. Maybe I should stay and help out, tell Mark I'd changed my mind. I could be here for Jess, too, when she had her heart broken by a feckless boy at university and needed the comfort of home. Surely that had to be a better formula for saving a marriage than tossing everything into the air and decamping to a boiling hot, politically intolerant country where I knew no one and would probably end up with food poisoning. I could see myself sitting alone in an air-conditioned flat watching BBC World News, waiting for Mark to come home every night.

Jess was in the kitchen when I got back, earbuds in, revising from bulging yellow files. I watched as she highlighted a paragraph of text, totally absorbed, unaware of anything around her. I remembered myself at her age, burying myself in textbooks, underlining passages in red and blue biro. In a few weeks she'd be gone from my life. If we moved to Cairo, I wouldn't see her until Christmas. Probably long after, knowing how avaricious the airlines could be over the holidays.

'Hi, Mum,' she said, taking out her earbuds and placing them carefully back in their case.

'Hello, darling. Last-minute revision?'

'I know, probably pointless,' she said, closing the file. 'Did Aunty Helen give you a hard time about Egypt?'

'She may have a point,' I said, flopping into a chair.

'You're not getting cold feet?'

'It does seem a little unfair to land her with Gran.'

'Well, as it happens, I have the answer to that. Check this out.' She held up the family iPad.

'I can't see without my glasses, what is it?'

'A map. And your passport to freedom.'

Five minutes later we rang Helen and put her on speakerphone.

'Aunty H,' said Jess. 'I've had an epiphany.'

'Congratulations.' Helen's voice echoed across the room. 'I remember those. I think I had one in my thirties.'

'It solves everything.'

'You know they said that about tea when it was first discovered? And the potato.'

'You move in with Gran!' announced Jess, proudly.

'Sorry, for a second there I thought you said move in with Gran. Is this your idea, Kirst?'

'Nothing to do with me,' I said.

'You divide the house,' said Jess. 'You have your half, Gran has hers. It would still be way bigger than where you are now.'

'I spent all my teenage years trying to get out of there, why would I want to go back?'

'For a start, there's the money you'd save on rent,' said Jess. 'But there's something else, too.' She leant in to the phone. 'Hallingham Academy is two minutes down the road. The boys could walk to one of the best state schools in the area, in the country in fact.'

The line went silent. Jess and I looked at each other. She held up crossed fingers.

'She'd never agree,' said Helen finally.

But Jess had thought that through, too. Helen would say she'd been turfed out of her flat because she'd failed to check the break clause. This would play into all my mother's instincts: the conviction her daughters were incompetent, landlords rapacious, and the only person capable of solving our self-inflicted disasters was her. Even Helen had to admit it might work.

'I'm not promising anything,' she said. 'And it doesn't let you off the hook, Kirst.'

'Absolutely.'

'But I'm prepared to give it a try. For Mum.'

After the call, Jess gave me a high-five. I smiled and told her how clever she was, but inside, part of me collapsed. The last hurdle had been removed. I'd have to go to Cairo – and never see Zac again.

'You are OK about this?' said Jess.

'Of course.'

'You don't look it.'

'It's a big step, that's all.'

'I think it's brilliant. I'm going to phone Dad and tell him.' She virtually skipped into the other room, leaving me staring blankly at her revision notes. For a moment I thought of calling Helen back, telling her it couldn't possibly work, that living with Mum would drive her nuts; I'd cancel Egypt and do my fair share of looking after her.

But even as the thoughts formulated themselves I knew they were specious, self-serving. While everyone else was jumping through hoops to make things better, all I could think of was my own pleasure. I needed to put that aside, be the better version of myself. And if that meant dealing with Zac, so be it. I'd made my decision to go with Mark and there could be no way back now.

I took out my secret phone. Zac replied within seconds.

CHAPTER TWENTY-EIGHT

The last time with Zac, I was almost as nervous as the first. When I suggested we meet after work, he chose a flat within walking distance of Paddington, down a side street lined with what must once have been workers' cottages, now nearly all turned into exclusive pied-à-terres for the Cotswold Crowd. I walked past a swarm of builders working on the one remaining unmodernised terrace, ripping everything out in a cloud of dust, dumping it in a huge skip. I crossed the road and checked the address; a discreet name on the bell confirmed it was the right house: Delacroix. Maybe that was Zac's real name. Perhaps he had intuited what I planned to say and invited me to his home for our last liaison.

Ringing the bell, I wondered if I should just have sent a text saying it was over. But I didn't want to take the coward's way out, like Khanda had. After all the pleasure Zac had given me, it was only fair I tell him face to face. It wasn't as if either of us thought the arrangement would go on for ever. I smoothed my skirt down; I had purposely chosen the plainest outfit I could find, the last thing I wanted was to risk feeling remotely sexy.

Zac answered the door in a suit and tie, ushering me through the narrow hallway into an open-plan kitchen. Not only had the whole back wall been taken off and replaced by glass, the ceiling had gone too, creating a double-height atrium.

'Wow,' I said, taking in the brightly coloured glass chandelier hanging on a long chain.

'You like it?' he said. 'Yours for three point two.'

So not the family home after all, I thought. 'Who has that sort of money?' I said, looking up at the balcony where the bedrooms must be.

'Foreign investors, mostly. Not that they'll ever live here. Probably no one will. They'll park the money for a bit, then sell it on to another investor.' He poured a glass of wine from an already-open bottle. Recently this had been how we started. Gone were the days of lust-filled scampers to the bedroom, ripping each other's clothes off en route. Now we sipped cold Chablis and discussed property prices. Is this, I wondered, savouring the subtle flavours of the wine on my tongue, the inevitable course of all relationships? From Dionysus to Mammon in a few short months.

I looked out of the expanse of glass, across to a fading mansion block with its tangle of confusing extensions and fire escapes. A couple stood on a narrow flat roof smoking, above them a man in a cut-off T-shirt leant out, cleaning his window with a cloth and spray bottle.

'Shall we?'

I turned to see Zac gesturing towards a glass spiral staircase. He looked like a bell-hop about to explain how the lights and air-con worked in hope of a tip.

'Do you mind if we talk for a second?' I said.

'Sure. Though I need to be out of here in an hour.'

'The thing is,' I said, twisting the stem of my wine glass, 'I have to go away for a while.'

'On business?'

'I don't exactly get to travel – as you saw. It's my husband. He's been offered a job abroad. And he wants me to go with him.'

Zac said nothing, tapped a finger on the granite island.

'Where is it?' he said. 'This "job"?'

I hesitated. 'The Middle East.'

He nodded, not looking up. 'I know,' I said. 'It's not exactly what I want, either. But we've had a good time, haven't we? Amazing, really.'

'So that's it? Just like that?'

'I don't have much choice.'

'Really?' His tone was harsh, clipped.

'We both knew it would have to end at some point.'

'Maybe *you* did.' He sounded sulky, like a disappointed teenager.

'Zac, don't be like that! It wasn't as if we were going to ride off into the sunset.'

'Might have been nice,' he said, looking up with a smile.

I laughed, took another sip of wine. I was so going to miss him. He walked slowly round the island, the fingers of one hand trailing across the surface. The next second, he was pulling me into him, his mouth on mine, forcing his tongue in. It was so quick I had to scramble to keep my balance. He pressed his knee forwards, forcing my legs apart. I tried to move away but his hand was behind my neck, holding me firm. Now his shoulders pushed in, pinning me against a chair.

315

'Or is this what you came for?'

'Zac! Get off me!' I said.

'That's not very friendly.'

His fingers tightened on my neck, pulling me in. I couldn't move, he was in control of every part of me. I could feel his erection against my thigh, my hand being crushed against the chair. I tried to twist free, but he held me firm.

'Zac, please . . . '

He frowned. 'I told you,' he said. 'It's George.'

'Right,' I said, forcing myself not to panic. 'Sorry. George.'

He smiled, but something about the way his mouth formed frightened me. His grip relaxed a fraction. I took my chance and stepped away.

'I should be going,' I said, picking up my handbag.

'You can't just go!'

'I have a meeting at two – they'll be wondering where I am,' I said, moving towards the door into the hall.

'Please!' he said. 'We both know that's not true. No one has any idea where you are.' Somehow he was in front of me again, his hands on my hips.

'I'd rather you didn't do that,' I said, fighting the urge to lash out.

'You sure about that?' he said, sliding his hands on to my thighs.

'Please don't touch me again,' I said, trying to keep my voice steady, though all I wanted to do was shout and scream.

'Kirsten, it's me,' he said, smiling. 'Us. Come on! This is crazy.' He stepped in further.

'I mean it,' I said.

'No. No, you don't mean it.' He was very close now, his hands reaching under my skirt. I took a breath – and shoved him with all my strength, pushing him back a step. He looked puzzled, as if this wasn't part of the script.

'Fuck – off!' I said.

He stared at me in disbelief, his lips forming themselves into a twisted smile. I dodged past him and ran to the front door.

'Kirsten . . . Kirsten, I'm sorry!'

I couldn't see where the handle was. Desperate, I swept my hand over the smooth surface, there must be a way out. I could hear Zac striding towards me.

'I thought you liked that stuff.'

I pushed at the door, kicked it. He loomed over me. I was trapped, his body filled the entire corridor and I still couldn't find the damn handle. I turned to face him.

'Zac . . . George . . . listen to me . . . '

He reached an arm forward. How could I have been so fucking stupid to come here?

CLICK!

He'd pressed a switch on the wall; I felt the door pop open against my back.

'Sorry,' he said. 'Misread it.' He took a step back. For a moment our eyes met, then I yanked the door open and burst out on to the street, almost tripping down the steps.

I didn't stop running until I reached the main road, with its clogged traffic and indifferent evening crowds. Panting, I slowed to catch my breath, glancing round, still terrified Zac might pop up out of nowhere. I dodged through a line of cars and jumped on a bus.

I didn't care where it was going, only that I was on it and he wasn't. My neck was sore from where he'd held it, my arms aching where he'd squeezed my biceps. There were bound to be bruises. He had never grabbed me like that before, not even close. I positioned myself behind the exit, so if by a miracle he did try to get on, I could jump off before he reached me. As we pulled into traffic, I stared through the graffitied window at the bustling crowds, at couples walking hand in hand, office workers hurrying to the Tube, friends on their way to the pub. I longed to tell someone what had happened, share with somebody, anyone, the terror that had almost paralysed me. But I had no one to tell, not Mark or Jess or even Helen. I thought of calling Dianne but could already hear her curt response.

I needed a friend, not an acquaintance or colleague. Someone I could talk to properly. A confessor, I suppose. I could feel the tears coming as it dawned on me I didn't have such a thing. Where had all my friends gone? There used to be so many: Janie and Frida, Tony, Esther, Karen. Not to mention Sally and Bridget. I'd had brilliant, intimate, life-affirming conversations with all of them, but I'd let parenting and work and marriage – and sheer laziness – get in the way until all my friendships had faded into nothing. Now there was no one I could turn to.

The bus lights flashed on and off. I looked up to see I was the only person left on board. The engine juddered into silence as the driver climbed out of her cab.

'Last stop,' she said, reaching for her radio. I stepped out of the open doors into the chill, no idea where I was.

'How do I get back?' I said to the driver.

'Back where?' she said.

* * *

I must have walked for fifteen minutes before I spotted a cab, its comforting yellow light ablaze. I ran across the road, waving my hand, hoping to God the driver wouldn't refuse to take me when he heard I wanted to go south of the river. He didn't, he just unlocked a door to let me in, pulled round in a smooth U turn and headed back the way he had come.

Settling into the warmth, I tried to steady my breathing.

'You OK, love?' said the driver, looking in his mirror.

I nodded, pulling the remains of a tissue from my bag.

'You sure?'

'My boyfriend tried to attack me,' I said, amazed to be telling a stranger.

'Are you hurt? You want me to take you to hospital?'

'No – thank you. I'm fine.'

'You should call the police.'

'I just want to go home.'

He drove the rest of the way in silence, pulling up right next to my house.

'How much,' I said, unzipping my bag.

'Forget it,' he said. 'It was on my way home anyway. I'll wait until you're in, OK?'

I made my way to the front door, took out my keys and turned to show the driver I was fine. He smiled, wound up his window, and all I wanted to do was cry at the thought that in this world there are people like Zac and people like him. And me.

I hauled myself upstairs, pulled the curtains shut and crawled into bed. I didn't remember my head hitting the pillow.

CHAPTER TWENTY-NINE

In the bathroom the following morning, I checked my arms and neck. While they still ached, the only sign of bruising was on the inside of one arm, barely noticeable if you weren't looking for it. I refused to think about yesterday. All that mattered was that it was over, the fever broken and, miracle of miracles, nobody had been hurt except me. Soon, I'd be waking to the sound of morning prayers echoing over Egyptian rooftops. Mark and I could start again. The last few months would fade into no more than a memory, one if not regretted, rarely thought about. I just needed to keep my head down and get through the next couple of weeks. I'd start by dumping that damn phone.

Opening a bag of cat litter, I contemplated driving to the Thames and melodramatically hurling the stupid thing into the swirling depths. But then a far simpler idea occurred to me. I fished out an old Sainsbury's carrier bag from under the sink, dropped the phone into it, then tipped the contents of the litter tray over the top. Good luck to anyone finding that I thought, tying it off and pushing it deep into the kitchen bin.

It was Jess's final day of exams. She had cruised through the previous weeks with an equanimity I had only dreamt of at her age. The last paper would be Applied Maths, though she seemed more concerned about her driving test, scheduled for the next day. Mark had promised to take her but then remembered he had a bike race, so I agreed to drive to the centre and wait. We'd have a celebratory lunch afterwards.

'What if I fail?'

'I've seen you drive,' I said. 'You won't.' Not my daughter. She couldn't fail at anything.

Thanks to a rare alliance between Southeastern trains and TfL, I arrived at work early. Sifting through my internal mail, I found a plain white envelope addressed to me in elaborate italics. My hand began to tremble. Please, God, it wasn't from Zac. I slid a finger under the flap, ripped it open, and took out a single sheet of A4.

On one side was a beautifully intricate drawing of my missing piece of sea-glass. Rendered in spidery Indian ink, it captured not just the shape but also the faint outline of the entwined couple within. I turned the paper over, it was blank on the other side.

'Thought it might help.' I jumped. Kevin was standing right behind me. 'You know, like a wanted poster?'

He must have been lying in wait, hiding round the corner by the noticeboard. He nodded at the drawing. 'Does it look right to you?'

'It's very accurate.' Almost like you had it in front of you, I thought.

'I have a photographic memory.'

I almost laughed. Did such a thing exist? 'Is that true?' I said.

He shrugged. 'Once I see something, I can bring it up in front of me whenever I want.'

'That's quite a gift, Kevin,' I said.

'We all have our talents, I guess. Anyway, hope it helps.' He heaved his new rucksack over one shoulder and sloped off. I thought of running after him, accusing him of stealing my precious talisman, but knew it would do no good. He'd hardly admit to his crime. I just hoped it was an elaborate ploy so he could miraculously 'find' it and give it back. As I screwed up the drawing and dropped it in a bin, I reasoned I'd be in Egypt soon, and never have to see Kevin again.

* * *

Peter Sanders had only been the Chief Medical Officer for a few months, but the job was already taking its toll on his face. Small patches of eczema had broken out at the edges of his mouth, and the skin round his eyes looked as if it had been attacked with sandpaper. When I explained I wanted to resign, he rubbed his whole face for what seemed minutes. He ended with a sigh, saying the timing was awkward, very awkward. Finding a replacement at this time of year would be a challenge.

I could have explained I had no choice, what with Jamie's accusation worming its way towards him through the convoluted NHS complaints system, but suspected that would have subjected his poor skin to further painful onslaughts. Besides, I needed a reference before Jamie's complaint reached him, or I'd never get one. So I told Mr Sanders that my husband had been offered a position abroad and I wanted to go with him for a year. Would it be possible to keep my job open? He was so relieved not to be abandoned for ever, he agreed immediately. Then I asked if he could send my reference direct to the hospital in Cairo. No problem, he'd just need an email address, which was precisely what I had hoped he'd say. I gave him the Gmail I'd set up on the train that morning, explaining it was the personal account of the head of HR. Mr Sanders didn't even blink.

When I broke the news to my team that I was leaving, Janice sighed even longer than normal, while the others mumbled congratulations, like fellow lifers learning one of their own has been pardoned. News travels fast in a hospital; on my way to lunch, Dr Svetkova stopped me in a subterranean corridor to ask if I knew the name of my replacement and when I said it wasn't up to me, she nodded briefly and went on her way without another word.

That evening, I was taking my usual shortcut through the underground car park when I thought I heard someone call my name. I looked round, expecting Kevin to come loping over, having picked up the news, but I couldn't see him. He was probably trying to spook me again.

'Kevin,' I said, making for the steps up to the street. 'I know it's you.'

He stepped out between two cars, his face silhouetted against the bright fluorescent light. But it wasn't Kevin.

'Hello, Kirsten,' said Zac.

My heart started to beat so fast I could hardly think.

He put his arms up. 'It's OK, I just want to talk.' There were dark rings under his eyes, the beginning of stubble on his chin. 'I want to apologise, for yesterday,' he said. 'It was totally unacceptable. I'm sorry.'

'Thank you,' I said, noticing how crumpled his suit was. Could he have slept in it?

'I didn't want any of that to happen. It wasn't part of the plan, you know?' He ran a hand through his hair. 'You should blame yourself for being so bloody attractive!' He smiled and for a moment there was a flash of the old Zac.

'It's OK. Really,' I said, determined to keep my voice even, reasonable. 'But you should go now.'

He shook his head back and forth, like a child who's realised the world isn't the way he imagined.

'I don't want to lose you. I *can't* lose you.'

'It's over,' I said gently. 'You know that.'

'We are *not* over,' he said, spelling out each word, his eyes hard and narrow.

I became aware we were alone amongst the rows of cars. I glanced round. The steps to ground level were a few yards away. It was early, there would still be people on the street. I took a step forward, but he was too quick and moved to block my way. I could smell alcohol and tobacco on his breath, mingled with the familiar aftershave.

'I have photos,' he said. 'Of us. I could send them to everyone you know in a heartbeat.'

'You do not have photos.' Even as I said it, I knew he could. I'd dozed off after sex enough times, it would have taken seconds to pick up his phone. I would never have known.

'Is that right?'

'Are you threatening me?'

'No, no of course not. I'm sorry. I want us to be together, that's all,' he said. 'I know you feel the same.'

'Look, Zac . . . '

'How many times? It's George!' A bubble of spittle appeared on his lips. I thought of making a dash for it, but there was no way I could outrun him and the noise of the traffic above would drown out any calls for help.

'Tell you what, George,' I said, forcing myself to smile. 'Why don't we talk about it over a drink?'

The muscles round his mouth relaxed a little. I took the chance to edge nearer the steps, felt the first hard edge under my foot. 'We could go to The Lamb,' I said, reaching for the metal rail. Any second, I expected to be dragged back, my head smashed into the concrete stairwell. I was halfway up now, could see the legs of pedestrians, smell the exhaust fumes. 'It'll be like old times,' I said, not daring to look back. A few more steps. Keep talking, keep reassuring. 'Do you remember the first time we met there?'

I emerged on to the pavement, never so grateful to see a rundown, polluted London street. A woman with a couple of kids and bawling pushchair was coming towards me; two young men barged passed, talking animatedly. I turned to face Zac.

'If you try to see me again,' I said quickly before I lost what little courage I had, 'I'm going to the police.'

The woman and her entourage were almost next to us now.

'You don't mean that,' said Zac, his hand reaching out.

'It's over,' I said, stepping into the gutter to let the push-chair past. 'Over.'

'Not for me. Never.' His lips were pressed tight, pale. I thought he might cry and for a mad moment wanted to reach out and tell him it would all be OK. 'I can't live without you!' he said. 'I'd rather die.'

I looked at him, saw he was a different person. A terrifying person. I bolted across the road, ignoring the hooting cars and I didn't stop running until I was deep in the anonymous safety of the Tube.

* * *

I was still shaking when I reached the car. I sat with the engine off, my hands tight on the steering wheel as if by sheer physical effort I could blank out what had happened. My first thought had been to call Alice at Amorem, but I didn't have her number. The only way to contact her was through the little phone and that could be in landfill by now. There was only one other person who would understand.

Dianne picked up immediately.

'Kirsten. Why are you calling me?'

'Sorry?' I said, thrown by her abrupt tone.

'We do not contact each other, remember? For both our sakes. I told you that.'

Had she? I had no recollection. 'What do you want?'

I explained as briefly as possible, trying to keep the melodrama out of my description of Zac's assault. The line went silent.

'Are you still there?' I said.

'That shouldn't have happened,' she said at last. 'I'm sorry.'

'I don't know what to do,' I said.

'Let me talk to Alice.'

'Maybe I should call her?'

'It should be me. I'll explain what happened and she'll deal with it.'

'How?'

'I'm not sure exactly, but I know they take that sort of thing very seriously.'

'It's happened before?' I said, surprised. The line went silent again.

'Something similar,' said Dianne, finally. 'And from what I can tell, they came down on the guy like a ton of bricks. Zac won't do it again.'

'But how can you be sure?' I said, aware of sounding like an inconsolable child.

'I'm going to phone Alice right now, OK? She'll know what to do, I promise. Can I phone you later? On this number?'

'Yes,' I said, suddenly exhausted.

'Kirsten, it'll be fine. I promise.'

*　*　*

It should have been the perfect evening. We had so much to celebrate: Jess finishing her exams, Mark accepting the job, me handing in my notice, but every part of me felt sick. What if Zac did have photos? He could easily have hacked into my contacts, too. He already knew where I worked, it wouldn't be difficult to find out everything else. As for Alice, what could she do apart from threaten to tell his wife? For all she knew, Zac might have told her himself already.

Mark had made another Arabic meal, more elaborate than before. He'd chosen a delicious Moroccan wine as well, and when I asked if that meant he was drinking again, he said no, but this was a special occasion. As we sat down, he produced two wrapped gifts. For me, a beautifully preserved

1877 edition of a Baedeker guide to Egypt; for Jess, a yellow toy Mini, with the promise it would become the real thing the moment she passed her test. Thrilled, she hugged him and I smiled and laughed and enthused, while inside all I could think of was Zac's face when he told me it wasn't over. The way every feature hardened. I told myself Alice would know how to deal with people like Zac, but I could still hear his last words, shouted at me as I dashed across the road: 'I *will* get you back.'

It would probably come to nothing. I'd broken up with enough boyfriends to know how meaningless parting shots can be. They loathe you, adore you, vow revenge, swear you will love them again, then they get distracted by work or another woman or a football match. More than likely, I'd never hear from Zac again.

'It's the director's cut,' said Mark. 'All two hundred and twenty-seven minutes.'

'I'm sorry?'

He held up a Blu-Ray case.

'Mum! Haven't you been listening to anything we've been saying? It's *Lawrence of Arabia*, the one you and Dad saw the night you got engaged.'

'Thought it would get us in the mood for Egypt,' said Mark.

We had watched it together at a BFI screening on the South Bank. I'd worn a dress from a stall in Kensington Market, Mark black 501s and a secondhand suede jacket. We held hands and whispered how lucky we were to have found each other. 'And Dad told you Lawrence was killed on a BSA motorbike,' said Jess.

'Brough,' I said. 'He died on a Brough Superior.'
'Must have been a fascinating date,' said Jess.

* * *

As Mark put in the disc and Jess dimmed the lights, my fears began to creep back. Any moment, Zac could turn up at the door and in moments lay waste to everything I most valued and cherished. I'd have no family, nowhere to live and no job to go to.

I should confess everything. Tonight. Throw myself on Mark's mercy as I had done before. A stolen milk jug might not be the same as serial, pre-meditated betrayal, but it could still be my best option. Mark could hate me, leave me, never speak to me again; at least I would have done the right thing. Honesty is rarely its own reward, but it can be comforting when you've lost everything else. The alternative, for Mark to find out from a drunk, destructive obsessive, was unthinkable. I'd do it later, in bed, when I didn't have to look him in the eye.

I glanced across the room at Jess, now absorbed in the film, and knew telling Mark would be the easy bit. She was the one who would never forgive me, not just for betraying her beloved father, but for destroying the family, driving a train through her childhood.

My phone rang loudly.

'Mum! No phones on movie night!'

'Sorry, sorry,' I said, extracting it from my pocket. Now it lit the whole room up with its glare.

'Jesus!' said Jess.

I checked the screen but didn't recognise the number. 'Hello?' I said.

'Are you alone?'

Alice's Scottish burr was unmistakable.

'One second,' I said, getting up, mouthing 'Helen' to the others.

'I'll pause it,' said Mark, reaching for the remote.

'And I'll get us some pudding,' said Jess. 'We know how long this is going to take.'

I hurried up the stairs to the safety of our bathroom and closed the door.

'OK,' I said, breathlessly. 'I'm on my own.'

'I have spoken to Zac,' said Alice. 'And the situation has been resolved.'

'What does that mean?'

'He understands.'

'What about the photographs?' I said.

'That was an empty threat. He has no photographs. I'm very sorry about this, Kirsten. I want you to know it's extremely unusual.'

'How can you be sure it won't happen again?' I interrupted. 'He knows my real name, where I work!'

'It won't happen again.'

'But how can you know? How can you?!' I was almost shouting.

'He's given me his word.'

'What the fuck difference does that make? He attacked me, for God's sake!' I caught sight of myself in the mirror, a middle-aged woman with a puffy face, squatting on a lavatory.

'Which he knows was totally unacceptable,' said Alice, her voice calm and reassuring. 'I realise this has been difficult for you, Kirsten, but it's over now. Zac understands he has as much to lose as you. He will not be bothering you again. I promise.'

I felt my body relax, became aware how tightly I had been holding the phone. 'As a sign of our goodwill,' said Alice, 'we would like to extend your membership.'

'No!' I said. 'I don't want anything to do with you.'

'If you change your mind, just let us know.'

'I won't.'

The line went silent.

'Take care of yourself, Kirsten. And again, my sincere apologies.' There was a click, and the screen showed she'd hung up. I leant back, took a deep breath. It was over.

When I went downstairs, Mark and Jess were sitting in the dark, a desert landscape frozen on the television.

'Finally!' said Jess.

'This is your mother's favourite scene,' said Mark. 'Isn't that right?'

'It certainly is,' I said, sitting on the sofa next to him. The TV came to life, played the long shot of Omar Sharif emerging from a shimmering desert. I snuggled into Mark, put his arm round me. No need to confess now. I could relax, go back to who I was supposed to be. Everything was going to be fine.

CHAPTER THIRTY

I'd hardly worn my running gear since Helen and I bought identical outfits in an end-of-season sale a few years ago. We'd promised each other to jog every Saturday. We lasted less than a month. When Tom announced he was leaving her, Helen decided she preferred Merlot to pounding the streets in the rain. I continued for a few more sessions before siding with the sisterhood and stuffing the whole elasticated jumble into a bottom drawer.

But now we were off to Egypt, I needed to get poolside-fit. The other night I had tried unsuccessfully to squeeze into my old bikini; either it had shrunk, or I'd ballooned. But I figured if I went running three times a week between now and leaving for Cairo, I could easily drop a size, maybe two. Which is how I found myself wriggling into a pair of garishly coloured leggings and strapping on my virtually-unused trainers.

Feeling not a little self-conscious, I stepped into the kitchen to find Jess working on her laptop, listening to music.

'Cool outfit!' she said, turning it down.

'You don't think it's too tight?

'You look great, Mum. You going to the park?'

'If I make it that far,' I said.

'Course you will.'

'So, what are you up to today?' I said, pulling a pair of headphones from my handbag.

'Mum! You know what I'm up to! The driving test?'

'Right, of course. Sorry. It's at one, isn't it?'

'We need to be there by half twelve.'

'Absolutely,' I said. 'And Jess, I want to apologise. For being grumpy recently.'

'You haven't. Not any more than usual anyway.'

'Distracted, then. Things have been weird at work.'

'Like the guy in Selfridges you mean?'

'Amongst other things,' I said, shocked she'd remembered. 'Anyway, everything's fine now. Full steam ahead for Egypt!'

She reached out, squeezed my hand. 'I'm happy for you, Mum,' she said, turning her music back up, then adding loudly, 'Half twelve, yeah?'

* * *

I'd planned to take a slow jog to the park entrance near the station, run through the woods, round the lake and end up at the café for a well-deserved latte, maybe even a sneaky flapjack. But I was already puffed by the time I got to the station and when I saw the little café was open, couldn't resist a quick fix of caffeine. For a second, a wave of nostalgia overcame me – it was where Jess and I always stopped when I took her to the park as a toddler. Coffee for me, gingerbread man for her. No point thinking like that, I told myself, I needed to concentrate on the future.

I had paid for my latte and was pressing on its plastic lid when I felt a tap on my shoulder. It was a second or two before I turned around and, when I did, I nearly dropped my coffee. It was Zac, peering earnestly at me. He launched into a barrage of questions as if we hadn't seen each other for years: how had I been; how was the family; was work OK? The rush of words was manic, overwhelming.

'What the hell are you doing here?' I said, my voice stupidly hoarse and trembling.

'And Jess, she must have finished her exams by now, no?'

I could feel the heat of the coffee through the paper cup and for a moment thought of throwing it in his face. Instead, I leant in.

'I told you, if you come near me again, I'm going straight to the police. You understand?'

He started to say something about meeting up 'properly', but I was already crossing the road. Safely on the other side, I glanced back. He stood staring at me, his jacket collar turned up, scarf flapping in the breeze. I tossed my coffee in a nearby bin and broke into a run, determined to get as far away as possible.

By the time I reached the main park, I was breathless, with a throbbing stitch in my side and a blister on my heel, right next to the one I got when shopping with Jess. But I didn't care, I knew I'd be safe there. A few years ago, the council had shut the golf course, turning it into 'London's Newest Green Space'. Ever since, it had been packed at weekends and today was no different. Grateful for the crowds, I limped past a group of men in colourful shorts playing Frisbee football, skirted round a half a dozen women doing yoga and made for a bench. I slumped down, my thighs throbbing.

A young couple jogged past like a pair of dressage horses, all legs and forelocks. Self-conscious about what I knew would be my bright-red face, I bent over, pretending to stretch. As I eased myself up, I saw a figure standing on the other side of the Frisbee players, staring straight at me. Although he was over a hundred yards away, there could be no doubt it was Zac. Who else stood like that, slightly lopsided, weight on one leg? Besides, I could see the red scarf round his neck.

My legs felt wobbly. Zac started to wave. A long, languorous wave like you might give from a liner pulling into harbour. Ignoring my stitch, I broke into a run, past a man teaching his child to ride a bike and nearly straight into an old woman picking up her dog's mess. I glanced back but couldn't see Zac; the Frisbee players had swarmed down their makeshift pitch, blocking my view.

A crack of thunder boomed above me and the air filled with giant, heavy raindrops. The path came alive with wriggling rivulets of water as parents grabbed children and couples ran giggling arm in arm. I hesitated, not sure which way to go; the nearest exit was the one I had come in by, but I couldn't risk going anywhere near Zac, and I knew the others came out miles from home. Lightning spiked across the sky, followed by another crack of thunder so loud it set off a distant car alarm. The whole place was on the move, everyone shouting and laughing as they ran for shelter through the warm, heavy rain. Zac could be anywhere among them. Then I remembered the park café. Ignoring the pain in my side, I started to run again.

Everyone seemed to have had the same idea. Outside the converted building, teenagers shoved each other under a broken gutter, laughing hysterically as the water cascaded over them, while nearby a gaggle of mums struggled to get their cumbersome buggies out of the rain. Inside, the air was thick with the smell of damp clothes and sweat. Everybody was talking at once, best friends in the face of the downpour.

I elbowed my way to the loos, pushing through the chaos of parents and kids to the safety of a cubicle. As I slid the bolt, I could see the shoes and squished down jeans of the person next to me, heard the sound of peeing, then the rattle of tissue being pulled out.

How long since I saw Zac – five minutes, ten? I reached for my phone to call Alice, she needed to get hold of him and tell him to back the fuck off. But I then I remembered I didn't have her number. I'd have to call Dianne again, get it from her. I was scrolling through my contacts when there was a bang on the door.

'How much longer are you going to be?' An angry female voice.

'It's coming, Mummy, it's coming!' squealed a girl.

'Well?' demanded the voice.

'One second,' I said, finding Dianne's number and tapping on it. The phone beeped, then the whole screen went black. I tapped it again. Shit! The bloody battery was dead.

'Oi!' Another bang. I pulled back the bolt, opened the door and stepped past the fuming woman without making eye contact. I peered into the packed, noisy café. There was no sign of Zac. I worked my way to the counter.

'Is there a payphone here?' I shouted to the waitress.

'What?' she said, above the noise of a hissing coffee machine.

'Phone! Do you have a phone?'

'No phone,' she said, thumping a milk container on the counter.

'What about that one?' I said, pointing at a handset on the wall next to her.

'Staff only.'

'It's an emergency,' I said. But she'd already moved off with her coffees, squeezing through the crowd. 'For Christ's sake!' I said.

'You can borrow mine if you like.' I turned to see a young woman with a baby strapped to her front. 'As long as you're not calling Rio.' She smiled, managing to hold out a mobile despite being hemmed in on every side. Taking it, I realised I didn't know Dianne's number either, it was on my dead phone. She had scribbled it on her name tag but what the hell had I done with that? It was probably in my handbag, back at the house. I was about to call Jess and ask her to look when I glanced over to the door and saw a flash of red through the jumble of bodies. I'd recognise that scarf anywhere.

'Fuck, fuck, fuck!' I said, pulling out of sight.

'Hey, mind the language!' said the woman, nodding at an older child holding her hand. I pushed the phone back at her, dodged past the register and ran into the kitchen. A huge man in a white hairnet, a tray of pastries in his hand, stared at me.

'Sorry, sorry!' I said, breathless. 'There's this guy out there, he's following me!'

Without a word, he put down his tray and ushered me into a storeroom.

'What he look like?'

'Sorry?'

'This man, what he look like?'

'He's tall, in a motorbike jacket. If I could borrow a phone to . . . '

Before I could finish, he'd shut the door and was gone. I looked around at the piles of boxes, the stacks of bottles wrapped in plastic. How had it come to this, hiding in a storeroom, in the middle of a park? I could hear the muffled sound of people in the café, the hiss of steam from somewhere, the distant drone of a plane going overhead. I glanced across the room to a door propped open with a large tin of sunflower oil and caught a glimpse of grass and beyond that, trees. The rain seemed to have stopped. Maybe I should run for it, I could probably get to the road before Zac worked out where I was.

'He not there. You safe now.'

I turned to see the man in the doorway, the waitress next to him. She was saying something about her ex stalking her for months until her brother and his mates slashed his car tyres.

'It's the only language they understand,' she said. 'Police don't do fuck all, do they?' She gestured for me to follow her. 'Come on, it's OK now.'

She led me into the café. People were streaming back into the sun-dappled park, the storm blown through as quickly as it had arrived. The waitress let me use the staff phone and even offered to get me a coffee. I tried Jess at home but she didn't answer so, feeling a tiny bit guilty, I called 118 118 and got Dianne's number. She picked up on the third ring.

'He's stalking me,' I said. 'Right now.'

338

'Kirsten? Is that you?'

'Whatever Alice did, it was fucking useless. I've just seen him!'

'Slow down. Where are you?

'Beckenham park – in the café.'

'So you're with people?'

'That's not the point!'

'Listen to me, you're perfectly safe, OK? Stay where you are, I'll come and get you.'

'What about Alice? I want her to know that . . . '

'I'll deal with Alice. Don't move. I'll be as quick as I can.'

She hung up. The waitress brought me a coffee, for which I felt pathetically grateful. Outside, the teenagers perched on picnic tables, tapping at their phones. Beyond them, mums pushed kids on swings and a pack of joggers fiddled with their shoes before setting off down one of the trails. There was no sign of Zac.

Nothing much happened for at least twenty minutes. An elderly couple appeared and bickered over what pastry to share, a girl came looking for her beanie, but that was about it. The waitress asked me if everything was OK though I could tell she had lost interest, probably thinking I had made the whole thing up. I felt overwhelmed with tiredness, all I wanted to do was close my eyes and sleep. I sat more upright to force myself awake but my mind kept wandering, my eyes drooping.

'Kirsten?'

I jerked up to see Dianne looking at me. 'Are you all right?'

I nodded. 'Has he been back?' she said.

.I shook my head. 'Did you get hold of Alice?'

'I left a message. Come on.' She held out a hand and helped me to my feet. I looked round to thank the waitress, but she must have been in the back somewhere. The next minute, Dianne was leading me across the damp grass.

'I want to call the police,' I said.

'You know you can't do that,' said Dianne.

'The guy's freaking me out!'

'Alice will deal with it.'

'No,' I said, stopping. 'She didn't and she can't. We need to involve the police.'

'And what exactly will you tell them?' said Dianne, turning on me. 'That a man you've never seen before is stalking you? Or that a guy you've been fucking on the side won't leave you alone? How do you think that would go down with your husband, with your daughter?'

'He assaulted me, Dianne! Do you need to see the bruises?'

She rubbed her face then reached for my hand. 'I'm sorry,' she said. 'But you must see how difficult this is, Kirsten, for everyone? Once the police start digging, God knows what they'll find. I don't want to lose my marriage. And I'm sure you don't want to lose yours, either.'

'No. . . '

'So we need to be careful, yeah? Let Alice do her job.'

'She said she'd spoken to him. That he understood.'

'I know.'

'So what the hell was he doing following me?'

Dianne sighed. 'I don't know. But please, give it one more chance. Let me talk to Alice, see what's going on. If it does happen again, we'll go to the police together, OK?'

I nodded. 'OK.'

'Thank you, Kirsten. Thank you so much.'

We didn't say any more as we made our way past the Mansion building and into the car park. Dianne stopped by a Mercedes and opened the rear door. There was a man in the driver's seat. I hesitated, suddenly uneasy.

'I don't drive,' said Dianne. 'So I asked a friend.'

The man turned around and smiled.

'Hi,' he said.

It was only as he turned again and I glimpsed the back of his head that I recognised him. He was the man Dianne had been having sex with on the bonnet of a car, maybe this very one.

I sat in silence as he drove the few streets to my house. Dianne offered to come in, but I wanted to be on my own. I mumbled a thank you and let myself into the hall.

I stood listening to the familiar sounds: the distant rumble of the boiler, the whir of the dishwasher, the creak of our bathroom window. I could smell fresh laundry, along with a comforting trace of bonfire smoke. I was home. All was well.

'Where the fuck were you?'

I span round to see a red-eyed Jess in the kitchen doorway. It hit me like a slap in the face. The driving test.

'Jess, I'm so. . . '

'Where the hell were you?' I could see she was close to tears.

'I'll call them,' I said. 'We'll get another appointment.'

But she was gone, stomping up the stairs, slamming her bedroom door. I felt beyond awful, wretched. I knew how long she had practised, how much today meant.

My first thought was to go to her, prostrate myself, admit it had been all my fault, promise to do whatever it took to sort this mess. But I knew when Jess was in this sort of mood it was best to leave her be. I slumped down. Maybe it wasn't so bad. If a missed driving test was the only fallout of my stupidly ill-advised affair, I'd got away with it lightly. I'd make it up to Jess. Spend more time with her, treat her to a fancy meal out, buy her a new outfit. Whatever she wanted.

I grabbed a used envelope from the bin and wrote a grovelling apology. I'd been a fool, inconsiderate, a bad mother. Could she ever forgive me? I left it outside her bedroom door and was stripping off my running clothes to have a shower when my phone rang. It was Dianne.

'Alice is going to talk to him again,' she said.

'It didn't work last time,' I said. 'Why would this be any different?'

'She'll see him in person.'

'So?'

'In his house. His wife will be there, and his child. He'll understand what's at stake.'

I stared at the pile of dirty running clothes by my feet. 'And if he does it again, we contact the police?'

'Absolutely. No question.'

* * *

As I changed into fresh clothes, I made a mental list of things to do before we left for Egypt. I didn't want to risk running in the park again, but I could use Mark's Peloton every morning. Then I'd do half an hour of Arabic and gen up on Cairo. By the time we left, I'd have a list of places to visit and things to do. I'd book our inoculations, order summery clothes and follow up on jobs. It would all be OK. As long as Zac stayed away.

Coming downstairs, I saw the front door was open a fraction, an extension cable sneaking through. I pushed it open to see Mark on the drive, power-washing an upside-down bicycle. What's he doing here, I thought. Wasn't he supposed to be out all morning?

'Hi,' I said, but he couldn't hear me above the roar of the machine. One of the bike's wheels was missing and a jet of water shot through the frame, slamming into the car, sending up a bloom of mist. Water dripped off the L plate and guilt swept over me again. I stepped out and tapped Mark on the shoulder. He jerked round.

'Jesus!' he said, turning the machine off. 'I didn't hear you.'

'How was it?' I said, trying to sound casual, normal.

'What?'

'Your bike race. Did you win? Is that why you're back early?'

'I fell off in the rain,' he said. 'Buggered one of the wheels.' He pointed at the hoop of twisted metal propped up against the wall.

'Are you OK?' I said.

'A few scratches, that's all.' He held up a grazed hand and was about to turn on his power washer again, when he hesitated. 'How did Jess get on with her test? Did she pass?'

When I told him what happened, he went silent. 'Why did you do that?' he said at last.

'I made a mistake.'

'For fuck's sake, Kirsten! You knew how important it was to her. You knew what time you had to be there.'

I mumbled an apology, shocked by his vehemence. Mark hardly ever swore, he thought it lazy and trite. 'I messed up, OK? We all do it.'

'Do we, though?' He turned round to look at me, the dripping lance in his hand. For a second I thought he might turn it on me.

'Maybe I'm getting old,' I said, forcing myself to smile.

'Is there anything you need to tell me?' said Mark, giving me the same look he had all those years ago, outside the department store – the stern teacher with the recalcitrant teenager. I longed to blurt it all out but knew that could only make things worse. Besides, I was almost home free. In a few weeks we'd be thousands of miles away and all this would be over.

'I'll make it up to her,' I said. 'And you.'

BRITISH
TRANSPORT
POLICE

Criminal Justice Act 1967 s9
Magistrates' Courts Act 1980 ss 5A (3) (a) and 5B
Criminal Procedure Rules r27.1 (1)

EXTRACT FROM STATEMENT OF WITNESS

Statement of:	Michael Henning
Age of Witness:	Over 18
Occupation of Witness:	Forensic Scientist
Date:	20/06/2019

This Statement, consisting of three pages, signed by
me, is true to the best of my knowledge and belief
and I make it knowing that, if tendered in evidence, I
shall be liable to prosecution if I have wilfully stated
in it anything which I know or believe to be false or
do not believe to be true.

On 20 June 2019 I was asked to examine a pair of
black denim trousers, marked MH/15, recovered in
the course of a post-mortem examination carried out
on 17 June 2019 by Dr Sheila Aston on an unknown
male.

I examined the outside of the trousers with a micro-
scope and noted all areas of deposited and stained red
paint and samples were taken for further comparison.

I designated areas 'A' to 'N' as identifiers and the areas of paint were classified according to colour. I compared the items of red paint found in areas A, B, F and G with a control sample of paint taken from a bridge over the railway at Ravensbourne railway station, Beckenham, which appeared to have been deposited as graffiti. This control sample is marked item GPB/3.

Applying both chemical and Fourier-transform infrared spectroscopy techniques to both the control sample GPB/3 and the samples found in areas A, B, F and G, I am able to say there is no support for the proposition that those samples and the control sample GPB/3 came from the same source.

The control sample of paint is of the type favoured by graffiti artists and is likely to have been applied by aerosol.

The samples from the trousers appear inconsistent with such paint.

CHAPTER THIRTY-ONE

It took several days to stop looking behind me every time I went out, not to check faces in the crowd for the one person I dreaded seeing. But whatever Alice said to Zac had worked – he didn't appear again. I hardly saw Mark, either. He buried himself in the practicalities of our trip, compiling endless to-do lists which he then methodically worked his way through. Determined to do my part, I applied for visas, registered with a change of address service and contacted the local estate agent to have the house valued for rental. Jess remained subdued for most of the next week, barely talking to me, directing all her comments through Mark, but once she had been offered a new date for her driving test, she began to thaw.

At the weekend, I helped Helen prepare Mum's place for her and the boys. I thought our mother would be all over it, bossing us about, maybe even changing her mind about Helen moving in. But she stayed uncharacteristically quiet, content to sit in her armchair listening to the radio as we buzzed about with bleach and brooms and pots of paint.

In our childhood, she kept the place spotless, full of welcome smells: baking bread, cakes, lavish fry-ups, the occasional bowl of popcorn if we were lucky. Now everything was dusty and sad, the windows dull, the rooms oppressive with damp and mould.

'You sure you still want to do this?' I whispered to Helen, tying off yet another black bin liner.

'It'll be great,' said Helen, who had embraced the idea of moving in with unexpected enthusiasm. 'We'll soon have it back the way it used to be.' She planned to take over her old room, despite Mum's being free, what with her having to sleep downstairs now.

'I couldn't use Mum and Dad's bed,' she said, pulling a face. 'It would be too weird.'

'You could buy a new mattress.'

'I like my room. Reminds me of the good times, BTFT.'

'BF what?' I said.

'BTFT: Before That Fucker, Tom.'

I laughed as she led the way up the narrow stairs to what had been my bedroom, tucked into the attic. With its sloping roof and dormer window overlooking the garden, it was smaller than I remembered. Helen poked the single bed with her foot.

'We'll get rid of that,' she said. 'Put bunks in, the boys will love them. And the whole place will need painting.'

'They might like it as it is,' I said.

Helen looked at the purple walls, the black skirting board. Part of my Goth phase.

'Hardly. You get started. I'll check the bathroom.'

I lay on my old bed, the mattress spongy with age, and ran my fingers across the stickers on the headboard. The hours I had spent there, listening to records, staring at the ceiling, imagining my bright future as a doctor. I tried to peer out of the window into the garden, but the glass was black with grime. I reached for the Windolene, sprayed on the foam and made a long, satisfying sweep of the cloth. I used to perch half in, half out of that same window, blowing illicit smoke into the night, dreaming of love and success and sex. Three decades on, I tried to think what I had achieved. There had been love, certainly, and sex. Success would be a different matter. But at least I hadn't been dumped in middle-age like Helen, or the victim of a double mastectomy like poor Bridget, or lived on my own watching box sets in my underwear, as I suspected Kevin did. If my career hadn't been all I hoped, it might not be too late. Maybe I could retrain, do something completely different. I caught my reflection in the now-sparkling glass and smiled. There was life in the old girl yet.

When I came downstairs, Helen was fiddling with the TV remote while my mother sat benignly in the corner, watching her.

'It's like she's put honey in it,' said Helen, stabbing at the buttons. I almost tripped over a large cardboard box by the door.

'What the hell's this?' I said, rubbing my shin.

'Your old stuff, it was in the landing cupboard.' The television came to life with a booming voice and distorted picture. While Helen and I winced at the noise, my mother didn't flinch. Maybe she was going deaf on top of everything else.

Later, as I prepared to leave, I had a hushed conversation with Helen in the hall.

'She hasn't been this bad before,' I said.

'I know,' said Helen.

'Are we losing her, Hellie?'

'That's why I want to be here, to keep her safe.'

I could see tears forming in her eyes. We hugged for a long moment, then the TV boomed again.

'She's found the remote, then,' said Helen, pulling away.

I laughed and heaved up the cardboard box.

'Call me if it gets too much,' I said.

'Will do.'

As I made my way to the car, arms clasped around the sagging box, I thought things were not so bad. Zac had gone, I'd made up with Jess – more or less – and, in a few weeks, I'd be off on an entirely new adventure with my husband, knowing Mum was in safe hands. I should have taken more pleasure in that moment because soon my whole world would fall apart.

CHAPTER THIRTY-TWO

I had been making good time on the way home, half listening to a radio documentary on Scythian burial mounds, when I hit stationary traffic. After about fifteen minutes, I'd made enough progress to see the blue lights of an ambulance reflecting off the trees. A police motorcycle blocked the road and an officer in leathers was turning people back. He approached my window as I wound it down.

'Sorry, no access,' he said.

'But I only live a couple of roads across.'

'I appreciate it's frustrating, but you can go round the park.'

'Officer,' I said, 'I'm really late, is there no way I can sneak through? It won't take a second.'

He bent down slightly, so he was looking directly at me. I gave him my best smile. 'Please?'

'I shouldn't be doing this,' he said, taking out his radio.

Five minutes later, I let myself into the house, thinking, just a few months ago I wouldn't have had the confidence to flirt like that. I could hear Taylor Swift playing in the kitchen and went through to find Jess lighting two large candlesticks, the ones we used for special dinner parties. The table was laid for five.

'Hey Mum,' shouted Jess above the noise. 'How was Aunty H?'

'What's going on?' I said, now spotting Mark by the stove.

'You're cutting it fine,' he said.

'Cutting what fine? What is all this?'

'Anne and Jeremy,' said Jess. 'Remember?'

'They'll be here any second,' added Mark, disappearing in a cloud of steam as he strained a large saucepan over the sink.

Anne and Jeremy were Jess's godparents, chosen by Mark with an uncannily fortuitous eye for the future: both were doctors. We only saw them occasionally but a month or so ago Jess had asked us to invite them round.

'It'll be *so* useful to pick their brains about medical school,' she'd said.

We'd agreed and then, in my case, completely forgotten. The doorbell rang.

'That'll be them,' said Mark. 'Can you get it?'

I made my way to the front door, briefly catching sight of myself in the hall mirror. My hair was a mess and my clothes dusty from heaving boxes around Mum's house. It didn't help to know Anne would be dressed to the nines. She had no taste but plenty of money, thanks to a lucrative private practice. I opened the door.

'Kirsten!' said Anne, clearly trying not to react as she took in my dishevelled appearance.

'Sorry,' I said. 'I haven't had a chance to change. Come in, come in. How nice to see you.'

'Managed to get across the border without showing our passports!' said Jeremy, holding out a bottle and a box of chocolates. I had never met someone so proud of an Islington postcode. Anne was wearing a bizarre parka-shaped mac with a giant zip all the way down the front. She looked like something out of Quadrophenia.

'Bottega Veneta,' she said, catching my look. 'Very light, very waterproof – wonderfully practical.'

And reassuringly expensive no doubt, I thought, as she started unzipping herself. I'd once seen an undertaker opening a body bag with more shape to it. Underneath, she had on a sparkly gold dress and tiny purple cardigan. She looked like a lava lamp. Jeremy, in a plain polo neck, was, as always, channelling Steve Jobs.

'Organic and vegan respectively,' he said, pointing to the wine and chocolates. 'Wouldn't want to pollute the House of Purity!'

What can I say, the man was a tit.

'Sorry we're late,' said Anne, as I took her bell tent of a coat. 'There was a massive traffic jam. We had to go miles round.'

'"Incident on the railway",' said Jeremy. 'We all know it means suicide. Why can't they say so?'

'Somebody died?' I said, remembering the flashing lights of the ambulance.

'It's fundamentally a selfish act,' said Jeremy, handing me a thin pair of leather gloves. Who even wears stuff like that, and in summer? 'Not only the inconvenience to the rest of us,' he went on, 'what about the train driver? Traumatised for life, I wouldn't wonder. If you want to kill yourself, take pills.'

'We don't know it was suicide,' said Anne, smoothing down her ridiculous dress.

'Course it was,' said Jeremy.

Zac's last words popped into my mind: 'I can't live without you! I'd rather die!' It was a ridiculous idea; whatever had happened by the railway had nothing to do with him. Why would it? Except the park entrance was right where the ambulance had been. What if his long wave that day had been a wave goodbye?

'The radio said it might be a graffiti artist,' said Anne.

'Serves them right if it was,' said Jeremy. 'Everybody's evening screwed up because some twat wants to spray a squiggle on a bridge. How selfish can you get?'

'Why don't you go through?' I said. 'I won't be a minute.' Even as I bolted up the stairs, I told myself I was being absurd. It had been a whole week since I'd seen Zac in the park. I shut the bedroom door, sat on the bed. He would never do something like that, he wasn't the suicide type. But what did I know? I'd once treated an amputee for over eight months, got her walking again, her life back to normal, then one Monday morning, for no apparent reason, she took twenty-four paracetamol.

I knew nothing about Zac, not his past, his mental health history or his relationship with drugs. He could have attempted suicide before or be on antidepressants or lithium, or an antipsychotic. I felt sick at the thought of what he might have done, yet a part of me was also horribly relieved by the prospect of never having to see him again, and with that came a wave of guilt so intense my head pounded.

I took a few deep breaths. There was no reason to assume anything had happened to Zac at all. I was being paranoid, no, worse than that, self-aggrandising. As if he would harm himself on my account. Ridiculous. He'd probably long since moved on. I picked up my phone, googled 'railway death Beckenham' then, when nothing came up, substituted 'suicide'. A dozen or so links appeared but all from years ago. Only when I checked Twitter did I find any mention of 'an incident on the railway', and then mostly rants from people stuck in traffic or on stationary trains. As I thought, no one had died. It was all nonsense, based on nothing but Jeremy's misanthropic speculations. I needed to get a grip, put the whole Zac obsession behind me and move on.

'Mum!' It was Jess, calling from downstairs.

'Coming!' I splashed my face with water, pulled off my jeans and grabbed a plain black dress. My heart sank at the thought of spending an evening with J & A, as they referred to themselves. They had always been smug and condescending, and Jeremy slightly creepy. Anne specialised in IVF while Jeremy was a colorectal surgeon who never tired of saying he'd worked his way up from the bottom. I looked in the mirror. My hair was still a mess but there wasn't much I could do about that. I pulled it through a scrunchy and headed downstairs, determined not to think about Zac again.

Jeremy spent the first course on broadcast, only requiring the occasional nod from his audience to spur him on to ever more fascinating medical anecdotes. Despite my efforts, I couldn't concentrate, my thoughts repeatedly drifting back to Zac. I needed to reassure myself he was OK, speak to him directly, in person. But, of course, I had thrown away my only means of doing that, burying it in a bag of soiled cat litter.

As Jeremy launched into the hilarious tale of a patient with a milk bottle stuck up his bottom – a story that not only was I pretty sure was apocryphal, but one I must have heard a dozen times over the years – I cleared the plates, urging everyone to sit tight. Scraping food scraps into the bin, I spotted the orange Sainsbury's bag nestling at the bottom. I was tempted to reach down and extract my little phone, but then heard guffaws of laughter behind me (Jeremy's mostly), and the next minute Mark was on his feet, sliding a baking tray from the oven.

There was no opportunity to check the bin again for over an hour, during which we were subjected to Anne's patronising guide to surviving medical school, interspersed with Jeremy's off-colour anecdotes about his sexual exploits as a student. Why anyone, ever, would want to have sex with him was beyond me. Anne might not have been a looker herself, but she could have done a lot better.

Jess lapped up Jeremy's jokes, laughing way more than politeness required; I could only assume she was drunk, though I hadn't seen her have more than a couple of glasses. If she seemed hyper, Mark was subdued. He tried to look interested, but I could tell his thoughts were elsewhere, as were mine. Anyone with an ounce of sensitivity would have picked up on all this, but J & A ploughed on regardless.

After two coffees and most of the port, Jeremy finally remembered he had theatre first thing – pity *that* poor patient, I thought – and announced they should make tracks. Coats and gloves were fetched and air-kisses exchanged, along with promises to meet up soon as it had been *so* good to catch up (this despite neither of them asking any of us a single question). Jess thanked J & A yet again for their 'invaluable' advice, while I beetled back into the kitchen to stop myself letting rip at Jeremy for being such an arrogant, tedious arsehole. The front door clicked shut, then Mark appeared.

'Jesus,' I said. 'Does he ever listen to himself?'

'Thanks for the support,' said Mark.

'Sorry?'

'You could at least have chipped in occasionally.'

'I was listening to what they had to say,' I said.

'On another planet more like.'

He was right, all I had been able to think of was how to fish out my phone.

'I thought they were brilliant,' said Jess. 'Thanks for inviting them, Dad. It's been a good day.' I watched them hug, desperately wanting them to go so I could pull out the Sainsbury's bag. It took another twenty minutes before they finally headed off to bed.

'Be up in a minute,' I said, then waited for the familiar creak of the floorboard on the stairs before running back to the bin and pressing the pedal with my foot. The lid hissed up. It was empty. I stared in disbelief at the shiny new liner. Mark must have taken the old one out when I was clearing the table.

Grabbing a pair of rubber gloves from under the sink, I opened the back door and stepped into the drizzle. The wheelie bins weren't where they should have been, next to the hose reel; they were standing neatly by the kerb, the way Mark always arranged them the night before collection: handle out, ready for the dustcart.

Ignoring the rain running down the back of my neck, I crept down the path and flipped open the grey bin, hoping to God Mark wouldn't look out of the bedroom window and see a madwoman in bright yellow Marigolds struggling with a bin liner. Heaving it onto the pavement, I tried to undo the knot, but my fingers were too slippery. I tore open the plastic and felt around in the damp, soggy contents, pushing aside rotting vegetables, smeary flyaway plastic film, the odd tin can. How did that end up in there? We were supposed to recycle this stuff. I dug deeper, felt a slimy lettuce slide through my hand but still couldn't find what I needed. It must be in the bag underneath.

I couldn't reach all the way down, so had to tilt the bin until I managed to get a grip on the next liner, but as I pulled, it snagged an edge, spilling the stinking contents all over the road. I didn't care, because clear under the light of the lamppost was the bright orange of the Sainsbury's bag. Tearing it open, I was hit by a wave of ammonia so strong I almost gagged. I put my hand in, moved my fingers through the clumpy cat litter until I felt the familiar oblong of my phone.

'Kirsten?'

I jerked round. It was Mark, peering at me from the back door. 'What on earth are you doing?'

'Hi!' I said, holding the bag behind my back and quickly standing in front of the mess I had made. 'I broke a glass. Thought I should put it straight in the bin.'

He stared at me. Had he seen the torn liner, the chicken carcass poking out from between my feet?

'Come on,' he said, holding the door open.

I pushed up the lid of the bin, letting it close with a thud and nudged the carcass out of sight at the same time. Heading back to the house, I managed to slide the phone into the palm of one of the gloves. In the kitchen, Mark had fetched a towel.

'Sit down,' he said, 'you're soaking.'

'It's OK,' I said. 'I'm fine, really.' But the next second I was in a chair with him rubbing my hair dry. I managed to peel off the glove and push the phone under my thigh.

'Better?' he said. I nodded. 'Time for bed, then.'

'I'll be up in a minute,' I said, not daring to stand up in case the phone fell to the floor. 'Are you OK?' he said.

'Just want to make myself a hot milk,' I said, thinking when was the last time I had done that?

'If there was something wrong, you would tell me?'

'What do you mean?' I said, worried he'd seen through my broken glass story and knew I had been rifling in the bin.

'You're not getting cold feet – about Cairo?'

'No, of course not.'

'Because I really do think it will be the best thing for us.'

I looked at his face, tried to gauge whether this was genuine concern or prelude to a barrage of questions designed to trip me up.

'Me too,' I said at last.

'Really?'

'Really.'

He leant in and kissed me. 'Thank you.'

The relief was like a shot of adrenaline, but I didn't trust myself to move until I heard the bedroom door click shut. The next second, I had the phone in my hand, shaking it dry, fumbling for the tiny 'on' button. Nothing happened. I tried again. Perhaps the battery had gone. I held it up to get a better look – which is when I saw the case was cracked, a twisted circuit board poking out at the side. A dribble of liquid oozed out, making a small yellow puddle of the floor.

I felt paralysed, didn't know what do. Without that phone I had no way of checking if Zac was OK. I spotted the iPad and picked it up to check Twitter, maybe there'd be something about the accident on the railway.

The complaints had dried up an hour ago, when the police reopened the road. I scrolled through the last entries, one of which said, 'As per' – and included a link to the Met's site. I clicked on it.

'*A section of Crab Hill was closed this evening between 18.25 and 21.10 following the discovery of a body on the Chatham line, adjacent to Ravensbourne station, Beckenham.*'

I stopped reading, unable to breathe. That couldn't be right. There had been no reports earlier, why had they changed their minds? And yet there it was: '*the discovery of a body*'. I glanced back at the screen.

'*The identity of the victim has not been established and police are appealing for witnesses. The one metre ninety male, believed to be between thirty and forty, was dressed in black jeans and a blue Ben Sherman shirt. Anyone with information, please call Bromley Police Station on 020 7946 0173 or dial 999.*'

I knew those clothes, had pulled them off Zac a dozen times. It couldn't be anyone else. I felt myself beginning to panic, my chest tightening, my pulse racing.

I yanked the cork from a half-empty bottle of wine and took a swig. Was I being irrational? Zac couldn't be the only man in London wearing jeans and a shirt. And if it *had* been him, they'd have found his wallet or phone. Anne said the victim was a graffiti artist. That made much more sense, they probably don't carry ID in case they get caught.

I took another mouthful of wine and felt myself tipping from tipsy to pissed. Might as well finish it, I thought, taking the now-empty bottle over to the recycling basket. Placing it amongst the dozen or so others, I had a flash of Zac lying dead and mangled on a mortuary slab. I felt a lump building in my throat, my mouth twisting at the fucking unfairness of it all. I had to know one way or the other. I called Dianne. It went straight to answerphone.

'Dianne,' I said, forcing my voice to remain calm. 'It's Kirsten. I have to talk to you. Call me. Any time. It's important.' I hung up, tossing the phone on to the kitchen surface. Had I sounded drunk? Slurred my words? So what. Maybe I should call again, keep on calling until she bloody well answered. But I didn't have to. My phone buzzed. I reached out, stubbing my toe on the damn cat's bowl as I picked it up.

'Kirsten? Dianne.'

'He's dead,' I said, rubbing my foot.

'What?'

'Zac. He's dead. I know he is!'

'Have you been drinking?'

'Will you fucking listen?' I said. 'He killed himself because of me.'

'Kirsten, you're not making any sense.'

'OK, OK,' I said, taking a deep breath. I closed the door into the hall, sat down and, as calmly as I could, told her about the news item, the police report – and the description of the man found by the tracks.

'That doesn't mean anything,' said Dianne.

'Don't you see?' I said. 'It's why he came to the park. To say goodbye.' I could feel the tears coming.

'I don't believe that for one minute,' she said, but I could tell from her tone of voice she was having doubts.

'I have to talk to Alice,' I said. 'I have to know what she said to him.'

'It's the middle of the night.'

'For fuck's sake, the guy's dead, Dianne!'

She didn't say anything. 'Hello? Are you still there?'

'I'll call you back.' She hung up.

I looked round the dimly lit kitchen, at the red lights glowing on the cooker, another on the burglar alarm, the occasional flash from the carbon monoxide detector Mark had insisted on screwing to the ceiling. It was my fault. I'd driven Zac to it. I hadn't even had the courage to talk to him myself, I'd made Alice do my dirty work. I thought of him standing on that bridge, his hands on the cold metal as he stepped over the railing.

The phone rang. I grabbed it before the first ring finished.

'It's not him.'

'What? What did you say?'

'It's not Zac. Alice called him just now. It's not him.'

I felt faint, reached for the island to steady myself.

'She spoke to him?' I said. 'In person?'

'In person.'

I laughed. My head suddenly light.

'This has to be the last time,' said Dianne. 'You are not to contact me again. You understand?'

'But . . . '

'I mean it, Kirsten. Do not call me.'

There was a click and the line went dead. I looked out of the window at the rain streaming past the street light, at the wheelie bin with its open lid, surrounded by the remains of the cat litter. Nothing had ever looked so beautiful.

And then I remembered: while Zac was alive, I could never be safe.

CHAPTER THIRTY-THREE

I hardly slept that night, the same thoughts churning round and round. I imagined Zac turning up on the doorstep with an ultimatum or, worse, waiting until I was out and tackling Mark, or even Jess. Should I head that off by confessing all? But if Alice had really spoken to him, it would be insane to bring the house crashing down for no reason at all. On the other hand, he'd taken no notice of her last time and there was nothing to stop him from turning up again. So I was back where I started, trying to imagine what it would like to sit my family down and tell them the horrific truth.

I must have slept eventually because when I woke sunlight was streaming through the window. Looking at myself in the bathroom mirror, I saw dark bags under my eyes, a face pale and creased. I was half dressed when the doorbell rang. It was Zac – it had to be! I pulled up the blind, tried to see if he was on the doorstep, but the angle wasn't right and I could only make out the dead potted plant that had been there for ever. I peered up and down the road. There was no sign of his motorbike, but he could have parked it on a side street, or walked.

'Kirsten? Could you come down, please?' It was Mark, calling from the hall in his formal, 'there-are-other-people-here' voice. I had a mad vision of myself climbing out the window, hotfooting it down the drive in my underwear.

'Kirsten?'

I pulled on a blouse and skirt and ran a brush through my hair. Stepping on to the landing, I could hear Mark saying something in low tones. I peered through the bannisters and saw a woman's legs. What the hell? I could make out a sensible skirt, sensible shoes. Professional. The police? I could feel my hand shaking, grabbed hold of the rail to stop it as I started down the stairs.

'And this,' said Mark, turning to me as I stepped into the hall, 'is my wife, Kirsten.'

He must have seen the confusion in my face. 'Amanda's from Cartertons. The estate agents?'

'Sorry,' I said. 'Still half asleep!' I had to stop myself grinning like a gormless lottery winner.

'We did say nine?' she said. 'I can come back later if you'd prefer?'

'No, no,' I said. 'This is fine. Absolutely.'

'Shall we start with the living room?' said Mark.

Normally, I would have been embarrassed by the mess in the kitchen, our unmade bed, the bomb site that I knew would be Jess's bedroom. But I didn't care. It wasn't Zac standing in front of me, or the police, just a harmless estate agent. I almost laughed out loud in relief. Even my hangover had miraculously vanished.

Amanda took less than five minutes to look round before sitting us down in the kitchen, tablet in hand.

'The catchment area is great,' she said. We've got the Montessori preschool, two academies and St Christopher's and Bishop Challoner for private, all close. Would you be looking to rent furnished or unfurnished?'

'Furnished, I suppose,' said Mark.

'Not sure that's a great idea,' said Amanda, glancing round. 'People are into modern stuff now. No offence.'

I looked at our homely kitchen, with its worn pine table and chairs, the wonky blind in the window, the family photos on the walls. Good enough for us, but no one else.

'You'd need to repaint throughout,' said Amanda, checking her tablet. 'And have the stain in the bath professionally removed. I'd also strongly advise installing a power shower and a new stair carpet. It's one of the first things people notice.'

'Sounds good,' I said. Anything to get out of the country as quickly as possible; I couldn't take any more sleepless nights.

'That's quite a list,' said Mark. 'How much would it come to, if we did it all?'

'Assuming you don't hit any snags, around five K.'

'And the rental income?'

'We'd probably market at nineteen hundred and expect to settle at seventeen-fifty to eighteen hundred.'

'From which we deduct your fees?' said Mark.

'We can't leave it empty!' I said, worried Mark might back out of the whole Egypt idea if the finances didn't work. Ignoring me, he turned to look at Amanda.

'We charge twelve point five for the full management package,' she said. 'But for new clients, I could reduce it to ten on a year-long, rolling contract with a six-month break clause.'

I could see Mark doing the maths. Once we added the mortgage payments and tax, it wouldn't leave us with much – certainly not enough to rent the sort of swanky flat in Cairo I know he had been checking out.

'That sounds fine,' I said quickly.

'Terrific,' said Amanda, producing her card. 'I'll have the team draw up a contract and put you in touch with a couple of contractors.'

'You don't think we should discuss it?' Mark asked me.

I took his hand. 'I just want to be on this adventure with you,' I said. And I meant it. I'd have given away the house for nothing to be out of the country, free to start over, to put the whole Zac debacle behind me and know he could never find me again.

*　*　*

Over the next few days, I decluttered cupboards, filled endless bin liners with rubbish and ruthlessly discarded half my wardrobe, all the while keeping half an eye on the news. At first, the 'incident' didn't merit much coverage, but with the police unable to establish the dead man's identity, the story gradually moved up the media agenda. One evening, bleaching tiles in the bathroom, I listened to an expert on the radio explain why dental records were no longer much help identifying bodies. Fluoride had so successfully reduced fillings that many people didn't bother with dentists any more. Later in the week, Sky News reported the police had DNA-tested a variety of items recovered from near the body, including a teddy bear, single flip-flop, paperback novel and a pair of knickers, but hadn't been able to make any useful matches. The investigation, it seemed, was getting nowhere.

The media, meanwhile, became fixated with the idea that the dead man had been a graffiti artist. A Network Rail official gave an interview about the dangers of trespassing on the railway, pointing out four young men had died in similar circumstances over the last few years; an arts programme featured a professor of cultural studies from an obscure university claiming the victim had died for his right to express himself, and a group of graffiti artists in melodramatic balaclavas paid tribute to one of their own, though none of them seemed to know who he was. But as the police failed to come up with any further leads, the story slipped down the pecking order. Within ten days it hardly featured at all.

Gradually my fears subsided, too, and I no longer spent every waking hour worrying that Zac might accost me on the way to work or jump out of a bush as I went to post yet another official form. Alice had done her job and he'd got the message. He probably had a new partner by now.

Mark and I continued to dig out obscure paperwork and fill in Byzantine forms. I stood in line at the Egyptian Consulate in Lowndes Street for hours, visited our local Post Office nearly every day and became so familiar with utility companies' holding music that I went to bed humming it. In the evenings, we sat surrounded by cardboard boxes and bin bags, sifting through embarrassingly large piles of accumulated junk until we were so tired we collapsed into bed.

As for Jess, once her exams were over, she was desperate to go to Ibiza with friends. It was expensive, but Mark said we'd pay and I agreed. She deserved it after all the hard work she'd put in. We saw her off at an absurdly early hour one morning, treating her to a taxi and the cliched parental talk to have fun but not do anything silly, advice which, I couldn't help thinking, I should have taken myself. I spent the rest of that day stumbling from room to room like a zombie, mourning the loss of my daughter, despite knowing she'd be back in ten days.

On my last Friday at work, I tackled the years of inconsequential detritus which had accumulated in my desk, half of which I couldn't remember putting there or why. In the end, I took out the drawers and upended them one by one over a bin. I peeled ex-patients' faded postcards off the wall, rolling the dots of Blu Tack into a lumpy, sticky ball, and dropped the lot into the same bin. By five o'clock, the place was back to the anonymous office I had moved into nearly fifteen years ago. I felt as I had leaving school, relieved and excited at the same time. Determined to embrace my future.

I was about to head for home when Janice popped her head in and said I hadn't signed the form to return my computer. Sighing, I went through into reception to be confronted by a roomful of people, all with drinks in their hands and a banner draped across the window saying, 'Good Luck Kirsten'. I could feel myself welling up. Apart from Janice, there were a dozen other colleagues from various departments and most of the consultants I had dealt with over the years, including Mike Denton.

'Sad day.'

I turned to see Kevin, in a surprisingly natty fitted jacket. Before I knew it, he was hugging me, his long arms reaching right around my shoulders. 'I'll miss you,' he mumbled into my neck.

'I'll miss you too, Kevin,' I said, extricating myself.

Someone was tapping a glass and the room hushed as a figure in the corner stood up. I was amazed to see it was Dr Svetkova, sporting what looked like a smile of all things.

'Thank you, thank you!' she said and then proceeded to give me a five-minute eulogy, saying what a difference I had made to so many people, how I'd turned the department around and been one of the most professional, conscientious colleagues she'd had the privilege to work with. I felt a tear running down my cheek and had to dab my eyes with the serviette Janice handed me. As I looked around at my cheering friends and colleagues, I wondered what the hell I was doing abandoning them. Surely I belonged here, not thousands of miles away in a foreign city where I'd know no one? But the sentiment lasted a few seconds at most. I took a mouthful of sparkling wine; I was doing the right thing, no question.

* * *

Arriving at Victoria Station, squiffy from a glass too many of Cava, I had to run for my train and ended up standing most of the way. I only managed to sit down for the last five minutes, opposite a man who insisted on holding his paper at arm's length, almost pushing it into my face as he ostentatiously folded back each page, running a thumb down the seam. I was about to say something when I saw a small headline that stopped me dead. 'Mystery Railway Body Breakthrough'.

I tried to read the article, but the man turned the page again and now the doors were opening for my stop. I grabbed my bag, stepping out just before they hissed shut. Standing on the platform, my legs felt weak and for a second I thought I might faint. Even though I knew it couldn't be Zac, I also knew I had to find out for sure. I was about to get out my phone to check the paper's website, when I saw an old woman fumbling for her ticket, a copy of the *Metro* under her arm.

'Excuse me?' I said, 'but could I look at your paper?'

Clearly thinking I was about to mug her, the woman took a step back, holding on to her copy even tighter. I smiled, tried to look non-threatening. 'I think my friend might be in it and I wanted to check if it was her. It won't take a second.'

The woman hesitated, then virtually threw the paper at me, before hurrying off. I flipped through the pages, my heart painful in my chest, but couldn't find the headline. I went back to the beginning, slowly turning each page, checking every headline. Time stopped. There it was, in small print underneath an article about a theatre opening. I scanned the first paragraph: 'graffiti theory ruled out . . . paint residues not a match for bridge . . . police back to square one.'

* * *

I drove home, determined not to panic. All the police had done was rule out the graffiti connection. That didn't mean it was Zac. How could it? Alice had spoken to him, seen him in his own house. This was a random death, nothing to do with me. Yet however many times I told myself everything was fine, a feeling of numbing dread kept sweeping through me.

As soon as I got home, I went straight for the iPad. The *Metro* webpage carried the same article, but with no more details, while the BBC and Sky had nothing at all. Fighting back a wave of nausea, I told myself this was a good thing. The less coverage the story merited, the better.

The doorbell rang but I ignored it – I was in no state to see anyone. It couldn't be Mark, he never forgot his keys, they were clipped to the ones for his bike padlock and Jess was still in Ibiza. It would be a delivery guy – he'd just have to leave whatever it was on the porch or put a card through the letterbox. I was checking Buzzfeed when the bell rang again, this time for much longer, followed by a loud knock. For Christ's sake! I made my way to the door, iPad still in hand.

A couple in black suits stood on the doorstep. He was short, compact; she Asian, tall and serious-looking. Jehovah's Witnesses maybe, or canvassers for the upcoming local election. Then they flashed their warrant cards.

'Mrs Norton?' said the man.

'Actually, it's Ms Callaway,' I said, trying to keep the tremor out of my voice.

'Apologies,' he said, offering his hand. 'DS Withers from the BTP.'

'From where?' I said.

'The British Transport Police. This is my colleague, Detective Constable Chowdhury. May we come in?'

'What do you want?' I said.

'It might be better inside, Ms Callaway.'

My God, I thought, this isn't about me at all. It's Jess, something terrible has happened to her.

'Is it my daughter? Is she OK?'

'It's not your daughter, no,' said Withers. 'May we?'

Mark, I thought, something's happened to Mark. I led them across the hall.

'Moving, Ms Callaway?'

'What?' I followed his glance into the sitting room, with its piles of removal boxes. 'Just having a clear-out,' I said, shutting the door and showing them into the kitchen.

'Is your husband in?' said Withers.

'He's at work,' I said. 'He's a teacher, at St Bartholomew's.'

They exchanged a look.

'Do you have a photograph of your husband, Ms Callaway?'

My mind went blank, then I remembered my phone. My fingers fumbled with the code, kept typing in the wrong one. He must have come off his bike again, that stupid, fucking bike.

'Sorry, sorry,' I said.

'It's OK. Take your time.'

I finally managed to open the photos app, held out the phone for them to see. 'Thank you,' said the man. 'No worries.'

'What does that mean?' I said. 'Is my husband all right or not? Has something happened to him?'

'This isn't about your husband, Ms Callaway.'

I should have felt relief. Instead, I felt dizzy. If it wasn't about Jess or Mark, there was only one other reason they could be here.

'I don't know if you've seen the news recently?' said the man. 'A few days ago, there was an incident on the railway cutting near Ravensbourne station.'

Cold sweat trickled down my back. I couldn't think clearly. It was like being stoned or exhausted, my thoughts a jumble of incoherent contradictions.

'Do you have a debit card ending 3821, Ms Callaway?' It was the female officer this time, staring at me with brown, doleful eyes.

'What?' Why would they ask that?

'It's a Visa card, issued by NatWest.'

And so it started, their polite, relentless questioning. Had I made a purchase at Cappa's Cuppa by Ravensbourne station? Could I confirm it was me in the CCTV footage? Did I know the man in the leather jacket? With every question, I felt more and more sick. I could hardly deny speaking to Zac, it was there in jerky black and white for all to see. But it would be a disaster to admit knowing him. Once they established that, the whole ghastly truth would come tumbling out. God knows where the idea of saying he'd asked for money came from, but I was grateful to have come up with something even vaguely credible.

The moment they left, I felt my insides turn to liquid. I ran to the loo, getting there just in time. My head throbbed as I tried to work out what the hell was going on. The police still clearly had no idea who the dead man was, they'd more or less said as much. All they knew was that I had spoken to someone at the coffee stall, who might – or might not – be the victim found at the bottom of a railway cutting. I knew it couldn't be Zac, Alice had spoken to him, Dianne had told me as much.

So what was the connection and why did they think I'd know anything?

My stomach went into spasm again and for a moment all I could do was screw up my face in agony. As the pain subsided, the truth became appalling clear: it made no difference that the police couldn't name the guy at the coffee stall or the body by the railway, because I could. I knew it with total conviction. Whatever Dianne said, they were both Zac.

CHAPTER THIRTY-FOUR

It was dusk by the time I drove over to Dianne's. At first, I thought she must be out. The lights were on, but nobody answered the door. I rang again and could hear chimes echoing deep inside. I was about to give up when I heard the sound of keys in the lock and the door opened. It was Dianne's husband, Henry, in a dressing gown, his hair wet.

'Sorry,' he said. 'In the shower.'

'Right,' I said, thrown. 'Sorry to bother you . . . '

'No, no, it's fine. Come in.'

As I stepped through a pleasant waft of shampoo and soap, it occurred to me they might have been having sex. Could my timing have been worse? 'Dianne will be down any minute,' said Henry. 'We've been for a jog.'

So that's what you call it, I thought. He mopped his brow with the towelling sleeve of his dressing gown.

'The girls are at a sleepover,' he said, for no apparent reason.

They were *definitely* having sex.

'Kirsten?'

I turned to see Dianne, immaculately dressed in a trouser suit, her hair perfect, even a touch of lipstick. I could never have turned things round that quickly. 'This is a surprise,' she said.

'We need to talk,' I managed, my voice sounding strange even to myself.

'I'll leave you to it,' said Henry. 'Good to see you again, Kirsten.' He scampered up the stairs, his bare white calves pale and spindly. Dianne waited until she heard the click of a door, then turned on me sharply.

'What the fuck are you doing here?' she whispered, and before I could answer, held her finger to her lips. She led me into the kitchen and shut the door. 'I told you not to contact me!'

'The police came to see me,' I said. 'Just now.'

She froze.

'What did they want?' she said at last.

'The guy I was seeing, the one you told me was fine? The one Alice "spoke to"? He's dead.'

'That's ridiculous.'

'They don't think so. They think it was his body by the railway cutting. What the hell's going on, Dianne?'

'Did you tell them about Alice? About me?'

'Of course not.'

She went to the sink, poured herself a glass of water without offering me one, drank it in one long gulp. I glanced at the fish in her aquarium, swimming aimlessly up and down.

'You need to tell me everything you told them. Every word,' she said, washing the glass.

I explained about the debit card, the CCTV footage, my ridiculous begging story.

'Did they believe you?'

'I don't know. Maybe.'

Dianne dried the glass, placing it back in the cupboard, upside down. I wanted to smash it out of her hand, her studied calmness suddenly infuriating.

'You said Alice spoke to him!' I said. 'You told me he was OK.'

She shrugged.

'Is that it?' I said. 'A shrug? I want to talk to Alice. Right now.'

'That's not possible.'

'Why the hell not?'

'She's left the country.'

'Bullshit,' I said. 'How can you know that?'

'Because I told her to. Because I employ her.'

* * *

Dianne refused to explain anything more in the house and shouted up to Henry that we were going to the wine bar for a drink. In fact, we sat in my cramped car, heater on, lights off as she laid it all out. She had run the service for years, organising the tech side while Alice met people in person. There had been no one called Livia, no cosy chat in front of a fire on the Isle of Wight. The whole thing had been Dianne's idea. When I asked if Henry knew, she shook her head.

'That's how it started. Me looking for an alternative.'

I tried to think of all the other lies she must have told me but kept coming back to the most important one.

'Did you know Zac was dead?' I said. 'Did you know it was him on the railway?'

'We still can't be certain it is.'

'But you suspected?' She nodded. 'For Christ's sake, Dianne! Why did you lie to me? Why would you do that?'

'To protect you. And myself. And by the way, his name's not Zac.'

'I know. It is – was – George.'

'No. He's called Stephen Hampton. Not that it matters any more.' She turned in her seat to face me. 'The point is, we need to handle this.'

'Excuse me?' I said, incredulous.

'If the police contact you again, stick to your story.'

I shook my head. 'I can't. I'm going to tell them everything. I have to.'

'Of course you don't!'

'They'll find out anyway.'

'Not if you're careful.'

I shook my head again, too tired to argue.

'Do you *want* to destroy your marriage, Kirsten? Because that's what will happen if you talk.'

'Not necessarily,' I said. 'They'd understand.'

'Please!' said Dianne. 'You think the police could keep something like this quiet, even if they wanted to?'

'I don't see why not, if I explain to them that . . . '

'Don't be so fucking naive! It'd be all over the papers in hours.' She took a breath, stared into the dark for a moment. 'If you go to the police,' she said at last, 'that's it. Your marriage is over, OK? Yours, mine and many, many others. Is that what you want?'

I looked at the red light of the heater knob. It flickered on and off, though I'd asked the garage to fix it the last time the car had been in.

'A man died, Dianne,' I said quietly.

'And you want to make it a whole lot worse for the living.'

We sat in silence, just the sound of the occasional car whooshing by. 'Look,' she said finally, her voice back to its usual calm tone, 'what's happened has happened, OK? We can't change that. What we can do is to prevent any more damage.'

'Did you kill him?' I said, not daring to look up.

'Excuse me?'

'The guy who drove me home, did he get rid of Zac? To protect all your precious marriages?' The thought had come to me the moment we'd got into my car; her 'friend' was a big man, powerful, much more muscular than poor Zac.

'How can you ask that? My God, is that who you think I am?'

'I have no idea who you are, Dianne. All I know is you pretended your husband was disabled and you encourage other women to be unfaithful. For profit.'

'Like you needed persuading! You sought me out, remember? I told you not to get involved; Alice told you not to get involved, but nothing would stop you. You had to have your bit of fun. If anybody's guilty here, it's you.'

I ran my hands around the steering wheel, shocked by the violence in her voice. Dianne sighed. 'I'm sorry, I didn't mean that. I should have stuck to my rule not to involve friends.' She took a deep breath, let it out through her nose. 'The truth is, Stephen – Zac – hadn't been in a good place for a while. You mustn't blame yourself.'

'I don't.'

'He wasn't in a happy marriage and was terrified of losing his daughter if he pushed for a divorce. That's why he signed on.'

'He told you that, right?' I said, staring at her, incredulous. 'And you were dumb enough to believe him? He signed up because he wanted sex, for God's sake – his daughter had nothing to do with it!'

'For him it did,' said Dianne slowly. 'His wife's Polish and he was scared she'd take their daughter back to Poland if they split.'

'Why would he think that? She might not even get custody.'

Dianne examined her perfectly painted fingernails for a moment.

'He had a history – with alcohol. A court wouldn't have been sympathetic.'

'Wait,' I say, struggling to get things clear. 'You knew he was an alcoholic, but you didn't warn me? You were supposed to vet these guys!'

'Ex-alcoholic. He'd been clean for a long time.'

It came back to me; Zac never finished a glass of wine, in fact I couldn't swear he ever took a sip. The first time we met in that pub, I was the one who'd drunk his beer. Why hadn't I put it together? The only time he smelled of alcohol was after I ended things. Could I have been responsible for his relapse?

'A couple of weeks ago he told his wife.'

'About me?' I said, feeling as if someone had slapped me in the face.

'Not specifically. Only that he had met someone. But it was enough. She flew back to Poland, with their daughter.'

I tried to think when that could have been, if it was around the time he'd turned up in the car park, or maybe even before.

'It was his worst nightmare,' said Dianne. 'And then you ended things – which is fine, I don't blame you – and he probably felt nothing could ever work out again. Maybe he had a few drinks and . . . ' She spread her hands. 'Life was just too difficult.'

I sat in silence, imagining his despair, his last few moments when all he could think of was ending it all.

'I should get back to Henry,' said Dianne, reaching for the door handle. She got out then bent down to look at me through the open door.

'Don't go to the police, Kirsten. If you do, I'll deny everything. You understand? You'll be on your own.'

* * *

The moment I got home, I went straight to the kitchen and poured myself a large glass of wine. Downing it in one, I refilled it to the brim. I couldn't make sense of what I felt, if I was mourning Zac, or relieved he couldn't harm me anymore; devastated never to see him again or terrified he'd somehow reach out from the grave and destroy me. And underneath it all, the nagging thought that I had colluded in his death, was responsible for a wife losing her husband, a daughter her father.

I typed Stephen Hampton into Google. 42,000 results in 0.57 seconds, leading with articles on the Dean of Peterhouse, Cambridge. A quick image search confirmed he wasn't the man I had been having sex with for the last few months. Nor, as far as I could tell, was it any of the next dozen or so entries. To narrow things down, I added 'London' and 'property' to the search field, then tried 'Zac', on the off-chance it might have been his middle name, but nothing came up. I tried changing the Christian name to George but could only find a nineteenth-century Australian Comptroller of Convicts and a bloke who wrote on ThunderCats. Either 'Zac' had managed to leave no internet presence at all, or his real name was something totally different.

'Look what I found!'

I span round to see Mark in the doorway – I had no idea he was even in the house. He had a photograph album in his hand, was holding up a page for me to see. 'Italy,' he said. 'Remember?'

It was a shot of the three us by a hotel swimming pool, Jess in the middle, holding our hands, smiling a toothy grin. 'Who took it, do you think?'

'The waiter,' I said quietly. 'We asked the waiter.' We'd been so happy back then; things had been so simple.

'That's right!' said Mark. 'Of course.' He turned the page, peering at more images.

'Let's go to Cairo now,' I said.

'Sorry?'

'We have all the right papers, we could go whenever we want. We could go this weekend.'

He said nothing, I could hear his finger tapping the page of photos. 'I just want to be there, Mark.'

He closed the album.

'I've been thinking the same.'

'You have?'

'If we're going to go, we might as well go. But what about Jess? We wouldn't be here for her results.'

'She could come out and see us. Flights are really cheap at the moment. She could get her results there.'

'Do you think?'

I reached for his hand. 'At least let's talk to her,' I said. 'I'm sure she'd understand.'

He nodded. 'Why not? We'll talk to her.'

I gave his fingers a squeeze, then went straight to the loo and threw up.

CHAPTER THIRTY-FIVE

Unable to sleep, I spent the night listening to rolling news stations through an old pair of earphones, hoping the litany of disasters from around the world might blot out thoughts of Zac. I was still awake at two and heard the headlines for the fourth time at three. I must have dozed for an hour or so, but at five was wide awake again. I glanced across at Mark, then remembered he wasn't there. Recently, unable to bear my endless squirming, he'd taken to slipping off to the spare room to get a decent night's sleep.

Downstairs, armed with a cup of coffee and the iPad, I checked flights to Cairo. There was plenty of availability. We could be there in a few days. Surely the police wouldn't bother me in Egypt and if they did, hadn't Helen said there was no extradition treaty? A quick search on the Foreign Office website confirmed she was right. It felt disloyal leaving Jess, but if I didn't go now it might be much worse for us all, including her.

I glanced at the kitchen clock. Still only half-past five. I topped up my coffee with hot water and padded into the sitting room where I had dumped the boxes from Mum's house, hoping to find distraction in memories of my youth. Easing open the flaps of the nearest box, I saw the familiar blue cover of an A-level physics textbook. I felt its weight in my hands, remembered lugging it back and forth to school, embossing the front with blue biro doodles as I sat on the bus. Opening it at a double-page spread on drag force in turbulent flow, I realised I had no idea what any of it meant. I tried another page, headlined 'The significance of Avogadro's constant as the number of atoms in 0.012kg of carbon-12'. It was followed by several lines of formulae that might as well have been in Chinese.

Had I ever understood any of this? What had been the point of all those lessons, the hours of revision, the nights spent cramming facts which, a few years later, let alone decades, would vanish with no trace? All I could remember were the months of anxiety. My education hadn't broadened my mind or honed my analytical abilities, it simply stuffed my brain with useless facts. If you couldn't regurgitate them on a specific day, within the space of a couple of hours, the whole enterprise became a monumental waste of effort. Which in my case, it turned out to be.

I tossed the textbook back into the box, heaved it up and headed for the garden. Mark had been having bonfires over the last few days, burning old bank statements he refused to trust to the bins. He'd cut a neat square in the vegetable patch we had nurtured together, back when we had time and enthusiasm for such things, before work and the internet neutered our ability to do anything other than stare at screens. I ripped out a couple of pages, put them on the dark pile of ash and set a match to them. They flared up, and soon I had a blaze good enough to throw dozens of sheets on at a time. The flames licked round the edges, fanning out pages like a careful reader, then turned a beautiful shade of yellow and orange. If I'd studied harder, I'd probably have been able to tell what chemicals were used in the ink by the colour of the flames.

As I watched wisps of smoke climb into the dawn sky, I was overwhelmed by a deadening melancholy. Thoughts of Zac pressed in, alone and cold by a litter-strewn railway track. However he had behaved, he didn't deserve to die like that. If I had been kinder, less brutal in my determination to end our arrangement, maybe he wouldn't have. It seemed impossible for a man with such passion, who took such joy in life, to become so overwhelmed by hopelessness he wanted to end it all.

But if not by his own hand, how did he die? Dianne could have been lying when she said she hadn't been involved; after all, she'd lied about virtually everything else. Perhaps she had sent her friend to reason with him and Zac, drunk and miserable, became aggressive. A single punch, an unfortunate fall and it would have been over in a moment. I could send the police an anonymous email, but I knew Dianne would deny everything and all I'd achieve would be to destroy my marriage and my family. The truth wouldn't bring Zac back, it would just spread more misery, like it had with Jamie and Michelle. I stirred the remaining ashes with a stick and headed inside.

Filling the kettle, I was suddenly furious with Zac for putting everyone through this: his wife, his daughter – me. And then I turned the fury on myself; I was as much to blame as him, maybe more so. It seemed impossible I had got myself into this position, me, who never actively wished anyone any harm. I was a good person, for fuck's sake. Who had I become?

A sharp sound jerked me back into the room. The door-bell. It couldn't be the post, not this early on a Saturday. Dianne's warning about the press came back to me. It would only take fifty quid to the right cash-strapped copper for a hack to end up on my doorstep. As I crept into the hall and eased the curtain back, the bell rang again. I peered out. It wasn't a journalist standing in the early morning sun. It was two uniformed police officers, the blue light of their patrol car lighting up the street behind them.

PART V

BRITISH TRANSPORT POLICE

Criminal Justice Act 1967 s9
Magistrates' Courts Act 1980 ss 5A (3) (a) and 5B
Criminal Procedure Rules r27.1 (1)

EXTRACT FROM STATEMENT OF WITNESS

Statement of:	Jayden Matthews
Age of Witness:	Over 18
Occupation of Witness:	CCTV Operator
Date:	20/06/2019

This Statement, consisting of two pages, signed by me, is true to the best of my knowledge and belief, and I make it knowing that, if tendered in evidence, I shall be liable to prosecution if I have wilfully stated in it anything which I know or believe to be false or do not believe to be true.

At 09.30 hrs on 20 June 2019 I was on duty in the police CCTV Monitoring Centre at Croydon when DS Withers contacted me by telephone and asked me to review footage recorded from the London Borough of Bromley's CCTV network extending in a two-mile radius from Network Rail camera ID 74B, located at Ravensbourne station, Beckenham.

DS Withers provided me with still photographs of a male in his thirties and asked for any images of the subject within the above-specified area recorded in the 24-hour period prior to 10.26 hrs on 8 June.

No images were available from the London Borough of Bromley's camera network.

I requested footage from privately owned and operated CCTV cameras within the same geographical area and time frame. I was able to provide images of a man resembling the male in the photograph from a camera installed at the Esso petrol station on the Bromley Road. On 8 June 2019, the subject appears on foot at 08.32hrs, enters the shop and leaves at 08.40 with a disposable cup and paper bag.

No other images were available from the footage provided to me.

I downloaded this footage on to a DVD which is now marked as item JM/2 and I handed it to DS Withers at 16.40 hrs on 20 June 2019.

Signed,

Jayden Matthews

Bromley Police Station

11.05, 22 June 2019

I wash my hands, wave them under the deafening dryer and head back to the interview room. DS Withers and DC Chowdhury are waiting for me. There's a faint smell of chips and I realise I haven't eaten all day. My clothes are sticking to me in the heat and I all want to do is go home, grab a sandwich and have a cold shower.

'All right, Ms Callaway?' says Withers.

'Fine,' I say, sitting down opposite them, bracing myself for more questions about the scarf or the footage of that damn coffee place. Withers smiles.

'We've had some good news, Ms Callaway,' he says, leaning back in his chair. 'There's been a breakthrough identifying the deceased.'

It's as if everything stops. All I can hear is white noise. Withers is talking again but I can't make out the words, only a muffled, unintelligible jumble. Chowdhury's nodding, looking at her boss, then at me. They seem to expect me to say something.

'Sorry, I didn't catch that,' I say, shaking my head as if I have an earful of water.

'I was just explaining how difficult it is to get anything out of the banks on a Saturday. You wouldn't believe the hoops they make us jump through.'

I hear myself say I don't understand, then Withers says they've found footage of the deceased making a purchase at petrol station. Once they had that it was simply a matter of persuading the bank to hand over account details.

'His name was Alan Swerford,' says Withers. 'Alan George Swerford.'

They're both watching me intently now. My mind's a mess, I can't work out what all this means or how I'm supposed to react. Dianne had said his name was Stephen. Why would she lie about that? Unless he lied to her. Or the police have got this whole thing wrong and it's someone else entirely.

'Does the name mean anything to you?' asks Withers.

I shake my head. Withers glances at his notebook. 'Mr Swerford worked for a company called Pershore Bespoke. Are you familiar with them?' I shake my head again. 'They're a property rental company, specialising in short-term lets, mostly at the high end of the market. Mr Swerford was their presentation manager.'

That would make sense, explain how everywhere we met had been so immaculate. Zac could have fluffed the pillows and cleaned the bathrooms himself.

'We're confident we have the right man,' says Withers, sliding a photograph across the desk. A beaming Zac stands with his arm round a young woman, a toddler between them. The woman's pretty, smiley, her arm casually resting round her husband's waist, leaning against him. I can see her wedding ring. I want to put my head in my hands and weep.

'What has any of this got to do with me?' I manage at last.

'It's a small thing,' says Withers. 'It turns out Mr Swerford was the registered owner of a Triumph Bonneville T100 motorcycle. Current recommended retail price, £8,300. He bought it on a personal purchase contract last summer.'

Chowdhury slides a photograph across the table. I recognise the familiar sleek lines immediately. 'A local PCSO reported it abandoned four days ago but it didn't get flagged until we lodged Mr Swerford's details on the PNC – that's the Police National Computer.'

'The odd thing is,' says Withers, 'it was parked over a hundred metres from the service station. He didn't drive there for fuel, he went by foot. We have footage of him on the forecourt, and inside. Purchasing alcohol.'

I desperately want him to stop, give me time to get my head round all this, but now he's talking again. 'You probably know the place. The Esso garage on the Bromley Road? It can't be more than a few minutes' walk from your house.'

My mind races. Zac must have been watching me, followed me from the house to the park. 'Probably just a coincidence,' says Withers. 'But there are some obvious questions which it raises. Like why Mr Swerford walked from there to the park – and then asked you for money to get home.' He turns down the edges of his mouth in mock bafflement. I want to tell him to cut out the theatrics but dare not move. 'I mean,' he goes on, 'why would he need money, if he had this splendid machine just minutes away?'

'Like I said, it was a con,' I say, forcing myself to look straight at him.

'Odd though. A con artist making a few quid when he owns a fancy motorbike.'

'Maybe that's how he paid for it,' I say, instantly feeling stupid for being so glib. 'Anyway,' I add quickly, remembering the explanation I gave last time, 'it was probably just a chat-up line.' I look at Chowdhury. 'Have you never been hit on, Sergeant?'

'It's Constable,' she says. 'And no, I have never been hit on by a man pretending to be a beggar.'

I shrug, knowing how ridiculous it must sound.

'Still,' says Withers, smiling, 'finding his motorcycle has been something of a moment for us. For one thing, it explains why he was wearing a leather jacket on such a warm day. Makes complete sense now, doesn't it, Constable?'

'Yes, sir.'

'And it's been helpful in other ways, too.'

I keep silent, knowing whatever he's about to say can't be good. 'It's enabled us to trace Mr Swerford's movements via the Met's network of traffic enforcement cameras. Him and his passengers.'

He stares at me like a chess master who has made a final, ingenious move, the one he's had up his sleeve from the start. I feel battered, physically abused. DC Chowdhury leans in.

'Kirsten,' she says quietly. 'May I offer you some advice?'

I nod and for the first time realise how pretty she is. 'You really should call a solicitor.'

CHAPTER THIRTY-SIX

Helen answers on the third ring.

'Hiya, how's it going?' she says.

There's the sound of running water in the background, she must be washing up or filling the kettle. I try to explain what's happened but it comes out in an incoherent rush. Helen stops me mid-flow and asks where I am. Then she tells me to stay put and say nothing – at all – until she gets there.

The Duty Sergeant has given us a meeting room, and now Helen and I sit opposite each other across a desk, like teacher and pupil. It takes nearly an hour to tell her everything, from the moment I saw Dianne spreadeagled across that car, through all the clandestine meetings, up to my last sighting of Zac in the park. She remains silent throughout, making the occasional note on an A4 pad. When I stop, she puts her pen down and looks up at me.

'Did you kill him?' she says.

'I'm sorry?'

'It's a simple question.'

'What sort of person do you think I am?' I say.

'I have no idea, Kirsten. I used to know who you were. But not any more.'

I take a breath. 'No, I did not kill him.'

Helen leans back, folds her arms. 'I swear on Jess's life, OK?' Jesus, how can she even ask?

'All right,' she says at last. 'Have the police arrested you?'

'I don't know.'

She sighs. 'Did they read you your rights?'

'No.'

'So you're free to leave, which is what we should do.'

'And if they do arrest me?'

'Then we deal with it, but my guess is if they had enough, they'd have done that already.'

'Probably only a matter of time,' I say sullenly. 'Once they have footage of us on his stupid motorbike, it'll all be over.'

'They're bluffing. If you were both wearing helmets they can't prove it was you – or him, come to that.'

'Who else could it be?' I say, incredulous she can be so dismissive.

'That's not our problem,' says Helen. 'The police need to prove beyond all reasonable doubt that you were the passenger, and he was the driver. Unless they have clear, identifiable footage of you getting on the bike, it won't be conclusive. Could they have that?'

'I don't know,' I say. 'Possibly. I mean, there might be pictures of me taking the helmet off, I suppose.'

'Even if there is, it doesn't prove anything – other than on one occasion he gave you a lift.'

'It proves I knew him!' I say, exasperated.

Helen sighs. 'Do you want to fight this or not?'

'Of course.'

'Then do as I say, OK?' She gets up and heads for the door. 'Don't move.'

I can hear her talking to Withers in the corridor. A few minutes later he comes in and tells me I am free to leave. He shakes my hand and thanks me for coming down. Chowdhury stands rigid next to him, impassive as ever. I get the impression she doesn't think this is over, not by a long chalk.

* * *

We drive back in silence, Helen concentrating on the road, me with my head pressed against the passenger window, staring mindlessly at the buildings as they slide past in a blur. I'm exhausted, tired to the bone. All I want to do is sleep. Helen is saying something, but I can't be sure what.

'Sorry?' I say.

'I said, why did you even start?'

'Start what?'

'For Christ's sake, Kirsten! What do you think?'

How can I explain what I barely understand myself? The me who dived into infidelity a few short months ago now seems an entirely different person, as distant as my childhood self.

'Why does anyone have an affair?' I say.

'Don't even try blaming Mark.'

'I'm not.'

'The fault lies with the cheater, Kirsten. Every time.'

This is about you and Tom, I think, not me.

'Have you any idea how lucky you are?' says Helen. 'To have Mark and Jess. How could you throw it all away for a shag?'

'It wasn't like that.'

'No? What were you after, spiritual enlightenment?'

I'm tempted to say in a way, yes.

'I wanted to keep my marriage together.' As I say the words, I hear how disingenuous they must sound to anyone but me, how crass and self-serving. Delusional.

'You never did appreciate what you had,' says Helen. 'Always had to have that little bit extra, whatever the risk, whatever the cost. Never satisfied, always wanting more.'

Could that be true? Is that who I am? Who I've become? Maybe it is. I have no idea any more. I've lost sight of myself, like you do a ship as it gets further and further away until you can't be sure you are seeing it at all, or just the sky and the sea.

Helen turns into our road, parking a few doors down from the house. We sit in silence, listening to the creak of the cooling engine.

'You're going to have to tell Mark everything,' says Helen finally, staring ahead. 'And then tell the police.'

'I can't.'

She turns to face me. 'Let me tell you what's going to happen if you don't. DS Withers will brief the press with everything he has: footage from the coffee place and the hospital; the scarf; the two of you on the motorbike. As soon as it's out there, people are going to contact him. People who remember seeing you and Zac together all over London. The police are not stupid, Kirsten. Really, they are not. They'll put it together and once they do, they'll come after you like a hurricane: making a false statement, wasting police time, perverting the course of justice. You do not want to go there, believe me.'

I feel like I used to when playing chess with Dad. In under ten moves he'd have me pinned down with no possibility of escape, then I'd flip the board over and storm off to my room, pursued by his patronising laugh until I blocked it out with the slam of a door. But there's no bedroom to hide in now. 'Come on,' says Helen, opening the car door. 'Let's get this over with.'

*　　*　　*

Mark isn't at home. Thank God.

'He'll be back later,' I say to Helen, slumping on to a kitchen chair. 'Help yourself to a drink.' But she's put the kettle on for tea and is now peering into the fridge.

'What do you fancy to eat?' she says.

'Nothing,' I say, my hunger weirdly gone.

'You can't think straight on an empty stomach. Here, at least have a banana,' she says, taking one from the fruit bowl.

I shake my head. I just want to crawl away and hide until all this is miraculously over. Maybe I could write it down, a confessional letter Mark can read later, without me having to be there.

'You're sure he doesn't suspect?' says Helen, dropping tea bags into a couple of mugs. 'I mean, I knew about Tom.'

'Sorry?'

'Before he told me, I knew he was cheating.'

'You said you had no idea until he confessed.'

'I know what I said,' says Helen, filling our mugs with boiling water and tamping the tea bags a couple of times with a spoon. 'I went through his stuff. What sort of cliché is that?'

I look away, knowing she's only telling me this so I don't have to think of what I'll say to Mark. She adds a splosh of milk to the teas and pushes one of the mugs towards me. 'I checked his phone, went through his bank statements, I even kept a record of the mileage on his car. I'd seen that in a film once. But there was nothing odd, nothing out of the ordinary. Then one Friday afternoon, after collecting the boys from school, I found a receipt for a hotel in his jacket pocket. It was such a dumb mistake on his part I was convinced he'd left it there on purpose, hoping I'd find it so he didn't have to confess. That's partly why I stayed quiet, I didn't want to give the bastard the satisfaction of thinking his pathetic scheme had worked.'

'Why didn't you tell me?' I say, distracted despite myself.

'That I'd found out my husband was having sex with another woman but still wanted to stay with him? I wonder.'

'When was this?'

'August the fifteenth.'

I try to remember back. 'But you came to Cornwall with us that summer. Both of you.'

'Not one of my favourite holidays.'

'You knew the whole time?' I say, fascinated. Helen nods. 'I had no idea.'

'I'm a good actress. And Tom, well Tom could win the Oscar for Cheating Scumbag Pretending to be a Loving Husband.'

'I'm so sorry, Hellie, that must have been awful.'

'Goes to show, doesn't it,' she says. 'You can never know anyone. Not even your own sister.'

We finish our tea and Helen washes the mugs, dries them and puts them back on their hooks.

'You should get back,' I say. 'Mark won't be home until at least six.'

'I'm OK.'

'What about the boys?'

'They can sort themselves out for once.'

I stand up, desperate to be on my own, to think through the awfulness of my situation.

'I think I'll have a bath,' I say.

Helen hesitates. I know she wants to leave but is worried I'll bottle it or do something stupid.

'Go on, go,' I say, holding out her handbag. 'I'll tell Mark everything, I promise.'

'On Jess's life?'

I nod.

'Call me when it's done, OK?' she says, then reaches out and gives me a hug. 'It's the right thing, Kirst. It really is.'

I wait by the front door until her car pulls away, then go into the sitting room and flop into the armchair. I should be planning what to say to Mark, thinking how to break the news that his trusted partner of twenty-four years has broken every one of her marriage vows. But I can't concentrate, can only think of Zac's – Alan's – twisted body, of his wife smiling into the camera while their little girl hugged her thigh. I feel more alone than ever. There's no one I can talk to. Then it hits me – there is someone.

I reach for my mobile and speed dial Dianne's number. It rings and rings, then cuts off without going to answerphone. For a moment I'm stumped, then remember when she'd first called me at home it had been from a landline. I scroll back through dozens of received calls until I reach one with the right date. A man answers almost immediately. He sounds breathless.

'Hello?'

I don't recognise the voice.

'Hi,' I say, 'can I speak to Dianne?'

'She's not here.'

'Oh,' I say. 'Do you know when she will be back?'

'She won't be.'

'Sorry, I don't understand. This is the right number for Dianne, Dianne Hendon?'

'It was, she doesn't live here any more.'

'But she's the owner.'

'I'm the owner. The Hendersons are my tenants, or rather they were until they did a runner.'

'What do you mean?'

'What do you think I mean, love?'

'Do you know where they went?'

'I wish. Maybe you do?'

I hang up. She's vanished, like she did at school that summer. And it's my fault. I drove her to it, just as I did Zac, insisting she did something about him then, when it went wrong, threatening her with the police. She could be anywhere by now, abroad probably, beyond my reach for sure. The only person left who can corroborate any of my story, disappeared for ever.

It serves me right.

CHAPTER THIRTY-SEVEN

It's dusk when I hear the click of the front door and creak of the hall floorboard. I've been sitting in the same armchair for hours, part of me dreading Mark's return, another part wanting it all to be over. He doesn't see me in the gloom as he reaches for the light switch.

'Could you leave it off?' I say.

'Kirsten?'

'You'd better sit down.'

'What's going on?' he says. 'Are you OK?'

I don't reply, then hear him sit on the sofa, the air wheezing out of the cushions as he lowers himself down. We sit in the dark, the street lamp outside throwing its eerie orange glow over the room, and I tell him everything, from the beginning. I don't spare myself, or him. I'm beyond all that.

By the end, I am almost hoarse. I've emptied myself out, now it's for others to decide what will happen. Mark says nothing. If it wasn't for the sound of his even breathing, I wouldn't know he was there. Somewhere in the house a window bangs. They said there might be a storm tonight.

'I wanted you to know first,' I say. 'And now I'm going to tell the police.'

'You can't do that,' says Mark quietly from the dark.

'I'll tell Jess when she gets back. She deserves to hear it from me. Face to face.'

'No.'

I look down at my hands. I have no right to make demands, not after what I've put him through 'All right,' I say softly. 'Whatever you think best.'

Listening to the house creak and sigh, I wonder where we go from here. Does one of us get up and pour a drink, ask what the other would like for supper? And then there's where to sleep. In the spare room, maybe, or a cheap hotel. I massage my leg; it has gone numb from sitting so long.

'That day, the Saturday, I went for a bike ride, do you remember?' says Mark.

'You fell off,' I say. 'In the rain. You hurt your hand.'

'I was less than halfway when Jess phoned, she sounded very distressed.'

Her driving test, I think. Another betrayal. 'She was in the car,' says Mark quietly. 'Our car.'

'She can't have been . . . '

'Please, let me finish.' I hear him uncross his legs. 'When you didn't turn up to take her to the test centre, she decided to look for you. She thought if she picked you up near the park you could still get her there on time.'

'Why didn't she call me?' I say.

'She did – you didn't answer.' He sighs. 'She knew she was taking a risk but the roads round there are deserted on a Saturday. When she didn't see you on the way over, she stopped near the park entrance to wait. Which is when it must have happened.'

'When what happened?'

'She phoned me because she'd had an accident.'

'Was she hurt?' I say. There's a brief silence before Mark continues.

'I told her to stay put, that I'd cycle over and find her.'

That makes no sense. Mark had smashed up his bike when he came off it in the race. I begin to feel dizzy, light-headed. I can't move, let alone speak.

'When I got there,' says Mark. 'Jess was all over the place. It took a while to calm her down, but slowly I began to piece it together. She'd just parked when there was a bang on the window. It was a drunk guy, shouting at her. She thought maybe she'd taken his space, but then he banged on the window again, yelling for her get the fuck out of the car. Jess was terrified. She locked the doors but he started pounding on the windscreen, smashing his fist into it until it bled. She was sure the glass was going to break any second. She tried to drive off, but every time she went forward, he stood in front of her. She put the car into reverse, slammed her foot down. Only she got it wrong. The car leapt forward. She hit him full on.' Mark takes a deep breath, as if trying to steady his own nerves. I can make out his silhouette on the sofa, see him run a hand through his hair.

It starts to make horrible sense. When Zac couldn't find me in the café, he must have left the park the same way he came in, by the station entrance. He would have recognised the car, assumed I was in it.

'Understandably, Jess panicked,' says Mark. 'Drove off without thinking. But, after a few hundred yards, she was shaking so badly she couldn't hold the wheel and had to stop. She knew she couldn't call the police, not without a licence or insurance, so she phoned you – and when you didn't answer, me. She was still shaking when I found her.'

I close my eyes, can see Jess sitting terrified behind the wheel, her whole world imploding. My poor, dear daughter.

Mark takes another deep breath, exhales through his nose. 'My first thought was to drive home, get her safe, but I couldn't leave someone out there, they might be bleeding to death. I told Jess to stay put, that I'd deal with it. I went back to where she thought she'd hit him, dreading what I might find, but there was nothing. No body, no blood, nothing at all. I must have looked for ten, fifteen minutes, checking both sides of the road. I began to think Jess couldn't have hit him very hard, that he must have wandered off, shaken but unhurt.

'I was heading back to the car, looking forward to telling her the good news, when I saw the toe of a trainer poking out of the undergrowth. I told myself it had to be one of those single random shoes you sometimes see. I pushed the bushes aside to check.

'It was a man in a motorbike jacket, lying on his back, his head facing the tracks. I knelt down, shook his leg. "Hey," I said. "Are you OK?" He didn't move. I took out my phone, switched on the light. His face looked OK, but his eyes were closed. I checked what I could see of the rest of him. His clothes were intact, there was no blood, no grazing. He could have been asleep or passed out. I could smell alcohol and thought that must be a good sign, maybe he was just drunk. I tapped his cheek. Then I hit him harder, a slap almost, but he still didn't move. That's when I knew he was dead.'

I hear Mark scratch his stubble, shift on the sofa. I hardly dare breathe.

'I had no idea what to do. When a train went past below, I found myself crouching down, worried someone might see me. Then it started raining, really pelting down. I thought maybe the guy had had a heart attack or died of alcohol poisoning and it had nothing to do with Jess. Maybe I could leave him there for someone else to find. There was nothing to connect us. But I remembered something Jess had said, about your mother's phone. How it tracked her every move. What if he had a mobile? Could it show he had been right next to Jess in some way? I told myself that was ridiculous but then thought what if someone tried to call him, worked out where he was? I couldn't risk it.

'I pushed my way in, pulling the bushes behind me in case anyone happened to walk by. I knelt down and went through his pockets. I found a wallet and almost opened it but then stopped. I didn't want to know anything about this guy, that would only make it worse. He had a phone in his jeans. Tiny, like a toy. I ripped it open, pulled out the battery and shoved it into my pocket.

'I was getting to my feet when I spotted something on his jacket. Specks of paint. Red paint. They had to be from our car. I was about to brush them off when I saw a whole lot more. I couldn't get rid of all of them, but I knew if the police traced them back to Jess, her whole future would be ruined, everything she worked for would disappear in a heartbeat. I was not prepared to let that happen.'

I hear Mark swallow. I want to say something but dare not interrupt.

'I knew I had to get rid of the jacket, but couldn't pull it off him. His arms wouldn't bend and I kept slipping in the mud, scratching my hand on the brambles. I was terrified someone would come along, ask what the hell I was doing. I yanked it as hard as I could, heard a crack.' Mark takes another deep breath. 'After that, it became easier. I put the jacket to one side and then I picked up his legs and . . . I pushed them over his chest.'

'Oh, Mark!' I say quietly. I want to reach out, take his hand, but he's too far away. He sniffs.

'He fell for what felt like an age, over and over, crashing through the undergrowth. And then nothing. Grabbing the jacket, I scrambled back up on to the road. Thank God, there was nobody there. I didn't know what to do with his damned jacket, so I bundled it up and took it back to the car.

'I told Jess I'd found the man she hit and he was OK, a bit shaken but with no real damage. I put the leather jacket on the back seat and draped my own over it. Jess was too out of it to notice what I was doing.' He stops. I can hear him trying to get his breathing under control. 'She hugged me and started crying; the shock, I suppose. I kept telling her everything was OK, that she had nothing to worry about; we'd reschedule her test and everything would be fine.'

'You did the right thing,' I say. 'There was no other—'

He cuts me short, as if he has to get everything out in one go or he'll lose the courage to say it.

'I couldn't let Jess drive,' he says. 'Even if she had been capable. I tried to put my bike in the back, but it kept sliding out. I push it hard and slammed the boot. I could see the spokes were all twisted and bent but the boot stayed shut.

'As soon as we got home, I gave Jess a shot of whiskey and told her to have a bath. Then I went back to the car, took out the jacket and tried to burn it in the garden. It took ages to catch and in the end I had to use some old turps it to get it going.'

We sit motionless. I can hear rain battering the windows, a boom of thunder sounding in the distance.

'It's my fault,' I say at last. 'All of it.'

Mark says nothing.

CHAPTER THIRTY-EIGHT

I don't remember the rest of the evening. I must have brushed my teeth, undressed, put on my pyjamas, but have no recollection of any of it. As soon as the light went out, I fell into a sleep so deep I could've been drugged. Maybe it was my body's way of telling me it couldn't take any more.

I woke not long after dawn, and have come into the garden. It's a beautiful summer morning, the world made clean by last night's storm. The bonfire where Mark burnt Zac's jacket, and I destroyed the last of my schooldays, has been flattened into a pancake of ash, pitted with hundreds of tiny holes by the rain.

I try to get my head around what Mark has – and has not – done. For nearly two weeks, he knew Jess killed a man, yet he said nothing. He should have told me as soon as it happened, the moment I stepped out of the house and saw him hosing down the car. Instead, he span me some nonsense about him falling off his bike. We had Anne and Jeremy to dinner just days afterwards, for God's sake, and he behaved as if nothing had happened. Did he really think if I knew, I'd go to the police and tell them what Jess had done? Or perhaps he suspected my involvement, though it hardly seems possible. His silence was either an act of supreme kindness or a cold calculation that I couldn't be trusted with my own daughter's future.

I poke the ashes with a stick and can make out the charred remains of my old textbook. If I hadn't confessed, Mark would never have told me the truth and we'd be off to Egypt with his secret – and mine – safely hidden from one another. He'd spend the rest of his life knowing he had lied to his wife and child, while I would bear the guilt of a snatched affair. Perhaps we would have both accepted those were prices worth paying.

I throw the stick into the dead bonfire and am about to walk away when something flashes in the pale morning sunshine. I bend down, gently brush away the ashes and pick out a dusty piece of glass. Licking a finger, I clean it off, hold it up to the light. The familiar entwined couple reveals itself. How could our little piece of sea-glass possibly have ended up here?

There's only one explanation – it was in Zac's motorbike jacket when Mark threw it on the fire. Zac must have stolen it from my handbag. Even as the thought occurs to me, I dismiss it. He never saw that piece of glass, certainly couldn't have appreciated its significance. Yet there it had been, lying in the ashes.

A memory comes back to me: the day Mark texted, saying my mother had gone missing. Entangled with Zac, I'd fumbled in my handbag for the phone, thinking it might be Jess. Unable to see in the dark, I'd turfed everything out on the bedroom floor. The little pouch must have slid under the bed. Zac could have found it when he cleared up and put it in his pocket, intending to give it back the next time we met.

As I run my fingers over smooth curves of the glass, a numbing thought begins to crystallise: Mark had been through Zac's pockets, had found his wallet and phone. What if he found this, too? I picture him opening the string on the velvet pouch, letting our private talisman slide into his palm. He could only conclude I gave it to Zac, and with that knowledge, everything else would follow.

My mind reels as I try to make sense of Mark's silence, of his decision not to confront me. In his position, I would have stormed in, demanding to know who this man was, why I had allowed him to destroy our marriage, threaten our daughter's future. But before I can think it through, I hear the doorbell. Who drops round this early on a Sunday morning? Only the police.

Making my way through the silent house into the hall, I'm not sure how much more of their relentless questioning I can take. I slide open the safety chain, unlock the Yale. It's not the police. It's Kevin, wearing some sort of Lycra outfit.

'Hi,' he says, hopping nervously from foot to foot in garish trainers. 'Sorry it's so early – triathlon day.'

I'm so surprised I don't even manage a hello. 'How's it going?' says Kevin.

'Fine,' I say, baffled by what he's doing on my doorstep on a Sunday morning.

'Cool. I just wanted to say goodbye.'

'Goodbye?'

'Yeah, I'm leaving the hospital. I meant to tell you at your party, but it didn't seem appropriate, you know.' He smiles apologetically.

'Where are you going?'

'America. Galina's got a job there, she's the brainy one, I'm just tagging along.' He glances over his shoulder and I spot a car with a couple of bikes strapped to the roof and a woman looking out of the window. Is that Dr Svetkova? What's she doing here?

'We're going to Boston. Not now, obviously! In a few weeks.'

I stare at the car, at the bikes, trying to take all this in. The woman waves and something finally clicks into place.

'You and Dr Svetkova, you're . . . together?'

'We hooked up before Christmas, at the nurses' party. I thought you knew?'

Of course! The new clothes, the haircut, the Tumi bag. All her. How on earth did I miss that?

'I heard about the cops and stuff.' He makes one of his sad faces.

So that's why you're really here, I think.

'Janice?' I say, guessing she must have told him where I live, as well.

'Yeah. And the Bish.'

'The Bish?'

'Bishaaro, the security guy at the hospital? He asked me for CCTV footage of our wing.' For some inexplicable reason, Kevin is now winking. 'I told him we had a problem with the IP address.'

I stare at him, trying to process what he's telling me. 'Was that the wrong thing to do?' he says, worried.

'No,' I say, finally understanding. 'No, not at all.'

'It was Galina's idea, really. She has this thing about state surveillance, what with coming from Bulgaria, I suppose.'

Kevin, Janice, Dr Svetkova – all protecting me. It doesn't seem possible.

'I don't know what to say, Kevin.'

'*Molya*! That's Bulgarian for you're welcome. I'm trying to learn it.' He taps the headphones hanging around his neck. 'Galina says I sound like a waste disposal unit with a spoon stuck down it, but it's a tough language.'

I feel my eyes well up and now I am properly crying, the tears streaming down my face.

'I'm so sorry, Kevin.'

He doesn't know where to look. 'Please,' he says, 'don't be sorry. It's cool. There's nothing to be sorry about.'

Nothing apart from being a self-regarding, self-obsessed, overly judgemental fool.

He produces a pack of Kleenex and hands me a tissue. I wipe my eyes.

'I'm sorry I didn't know about you and Dr Svetkova,' I say.

'Well, you and me didn't get to talk that much, did we?' he says.

I want to reach out, hug him, tell him how grateful I am, how sorry, but he's started down the path now.

'Got to go – swim starts at half-past! I hate that bit, to be honest! You take care of yourself, yeah?' he says. 'And don't let the bastards win!'

I watch as he opens the car door and gets in. Dr Svetkova – Galina – leans over and kisses him.

'Who was that?' Mark has silently appeared from nowhere.

'He's from work,' I say. 'A friend from work.'

* * *

Later, I find Mark in the kitchen, methodically going through his coffee machine routine: grinding the beans, tamping the grounds, turning and twisting polished chrome dials. I take the sliver of glass and place it silently on the counter. He looks up, surprised.

'I thought I'd lost it,' I say.

'Uh-huh,' he says, placing a cup under a nozzle and pressing a button. The machine grinds and gurgles as black liquid dribbles out. How can he remain so calm?

'I thought you might have come across it?'

'Nope.' Now he's frothing milk in a stainless steel pot, jiggling it up and down under a gush of steam. I stare at his face but only see concentration, no hint of duplicity.

'Aren't you curious where I found it?'

He bangs the pot on the counter like a pro. 'Your bag? At work?'

He *doesn't* know. He never saw it. The thought rushes through me like a blast of water clearing all before it. Mark pours his coffee into a mug before carefully adding the milk.

'Mark,' I say, reaching out an arm. 'I want to say . . . I'm sorry. So, so sorry.'

He glances at me, then shrugs, as if I've apologised for breaking a favourite glass or forgetting to empty the washing machine. 'Can we talk about . . . '

'Not now, Kirsten,' he says, cutting me off. He starts up the stairs with his coffee, taking the steps two at a time. 'I'm on a call.' And he gives me a smile. A smile! I am more confused than ever. Have I got my husband as wrong as I did Kevin? Misjudged his every move? All Mark has ever done is look out for me, and then he did the same for Jess.

What greater constancy could there be? What better proof of love?

I lay the table for breakfast and, on a whim, check to see if we have the ingredients for savoury pancakes, Mark's all-time favourite. There's just one egg, so I grab my purse and hurry to the Co-op. It'll only take a minute or two and be so worth it to see his face. Paying at the till, it feels both surreal and reassuring to be doing something as mundane as food shopping. For the first time in months, I can see a way forward, a way back to how things used to be. Mark and I will sit down together and hammer out our future over plates of steaming pancakes. After all, we want the same thing – to save Jess, to save ourselves. It must be possible.

* * *

Hurrying home, I step into the hall with the shopping to hear Mark's voice from the kitchen. He's talking quickly, emphatically. I open the door expecting to see Withers and Chowdhury perched on our stools, midway through quizzing him. Instead, it's Helen who turns to see me.

'I've been trying to tell him it's a crazy idea,' she says.

'I'm sorry?' I say, the flimsy plastic bag cutting into my fingers. 'What idea?'

Helen looks at Mark.

'You haven't told her?'

He shrugs. I begin to feel nervous.

Helen sighs. 'Mark called me this morning to tell me what happened with Jess.'

'Right,' I say, thinking that's good. We need professional advice and Helen's the obvious choice.

Helen turns to face Mark. 'Are you going to tell her or am I?'

'I don't want Jess involved,' he says, looking straight at me. 'So I'm going to tell the police it was me driving. That I was responsible for everything.'

'Like I said,' says Helen. 'Crazy.'

'Why didn't you discuss this with me?' I say, my head reeling.

'Or indeed Jess,' adds Helen.

Mark holds up his hand. 'Jess doesn't need to know. I've sent her enough money so she can stay in Ibiza until this is over. There'll be plenty of time to explain later.'

'It's an insane idea,' says Helen. 'Illegal, ill-advised and almost certain to fail.'

'It's non-negotiable,' says Mark.

Helen sighs. 'You realise I can't represent you?'

'You mean you won't.'

'No, Mark, I mean I can't. I cannot say something in court which I know to be a lie. It would be unethical and against my professional code of conduct.'

I sit in silence as they bicker back and forth. I might as well not be here.

'Lying to the police is a serious offence,' says Helen. 'If they find out, you could go to prison. Are you willing to risk that?'

'Absolutely.'

'Mark!' I say. 'You can't go to prison for something you didn't do! Why don't we just tell the police what happened? It was a mistake, Jess panicked. It was an accident!'

He turns to me, the trace of a smile on his lips. That same smile.

'Do you really think you're entitled to a view? After what you've done?'

I feel numb, unable to reply. Mark's talking to Helen now, asking what they need to do next.

'We have to find you another solicitor,' she says. 'And whatever you tell them will need to be watertight. No inconsistencies, no time jumps, no bits which don't make sense. You think you can do that?'

'Let's find out,' says Mark.

As they work on his story, I feel as if I'm watching a film or looking down on myself from a great height. Mark's version is so detailed, so consistent, he must have been thinking about it for hours, days even. He tells Helen he fell off his bike in the rain, damaging the back wheel. When he got home, Jess was asleep and I was on my run. Then I called on the landline to say I had hurt my foot in the park (how long did he take to come up with that?), so he drove over to pick me up from the entrance by the station. As he carefully recounts each detail, even suggesting the police could check phone records to back up his story, I feel sick and useless and guilty. All this is my fault, yet I have no control. Maybe Mark's right, I don't deserve any.

Helen scribbles notes as he tells her exactly where he parked, and how, when he was reversing, a drunk leapt out of nowhere.

'You know the rest,' he says, moving a hand over his face. 'I got the wrong gear, panicked when I hit him, then went back to see if he was OK.'

Helen looks up from her notes. 'When you realised he was dead, why didn't you call the police?'

'I suppose the same reason I drove off. I panicked.' Mark says it with such simplicity, such conviction that if I didn't know better, I'd believe it myself. His whole performance has been perfect.

'You removed his jacket and pushed him down the embankment to cover your tracks?'

Mark nods. 'I thought the police would assume it was a suicide.'

Helen puts down her pen.

'It's not enough.' She turns to me. 'Not without your corroboration.'

'What do you mean?' I say.

'You need to make a statement admitting to the affair and explaining how when you ended things, the guy wouldn't accept it and began stalking you. Which is pretty much true, right? Then that Saturday, you saw him again in the park. We'll suggest he spotted your car, assumed you were in it, and lost the plot.' She looks back through her notes. 'It'll help he was over the limit.'

'His name was Alan,' I say, but no one is listening.

Helen makes me go over my story again and again. I can't concentrate, keep forgetting details, but she won't let up.

'How hard can it be, Kirsten?' she says. 'All you have to do is tell the truth!'

'You're forgetting something,' I say. 'How did I get back from the park if I hurt my foot?'

'I picked you up,' says Mark, without a second's hesitation.

'And did you tell me what you'd done?'

He looks straight at me.

'Of course not, I wanted to protect you. That's why you lied to the police.'

When I finally manage to get through the whole thing without a mistake, Helen makes a call and the next thing I know, we have an appointment to see Withers. Helen says she'll drive.

I stare out of the car window as the familiar landmarks slide past: the Taj, the Co-op, Cartertons the estate agents. I can't believe this is happening, and so fast. By the time we get to Bromley Police Station, it has started to rain. Mark's new solicitor is already there, parked up opposite. We squeeze into her car and she introduces herself as Andrea Holden, awkwardly shaking hands over the seats. According to Helen, she's one of the best criminal defence solicitors in the business. We're lucky to have her.

I sit in the back, listening to Mark repeat his story yet again. He's articulate and consistent, with a hint of contrition for the awful thing he did. Andrea asks a few questions but Helen has rehearsed him well, they are minor points, easily clarified.

As Helen fills Andrea in on my affair, I silently count to a hundred to block out the humiliation.

'So what we have,' says Andrea, twisting to face me, 'is a man who wouldn't take no for an answer. A man who had not only previously exhibited violent behaviour but also had a tendency to lose control. Would you say that was fair, Kirsten?'

They are all looking at me now. Had Zac been violent? Or just passionate? Out of control, or driven by his emotions?

'Kirst?' says Helen.

I look at Mark, doing his best, taking the blame for his beloved daughter, for me.

'Yes,' I say. 'That's fair.'

* * *

I recognise the officer on duty at the desk; Sergeant Bloxham and I have become familiar with each other over the last twenty-four hours and it's good to see a friendly face. Andrea introduces herself, explains we have an appointment with an officer from the BTP to make a voluntary statement. The sergeant tells us to take a seat. Helen asks if it's OK to vape in here, but he says he'd rather she didn't, so she steps outside.

I pretend to study the faded public safety posters: 'Run. Hide. Tell'; 'Communities Defeat Terrorism', trying not to listen to Andrea and Mark's last-minute confab. I feel for the reassurance of the sea-glass in my pocket, turning it over and over in my fingers. They're talking in whispers now, nodding, agreeing – and ignoring me.

Spotting Helen outside, I go to join her. We stand under a dripping overhang, staring at the rain falling relentlessly on a badly parked police van.

'Can I have a go?' I say, nodding at her vape.

'You don't even smoke,' she says.

'So?'

Helen hands over her shiny metal device. It's surprisingly heavy. I take a deep drag and cough so much I feel my liver might flop on to the pavement. Then my mouth goes dry, as if it's been filled with blotting paper.

'Nice,' I finally manage, handing it back.

'Twat,' says Helen and we both laugh. I glance back at Mark and Andrea, still in earnest conversation.

'Why do you think he's doing this?' I say.

Helen shrugs. 'Love?'

'For me?'

She says nothing, takes another puff on her vape.

'When Mark says jump, I jump. Isn't that what you're always saying?'

'This is hardly the same.'

'Isn't it?'

We share a look, then Helen puts her vape away. 'We should get back in.'

As we step into the dry, I look over at Sergeant Bloxham. He catches my eye and smiles. DS Withers has appeared, is talking to Helen, who's introducing Andrea and they're pointing at Mark.

In that moment, everything is clear, obvious and certain. I know exactly what I have to do.

'Sergeant Withers?' I say, standing, my arm outstretched. He has no option but to take my hand. 'May I have a word?'

He looks puzzled, glances at the others who don't know what to make of my intervention. 'It won't take long,' I say, heading for the door I know leads to the interview rooms. Withers shrugs, he can hardly say no, not after the hours we've spent together.

He leads me into the familiar room and closes the door.

'The thing is, Sergeant, I have not been entirely honest with you,' I say, pulling out the chair I have sat in so many times. I tell him everything. About the affair, the stalking, how I drove to the park that day, how Zac attacked me in my car and I smashed into him; how I looked to see if he was OK and, finding he wasn't, took off his leather jacket and rolled him down that terrible incline.

Withers listens in silence. I can tell he believes me. So much of it makes sense, confirms what he suspected all along.

'I'm sorry I lied to you,' I say. 'I panicked.'

When we come back out into reception, Withers announces I have been arrested and charged. Everyone leaps to their feet. Andrea's on to him with a barrage of legal questions, Helen keeps saying, 'What have you done? What have you done?' And Mark? Mark stands motionless, unable to believe I've finally taken control.

CHAPTER THIRTY-NINE

The court hearing is a few weeks later and surprisingly quick. With a guilty plea and no jury, the judge sits alone to decide my sentence. Andrea Holden, who segued effortlessly from being Mark's brief to mine, came up with impressive character references along with a list of mitigating circumstances. I'm a professional of good character with many years of dedicated public service; mother to a teenager daughter at a crucial point in her young life, not to mention a penitent who made a full and frank confession (she skates over my dissembling in numerous police interviews). Lastly, and perhaps most persuasively, I am a woman who has been subjected to a premeditated, unrelenting campaign of intimidation by a ruthless stalker.

Andrea warned they could throw the book at me: causing death by dangerous driving, failing to report an accident, leaving the scene of an accident, failing to report a death, concealing a death, even prevention of lawful burial. But the judge is remarkably sympathetic, says she understands the pressure I was under, acknowledges I had been the victim of unwanted attention and, most important of all, accepts I did not intend to take a life. Her summing up is fair, the sentence what I deserve. Andrea is sanguine;

three years is in line with her prediction and, with good behaviour, I should be out in a third of that time.

I'm allowed a few minutes with Mark before I'm taken away. I hadn't been able to face seeing him before sentencing and suspect he felt the same. I moved in with Helen, much to the confusion of my mother who thought we were all on holiday in Wales. I know Mark can't understand why I chose this path, that he thinks I have been foolish and contrary – a favourite Mark word when it comes to me. I do owe him an explanation but cannot bring myself to tell him the truth behind the epiphany I'd had watching him and Andrea decide my future in the police station.

Within a few seconds, so many things had become clear, as if a cataract had been removed and the world snapped back into focus after years of blurriness. I saw that Mark had never moved beyond the moral certainty of adolescence, when you know what is good for everyone except yourself. From the day he saw me sneak that milk jug into my bag, he had a vision of me that was at odds with who I really was. Or ever could be.

I understood, too, that under much of his approach to life lay an urgent desire to hold on to both his youth and those certainties, whether it was a punishing exercise regime, obsessive self-improvement or staring at porn. Mark never wanted a real-life woman with all her imperfections, a human being growing old in front of his eyes, refusing to be the person he wanted her to be. Better to satisfy himself with images of compliant young women, their perfection frozen for ever by the camera. I never stood a chance. No living, breathing woman would. At least my sexual exploits had been real and tangible, flawed maybe, but with a human heartbeat.

I can't bring myself to tell Mark any of this. What good would it do, at this point in our lives? I know he has, in his own way, wished me well. It's what he used to say: I want you to be the best version of yourself. And there lay the problem: he wanted me to be *his* best version of myself, not mine. I can't do that any more.

So instead, I take his hand.

'I have something of yours,' I say. And press the sea-glass into his palm.

* * *

At first, they sent me to a high-security prison near Hull. It was loud, confusing and terrifying. Any Shawshank fantasies I might have had about teaching old lags to read and write were soon dispelled. While no one jammed a sharpened toothbrush into my thigh or slashed me with a dismantled razor, I was pushed and shoved enough to have an impressive array of bruises by the third day. But things calmed down with every new intake of inmates – bullies like nothing more than fresh meat – and I rapidly learned to keep out of their way.

Most of the women were no trouble. They were nearly all young, damaged and resigned, each with their own heartrending story. If they shared one thing in common, it was that they had committed crimes on behalf of men. Whether it was dealing drugs, shoplifting or selling themselves, they invariably did it to support the drug habits of their boyfriends, who more often than not, rewarded them with physical violence. I felt lucky; at least no man had punched the shit out of me every Saturday night.

My worst fear wasn't being attacked, it was that Jess would never speak to me again. Thanks to my guilty plea, the press soon lost interest, and I'd insisted on being charged under my maiden name so there would be nothing to connect Jess to the case. Even so, I convinced myself she would cut me out of her life. However grateful she might be for me taking the blame, she would never be able to forgive me for what I'd put our family through. She was right. If it hadn't been for my adultery, none of the awful consequences would have followed. A terse email from Mark had informed me she got the grades she needed – by some margin in fact – so would be going to Bristol Medical School. I fully expected that's how it would be from now on, any news of Jess filtered through Mark.

I couldn't have been more wrong. Jess came to see me the day she flew in from Ibiza, straight from the airport. She was brown as a berry, her hair cut short. She looked wonderful. At first, it was difficult to be open, what with a warder standing by the door, pretending not to listen. But we only had forty minutes so I couldn't afford to be precious. I told her about Zac, why I got involved, what we did together, how I had ended it. I saw no point in lying, hiding the seedier details – she was an adult now. I fully expected her to kick the chair over and demand to be let out. Instead, she reached over and took my hand.

'Poor Mum,' she said.

Even the warder must have found it moving, because she waited a full ten seconds before reminding us touching was not permitted.

A few days later, via Skype, Jess told me how grateful she was, how she owed me a debt she felt unable ever to repay. I told her it was nonsense, that love knows no debt and it had, in fact, been her father's idea to take the blame. Besides, if it hadn't been for my own reckless behaviour, there would have been no need. We speak most weeks now. She's doing well, loving her course. I ask about Mark, how he's getting on in Cairo. Apparently, he's been put in charge of timetabling.

Jess asks if we will ever get back together.

'I don't think so, darling,' I say. 'Your father's a good man, just not good for me.'

* * *

A month ago, they transferred me to an open prison. In some ways, I'm happier here than I've been for years. Certainly fitter. There isn't much to do apart from work out in the gym, read and listen to podcasts and, of course, think.

I've become friendly with one of the warders, Brenda. A tiny woman who presents herself immaculately despite the challenges of her uniform, she bonds with inmates by offering hints and tips on beauty regimes. I have never had such good hair and nails – or body come to that.

Brenda is a fan of the self-help book, regaling us most mornings with gnomic insights such as, 'You have to look through the rain to see the rainbow', or 'Yesterday is history, tomorrow a mystery and today a gift'. Personally, I find her views on gels versus acrylics more insightful. She did offer some useful advice the other day, however. She popped into the kitchen to see how I was doing with my new duties there.

'You should keep a diary,' she said.

'So it can keep me?' I said.

'Because when you're out, you'll forget who you were in here, and then all you'll have done is be punished.'

As often with Brenda, the phrasing might be convoluted but the sentiment was true. I had Jess send me half a dozen spiral-bound notebooks and ever since have been jotting down my thoughts. Many have been about Zac, not in any romantic way, but trying to understand how the two of us ended up where we did. One thing I now know for sure is he did not deserve to die like that. His sin was no worse than mine and, in some ways, more forgivable. He was not the monster they made him out to be at my hearing, just a man whose passions would not let him live in peace.

I did think of writing to Zac's wife, but who would want to hear from the woman who cheated with her husband and was then responsible for his death? As Brenda put it, 'value the peace of mind of the other, rather than crave your own forgiveness', which I didn't follow at first but now think I begin to understand. The truth is only as useful as it is helpful; if it burdens more than it enlightens, it is probably best left unsaid. I tore up the letter I had started.

As for the 'problem' that landed me here in the first place, I can't say the urge has entirely gone away, but with no opportunities to pursue it, or at least none which appeal to me, desire has, thankfully, taken a back seat.

Helen's still living with our mother, which, miraculously, seems to work. Mum has company, the boys love their new school, and Helen enjoys being back in a family home. We decided not to tell Mum where I am. Helen says if we did, she'd have forgotten by the next day. As far as she is concerned, I'm away on business or seeing friends or on holiday. Not that she asks very often.

Helen visits when she can, but she's a busy woman now; Andrea offered her a job at her law firm. Helen appears genuinely happy and thinks if she plays her cards right, she might – whisper it – make partner one day. She's off the booze (mostly) and even back on a couple of dating sites.

Dr Svetkova – Galina – has taken up a post at the Wyss Institute, part of Harvard University, working in their neuro-prosthetics department. Her speciality is amyotrophic lateral sclerosis, using MRI scans to map sensory pathways – or so Kevin tells me. He's just thrilled to be within spitting distance of MIT, where he's auditing a couple of classes on AI. As he said in his last email, it's like his dream life has come true, twice over. I'm happy for him.

Over the last few months, I have taken a couple of courses offered by the prison's education service. I saw myself learning Spanish so I could relocate to South America, or getting an Open University degree in environmental studies and working for the National Trust in a rent-free pile somewhere on the Yorkshire Moors. None of those ever came to anything, and I've learned the most from a young woman called Gail, serving eighteen months for financial fraud. In return for helping with her frozen shoulder, she's been giving me computer lessons. There's not much I can't do on the web now.

One wet Monday afternoon, she was explaining how carding forums work when Brenda appeared and told me

I had an unexpected visitor. As I walked across the yard to the 'liaison' building, I wondered who it could be. Not Jess, she was up to her eyes in end of year exams, nor Helen, she always sent a message via the prison's email service first, and certainly not Mark, our communication, while civil, would never be so personal. Besides, he was still in Cairo, having recently extended his contract at the international school.

At first, I didn't recognise the woman waiting for me in the small visitor's room. She stood silhouetted against the light and all I could make out was a puffa jacket.

'Hello, Kirsten,' she said.

'Dianne!' I said, instantly knowing the voice.

'I hope you don't mind me coming to see you,' she said, stepping out of the light.

'No, no, of course not.' She looked older, her face pale despite the make-up.

'I wanted to apologise. For disappearing like that . . . '

'There's no need.'

'There is. I shouldn't have done it. I'm sorry.'

I nodded, not sure what I was supposed to say.

'I shouldn't have involved you in the first place and then to vanish . . . that was unforgivable.'

'I'm sure you had your reasons,' I said, thinking of all the other marriages she must have been responsible for.

'All the same . . . '

'Dianne, whatever happened was my choice. My responsibility.'

'I don't know,' she said, rubbing the finger where her wedding ring used to be.

'In fact, I'm grateful to you.'

'To me?'

'You know what they say, it's OK to make mistakes, just don't make the same one twice.' One of Brenda's simpler aphorisms.

'Right,' said Dianne, though I could see she didn't quite understand. Maybe she would later.

'And how are things with you?' I said.

She stared at her fingernails for a moment, unpainted now, cut short.

'Henry and I split.'

'I'm sorry.'

'Me too,' she said. 'He got custody, as well. I could have fought for the girls but under the circumstances . . . actually, Henry has been very fair. I still see them . . . ' She trailed off and we sat in silence for a while, perhaps both thinking of what we had lost.

'And the business?'

'That's all gone. I had to reimburse a lot of people. It hasn't been easy.'

'No, I can imagine.'

'It's all been a bit shit, to be honest. But I've got a new job, and I've been seeing a therapist online.'

'Which is why you're here?'

'You always were the bright one.'

'Apart from ending up in prison.'

We laughed and it almost felt like old times.

'What will you do when you get out?' she said. 'Go back to the NHS?'

'I doubt they'd give me a job and, to be honest, even if they did, I wouldn't want it. All that seems a lifetime ago, I couldn't go back.'

'So what will you do?'

'I've been working on a few ideas.'

*　　*　　*

Which is how I find myself sitting in a rooftop restaurant, fitted out with heaters and Christmas lights, opposite a well-preserved man in his fifties. He's good-looking, if not entirely my type, which is probably no bad thing considering how *that* turned out.

All the safeguards are in place this time; I've done everything possible to make sure there will be no repetition of the Zac problem. Thanks to Gail's computer classes, I know a surprising amount about this man. There are no drug or alcohol issues, he has an impeccable employment record, is a regular donor to several charities and a lifetime member of the National Trust. I even know his real name.

We've been chatting for a while now and I can tell he's interested, keen to cut to the chase. But he needs to know this is not a game, that inevitably there will be consequences. I lean back, put on my serious face.

'The thing is, Charles,' I say, 'infidelity changes people. They become someone else. Once you make the decision, there's no way back.'

'I don't want to go back,' he says.

I smile. 'Then that's fine. Why don't I take you through the rules?'

Acknowledgements

There are a number of people without whom I would never have started this novel, let alone finished it. First, my tutor on the Faber Writing Course, Shelley Weiner, who gave me encouragement, advice and wisdom in equal measure.

My fellow students were wonderfully supportive and insightful, particularly the group that continues with regular meetings now the course has finished: Bethanie Alhadeff, Alison Cable, Paul Clabburn, Stuart Clark, Tiffany Flynn, Melanie McDonald, Suzy Oldfield, Eve Richings, Carol Sadan, Joanna Wood and Lizzi Zita. All took the time to read early drafts, which I now blush at. Their attention to detail and editorial insights have been truly invaluable and I know they improved the final version immeasurably.

I wouldn't have been able to attempt any of the police procedural elements without the help of my police advisor, Graham Bartlett. A detective with 30 years' experience, he not only has an in-depth knowledge of the world of police and crime, but as an author himself understands the requirements that fiction brings. Any technical mistakes which remain are entirely my own.

I owe an enormous debt to my agent, Ben Dunn, who not only took a risk picking up my idea from the Faber 'Writing a Novel' publication, but arrived at our first meeting with a bottle of wine and ideas about the ending. What more could an author want? His combination of editorial nous and commercial instinct is as rare as it is enviable. Thank you, Ben.

I was thrilled when Jon Elek at Welbeck agreed to publish the book. He has been a consistent and unrelenting champion since day one and I feel very lucky to have such a talented and committed publisher on my side. Everyone at Welbeck has been consistently helpful, professional and welcoming – all without us ever meeting in person, thanks to Covid.

I would also like to thank my editor, Niamh Mulvey. It has been a humbling experience to be edited by someone so dedicated, knowledgeable and downright clever. Niamh's insights into what I was trying to do, but not quite achieving, were extraordinarily helpful. Where I struggled, she brought clarity, and I know the book is many times better thanks to her editorial skills.

I have been lucky enough to have several friends willing to read the novel in manuscript form and offer their insights, not just as notes, but over several long meetings. I found these both stimulating and helpful. Their thoughts and solutions enabled me to return to my desk with renewed enthusiasm. A big thank you to Stephanie Calman, Peter Grimsdale and my screenwriting partner, Philip Greenacre.

I'd also like to thank my daughter, Ella, who put up with my endless witterings about plot problems on numerous walks and car journeys. She came up with many ingenious answers, several of which I have unashamedly stolen. But no, you can't have 10%.

Lastly, I must thank the one person without whose support – in every conceivable sense – none of this could possibly have happened. From her early question, 'Why don't you write a novel?', through her highly insightful comments on the story, to her patience while I wrestled with yet another draft, my wife, Pippa Harris, has been committed, supportive and loving. I don't just feel fortunate to have you in my life, I feel honoured.